HEAVEN'S CROOKED FINGER

HEAVEN'S CROOKED FINGER

AN EARL MARCUS MYSTERY

Hank Early

CROOKED
LANE

NEW YORK

Published in the United States by Crooked Lane Books, an imprint of The Quick Brown Fox & Company LLC.

Crooked Lane Books and its logo are trademarks of The Quick Brown Fox & Company LLC.

Library of Congress Catalog-in-Publication data available upon request.

ISBN (hardcover): 978-1-68331-391-5
ISBN (ePub): 978-1-68331-392-2
ISBN (ePDF): 978-1-68331-394-6

Cover design by Melanie Sun
Book design by Jennifer Canzone

Printed in the United States.

www.crookedlanebooks.com

Crooked Lane Books
34 West 27th St., 10th Floor
New York, NY 10001

First Edition: November 2017

10 9 8 7 6 5 4 3 2 1

For Joy, with all my love
And to the memory of my two North Georgia grandmothers,
Opal Rogers and Gertrude Mantooth

1

My first realization that heaven—at least my father's version of it—didn't hold anything for me came thirty-three years ago when I was seventeen, on the day I picked up my first venomous snake with my bare hands in front of Daddy's church. It was a moment I'd imagined and dreaded since I could see over the church pew and watch my father stalking from the pulpit to the front row, wearing the church's old brown carpet thin, shouting so fervently, with such conviction, that I became certain I had to feel that conviction too, and if I only could, the world would fall into place, and my father would love me once and for all.

When I was a child and I watched him holding those serpents, I was sold. The words no longer mattered. It was a visceral thing, a tingle deep inside me, an itch, a fiery rash swelling across the hidden skin of my heart. It would drive me insane unless I scratched it. The year prior, I'd watched my older brother, Lester, shaking as he lifted the cottonmouth high over his head. Eventually he relaxed, even grinned, as the snake remained passive, its wickedness calmed by my brother's apparent faith. He was saved, a child of God, but maybe more important in the patriarchal world of North Georgia, he was a man of God. He changed. The distance that had existed between him and my father diminished, and I was left alone, isolated with an odd mix of longing and dread.

My father lived his entire life in preparation for his death, a North Georgia mountain preacher who believed in the almighty power of God and the strictest interpretations of good and evil. If he ever found a gray area in all his days, I wasn't privy to it; there was the Holy Scripture and there was everything else. There was this world and there was the next, and everything in this world was simply a test for the one that followed. If you passed the tests, you made it to heaven and everlasting peace. If you failed even one of the tests and didn't get right with God, if you didn't fall on your hands and knees and ask for his forgiveness, you were damned to a hell worse than the one Dante described. In Daddy's hell, there was nothing but constant torture and excruciating pain. I remember falling once as a small boy, cracking my chin open on the rusted edge of a shovel left carelessly on the ground by my brother. Daddy picked me up and held me high like he always did as if somehow trying to remind God that he worried for me, that he prayed for me daily, and that he'd yet to see any of the fruits of those ministrations.

"Feel that?" he said, his voice a low and rough rumble that always sounded like the purr of a muscle car just before you really made the engine work. He only let his voice fly in front of his congregation, and then that low rumble stretched out sonorously over us and settled in the spaces between our thoughts and the ceiling of the little country church on the side of Ghost Creek Mountain, a comfort and a threat, all tangled together.

I nodded furiously at him. I felt it.

"That's hell, boy. Except hell is a thousand times worse, and there won't be nobody to pick you up and dust you off and tell you it'll get better. It won't get better. Not in hell. There's no end to it."

Later, I would learn the steel blade of the shovel had connected with bone, leaving the tiniest of cracks, enough to disrupt a growth plate and cause one side of my lower jaw to grow longer than the other, giving me an eternally crooked smile.

When my turn to touch the snake came a few years later, I was a jaded teenager, probably already an alcoholic, my desperation for my father's love by then soured and replaced by a sharp and defiant hate. But maybe, I reckoned, power lay at the heart of that action after all, because didn't facing danger equal faith? And faith was the key I'd always lacked, the key that would unlock all doors, the one thing that would make me a part of my father's world. In many ways, the opportunity to hold that snake in front of the church began to feel like my very last chance at salvation.

On the morning I was supposed to take up the serpent, I vomited in the dank bathroom at the far end of the Church of the Holy Flame, wiped my mouth clean, glanced into a mirror smeared with dead insects, and promised myself I'd believe as hard as I had to and then some. I'd trust God completely, so he would seal the lips of the serpent, and instead of its venom, I'd be filled with the Holy Spirit, the secret wind I'd never known before. According to Daddy and all the men I knew, this had to happen soon or it would be a bad sign.

I was sweating when the door to the inner sanctuary swung open, and I saw the throng already swaying to the sporadic thunking of Aunt Mary Lee's arthritic fingers on the tuneless piano. Daddy held two snakes, a large rattler he'd been using for years and a smaller cottonmouth found years ago in some brush down near Ghost Creek. Stepping into the sanctuary, I believed I felt it. The wind. Daddy said it was a breath, and when it took a hold of you, you might feel your feet lifted off the ground, your lungs expanding with the fresh air of heaven. I waited, closing my eyes, willing it to come in.

I had always wanted to believe in something. I still do.

I scanned the throng of congregants, looking for a kind face. I only saw two: my mother and Lester. Despite Lester's newfound closeness with Daddy, he always had time for me. We were only a year apart and were close in a way I truly miss now. I knew he'd been counting on this moment for a long time, hoping all would go well, that I would join him and Daddy as a man of God at last.

My eyes also fell on Lester's girlfriend, Maggie Shaw. Maggie was the only girl who really mattered in our little community. She was in my grade in school, but because of her long blonde hair, quick smile, and womanly figure, she drew the attention of boys—and men—much older than she was. Even then, she was considered a threat to the godliness of male congregants young and old alike, though she had not yet been vilified like she would be in the coming weeks. I spotted her in the congregation, sitting with her mother and father, both founding members of the church my father led. I knew they were deeply disappointed in her flirtatious ways and worked diligently to keep her away from the opposite sex, because nothing was more sacred for a young girl in the Holy Flame community than purity. They had no idea about Lester and Maggie's clandestine meetings in the church cemetery after dark. As far as I knew, nobody did other than me.

It was just one more way in which I was deeply envious of my brother. Not only had he made the transition within the church, he was also spending time alone with Maggie. I didn't even try to imagine what they might be doing during that time. That would have driven me crazy. I know now I didn't love Maggie, but I wanted her with a power that can sometimes eclipse love. Often I dreamed of escaping this place with her. We'd go to Chattanooga and live in sin, an idea I found at once both reprehensible and deeply compelling. In the weeks before holding the snake, I'd crept away when Lester did, but instead of following him to the churchyard, I went to Ghost Creek and lay thinking of her until my urges overcame me and I felt better—at least temporarily.

Yet as much as I wanted Maggie, I realize now I wanted something else even more. That itch, the one that ran across the skin of my heart, would not stop tormenting me. I had to scratch it. I had to make it stop. I craved Maggie, but I craved my daddy's love more.

Aunt Mary Lee slowed the tempo, and Daddy began to speak. At first, he only moaned, and I knew this was the spirit working its way through him like fingers kneading dough. Soon the moans took shape, and I heard words.

"Come and take us, God. Come and take us now. If your will, God, be for this serpent to strike, may he strike my son dead, just as Abraham presented his own to you, God, just as he raised the weapon and you stayed his hand, I commend this boy unto your will, Lord, unto your perfect mercy, but even more so to your absolute justice."

Then he closed his eyes, and the other words came out. These were the words that made my head spin, made me feel useless and afraid, because Daddy was gone, and what remained was some other alien thing, ancient and trembling beneath the ages. We had prayed the prayer of salvation so many times, but Daddy said you just had to keep at it until it stuck, until your doubt went away and you felt the spirit of the Lord take up residence in your heart. When that happened, he said, your sin would fly out of your mouth so fast, you'd nearly choke on it. Once in the middle of a tornado, he made Lester and me go outside and kneel, naked to the elements, and repeat words after him. Sometimes he did it that way, feeding the words to us, but other times he wanted to hear them come from us. Our own faith. That was what he always said—"It can't be mine, boys. It has to be your own."

Another time, when Mama had come home drunk, he'd slapped her and then pulled us into their room, where he made us kneel beside him and pray and pray. It was for our salvation and his forgiveness. Mother lay on the kitchen floor, blissfully unaware of it all. At the time, she'd been six months pregnant with my little sister, Aida, who would only live for a few hours.

Daddy went on for some time. I closed my eyes and let the sounds float over me, hoping to catch even one of them and tuck it inside, hold it, feel it, and be filled. When the tongues ceased, he beckoned me. Mary Lee's pounding began again in earnest, and I wondered if she'd fall prone like she'd done before, legs wriggling insect-like as she landed on her back.

As I approached, Daddy took the cottonmouth and kissed it on its head. Its tongue flickered against my father's chin, and for a moment, I believed I understood it all at last. The snake was a magnificent creature. To be so close to it, to feel its tongue against your flesh, must be a feeling of supernatural grace and power. I wanted that.

When he held out the snake for me, I did not hesitate. I took it in my hands, feeling its otherness in the slick of skin, the cold languor in which it lay nearly dead in my palm. I turned it around so it would face me. I so wanted to be like my father, to please him, to find him where he was, wrapped in something so transcendent, I would never want to leave.

The eyes of the snake were flat—so flat, I believed Daddy had given me a dead creature, and I almost dropped it. Later, I would realize the eyes reminded me of my own when I looked in the mirror, that in many ways, I was already dead inside when I touched that first snake.

The serpent twisted in my hands, and I gripped it more tightly. The slack eyes found mine, and when they did, they held me in such contempt that I knew everything was wrong, not just in me, but in all of us. The breath I was waiting for would not come, not like this, not now. Again I scanned the congregation, desperate for a friendly face. I found none. My mother had covered her eyes, and Lester looked at my feet, wincing.

The cottonmouth opened its jaws and showed me the gleaming, wet cotton inside its throat, and I began a journey past the fangs and into its belly. Years seemed to pass as I made my way through the cavern of its open mouth and into its hollow length.

I believe a part of me is still trapped there.

And maybe that's why I'd never been able to quit drinking. It seemed like the one place to escape the thoughts of hell, the sense that I'd never tap into the salvation Daddy wanted for me. So many times I had said the prayer, and each time it never seemed good enough. I'd do something stupid or selfish or mean. I'd lash out in anger toward him—I'd been born with my father's temper, just not his faith—and this would cause him to quote scripture about discipline and how it was his fault I'd not come to the Lord yet. Then he would begin to cry, nearly sobbing, as he made me hold the lowest limb of the oak tree in the side yard while he pulled my blue jeans around my ankles and tore the flesh off my ass with a switch as thick as cord rope.

When the snake struck, I barely felt anything. I'd heard a venomous snakebite is one of the most painful injuries a person can suffer. I believed that, but for me it was only a prick before a veil fell over me and the room turned to shadow. All the people were gone. Not even my father remained. I dropped the serpent and fell to the floor. I lay there for a long time, watching shadows. Most of the shadows were children, and after a while, the realization dawned on me that the children were lost, trapped in a limbo so profound, to this day, I cannot bear thinking about it. When we were kids, Lester and I took to sneaking out of the long Sunday services in that hot and dusty church. We would slip down to Ghost Creek, so named because there was supposed to be a ghost of a girl who'd killed herself roaming its banks, still looking for whatever she'd not been able to find in her short life. I was fascinated by that nameless girl, that ghost I never saw but felt more surely than any spirit my father wanted me to feel. No one seemed to know the details of her longing, so I imagined what they could be, sitting on the bank, passing the bottle we'd stolen from the local moonshiner, Herschel Knott. I figured she wasn't really looking for anything physical. Why would a ghost, I reasoned, need anything of this world? No, I decided it had to be escape she was looking for. Stuck between heaven and hell, that was her prison. She didn't care for either, and now she drifted along a creek because it was beautiful, because it was a promise she felt had been broken. That was what I'd come to feel too: betrayed, left in limbo between my father's angry God and the hope of another, better one. In some ways, everything that came after the snakebite was a shadow world, and I moved through it like a ghost, searching for a light to shine, for some tiny morsel or scrap that would help me believe the journey was worthwhile.

When I woke five days later, I discovered Daddy had refused to take me to a hospital and had instead left it to God to decide my fate. And as he'd done so many times before, God had decided to torture me.

He let me live.

2

The letter came on a Saturday morning in an oversized white envelope. I did not open it right away.

I'd spent the morning following a city councilman who was clearly using city funds to entertain a high-class escort. I'd taken several photos of him walking in the park with the woman. I'd planned to go through them over a quick lunch at my apartment before taking the best ones down to the mayor's office in hopes of getting paid. I had plenty of work, but there never seemed to be enough money. Probably would have more if not for my infatuation with beer and bourbon, but then again, I'd tried quitting once. It had gone poorly, causing me to quickly come to the decision that nearly anything would be preferable to going without alcohol.

Some people can reform, and some people just get by the best they can with their flaws. I'm the second kind.

I put the letter on my kitchen table—pushing aside a stack of tax returns I'd been going through for another case—and stared at it.

The writing on the front was unfamiliar. The return address was not.

12 Old Fields Road
Riley, GA 30710

I held it up to the light and shook it. Then I put it back on the table and looked at it some more. I decided whatever was inside would go

8

better with whiskey, so I poured myself a double and tossed back half of it before ripping the envelope open.

Inside was a letter and another envelope. The second envelope was labeled with only my first name, *Earl*. I put it aside and looked at the letter.

Mr. Marcus,

My name is Mary Hawkins. My grandmother is Ms. Arnette Lacey. Like me, I believe you know her best as Granny. She still speaks of you fondly, and I feel like I know you because she's told me so many stories. The good news is that Granny is still very much the woman you will remember from your years living in her home. Her mind is still sharp. The bad news is her body is not doing well. She has pancreatic cancer, and the doctors are not giving her long. She would like to see you again before she goes. Please consider coming down for a few days at least. I hope you don't mind that I looked you up in order to find your address (I'm a sheriff's deputy here in Coulee County). I know you are probably busy with your own cases in NC, but it would mean the world to her if she got to see you again.

I should also mention the other letter I have enclosed. According to Granny, this was delivered to her by a man she did not know a few weeks before she got sick (this would have been around April). The man asked if she could make sure you got it. Okay—just a warning—this is where it gets a little weird. Granny said she had a bad feeling about the man. She said she wasn't sure she wanted you to get the letter. I think her exact words were, "He finally escaped, and I think somebody's trying to pull him back in."

After she got the diagnosis, she decided it wasn't hers to keep from you. So she asked me to include it. I have no idea what's inside or who it's from.

What I do know is Granny grows worse every day, and your time is running out if you'd like to see her again. Please call me if you can come.

Mary Hawkins
470-488-4842

I drank some more of the whiskey. I'd known this day was coming and was pleased Granny wanted me to be there. I would book a flight to Atlanta tomorrow. The mayor's office could wait.

I regarded the second envelope, the tight blue script on the front. *Earl.*

Somehow I understood what I'd find inside was also a long time coming, that it would change me—or attempt to. I understood reading it could change my mind about going home. Even if it meant not getting to see Granny, the woman who had taken me in when I was learning to be a man and held my hand until I'd had the strength to grow up.

Briefly, I considered throwing the envelope away unopened. I could still go visit Granny, and if she asked what was inside, I could make something up. I could tell her it was from my brother, Lester, about my father's estate. Easy enough.

But she wouldn't believe me.

And worse, I wouldn't ever know.

Because it might be from Lester, and if it came from Lester, it meant there was a chance—however small—that he'd forgiven me.

Pushing the unopened envelope away, I downed the rest of the whiskey and poured another glass. I took out my cell phone and dialed Mary Hawkins's number. I looked out the kitchen window at the parking lot as I waited for her to answer. This was nothing like the place I had grown up. I'd spent most of my formative years having never even seen a parking lot, much less an apartment building. We lived in the mountains, where the roads were dusty and the sky seemed close enough to touch, so close that when it stormed and Daddy pointed at the lightning, saying it was the "crooked finger" of heaven, I believed heaven might be just at the top of the mountain, and one day I'd climb it and see God for myself.

*　　*　　*

Mary Hawkins didn't ask about the other envelope, and I didn't ask her how an African American girl had ended up working for the traditionally lily-white Coulee County Sheriff's Office. Granny had been the only person of color I remembered in the mountains, and she'd lived as a pariah, begrudgingly accepted because of her skill as a midwife.

I told Mary I'd try to be there by tomorrow evening. She said that was fine and that she would tell Granny right away.

When I ended the call with Mary Hawkins, I was still left with the other envelope. It had not vanished, as I'd hoped. It would not vanish. In a lot of ways, I realized, that envelope was like my past. I could put it aside, ignore it, drink enough to forget it, even throw it away, but that didn't mean it was gone, that it wouldn't still be waiting for me when I finally couldn't run anymore.

I picked up the envelope and tore it open.

3

Inside the envelope was a photo of my father.
My *dead* father.

He was standing in front of a stack of giant rocks somewhere up in the mountains. A vine-covered rock outcrop partially blocked the blue sky behind him. In the left-hand corner of the photo, the sun was smashed into a flat yellow flare. Daddy was smiling and looking right at the camera. He was thin and pale, but he was alive. On the back of the photo was a note scribbled in the same tight script that was on the front of the envelope.

Look at the time stamp. Compare with date of death. Proof he's alive. Need help finding him again. Please come.

Bryant McCauley

I looked at the time stamp. March of this year. Daddy died at the end of February. He went missing a few weeks earlier, and after a two-week manhunt, his body was found near the top of Pointer Mountain, where I'd grown up. The crows had gotten at him, and most of his face was gone, but he'd been carrying the Bible he took with him everywhere, and several people, including my brother, identified him. And now this. A photo of him—face intact, alive—nearly a month later. I laughed.

The photograph could have very easily been faked. After all, it was from Bryant McCauley, a man who looked up to my father as more than just a preacher. Hell, McCauley looked at Daddy as more than human. He'd been one of the first to believe in my father's "words of prophecy" and in my opinion was nearly as responsible for the radical turn the Holy Flame took in my teen years as anyone else, including my father. A charismatic leader always has to have that first follower everyone else can look to as an example. That was Bryant McCauley. He was the kind of man who would follow another man right off a cliff and then chastise everyone else for being too foolish to come along.

So yeah, I could totally see this as a fake, as McCauley's demented and desperate way to keep my father alive. Except . . .

I looked at the photo again, leaning in to study the rocks behind my father, the vivid blue of the sky, the overall clarity of the photo. I had some experience with verifying photos, and my initial impression of this one made me think it was legit.

Which scared me a little.

I looked closer. There was no way to tell for sure unless I took it to a lab.

Don't even think about it, Earl. Just get rid of it and forget all about it. Make the smart choice.

And maybe I would have followed my own advice if not for the dream.

Ever since the cottonmouth bit me, my dreams had changed. Sometimes they were just more intense, more foreboding. Other times certain dreams would not leave me alone, repeating over and over again, night after night, until I could see them in my waking hours. These were the ones that worried me the most, because more than one of them had come true, at least partially.

The dream I'd been having lately wasn't specifically about my father. It was more about an old well. He was always in it, standing beside the old well atop a rainswept mountain. I watched as he turned the hand crank attached to a rope and raised the shaky dipping bucket. I could hear it clanging against the sides of beveled stone. I knew inside that bucket was something I did not want to see, something so abominable that I'd never be able to live with the memory. Yet in the dream, I was transfixed, unable to move away or close my eyes. And then, just before the bucket broke the lip of the stone well, there was a flash of light, so bright I still felt dazed upon waking. That was all, the dream in its entirety, and I'd only had it five or six times in all the years since the snake bit me. Then the news of my father's death a few months ago reached me, and the dream came back with a vengeance. Every night, the bucket was a little closer to reaching the top. Every night, I felt sure I'd see what was inside, but thus far, the dream had always ended just before I could catch a glimpse. I remained haunted by the imagery, by the bucket, whose contents I never saw.

And that image of my father, hauling the unseen up from the depths of the well, was the first thing I thought of when I saw that photo.

I pushed it away and closed my eyes, trying to clear my mind. I wanted to be rational. The dream had nothing do with the photo McCauley had sent. It was just a dream, and this was just a doctored photograph.

In my childhood, Daddy had taken Lester and me on long excursions high in the mountains. His goal on these trips was to teach us about the area, to show us how to live in the wilderness, but mostly he wanted to use the time to talk to us about heaven and hell.

Well, mostly hell.

I remember a lot from these trips—a swinging bridge thrown across a deep gorge my father called Backslide Gap, a bald mountaintop surrounded by pine trees that made me feel like I was inside a great wooden fence, and a dark spot in the shadow of two mountains that Daddy said never received direct sunlight. He used each place as a metaphor for faith or, more often, the lack thereof.

I would have remembered the well, which made it clear to me it was just a dream and nothing more.

I looked at the photo again. And the place in the photo: I would have remembered it too. It was a bald spot—not a tree in sight—and the rocks behind Daddy opened up at the base, a tiny split that looked like a tunnel leading into a dark place.

I decided I owed it to myself to find McCauley and see what was happening. I was going, after all; what would it hurt to track down McCauley and tell him to leave me the hell alone?

Sighing loudly, I turned the photograph over. It would be nothing. Just a crazy man still clinging to the past.

That was all.

The only problem was I wasn't completely sure who the crazy man was, me or Bryant McCauley.

4

When I'd last seen Coulee County, nearly thirty years ago, it was one of the smallest counties, both in actual size and population, in Georgia. As I entered it again, very little seemed to have changed. The egg-shaped county was still neatly divided by the eastern edge of the Appalachians. West of the mountains lay the civilized part, better known as the townships of Riley, Cummings, and Brethren. The side with the mountains, where I grew up, was basically a dusting of tiny communities tossed without much rhyme or reason throughout the peaks and valleys of what the locals called the Fingers. There were five mountains in Coulee County, and each mountain was identified as a different finger. I came up on Pointer Mountain, also known as Ghost Creek Mountain because of the long creek that ran along its southern face. At the time, Pointer was home to half a dozen homes and a single trailer park at the foot of the mountain. An outsider would be forgiven for assuming Thumb Mountain and Birdie Mountain were on either side of us, but the Fingers didn't follow the normal human anatomy. Instead, to the south was Small Mountain, which best as I could tell was supposed to be the pinkie finger. North of us was Ring Mountain, so named because of the bald ring near its peak. Beyond that were Possible Mountain (some folks said it was supposed to be "Opposable," as in opposable thumb, but through the years, it had been bastardized into "posable" and finally "possible") and Long Finger Mountain. Long Finger was the only mountain of the five that actually contained something resembling a finger, but you had to be in just the right place to see it. Daddy had showed it to me and Lester once when he took us on a ride up Possible Mountain and gestured across the valley through the early morning mist to a stream that glistened like a silver scar.

"That there," he said in his low, hypnotic voice, "is where God touched these mountains with his own finger."

Lester and I were silent, but I remember imagining a giant finger coming down from the sky and touching the mountainside, leaving the stream of silver water like a never-ending fount of tears. I could still see it just like it was yesterday.

I purposefully drove past Pointer and my childhood home and instead headed straight for Ring Mountain, where I'd spent the last three years of my time in North Georgia. Ring Mountain and Possible Mountain were the least settled mountains of the five. Thirty years ago, most parts of Ring were only accessible by foot, something I desperately hoped had changed. Fifty was too old to be climbing mountains, even if I did run a couple of times a week and work out with weights when I couldn't sleep at night.

I started up the old logging road, dropping the truck into second gear as the ground rose sharply beneath my wheels. It was midsummer and hot, but as I gained altitude, I cut the windows down and let the cooler air come in. Immediately I was struck by the smell of honeysuckle and blackberry and something earthier that might have been the soil itself. I was home, and the realization hit me in a way I wasn't prepared for. The smell and the feel of that breeze on my face. God, I felt old and young all at once, and the tension of the last thirty years caught fire inside me. I pulled over to the side of the road and sat there, inhaling every last drop of the mountain air, gazing up at the treetops, the blue sky beyond the network of branches, and I barely noticed when the tears began.

There were so many emotions, but perhaps the greatest was simply realizing how much I'd loved this place and how, under different circumstances, I might still be here. Would I have become a preacher like Lester if I'd stayed? The thought of such a life filled me with a deep melancholy—no matter what I did, what choice I made, I would still be left forlorn and unhappy, I thought, simply because I'd been born in these mountains, to a man whose very existence had become the stuff of myth and legend.

I thought of the photo again, of McCauley's short note. *Need help finding him again.*

"Asking the wrong man," I said aloud. "I lost him a long, long time ago."

After a few more moments, I pulled back onto the road and continued on to Granny's house.

*   *   *

Years ago, there had been no way to reach her house except for on foot. The logging road they'd used to bring the materials to her home in the 1940s had eroded right off the side of the mountain by the time I was born in 1965, and since it was just an old black woman living alone, no one bothered to add another one. It suited Granny fine, though. She walked everywhere and often claimed it was the walking that kept her in such good shape. It was definitely something. When I'd moved in with her in 1983, she was seventy-four years old but looked closer to forty-five. Men twenty years younger than her often visited in the night, though she always played innocent if I asked about any of them, using the same line she always used: "We're just friends. Sometimes friends need to spend the night."

She would be over a hundred now, but I wasn't surprised at her longevity. She'd always lived like a much younger woman. Over the three years I'd lived with her, she revealed that she'd had two children—a boy and a girl—and they'd both been born when she was in her late forties. The boy had moved to Atlanta, and he'd often come up and visit with her on Sunday afternoons. Sometimes he'd bring his young wife, a beautiful white woman with red hair and an easy manner, and their daughter, a cutie I remembered playing peekaboo with on more than one occasion. I felt sure this was Mary Hawkins, the woman who'd sent me the letter. She'd be around thirty-five or so now. Still a youngster, but at least old enough to have worked a few years as an officer somewhere else before making the transition to Coulee County.

I was pleased to see in the nearly thirty years I'd been away, someone had built a road that ran nearly to Granny's front door. It was a dirt road, and there'd been some rain of late, so the rental would need a good scrubbing before I went back to the airport the next day, but it sure beat walking the last three miles.

Her house was unchanged. Still a little log cabin, situated in the perfect shade of two of the largest live oaks I'd ever seen. When I left, Granny hadn't had running water or power, and I didn't see any evidence she'd upgraded. In fact, the only thing preventing it from being 1983 all over again was the Chevy Tahoe parked out front. It read "Coulee County Sheriff" on the side, and I was pretty sure it belonged to Mary Hawkins.

I parked beside it and checked myself in the mirror before getting out. This was something I rarely did in North Carolina. Hell, I couldn't give two shits how I looked. It had never been my way, something that used to drive both Daddy and Lester—who believed in always looking your best—crazy. But this time it felt . . . almost necessary. I had to take stock of how I'd changed in thirty years. It was an urge—no, an obligation—I couldn't explain.

It wasn't exactly a pretty picture. My attitude about my beard was essentially the same as my attitude about my clothes. I let it be. I saw now that it was a scraggly gray mess. My skin was darker, marked with sunspots from years out in the sun without the first thought of sunscreen. My eyes were narrow—probably too narrow—and I tried to widen them, to look more alert, but it made my head hurt, so I just let them be. I'd suffered plenty of injuries over the last thirty years working first as a bouncer at a nightclub before becoming a full-time private investigator, but all the significant ones were below the neck. I only had one scar on my face, and it was not new. Just above the beard on my right cheek, my skin puckered into a tiny pink knob, and if I looked hard enough, I could almost see where the two fangs had broken the skin and injected the venom that had knocked me on my back for five days. Thinking of the cottonmouth again made me think of Daddy. I'd promised myself on the flight down that I'd see Granny tonight and track down McCauley tomorrow. I'd meet with McCauley and tell him I wasn't interested in hearing any more about my dead father and suggest he get some psychiatric help. After that, I'd head back to North Carolina with a simple resolution: never come back.

Granny was the only thing I had here anyway, and she'd be gone very soon.

5

Mary was a small woman like her grandmother. Her skin was lighter, and she had a smattering of freckles on either side of her nose. When the light hit her hair right, it was reddish brown instead of black. She was dressed in faded blue jeans and a top that hung down past her hips. She was barefoot, and each toenail was painted a vivid pink. If she hadn't already introduced herself in the letter as a sheriff's deputy, I wouldn't have believed it was possible.

But then she approached me, upright, sure of herself, a large smile that held just enough in reserve, and I could see it. I could also see—with very little doubt—she was a good cop, something that made it even more unusual that she'd end up here in this hillbilly cluster of . . . whatever it was that was here.

"I'm Mary," she said. "Granny is so glad you came."

"Earl," I grunted and took her hand in mine.

"She's in the kitchen. She can't wait to see you."

"The kitchen?"

"That's right."

"I thought she'd be in bed."

"Wait, you are Earl Marcus, right?"

"I already told you—"

"Because Earl Marcus would know Granny doesn't stay in bed for anything."

I smiled. She had me there. The woman was a special breed. She never sat still or slept in. Or went to bed early. It simply wasn't in her DNA.

I followed her into the old kitchen. Granny was seated at the same oak table she'd had when I'd lived here so many years ago. I felt my heart catch in my chest when I realized how old she looked. And it wasn't even the age. I'd expected that. It was the way she looked, her whole aura. She was feeble, beaten down at long last by all those years. Still, when she met my eyes, she brightened, and for a moment, the years fell away, and her gaze was the same I'd always known.

She tried to get up, but I moved quickly across the room and leaned over to embrace her. She smelled just like she always had—a combination of rosewater and old mahogany.

"I'm so glad to see you again," she said, patting my head. "So glad."

"Me too," I said. "Me too."

*   *   *

The three of us sat at the table and sipped moonshine. Granny had sworn by the stuff since she was a young woman and often drank three or four fingers before bed each night. Mary shook her head when her grandmother asked her to get it out, but Granny quickly admonished her, saying it was a special occasion, and besides, moonshine was "good for you of an evening."

I couldn't help but smile. Granny had so many things that were good for a person if taken of a morning or evening. Coffee or even just hot water of a morning would cure constipation. Spinach of a morning could cure a hangover quick. And a dose of honey straight of an afternoon could make a person happy—at least that was always how it worked for her. As far as I could tell, "of" was her shorthand way of saying "every." I still don't know if this was something she'd heard before or just her own distinctive kind of dialect.

She asked me to tell her what I remembered about the good times. "Don't think nothing about the time before, when you were messed up with that church," she said. "Now's a moment for good things. We'll have a talk later about the ugly stuff."

That was foreboding, but I took her advice and put the thoughts of Daddy and everything that had happened after the cottonmouth out of my mind.

I told stories well into the afternoon and into the early evening, recounting the time the black bear had tried to climb through the kitchen window to steal one of Granny's pies and she'd had to fend it off with nothing but a broom and frying pan. I told about the time Granny had fallen and sprained her ankle on her way back from delivering a baby over on Possible, and I stayed up all night worrying about her. Eventually, I'd grabbed a flashlight and taken off down the mountain, doing my damnedest to guess the route she would have taken. I searched the mountainside for nearly five hours when I heard a dog barking over beside a little creek.

Granny interrupted this one to explain that the dog—"a mongrel sent straight from God's right hand side if there ever had been one"—found her and sat there beside her for the whole night until it heard me "clanging around through the woods like a parade."

"He barked and barked trying to get Earl's attention. I wasn't so sure I wanted whoever it was to come down and find me. But that dog sure knew." She smiled at Mary. "Look at him. He's still a nice-looking man, but thirty years ago, he was stout enough to carry me home in his big old arms."

"And that dog," I said, eager to get the spotlight off my looks, "never would leave her side until the day he died."

Granny shook her head. "Died by my side. Didn't leave me until he was in the ground."

We went on and on, and it was the best feeling I'd had in a very long time.

*   *   *

At some point, Mary said she was going to cook some supper, and Granny asked if I'd help her out to the yard. "I like to watch the sunset these days."

She held onto me, and I helped her out to the cast-iron rocker that faced the west. We sank into it, and she put her hand over mine.

"Mary is a good girl," she said. "She moved her whole life up here to be with me. Left a good detective job in Atlanta to come take care of me. That ain't ordinary for today's world."

I agreed. It was more than just an average sacrifice. To come here, to live among these people, this insular environment. "Has it gotten better?" I asked.

"You mean the racism?"

I nodded.

"It's always getting better, but it's still there, and really a little racism can hurt just as much as a lot. But she's uncommon strong. She'll do all right. Besides"—Granny smiled weakly—"they say it'll only be another few weeks."

My hand found hers, and I squeezed gently.

"You got the letter?" she asked.

"I got it."

"I don't know the man who brought it. Must have never had children, or if he did, he must not have stuck around long enough to see me deliver them."

"I'm pretty sure it was a man named Bryant McCauley. And no, I don't believe he ever had kids. His wife died when she was very young, and he wasn't the kind of man to remarry."

Granny nodded. "You still having those sightings?"

I thought about my reluctance to open the envelope from McCauley, the dream of the well that had restarted right after Daddy died. Granny would have called both of those examples the "sight."

"No," I lied.

She said nothing, and I knew she didn't believe me. After a moment, she gestured to the setting sun. "You don't miss that?"

I wanted to but couldn't bring myself to lie this time. "Yeah, I absolutely do."

"I still have the sight," she said.

I waited, not surprised by where the conversation was going but feeling a slight chill nonetheless.

"I saw that man come before he showed up. I saw trouble all over him. It's why I almost didn't send you the letter." She sighed, or maybe it was a grunt. I looked at her face, and it was tight, her eyes distant. The moment passed, and she grinned again. "Pain is always there, but sometimes it bears down a little."

"Let me get you some medicine."

She waved me off. "You can bring me another glass of that shine, but first tell me you'll be careful."

"Careful?"

"When you go looking for that man."

I shook my head. "I'm going to pay him a visit tomorrow and tell him I'm not buying what he's selling. Then I'm heading back to Carolina."

She closed her eyes and nodded. Her hand tightened over mine. "Just promise me one thing, okay?"

"Sure, Granny. Anything."

"Be careful. Nothing is like it seems."

I scratched my beard. "I'll be careful, but tomorrow night, I'll be back in North Carolina."

She nodded. "Okay. Sit with me for a while. Let's watch the sun disappear. It's something I won't see too many times again."

That was what we did until Mary called us in for supper.

6

It was nearly one in the morning when we put Granny to bed. Mary kissed her on the forehead, and together we walked back into the kitchen.

"You have a place to stay?" she asked.

"Well, I'd planned to get a motel room down in Riley, but it might be a little late for that now." I looked around. "I reckon the sofa is still as comfortable as it used to be. Will that work?"

"Sure. I've got to work in the morning, but Leigh Ann should be by at around eight. I'll text her and let her know you'll be here."

"Leigh Ann?"

"You didn't think you were the only person Granny ever helped, did you? Leigh Ann Mears. Sometime in the early nineties, Granny went down to the valley to help deliver her baby. The husband was drunk when she showed up. Drunk and abusive. Granny called the police, something Leigh Ann hadn't had the guts to do. Turned out, the husband was connected in this area, and the police let him go the same night. Granny—you know about the way she sees things—felt like that might happen, and she waited at the home with Leigh Ann and the newborn boy. When the husband showed up later that evening, drunk as usual, Granny met him at the front door with his own .22. She didn't waste any words before squeezing off two shots. She didn't hit him, but they must have been close because he took off running and didn't come back for a few weeks. Served the asshole right."

"Wait," I said, "he didn't come back for a *few weeks*? Does that mean he did eventually come back?"

"They always come back, yeah. He decided he wanted the kid. And he got him too. According to Granny, knowing the right people in these mountains is far more productive than being in the right."

"I wouldn't disagree with that. Unfortunately."

"Anyway, Leigh Ann was devastated. But Granny took her in, saw her through the depression."

"And the kid?"

Mary smiled, and it was something to see. The dark den seemed to brighten with her face. "It ain't all bad in these mountains. The father fell off the side of the mountain. That's no joke. He literally lost his balance while being an asshole in front of some of his friends and fell to his death. The woman he was seeing at the time didn't want any part of the little boy. She dropped him off at Granny's doorstep."

I nodded, amazed again at the life Granny had lived.

"Well," Mary said, holding out her hand, "it was really nice to meet you. I enjoyed the stories. It felt like I was there. I'll be in touch when she passes. I'm sure you'll want to come to the funeral."

I shook my head. "No. I'm not coming back."

Mary looked disconcerted. "Okay. I just thought . . ."

"It's personal. This place don't hold the best memories."

"Sure, I understand," she said, but her face told a different story. I couldn't help but think I'd disappointed her.

"Before you go," I said, "could you help me find someone?"

"I'll do my best."

"His name is Bryant McCauley."

Mary's eyes grew large. "Did you say McCauley?"

"Yeah, you know him?"

"Bryant McCauley, the nutcase from Pointer Mountain?"

"Yeah, that'd be the one. He sent me the letter, and I wanted—"

"Let me see the letter."

"Excuse me?"

"I need to see the letter."

"I don't have it. I left it in North Carolina. Actually, I burned it and put it in the trash."

Mary's wide eyes got wider, and her mouth dropped open. "You did what?"

"I burned it. Why do you care?"

"Why do I care? That letter could mean everything."

"I don't understand."

She sat down on the couch. "Bryant McCauley's been missing since late June."

7

Daddy always preached that being lukewarm about God was worse than full rebellion, but like a lot of things he said, his actions didn't back it up. Before the snake had bitten me, I'd been unsure of nearly everything, but after I woke up from my five-day sleep, I possessed a clarity I'd never known before or, frankly, since: I wanted no part of my father or his church. I'd burn in hell before I let myself follow his God.

At the time, it was pure rebellion. I lacked the insight and experience time would offer, the wisdom to see that the Holy Flame was the kind of crippling religion that nearly always lifted up one person, and it wasn't Jesus Christ—it was my father. Was it a cult? I wasn't sure. Was it poison to the soul? Absolutely.

Yet in his own twisted way, my father was able to convince himself that everything he did was noble and right. After all, nothing could be worse than the hell he believed in. And he really *did* believe in it. It wasn't abstract with Daddy. It wasn't some metaphysical argument. It was a *physical* one. Daddy believed hell—all that burning and damnation and eternal suffering—was always just a breath away. Over the years, as I thought about him with the benefit of some distance, I determined there was nothing Daddy wouldn't try in order to save a soul. There was a strange nobility in that.

But there was also a kind of wicked arrogance, a world view that was so stunningly close-minded, it bordered on outright disdain.

When I finally woke from my five-day slumber, my brother Lester was there beside me. He smiled and thanked God I was alive.

"You made it," he said. "God saved you. He brought you through the dark valley, Earl."

I opened my mouth to speak, but the words wouldn't come. I was dried out, my lips nearly stuck together. Lester fetched a pail of water and dipped a rag in it.

"Take it slow," he said. I sucked hard on the rag. The water brought me alive, brought me to my senses.

"How long?" I managed to say.

Lester was still grinning. "You were in the valley for five days."

"Five days? Why didn't anyone take me to town? To the hospital?"

Lester's smile wavered. He didn't answer, but he didn't have to. I already knew the answer. Daddy didn't believe in doctors. "My faith is in the great physician," he'd say. "Not some heathen college student." Daddy held college students in great disdain, not because they were intelligent—Daddy always liked to surround himself with smart people—but because they put their faith in science and books instead of God's word. I never knew Daddy to waver on this point, and at least once, his reluctance to seek medical treatment had been fatal.

"He doesn't love me," I said, suddenly able to give voice to the festering sorrow I'd felt in my gut for a very long time. "If he did, he'd have taken me to the doctor."

"No, no, no," Lester said, and there was something like desperation in his voice. He wanted badly for me and Daddy to reconcile, for me to cross that threshold and become a man of God like he was. "Daddy did it out of love. Don't you see? He loved you so much, he did whatever it took to make you see God. Don't let this work lay fallow, Earl. Accept this gift."

"Gift? You call this a gift? He handed me a cottonmouth, and then when it bit me, he left me exactly where I landed. For *five* days, Lester."

"He did it for you, Earl. To prove God's power to you. So you'd finally accept him. Can't you see the beauty in that?"

Before I could tell him no, the sanctuary door swung open, and my father strode in, flanked by his closest advisors, three men who all aspired to his glory but fell short in different ways. One of them, his older brother, Otis, was cursed with a nearly identical physical appearance as my father, but he possessed none of his charisma. I'd always found it fascinating how he deferred to my father despite being nearly four years older. But what choice did he have? Daddy's influence stretched throughout the Fingers, and to create conflict with him was to lose. No, not just lose—it was to be destroyed. Daddy didn't have enemies because he annihilated them. Otis was smart enough to know this, and he submitted to my father begrudgingly, making their relationship a fascinating one that, throughout the years, would prove nearly as complicated as mine and Lester's.

The other two men were friends. There was Hank Shaw, a man who'd never seemed particularly religious but was a crucial ally for my father because he was—at the time—on the fast track to being sheriff in Coulee County. Daddy coveted friendships with powerful men because it helped legitimize his church, which was frequently seen as a fringe branch of the Pentecostal Church. In some ways, Shaw and my daddy were like two sides of the same coin. Shaw needed a religious friend, someone who could make him feel better about himself, and he found a willing ally in my father.

Billy Thrash was more complicated. He and Daddy had grown up together, and their bond was deep. Thrash was a gregarious man, quick to smile and slow to anger. When Daddy pushed people away with snap judgments and unconsidered pronouncements, Billy was always there to pull them back into the fold. And it almost always worked.

My father held up his hand, signaling for the other men to stay at the rear of the sanctuary. He nodded at Lester, who rose immediately and left without a word. Daddy sat down on the front pew, a few feet away from the pallet where I lay.

I tried a weak smile, but Daddy didn't return it. He hardly seemed to look at me at all. Instead, he knelt beside my makeshift bed and bowed his head. He was silent for a moment before looking back up. I'd never seen my father pray silently before, and I knew it was done on purpose. Everything Daddy did was for some effect.

After the prayer, he looked at me again. He seemed to be waiting for me to say something. I had no idea what he wanted, so I remained silent, feeling something like irritation beginning to build toward actual anger, which was a feeling I'd long harbored toward my father but also one I hadn't allowed myself to ever show in his presence.

"You ain't got nothing to say?" he said in a low, contained rumble.

"No, sir."

"Well, don't that beat all."

"Don't what beat all?"

He scowled at me, and for a moment, I was sure he was going to slap the side of my face that the snake hadn't bitten. Or maybe he'd slap the side with the snakebite. He certainly didn't seem aware of my pain, the close call I'd had with death.

"The Lord give you a second chance, and you ain't got nothing to say?"

I just looked at him.

He stood up and turned his back to me. Then with a movement so sudden it made me jump, he reared his leg back and kicked the hell out of the first pew. There was a loud thud and the sound of wood splintering. He looked down at me and shook his head before grunting and kicking it again. This time, his boot went through the pew clean and came free on the other side.

Billy Thrash started from the back of the sanctuary, but Daddy shouted him down. "Stay there, Billy. I need to be alone with him. I want him to look me in the eye"—he spun around, dropped to one knee, leaned forward, and spat the next words into my face—"and tell me he is going to turn his back on God after what he done for him."

His vitriol surprised me. Despite all his talk of sin and damnation, Daddy had rarely seemed so furious.

"Daddy . . ." I said.

"Don't you 'Daddy' me, boy. You better talk to God."

"What?"

"God brought you back from the dead, son. You know how many people lay prostrate praying for you? Do you know?"

"Wasn't anybody here when I woke up but Lester," I said.

He slapped me. He hit my good cheek, but that didn't make it any better. My head snapped back, and I started crying. He grabbed my shoulders and picked me up. He faced me, squeezing my chin with one hand, his other wrapped so tightly around my arm, it went instantly numb.

Something hit me then. It hit me hard. Something I'd never expected, but when it came, it felt like it made sense, like it fit. It was an interior righteousness; it fairly bloomed inside my body and pushed against my pores, and I felt like I might burst with it. I've spent most of my life trying to find that same righteousness again. It was a kind of faith, really, the kind of faith strong enough to look evil in the eye and speak the truth.

"God didn't save me," I said. "I just lived. I could have just as easily died. Just like Aida did."

The next blow knocked me down.

I hit the hardwood floor, completely missing the mattress.

"You don't never disrespect her name like that again," he said, "or I will make you pay, by God."

I just stared at him from where I lay. I refused to break eye contact with the man I both loved and loathed in equal measure. I knew if I looked away first, it would signal something—it would mean something irrevocable had happened inside me, something that would taint the rest of my days. I would be a coward in my own eyes and not just his.

He seemed to sense this and bore his awful gaze into me. His lips quivered with rage, and his eyes seemed to grow rounder and bigger as a single vein pulsed just to the right of his temple.

"I hate you," I said. There was no heat in the words. No anger. They were matter of fact, and that was how he knew I spoke the truth.

"The only thing I can figure," he said, letting his voice drop back into neutral, back to the slow purr that had seduced so many good folks in these mountains over the years, "is that God left you alive to make a point. He wanted everybody who ever met you to see what sin does to a person. He wanted everybody in these mountains to be able to point to a living embodiment of what it means to be damned."

He turned to walk away. My whole body let go into deep, rib-rattling sobs. He stopped upon hearing my cries. I watched as his body tensed and he rolled his neck. Then all at once, he spun around. I opened my mouth to say something—I have no idea what—but I never got a word out.

His big boot came crashing into my face, and I was knocked right back to the place I'd spent the last five days: darkness.

8

Mary tossed back the rest of her shine and met my eyes. "You burned it? Are you shitting me?" We'd moved back to the kitchen and were talking in hushed whispers for fear of disturbing Granny.

"No. I didn't want to see it again."

"See it?"

"It wasn't a letter. Not really."

"What was it?"

"A photograph."

"Of who?"

I poured her some more moonshine. "You might need another drink."

"I'm fine. Tell me."

I decided to tell her as little as possible. This woman didn't deserve to have the pain of my past inflicted upon her.

"It was my father."

"Your father? Didn't he die a few months back?"

"Yeah."

"Up in the mountains. The crows got to him?"

"Yeah."

"Oh, Jesus, I'm sorry. I didn't mean . . ."

I waved her off. "Granny really didn't tell you very much about me, did she?"

Mary shrugged and brushed back a pile of her brown hair. She was the kind of woman who could drive a perceptive man crazy. The little

35

things all added up to something special—the light freckles, her honey-colored skin, the small gestures she made that were at once efficient and completely feminine. I made myself look away from her.

"Let's just say me and my father had our issues. Anyway, on this photo, the time stamp was about a month after they found his body."

"That doesn't make any sense."

"No, which is why I wanted to talk to McCauley and tell him to leave me out of his crazy fantasy. My father had a strange effect on a lot of people. Bryant McCauley was just one of the more extreme cases."

"And there was nothing else? Just the photo?"

"He sent a note too. I burned it as well."

She laughed and leaned back in her chair.

"What?"

"Oh, nothing." But she was still laughing. It wasn't cruel, at least not purposefully, but it dug into me nevertheless.

"No, you're laughing. What's funny?"

"It's just, I thought you were a detective."

"I am a detective."

"Fine. I'm sure you're a good one too. But it was a mistake to burn the stuff. I've been working on that case for two weeks, and I've got nothing. Can you recall what the note said?"

I swallowed, deeply displeased with how the trip was going. I'd promised myself I'd speak with McCauley and get the hell out of town, a plan that seemed more unlikely by the minute.

"Something about him needing my help. He said he'd lost my father, and he needed my help finding him again. Something like that."

Mary considered this. "Doesn't help us much, does it?"

"Us?"

"Aren't we both looking for Bryant McCauley?"

"No. I *was* looking for him. My flight leaves at four tomorrow afternoon."

Mary drank some more of her shine and passed the jug to me. I didn't bother pouring, drinking straight from the jug instead.

"Okay," she said. "I'll go ahead and ask."

"Ask?"

"Yeah. I was hoping you wouldn't make me, that we could, you know, just sort of mutually agree and avoid the awkward conversation, but . . ."

"I don't know what you're talking about."

"I'm talking about you hanging around and helping me track down Bryant McCauley."

"Don't you have a partner or something?"

"Nope. I'm a transfer, and not just any transfer. My chief in Atlanta nearly had to call in every favor he had to get me here. It still wasn't enough. Wasn't until one of the other deputies went AWOL that Shaw finally relented. All of that would be bad enough for getting along with my new colleagues, but there's more. See, if you haven't noticed, my skin is a little too brown for these parts, and I'll be perfectly honest with you, Sheriff Shaw is a racist prick."

I covered my mouth to keep from laughing. It didn't work.

"What?"

"It's just that . . . well, it's funny on a lot of levels."

"I hope one of those levels isn't the 'racism is funny' level."

"No, racism is definitely not funny. It's just Shaw. He's always been an asshole. I laugh because I agree wholeheartedly."

She eyed me with something between impatience and outright disdain. "I don't see how that's funny."

"You're right," I said. "Sorry."

"Anyway, as I was saying, I'm not exactly Ms. Popularity at the sheriff's office these days. I could request some support on this one, but it would only make me look weak. Shaw says he gave me the case because McCauley was a fool. Said he should be easy enough to track down."

"But he hasn't been," I said.

"Right. And I figured . . . well, you know these people. You're not an outsider. You're—"

"Let me stop you there," I said. "I'm something worse than an outsider—I'm a pariah."

"Fine," she said. "Granny said—" She stopped.

"What? What did Granny say?"

"Never mind. Can I grab the couch? I don't think I'm in any condition to drive."

"Sure, but I want to know what Granny said."

She shook her head, but maybe the alcohol hit her because a minute later, she said, "Granny said you were a good kid, but she worried about you. She said she feared you might be damaged."

"Damaged, huh?"

"I shouldn't have said that."

"No, it's fine."

"I'm sorry. Listen, it was unfair of me to try to pressure you to stay. You have your own life now. It was kind of you to come." She stood and leaned over to kiss my forehead. It was just a friendly peck, but I had to resist the urge to try to turn it into something more.

"Good night, Earl. I'm glad I got to meet you. I appreciate you coming."

I watched her head into the den and collapse on the couch. I turned back to the bottle, lifting it to feel how much was left inside. Plenty, I decided, and took another swig. I stood and eased into the den. Mary was already asleep. I found a light blanket on the back of Granny's old chair and spread it over her. Then I went back for the moonshine and settled down in the chair to try to drink myself to sleep.

9

woke from a deep, dreamless sleep when I heard a dog barking outside. There was an intense moment of dislocation in which I thought I was in North Carolina and then I thought I was in my boyhood bedroom before finally realizing I was at Granny's.

I rose and tried to make it over to the window. I tripped over one of my own boots and banged my knee on the coffee table. Mary groaned in her sleep but didn't wake up. I made it to the window and saw the storm coming on hard and fast. Lightning struck the top of Possible Mountain. The night went electric white, and I saw the figure of a man standing a few yards away from Mary's truck. I jumped back, wishing I'd brought my .45 with me, but I'd seen no reason to bring it on such a short trip.

The dog started barking again, and I wondered why I was the only one awake. I waited by the window, but I couldn't see anything in the gloom. Lightning flickered in the yard. I braced for anything, but this time there was nothing out of the ordinary. I must have imagined the figure the first time.

The barking was coming from the other side of my rental. I swung the door open and felt the rain blowing slantwise across the yard. I stepped off the stoop and whistled sharply.

The dog whined softly at the sound and then began to growl. My eyes had adjusted to the darkness enough to see it backed against the rear tire of the rental. It swatted at something with a big paw before lurching back with a whimper.

Moving as quietly as I could, I went around to the back of Granny's house and found a spade hung under the eaves. I took it down and weighed it in my hands.

The dog whined again. I moved faster, knowing my time was limited.

I slowed my pace as I neared the truck. Another spark of lightning showed me what was menacing the dog—a rattlesnake, coiled and ready to strike. The dog was large, but I knew it wouldn't be any match for the snake.

I lurched forward with everything I had, bringing the spade over my head and down, driving it into the snake with all my momentum. The spade split the serpent cleanly in two. The dog jumped away, cowering beneath the rental. I reached for it. It snapped at me, and I jerked back my hand, thankful its teeth had done little more than graze the skin between my thumb and forefinger.

I made a low clucking sound and came at the big dog more slowly this time, letting him smell me. He growled at first but didn't snap. I got a hand on his fur and stroked him slowly for a long time. Behind me, the snake's body continued to writhe in its death throes. I kept petting the dog, murmuring softly until I sensed him relax. I pulled his body from beneath the truck and carried him inside.

I laid him on the kitchen table to inspect him. His torso and legs looked good. I ran my hands along either flank, and he looked up at me, meeting my eyes. That was when I saw it.

The snake had bitten him on the side of his face.

I felt panic surge through me. I didn't know what to do, how to react. But before I could botch it up, I heard Granny's calm voice. "There he is. The pup been running around my house for days."

"Pup?"

She nodded. "What happened?"

"Rattlesnake."

Granny pulled herself into the kitchen, grasping the kitchen counter to keep her balance. She reached the table and examined the bite. "We don't have long," she said. "Get me a syringe from over by the stove. Fill it with moonshine for me."

I did as she said, thankful for this amazing woman who had never met a situation she couldn't handle.

"Now some gauze and tape. Over in the drawer. There. Scissors too." I fetched the other supplies and watched as she worked, first cleaning the bite, then covering it with a compress.

The dog—the puppy—was clearly some sort of mongrel. It had short light-gray hair and a muscular body. Its large head and eyes seemed friendly and calm—or maybe it was just the shock. I guessed it had some mastiff in it, but the sharply pointed ears made me think German shepherd.

"He's been coming 'round for a few days," Granny said. "I don't think he's more than a few months old. Gonna be a big one."

"Is he going to make it?" I asked.

"I got a feeling he will," she said, stroking his midsection with one of her gnarled yet somehow expert hands. "You made it, didn't you? Besides, I don't think he got much of the venom. Sometimes snakes do that. Bite dry or nearly dry."

I touched the scar on my face, my hand moving there almost unconsciously.

"This dog here," she said. "He's yours."

"Mine?"

"That's right. No denying it. He's your mirror image." She reached up and touched the right side of my face and then nodded to the gauze just below the dog's left eye.

"I can't have a dog," I said. "I'm going back to North Carolina tomorrow."

"Now why would you do a thing like that?"

"There's nothing for me here, Granny. Except you."

"Not true. Your kin is here, and whether you like them or not, you can't ignore them. That church your daddy started is still going strong. Your brother is preacher now. You knew that, right?"

"Yeah. Sure."

"Well, that's your family."

There was an awkward silence in which her last sentence seemed to take on layers of unexpected meaning. *Your family.* Was she suggesting I was somehow responsible for their behavior?

"When's the last time you've talked to any of them?"

I sat down. The dog was breathing heavily now, sleeping.

"I talked to my cousin, Burt, when Daddy died."

"Your cousin?"

"Yeah."

"What about your brother?"

I felt myself flushing red. As much as I loved Granny, she could be infuriating sometimes, especially when she refused to stop pressing certain buttons.

"No."

"How old are you?"

"Fifty."

She whistled. "Where do the years go?"

"Good question."

She adjusted the gauze over the bite and pulled up one of the dog's eyelids for a quick check.

"You know," she said, "you may not get another chance."

I opened my mouth to answer, but nothing came out.

"There's no harm in reaching out."

"What's this?"

I turned and saw Mary. Her hair was wild, and her eyes were half shut, but somehow she was still attractive.

"This big guy got bit by a snake," I said.

"Just like his master," Granny said, grinning.

Mary looked confused, and I touched my face again. "I was bit when I was a teenager. But the dog isn't mine."

"Sure he is," Granny said. "Now I'm going to leave him to your care. He'll sleep for a bit, but watch him. If he shows signs of distress, wake me up. I gotta get some sleep."

"I'll help you, Granny," Mary said and took her arm, guiding her back to the bedroom. I was left alone with the dog—*my* dog—in the

42

kitchen. Thunder boomed out over the valley, and the dog whimpered. I pulled up a chair and laid a hand over his belly to let him know I was there.

I thought about what Granny had said. *You may not get another chance.*

I didn't go back to sleep the rest of the night.

10

The next morning, the dog was sleeping well, and I moved him to the den and let him sprawl out on the floor. Mary stirred and asked if Granny was up yet.

"Not yet."

"Good. She needs her sleep." She sat up. "I'll take the dog with me today. Drop him off with a friend of mine who'll make sure he gets treatment and a good home."

I nodded. "Thanks. I appreciate that."

"So you heading back today?"

"That's the plan."

"Well, if you get any more letters, you know where to find me."

I scratched my head. "Sure do."

She stood up. "I've got to get moving. Actually, if I gave you the address, would you be able to take the dog to my friend? I'd love to have time to go by my apartment and take a hot shower."

"Sure thing."

"And you can wait for Leigh Ann, right? She'll be here at nine."

"I don't see why not. My flight doesn't leave until four. I figured I'd head back to Atlanta around noon since McCauley is MIA."

I watched as Mary turned away to adjust her shoulder holster. She unbuttoned her shirt and reached in with one hand. She rebuttoned it and turned back to me, running a hand through her frizzy hair.

"Don't you want to see anyone else while you're here? I mean, I hope you don't mind me asking, but haven't you kept up with anyone else over the years?"

"Not really. I have a cousin, Burt. He came to see me in Carolina a few years back. Brought the family. Maybe I should drop by and see him." I said it almost as much to myself as I did to Mary.

"Granny said your brother was the preacher at the Holy Flame," Mary said. "I met him once."

"Oh, yeah? What was the occasion?"

"We were investigating a runaway. Actually a pair of them. Both girls and their families attended the Holy Flame. Lester wasn't what I expected." She slipped into her shoes, a sensible pair of flat sandals. "Of course, neither are you."

"What's that supposed to mean?"

She shrugged. "I don't know. I mean, I kind of pictured you different. You're not as old as I thought you'd be. And after meeting Lester, I thought you'd be . . . just different."

"Well, I am a very different man than my brother. We've had different paths in life."

"I suppose." She seemed to think for a moment. "It's none of my business, but since we've just spent the night together—sort of—I'm going to ask, what's the deal with you and your brother? Granny mentioned there was some big rift."

"Big rift? Nah, we just haven't spoken for thirty years. We're fine."

"I'm being serious."

I shrugged. "So was I. Look, I've already said it—we're different people. End of story."

"Fine," she said and held out her hand. "It was nice meeting you, Earl Marcus. I would have loved to get to know you better."

I took her hand. "Same to you."

*   *   *

45

Leigh Ann was late, but it didn't take me too long to understand this wasn't unusual. Leigh Ann was a hot mess. She wore a tight, flowery dress that accented her rather large hips and breasts. She made smoochie faces to the dog, who was just starting to wake up. When I introduced myself, she embraced me so hard, I though one of her breasts would pop loose.

"I've heard *sooo* much about you, Earl. What are you going to name this precious dog? Now tell me about yourself. Granny said you were some kind of detective. Where was it, North Carolina? Big city, I guess?"

She might have gone on, but I told her I had to get moving. I scooped the dog up as she hurried to get the door for me.

"Well, don't be a stranger," she said. "Come back soon so we can get acquainted."

I smiled and promised her I would.

At the time, I thought it was just a polite lie.

*   *   *

I've always heard if you don't want to keep a stray dog, you shouldn't name it. That was why I knew I was in trouble when the name hit me halfway down the mountain.

"Mongoose," I said. "Who fought the rattlesnake and lived to see another day."

He looked up at me and wagged his tail.

"Goose," I said. "I like it."

Goose tried to sit up, but I reached over and petted his head until he lay back down. "Just relax, buddy. Relax." He seemed to understand, because he closed his eyes for the rest of the drive.

Fifteen minutes later, I arrived at a nice brick home nestled along a hidden ridge. A woman was working in the yard. She looked to be in her midsixties. She waved when she saw me.

"You're Mary's friend," she said. "She said you wanted me to find a home for a dog?"

"Maybe not. Could you just see about his injury? Hang on to him for a couple of hours? I'll be in touch."

"So you want to keep the dog?"

I didn't hesitate. "Yeah. His name is Goose."

"Goose?"

"What? You don't like it?"

She shrugged.

"Just take care of him for me."

"Sure thing."

I opened the passenger side of my truck and was surprised when Goose jumped out and walked on unsteady feet over to a tree and lifted his leg.

"He looks like he's got German shepherd in him," she said. "And I don't even know what else."

"I was thinking mastiff."

"Maybe. He's going to be big for sure."

"Hell, he already is." I tried to hand her some cash. "For your trouble."

She shook her head. "It's no trouble. I love him already."

I almost said, *Me too*, but I wasn't ready to admit it out loud. I wasn't sure why. Maybe admitting that would be admitting I'd completely lost control of this visit. I'd been sure of my plan when I'd left Charlotte yesterday. Now everything seemed up in the air.

11

I had a few hours to kill before my flight, so I drove aimlessly for a while, trying to think. The rational side of me knew I shouldn't waste one more second here. It was like standing at the entrance of a bad dream and realizing the whole experience could be easily avoided. Yet there were things worse than bad dreams. There was life and trying to live it without closure. I didn't believe my father was alive, but that didn't mean the *possibility* wouldn't haunt me.

So I just drove. I tried not to think and to instead enjoy the scenery, the brief glimpse of a place that, under different circumstances, I could have loved.

Before I knew it, I was on Pointer Mountain, heading up to the old church.

Despite my better instincts, I couldn't resist. I'd not been inside its doors since I was seventeen, and I was curious to see if the reality of it matched the version I'd kept for so long in my memories. Burt told me it had been badly burned in a fire in the late nineties and Daddy had moved the congregation to a bigger and better facility on the outskirts of Riley, so I felt like it was a safe place to try to deal with some of the demons of my past.

The first thing I noticed when I pulled up was the old churchyard. It was well taken care of, something I probably should have suspected, knowing Lester, but it stood in stark contrast to the rest of the area, which was overgrown with kudzu and every kind of creeping vine.

I stopped the rental in front of the old church and took it in. The fire had burned off the back half of the building, but the actual sanctuary was still standing. I got out of the truck and immediately felt the heat. I went back for my Braves hat and then headed over to the cemetery. I walked straight to Mama's grave. She'd died of pneumonia a few years after I'd been bitten by the cottonmouth. I'd missed her funeral—not by choice—and it was something that ate at me nearly every day.

I turned back to look at the old church. For a moment, I swore I heard the strains of an old gospel hymn coming from within the moldering walls. It was very faint, little more than a whisper, so I let it go despite the uneasy feeling it gave me.

Beside Mama's headstone was another, larger one. It marked the grave of my father. I knelt in front of it and read the inscription.

Ronald Jackson Marcus 1940–2016
God's True Servant

"So when this corruptible shall have put on incorruption, and this mortal shall have put on immortality, then shall be brought to pass the saying that is written, Death is swallowed up in victory."

Daddy had always claimed death was the ultimate victory. It was only then that our salvation would come to fruition, and only then would we at last be able to drop the heavy burdens of our earthly existence.

Except he had meant more than that, hadn't he?

Even as far back as my teenage years, he'd told his intimate friends that he believed God had chosen him to defy death. That he could say it with a straight face revealed not only his prodigious arrogance but also his willingness to fall into his own echo chamber without even the slightest nod toward self-examination. Daddy's words were like the chicken and the egg paradox. It was a fool's game to try to figure out if he spoke his beliefs or simply believed what he spoke.

"Can I help you?" came a voice from behind me.

I was so startled, I stepped back and banged my heel against another headstone.

I turned and saw a tall, rangy man wearing large sunglasses standing behind me. He had on a pair of old farmer's overalls and a black T-shirt underneath. His hair was as black as the T-shirt, and his face was gaunt, his lips a pale pink. His age was nearly impossible to determine, and later it would dawn on me exactly why: there was something about the man that seemed to suggest he had already died and been reborn, not in some glorious fashion, hauled up from the earth whole by God himself, but in some hardscrabble, backcountry, middle-finger-to-death way. I suspected the rebirth might be a film that could only be played once because the scene (flickering in spasms of white light against a dirty wall inside some godforsaken place in these very mountains) would break the projector and, possibly, the viewer's sanity.

He just stared at me, his mouth set in straight line, those large shades hiding any thought or expression or humanity. For a moment, I could only stare back, unable to act on the overwhelming urge to get in the truck and head to the airport as fast as the rental would carry me.

The man was a ghoul, a mountain zombie of a man, a scene spliced onto the cutting room floor straight from a horror film.

And yet, despite all that . . . I recognized him.

"I'll be on my way," I said, finally finding my voice.

"Who are you?"

"Earl," I said, but that somehow seemed insufficient. My last name was out of the question, but it still felt like I needed to say more. "I'm just visiting my mama's grave."

He nodded.

"Well," I said, "I'm going to head back to my truck now."

He didn't move, which was unfortunate because he was blocking the path to my truck. I'd have to go around my daddy's headstone to get over there, and it felt like doing so would show him I was scared.

Like he didn't already know.

"I'm sorry," he said, and his voice was the kind of voice that stuck to your eardrums. I recognized it. There was no forgetting that kind of deep, slow drawl.

"For what?" I said.

"I think sometimes I startle folks."

"Naw," I lied.

He shifted his feet slightly, holding his hands out to the side until he felt a headstone with each. It was then I realized what was off about him: he was blind. I was a fool to have missed it. The shades, the way he didn't seem to understand he was blocking my exit.

Or maybe he did understand. Maybe I wasn't giving the blind enough credit.

"You sound familiar," he said and moved closer, deftly sidestepping the same grave I'd banged my heel against. He held out a skeletal claw, and I saw his veins were visible like thick purple worms beneath his pale skin. "I'm Rufus Gribble."

I held out my hand and felt his enfold mine. He pumped once and then let go.

"What did you say your last name was, Earl?"

"I didn't say, actually."

"Well, will you say?"

"Look, I'm just passing through. I don't want any trouble. Just wanted to see my mother's grave and then head out."

"You must have gone to the Holy Flame," he said.

"No . . ."

"Sure you did. Ain't nobody buried up here 'less they went to the Flame. You say your name is Earl?"

"I gotta get going," I said.

"Hell, you ain't Earl Marcus, are you?"

"No. You've got me confused."

"Oh, I hear it now." His face brightened a bit. He almost looked . . . normal. "Your voice. It's changed. Lost a little of its hillbilly, gained a little city, but I'm going to say you're the prodigal son, come back after all these many long years. Yep, I don't doubt it now. Earl Marcus."

51

How could I keep denying it? "Yeah, that's me."

"You don't remember me, do you?"

"Can't say that I do."

"I ain't surprised. I look a sight different. Or so I hear. Let me see if this helps. I always sat right up front with my mama. Wore a suit and tie every service. Hell, you probably hated me. I was one of them pious motherfuckers."

And that was all it took. I remembered him. And to say he'd changed was an understatement. He'd been overhauled, re-created. I had hated Rufus once. I'd hated him the same way I hated everybody that bought into my father's shit. But Rufus was special. He'd always been Daddy's special snowflake because he never rocked the boat—always on time, always with his pretty mama. I did remember exactly where they sat—first row, right in front of Daddy. I even remembered when Rufus held his snake in front of the congregation. I must have been eight or nine, which meant he was about nine or ten years older than me. I couldn't get over his transformation. He'd been nothing but a feckless choirboy when I last saw him. Now . . . now, he was something else.

I couldn't even say what. But it definitely wasn't a choirboy.

"I look different, don't I?"

"Yeah. You, uh, you live around here?"

"Matter of fact, I do. I heard you were a big detective up in North Carolina now."

"Yeah," I said. "I'm a little surprised anyone kept up."

"We ain't all fundamentalists anymore."

"Well, I suppose that's progress."

He grinned, and when he did, he was transformed to a man who kept his joy close to his vest for fear of losing it.

"Well, that's all we can hope for, right? Progress. Nobody gets to change where he starts, but every man can control where he goes."

"Yeah, I guess that's right."

"You say you're here visiting mama and daddy's graves?"

"Yeah, it's been a while."

"A while? That's an understatement. You didn't even come back for your daddy's funeral."

"Well . . ."

"Not that I blame you. He was a special kind of asshole, that one. After seeing what he did to you, I finally found what I needed inside to get the hell out. You inspired me. Bet you didn't know that, Earl Marcus."

"No, I didn't know that."

"Yep, I left the church on a Sunday when I was twenty-six, not long after you left yourself. I got myself lost in these mountains, and that's not just a figure of speech. I tried to get lost, and lost I was. It felt like something I had to do. I'd spent my whole life pretending I was found, that I had it all figured out—'cause that's how Mama raised me, and I didn't question it, at least not very much—so it felt like the right thing to do, to get lost. To just embrace it, you know?"

It made a weird, poetic kind of sense, and part of me envied his clearheadedness. I might have been his inspiration, but when I quit the church, it was a true struggle. I vacillated between feeling damned and feeling free, but mostly I just felt miserable, isolated from everyone who loved me.

And guilty. I felt very guilty.

There was a long silence. I looked at Rufus, and it was almost as if he was remembering my guilt too.

"You had a hard road," he said. "But I'm glad you come back. Want to come in for a drink?"

"Come in?"

"Yeah, I didn't tell you? I live in the old church."

"You *live* in the old Holy Flame?"

He grinned. "It keeps me honest. Plus, it's in a great location. Ghost Creek less than three hundred yards that way. Good fishing. Easy access for my visitors. And I can walk to work."

"Work?"

"Your brother pays me a hundred dollars a week to keep this cemetery up."

"But you're . . ." I hesitated. I didn't know what the rules were about these things.

"Blind? You are an observant man, Earl. But that's the best part about this cemetery. I had what you might call a death fetish when I was younger. Oh, you probably don't remember because you were just a kid, but I used to come out to this graveyard all the time and just sit, reading the headstones, thinking about the people, their bones, how they felt in the moment they realized their life was ending. I got the whole thing memorized now. Besides, if I mess up, I always know it because I run up against one of the headstones. You like whiskey?"

"Are you kidding?"

*   *   *

And that was how I ended up not only missing my flight back to Charlotte but also making peace with the old church.

Well, "peace" might be too strong a word. Call it a temporary cease-fire.

We drank and told tales of the very old days, mostly him filling in the blanks of stories I only half-remembered from my childhood. We kept it light, and at no time did he mention his blindness, just as I never mentioned what happened to me after the snakebite. Likewise, we each accepted the other's silence on these issues. It was a kind of mutual, unspoken distance that somehow brought us closer together. We understood some things were better left alone.

It was dark inside the old sanctuary, which I supposed made perfect sense for a blind man, but he lit a few candles so I could look around. The memories came back so fast and strong that I could see them like patterned images backlit by the flickering candles: the approximate place I used to sit with Lester and Mama near the front of the sanctuary; the congregation rising as one when Aunt Mary Lee began her hesitant fingering of the old piano; Daddy's smiling yet severe face as one of the ushers—sometimes even Rufus—placed the wooden box of serpents at his feet; my mother's hand on my back, reassuring me during a moment that was supposed to about grace but felt more like condemnation; Lester and me slipping out the back door as teenagers, hearing the sounds of my father's sermon ringing in our ears even as we left the little church behind and slipped away to Ghost Creek to drink moonshine pilfered from Herschel Knott's private stash.

I saw faces, flickering past, pale and ghostly, the congregation of forty years ago—Billy Thrash, smiling like a fool, his arm around his first wife; the Bronsons, Mr. and Mrs. and the three boys, heads thrown back in the wild fervor of a praise song I couldn't hear; Maggie, before she started dating Lester, sitting beside her father, Hank Shaw, her head tilted to one side, an expression of sarcastic amusement on her face. She'd never bought the show, I thought.

Well, that wasn't true. She bought it in the end.

In the end, you always buy it. One way or the other.

"You okay?"

I snapped back to reality. "Yeah," I said. "Can you pass that bottle?"

"Incoming," Rufus said.

We drank the rest of the afternoon and far into the evening. When I finally rose to leave, I realized two things: First, despite the initial fear I'd felt upon encountering him, I believed I'd found a kindred spirit in Rufus. The second was a little more jarring—I'd missed my flight back to North Carolina, and perhaps because of the whiskey, I wasn't all that concerned about it. If I'd believed in such things, I might have said meeting Rufus was a clear sign. I'd stay for a while. At least a few days, just long enough to erase any doubts—however small—that my father wasn't really dead.

12

In the days following the snakebite, I was increasingly ostracized by most of the community. Daddy made no secret of my rebellion. I'd thought he might be embarrassed to have a son in open defiance of him, but he seemed to almost revel in it, refusing to speak to me directly. Instead, he relayed what he wanted me to know through Mama or Lester, who cooperated willingly, if not enthusiastically. I didn't blame either one of them. There was a stiff price to be paid for crossing the man known throughout the Fingers as Brother RJ, and I was experiencing it firsthand. As was always the case, his followers were quick to emulate his behavior, and soon almost everyone in our little mountain community was ignoring me.

Everyone except Lester and Mama, the same two people who would also continue to stand by me. Mama would die a few years later after a bitter battle with pneumonia. Like he'd done with me after the snakebite, Daddy forbade her to see a doctor. She died in his arms, his face turned up to heaven, praying for her. He was unshaken when she passed, telling the congregation that God had willed it and that it was a serious sin to grieve in the face of God's will.

Daddy told me I wasn't welcome at the church again until I let go of my anger and accepted the will of God. I told him it would never happen, but he seemed unfazed by the pronouncement, something that would trouble me in the years to follow: What if he knew something I did not? What if, after all, he was right, and God had spared me from death, saving me for some secret purpose?

I spent the hours when everyone else was in church down at Ghost Creek with a bottle of something strong and a fishing pole. Sometimes I dreamed about Maggie. If not about her precisely, about meeting a girl like her one day. She was everything I wanted: beautiful, unafraid, wild, a free spirit in the face of Daddy's rigid proclamations. I believed she was uniquely suited among all the other people I knew to escape this place. At the time, I would have settled for a different kind of escape, the one that lasted only a few moments but was sweeter than anything else offered by this world, or at least that was the way I'd imagined it. I'd soon find out I wasn't far wrong.

When Lester slipped into my room late one evening, I half-expected him to tell me he was going to follow Daddy's lead and give me the silent treatment too, but instead he came in grinning, something he'd done very little of since adopting a more "adult" manner after becoming a "man of God." When I'd mentioned his behavior change a few days before, we'd had a huge argument, culminating in trading blows on the front porch. Daddy had broken us up with one simple admonition directed at Lester: "You can't fight with a child of the devil, son. Best to leave him be. Keep your distance. Stay in prayer."

Now Lester seemed unaccountably filled with joy. He slapped my back so hard, it hurt. "I'm going to do it," he said.

"Do what?"

"You're the first person I'm telling."

"I don't know what you're talking about."

"I can't tell nobody else because they wouldn't understand."

I just shook my head. I might have gotten angry under ordinary circumstances, because even then patience was not one of my virtues, but he was so damned happy, I couldn't help but be happy with him.

"Maggie has been ready for a while now."

"Ready?"

He sighed, trying to be serious, trying to act like a "man of God," but the smile just would not go away. "You know . . . sex. She was driving me crazy with it. I came close to giving in. You know? I mean, how could you not? But God has kept me from sin, and now he's shown me another way."

"Another way?"

"I'm going to ask her to marry me."

I was stunned. Lester was going to graduate in a few months, and I knew he had plans to go straight to the police academy and try to get on at the sheriff's office, but it was still a shock. He was in high school. Marriage? It didn't make any sense.

"Aren't you happy for me?" His grin was so big, so genuine, I couldn't be anything but happy for him.

"Yeah. I am happy for you, Lester. I think it's great."

He slapped me on the back again. "Things are working out," he said. "Don't you see how God has blessed me? I know you can see that, Earl."

But I couldn't see it. All I saw, beneath the happiness, was a deep sadness. It was coming on like the undertow swirling beneath the tide. He didn't even know it yet, but somehow I did.

It was one of the first and strongest premonitions I'd ever had. Over the years, I got used to them. They became a normal part of my existence. Most were vague, barely more than a feeling of dread creeping over me, but some seemed to be directed at someone I loved. And the first one was aimed right at Lester.

I should have said something to him. I should have done a lot of things that I didn't do over the coming days, but instead, I remained silent, trying to pretend—for the moment, at least—that the natural order of the world was for things to work out for the best, instead of the other way around.

13

When I heard the gunfire, I was sprawled out on the same pew where I'd sat for years with my brother and mother watching Daddy stalk from the pulpit to the piano, sometimes holding up a poisonous serpent and other times wielding his leather-bound King James Bible like a weapon more dangerous than any snake.

"Goddamnit," Rufus said.

"What is it?" I sat up and reached for my .45 before remembering I'd left it in North Carolina.

"Just some goddamned thugs," he said. He moved past the pew and over to where the old piano used to sit. There was a sawed-off shotgun leaning against the wall. He picked it up and carried it back to his bed—two pews he'd pulled together and laid a mattress over.

Another shot went off. Somebody whooped loudly.

"They live across the creek. Remember Herschel Knott's place?"

"Yeah."

"One of them is his boy. After Herschel died, about a half dozen of them moved in. Raise hell every damned night."

"They ever bother you?"

"These fuckers bother everybody. Call themselves the Angels of the Pass. Fuck if I know why. Once, I caught one of them inside here, trying to go through my things."

"What did you do?"

"I shot the bastard." He shrugged. "Don't know if I hit him or not, but I sure tried. I reckon I missed 'cause I never found no body or blood."

He laughed. "That's the part that gives me an advantage, believe it or not. Getting shot at by a blind man with a sawed-off will make you get on pretty quick. Since that night, they've mostly stayed on their side of the creek, but sometimes when they get drunk, they load up in their jacked-up trucks and drive by the church, shouting shit and throwing bottles and rocks and God knows what all. Busted the stained glass, and I was pulling shards out of my neck and back for days."

"Did you call the sheriff?"

"Well, I ain't got a phone, so by the time I hiked down to Jessamine's Bar, a couple hours had passed, but yeah, I called. Called the very first time those assholes drove by the church. They sent a deputy right out. He asked about a dozen questions about what I was doing here. I had to dig up the lease agreement to show him I was in my rights to be here—if he didn't like it, he could take it up with Pastor Lester. Once I showed him that, he changed his tone a little and said he'd go over and talk to the boys. That stopped them for a week or two, but it wasn't too long before it was happening again."

As if to make his point, I heard a truck revving its engine. It was so loud, the walls of the church shook with the sound.

"I offered to buy them some goddamned mufflers," Rufus said, "but they didn't think it was very funny."

"Jesus. I know a deputy. I'm going to talk to her about this."

He waved the idea away. "I talked to Shaw himself about it last week. He all but said I was on my own. Said this wasn't a priority."

"That's not right," I said.

"That's Shaw. He ain't never liked me." He fell silent, as if realizing that if the sheriff didn't like him, Shaw would almost certainly despise me.

"I know the feeling," I said awkwardly.

The engine revved again, and I heard the truck coming this way. "Fuck it," I said. "I'm going to tell them to get the hell away."

"I recommend just waiting them out," Rufus said. "It's what I do. They'll sling mud all over the place and tear up the grounds, but they always stop short of coming in. Like I said, a blind man and a shotgun make for a scary combination."

"What about the cemetery?" I said.

"They leave it be too. It's where your daddy is buried. Or used to be buried, depending on who you ask. Them boys are heathens, but some of them still hold the old fears. Hell, their leader is Billy Thrash's grandson, Ronnie. You probably remember the daddy. His name was Billy too, but he always went by John. Hell if I know why."

I did remember John Thrash. He was a few years older than me and always seemed distinctly uncomfortable in the church. But I couldn't focus on John Thrash. Something else Rufus said grabbed my attention.

"Go back," I said.

"Back?"

"You said, 'Used to be buried, depending on who you ask.'"

He winced. "It's just silly rumors."

Someone whooped over the din of the engine and then leaned on the horn.

I realized there was something new for them to desecrate—the rental truck. "Hold that thought," I said. "Can I borrow your shotgun?"

He shrugged. "You sure about this?"

"Absolutely."

He handed me the sawed-off, and I broke it down quickly, checking the breech to see that it was loaded. I cocked it and headed down the aisle, toward the front door.

*　　*　　*

There were two big trucks, jacked up higher than made any good sense. They were on either side of my rental. Somebody was leaned out the passenger side window with a can of spray paint, giving it a good shake.

I pointed the sawed-off at the starry sky and squeezed off a shot. The night shook around me. The sound echoed off across the valley. The man with the spray paint dropped it on the ground and slid back inside the cab.

The trucks stopped revving. Silence grew big all around, save the deep growl of the trucks, but it was a low purr compared to what it had been.

"You got buckshot on my truck," one of the men shouted.

I lifted the shotgun, aiming at the voice, which best I could tell, came from the driver's seat.

I loaded another shell into the breech and cocked the weapon with a satisfying crack. "More where that came from," I said, keeping my voice perfectly calm. There were a lot of things that shook me up these days, but dealing with situations like this rarely did. Part of it was that I didn't hold my own life in very high regard. I didn't have a death wish or anything, but I'd just stopped giving a fuck about guys like this. If one of them wanted to shoot me, then he could shoot me, but I'd be damned if I'd let them run all over me.

The ones willing to take it to the limit existed, of course, but they were few and far between. I was counting on that being the case with this crew.

"Go on, now. There's a blind man who lives here, and you are disturbing him. I'm going to be checking up on him from time to time. Don't let me see you bring either one of these pieces of shit across the creek again."

Someone chuckled. I looked around and saw a figure approaching from my left. I stepped back, surprised, and bumped into Rufus, who was now standing behind me, quiet as a damned panther.

"Apologies," a man's voice said in a slow drawl.

I aimed the gun at the man as he stepped out of the shadows and into the headlights of one of the trucks. "Kill that shit," he said.

The drivers of each truck turned them off.

"And the lights," the man said.

We stood in darkness. The man flicked on a light from his phone and held it out, illuminating himself.

"See, no weapons."

I nodded. He was younger than his voice sounded and had long black hair, combed straight back. He wore a pair of loose sweat pants and a dark T-shirt.

"Sorry about this," he said. "Boys were drinking, and . . ." He held out his palms and shrugged. "Be honest, this fella freaks 'em out a little.

Word in the hills is he ain't right in the head . . . and shit, look at him."
He turned to the trucks. "Get out of here."

"Aw, shit, Ronnie," one of the men said. "He shot my truck."

"Well, goddamn, Beard, that's what you get for nearly knocking
the doors off a man's home." He winced, looking the old church over.
"Though why a man would want to live in a place such as this is a mystery to me."

"Fuck off," Rufus said from behind me.

"He speaks," Ronnie said.

"I do a helluva lot more than that."

Ronnie chuckled. "I'll bet you do."

"This funny to you?" I said.

Ronnie turned to me, still smiling, and in the dark, his grin looked
like a sharp slash. I couldn't even see his teeth. "Sure it's funny. The
world is funny. Look the hell around you, man. You ever turn on
the news? The Middle Fucking East? Heard tell there's scientists working on robots that'll be smarter than we are one day. Probably going to
end the world. But they keep on trying to make them," he said, pausing
to glare over at the two trucks that still lingered in the yard. He shooed
them with both hands and laughed again. "So, yeah, it's funny."

There was some grumbling from within the two trucks, but ultimately, they decided to give in when Ronnie continued to glare in their
direction. I watched, still clutching the sawed-off, as the trucks drove
back across the creek and disappeared into the trees.

"But again," he said, "I apologize. And if my laughter offends . . .
well, fuck the hell off."

"Shoot his ass," Rufus said.

I shook my head, deciding not to let him bait me with the last bit.

"Seems like if you were sorry, you'd keep it from happening,"
I said.

"You know," Ronnie said, "we're just spinning our wheels on this
topic. Why not change it? Hell, I don't even think me and you have been
properly introduced."

"You're Ronnie Thrash," I said.

"Right. And you are?"

"Pissed."

He laughed again.

"You and your sycophant thugs need to stay the hell away from my friend's home."

He stepped forward, edging in on my personal space. He wasn't used to being talked to this way. That much was obvious.

"Why do you insist on being an asshole? It ain't neighborly."

I handed Rufus the sawed-off. "I prefer the term 'dick.' Assholes get fucked," I said. "Now get the hell back across the creek."

He stepped a little closer to me. I knew how these things went. He didn't want to fight. He wanted me to show weakness. If he'd wanted to hurt me, he would have done it already. I stared at him, eye to eye.

"I come over here to call them boys off, and this is how you thank me?"

"I ain't thanking you."

He smiled a little. "You got a comeback for everything, don't you?"

"Just the stupid shit."

"Earl," Rufus said, "if you're going to kick his ass, do it nice and loud. I want to hear it."

Ronnie cocked his head to one side. "Earl? You wouldn't be the famous Earl Marcus, would you?"

I said nothing, proving I didn't always have a comeback.

"Well, shit. I want to shake your hand."

And he did too, grabbing and pumping hard. "My daddy—God rest his drunk soul—told me all about you. Said you were one of the greatest men he ever knew."

"That don't say much about your daddy."

He laughed. "Naw, naw, I guess it doesn't. Be that as it may, you are a legend 'round these parts. What brings you back?"

"It's personal."

"Sure, sure. Hey, me and you have got a lot in common, Earl."

"I don't think so."

"No, hear me out. My granddaddy is Billy Thrash. Once my daddy died, he tried to step in and pull me into that shitshow of a church. Hey, is it true you told your daddy to go to—"

"Just get on out of here and leave Rufus alone."

"Ten-four, buddy. But let me ask you something first—do you think your daddy came back because of you? It's what I heard. Folks say he had unfinished business. Souls that needed saving. I reckon you'd be first on that list."

"I don't know what you're talking about."

"I heard he wasn't going to go to the grave unless each and every one of you was saved."

I said nothing.

"I never imagined you'd be so quiet."

"Time for you to go."

"Sure. If you need anything, I'm just across the creek."

"Stay there."

"I'll do my best."

"I'd like a firmer commitment than that."

"Hey, Earl, I can't see the future. The world is unpredictable. I'm just a culmination of all the bad shit that ever happened to me." He spat out into the churchyard. "Same as you."

"Me and you ain't nothing alike."

"Oh, I wouldn't be too sure about that. Hey, here's a question—where the hell you been all these years?" he said.

"I been away, spending all my time rounding up assholes like you."

He laughed. "Another good comeback." He looked me over and smiled as if he were in on some private joke at my expense. "You're pretty good at them. I'll give you that. But most of the time, they're just for cowards looking to hide weakness."

With that, he clicked off the light on his phone and started back toward the creek. Just before stepping across, he turned around again. "Say hi to your daddy for me. Tell him I don't care if he's dead or not—I'm going to put a bullet in him if I ever see him again either way."

14

Back inside the dark church, we sat down on the front pew, too amped up after the encounter to consider sleep.

"I heard the rumors about a week or so after they found his body. There's a kid that helps me out around here some. Lester sent him. Good kid, but he goes to the Holy Flame, and you know what that does to a person. Anyway, he said there were folks claiming to see your daddy up in the mountains. Others said he rose again, right out of the grave, and ascended to some special place. Apparently somebody's been talking to him, relaying his message back to the church."

I shook my head in disbelief. "You're kidding."

"I wish I was. Hell, you ain't really surprised, are you? I mean, as far back as I can remember, he'd been saying he was going to beat the grave. This is just some of the idiots making it come true."

"What does Lester think of it all?"

He shrugged. "You'll have to talk to him, but by all accounts, Lester is one of the more reasonable voices over there these days. Now keep in mind, reasonable is a relative term with those fools."

"What about a man named Bryant McCauley?" I asked.

"What about him?"

"You ever meet him?"

"Of course. He's an old-timer and as crazy as any of them."

"Did he believe my father had 'ascended'?"

"You like eggs? I've got a gas burner, and I figured, if me and you ain't gonna sleep no more tonight, might as well fix some eggs."

"That's fine. Can you tell me about McCauley?"

He stood up and moved over to where Daddy used to stand holding the serpents. He knelt and fiddled with an old camp stove, getting it lit and cracking some eggs over a hot plate.

"McCauley was a fool, but he was always a good-hearted one. He never meant no harm, I don't think. As to whether he believed in the ascension or not, I'm going to say yes, just because he wasn't the kind of man to disbelieve anything. But I can't say for sure. I ain't heard from him since before your daddy died."

"He's missing," I said.

Rufus pushed the eggs around, keeping them from the edges of the hot plate. The first signs of the sun were grazing the stained glass, offering a kind of rainbow of illumination. Rufus had taken off his shades, and I was surprised to see what looked like chemical burns around his eyes, reminding me that he'd not yet offered any information regarding his blindness. Not much felt taboo with Rufus, but somehow that topic did.

"Missing, huh? Not surprising, I guess. He always had a screw loose. Why the interest in Bryant?"

I told him about the photo I'd received.

He listened, turning the eggs over on the hot plate as I talked. I told him about meeting Mary and finding out she'd been looking for him for the last two weeks.

"She the new gal?" Rufus said.

"Yes, Mary Hawkins."

"How's she look?"

"What?"

"Come on, throw an old horny blind man a bone. Describe her for me."

"She's about six two, maybe two hundred fifty. A face like a sick armadillo."

"You're full of shit."

"Okay, okay. She's . . . on the short side, I guess. Skin like dark honey. Some freckles right around her nose, but you have to be up close to really notice them. I like her hair. It's sort of frizzy, hangs down just to her shoulders. Red highlights when the sun hits it right. Her eyes are dark brown and big."

"And the body?"

"It's very nice," I said.

"Can you be more specific?"

"Compact but lean."

"Her rack?"

"Come on."

"You come on. You ain't for equal rights?"

"What?"

"Equal rights for the blind. You get to look at it but I don't? That don't sound much like equality to me. Tell me once, I'll never ask again; it'll go into the mental-image bank, and it'll be mine forever." He tapped the side of his head.

I tried not to laugh. "Fine. Her breasts are nice."

"Natural?"

"I'm assuming so. I haven't actually studied them."

"You'd know if they were fake."

"Probably."

"So give me the bra size?"

I shrugged. "C-cup?"

He grinned and leaned his head back on the pew. I guessed he was putting it all together inside his "mental-image bank."

"Thank you," he said. "I've got her now."

"You're welcome," I said, electing not to tell him how deeply weird that had been. Instead, I tried to go back to the subject: "If you were looking for McCauley, where would you start?"

He stroked the rough stubble on his chin. "I guess there's several places I'd start, but I'm going to assume they already checked his house and didn't find nothing. After that, I'd go to his fishing shack."

"Fishing shack?"

"Yeah, he and your daddy liked to go fishing over on Small Mountain. You know Silver Lake?"

"I think I remember it. Right off the county road?"

"That's it. But to get to the shack, you have to get to the other side of the lake. The best way to do that is to go down the back side of Pointer on the little logging road. It'll take you right to it. And it's just a little shack, from what I hear. I ain't never seen it, of course." He grinned at me, and I couldn't help but grin back.

I was home. And I was going to stay for a little bit, at least until I resolved some things. Like what happened to Bryant McCauley, for one. I also wanted—no, *needed*—to find a way to put these rumors of my father's ascension to rest once and for all. Maybe it wouldn't have bothered me half as much if it hadn't been for the dream and the well.

And the bucket that, even in my waking hours, seemed to be slowly coming to the surface.

"You up for a little ride?" I said.

"Sure. Let's eat first. And then maybe we need to go by the pawn shop."

"What for?"

"Get you a firearm. You done made an enemy in Ronnie Thrash." He laughed. "As if you needed another one."

*　　*　　*

We swung by the "pawn shop," which was nothing more than a double-wide trailer on blocks with a large posterboard attached to one of the windows that read, "Als' Fire-Arm's and Pown." It looked like it had been written by a fourth grader who was well on his way to failing the year. For the second time.

"I don't know about this place," I said.

"Well, I heard it was a pawn shop," Rufus said. "Was I misled?"

I winced. "I think you might have been." Still, I did need a gun, and at the moment, I wasn't going to be too choosy about where I got it from. At least, I reasoned, whatever gun I bought here wouldn't wind up in some criminal's hands.

Al was asleep on his couch but woke right up when he heard us banging on the door. He looked us over when I asked to see the handguns and apparently decided we were reliable enough. He led us to the kitchen and pulled out a large tool chest from beneath the sink. He lifted the handguns out one at a time until the kitchen counter was covered in them. I inspected a Glock .45 caliber, but it didn't feel weighted right. After checking out a few more .45 calibers, which was what I preferred, I settled on the newest-looking piece, which was also small enough to keep hidden, a Smith & Wesson M&P 9mm. I bought some ammo and a shoulder holster. It cost me nearly three hundred dollars, most of the cash I'd brought.

"You didn't buy it here," Al said. He sounded almost bored.

"Of course not," Rufus said. "Besides, I never saw you."

"Good one," Al said, but he didn't laugh. Instead he just headed for the couch to lie back down.

*　　*　　*

The fishing shack sat a couple dozen feet from the shore. It was just large enough to squeeze a set of bunk beds inside as well as a cooler and some other equipment, all of which appeared to be completely abandoned.

"Anything?" Rufus asked.

"Not sure yet." I stepped inside and opened the cooler. It was filled with old water and a dead fish. I shut it quickly.

"Jesus," Rufus said. "There's dead fish in here."

"Just one." I sat down on the bottom bunk and looked around. There was some scribbling on the wall above the cooler. It was tough to read because the wood planks were a faded chestnut and whoever had done the writing did it in pencil. I leaned in close, squinting.

It was a list, and some of the items had been crossed through. Those were nearly impossible to read, but a few near the bottom were still legible.

—the girl
—find map (Miss Laney)
—Earl again

70

My name was underlined at least three times.

So he'd written my name down on this list. Why? To remind himself to reach out to me? And why *again*? Had he previously tried and failed? And what did *the girl* mean, not to mention *find map* and the parenthetical *Miss Laney*?

"Hey, you ever hear anything about a map?"

"You'll have to be more specific," Rufus said.

I tried to think how to best frame the question. "Anything about a map and my father? Or do you know who Miss Laney is?"

"Miss Laney? That's an easy one. She started coming after you, uh, left, but she never missed a Sunday. Sat right up front, hung on your daddy's every word. She was the first one to start taping the sermons. That was after I left, though."

He screwed his face up in an expression I took for deep contemplation. "As for the map . . . let me think on it. Sounds like something I heard once."

I leaned in again, trying to read some of the bullets that had been scratched through. It was no use. A letter here or there, but not nearly enough to make anything out.

"There was that thing in the newspaper," he said.

"Newspaper?"

"Yeah, your daddy was a celebrity for a while."

"What for?"

"What for? He used the power of the Lord to face down some pot dealers. It was big news at the time. Hell, it was one of the things that helped him become more than just a man."

"What did it say about a map?"

"I can't actually remember. But I reckon you could find the article if you really wanted to. Didn't you say you were a detective?"

I ignored the jab, my mind already turning to the old library in Riley.

15

Rufus said he'd pass on the library but invited me back to crash at his place that evening. "That is, as long as you don't mind the bad memories."

I told him I didn't and that I'd definitely be back, as long as he didn't mind me bringing along a dog.

"How does a man visiting from North Carolina already have a dog?"

I told him what happened the night before.

"And you already named this dog?"

"Goose," I said.

"You sure this ain't a bird?"

I told him I was pretty sure and thanked him for opening up his home to me.

"It's as much yours as it is mine. Your daddy built it with his bare hands, from what I hear."

"My father could do just about anything if he believed it was God's will."

"There are no limits to how completely a man can fool himself."

What I didn't tell him was that I wanted to be there as much for him as for me. He could make all the jokes he wanted about how scary a blind man with a sawed-off was, but I didn't think he was safe.

As a precautionary measure, I even drove down by the creek until I could get a glimpse of Herschel's old place through the trees. The two pickups were parked in front of the house, and it didn't appear any of the men had even stirred yet. Probably still sleeping it off, I assumed.

Probably wouldn't be up until evening, and I planned to be back by then. Of course, the likelihood of me being able to stand guard through the night was very slight. Maybe twenty years ago I could have tolerated three all-nighters in a row, but I was already feeling the gravity of sleep pulling me down.

In Riley, I stopped at a coffee shop and took the opportunity to call a few clients in Charlotte to let them know I hadn't forgotten them. They weren't happy, but they were willing to give me time. I'd worked for these clients before, and I'd built up enough goodwill with both of them to take a few days. But just a few. Both clients had other options, something I'd have to consider soon.

I bought an espresso to go and drank it on the way to the library. It was a short walk from the coffee place. Riley had done well over the last thirty years, retaining its small-town charm but infusing it seamlessly with modern amenities. It was the kind of place you might come antique shopping and run into some college kids who were here to hike the nearby trails. It was pleasant, and I felt myself relaxing a little as I headed up the steps to the old library.

That feeling didn't last very long. A familiar voice called out from behind me.

Repent, the same voice had said to me thirty-three years earlier.

I turned around slowly.

"Earl Marcus? I thought you'd never come back to this place again."

I recognized the man even though I had not seen him since I was seventeen. We'd called him Choirboy then, just not to his face. To his face, we tried to say as little as possible. In fact, we tried not to look at his face at all.

His real name was Chester Dunkling, and I'd always remember him for two things: being a head taller than everyone else our age and taking all the fire and brimstone bullshit my father preached as seriously as anyone I'd ever known.

He shook my hand, and I tried to read him. Time does a lot to someone, but it can't hide a person's true character. I saw in those eyes the same thing I'd seen so many years ago.

73

Repent.

You can't make somebody repent.

Sure you can. Watch me.

He had proceeded to pick me up and turn me over, holding me out over the gorge they used to call Backslide Gap. I screamed and yelled, but it was no use. Choirboy wasn't going to put me down until I repented.

Repent. Repent. Do it.

He wouldn't stop saying it. As determined as I was to not give in, I was more frightened his arms would give out before his stubborn desire to see me repent and that I would die before I ever made it to thirteen.

So I repented. I told him I was sorry. I told God I was sorry. What I didn't tell him—and was damned glad he hadn't noticed—was I had absolutely no idea what I was repenting for.

But it had worked. He put me down and gave me a hard stare.

God forgives you.

I wondered if God had forgiven him yet.

"You come back to make amends?"

I shook my head. "No. Just to tie up some loose ends. I'm not staying long."

"You should make amends, Earl."

"I don't have anything to make amends for." It had been my line thirty years ago, and it was still my line. For everybody except Lester. Lester was different. One day, I hoped he'd forgive me for what I had done.

"I hate to hear that," Choirboy said. He still looked the part. Tall, clean cut—wearing a pair of tan slacks hiked up nearly to his navel and a plain blue button-down oxford cloth shirt. His hair was parted neatly to one side and colored black to look like it had so many years ago.

I felt a distinct and powerful urge to get away from him, to put some distance between myself and this distasteful embodiment of a past I'd tried so hard to forget.

"I just want you to know, Earl," he said, his voice a low drawl, "God will take you back if you repent, but he has limits. His judgment is pure."

"That's good to hear, Chester."

74

He smiled. "Oh, folks just call me Choirboy now." He tilted his head to one side, in what seemed like an oddly robotic attempt at a human gesture. "It kind of stuck. I like it. Lets people know right up front what I'm about."

"And what's that, Chester?"

His smile vanished. "Doing the Lord's work."

"It's good to know some people never change."

"I agree. Like your daddy, for one. He's still the same today as he was when he baptized me in Ghost Creek."

"Except he's dead."

Choirboy smiled expansively, showing off clean, straight teeth, like well-polished tombstones.

It was one of the most disarming smiles I'd ever seen, and I was truly thankful when the library door swung open and hit my shoulder.

A young woman came out. "Excuse me," she said. She glanced at Choirboy and moved quickly on past.

"I got some stuff to do," I said.

He kept on smiling, not speaking, so I grabbed the door before it closed and slipped on inside, to what I hoped would be friendlier faces.

Just before the door swung shut behind me, I could have sworn I heard him say it again, or maybe it was just the old memory bubbling to the surface. Either way, it sent a chill through me, and I wanted to plug my ears.

Repent.

*   *   *

I didn't fare much better inside the library. I approached the front desk to ask a small blonde-haired woman where I could find the microfiche, but when she turned around and smiled pleasantly, the question I'd planned to ask got stuck in my throat.

Her smile disappeared immediately once she recognized who I was.

"May I help you?" she said, and I realized she was just going to pretend she didn't know me.

"How have you been, Mrs. Shaw?" I said.

"It's not Shaw anymore." She didn't offer her new name.

"I'd like to try to explain what happened."

"I'm not interested. Do you need some help?" She barely opened her mouth when she spoke, and her voice literally quivered with hate.

I winced and shook my head. "Your microfiche?"

"Why are you even here?" she said, ignoring the request she'd demanded I make.

"I'm here . . ." I was about to say *for Granny*, but then I remembered Granny was a reviled figure among people associated with the Holy Flame. I just shook my head. "I'm here for work."

"Work?"

"Yeah, I'm on a case."

"You some kind of cop?" Her voice was loud now, and people looked up from what they were doing to watch our conversation. She was visibly angry.

"I'll just find it myself," I said.

"I don't want you here." She turned around, looking for someone who'd help her. A young man wearing a suit came out from the rear of the library.

"What's the trouble?"

Maggie's mother clenched her fists together and glared at me. She said nothing else. Even when the young man repeatedly asked her if she was okay.

I took that opportunity to slip away and look for the microfiche.

*　　*　　*

Rufus had narrowed the time down to the early nineties, and he said he remembered it was in one of the smaller local papers, maybe Riley or Dalton. I got to work, still buzzing from the espresso and the awkward encounter with Maggie's mother. It felt weird to me that I could be away for thirty years and come back to the exact same vitriol. Yet it wasn't surprising, which explained why I'd resisted coming home in the first place.

I worked for nearly three hours before the library page stuck her head into the back room and said, "We're closing in fifteen minutes."

After that, I worked quickly, squinting hard into the machine, hoping something would catch my eye. And it did.

The headline itself was classic RJ Marcus.

Old-Time Religion Wins Against Mountain Drug Dealers

I took out my phone and snapped a photo of the screen. I checked to make sure it was clear enough and then took two more before giving the reel a good spin so nobody would know what I'd been looking at and then left the library.

I didn't look at the front desk as I slipped out the door.

16

To say Mary was shocked to see me was an understatement. She looked like she'd seen a ghost when she answered the door and I was standing there. And if I didn't know better, I could have sworn she looked pleased. I'd gone by to pick up Goose first, and he nudged her knee until she knelt to pet him.

"You miss your flight?" she said.

"You could say that."

I stepped inside and heard Granny call from the kitchen. "What did I tell you?"

"Shush, Granny."

"You two have a bet or something?" I said.

"She was just convinced you'd come back. Apparently, she's also convinced you and me should date." Mary smiled and pulled her hair back. "She's old, what can I tell you?"

"Well, she was right about me still being here."

"I see that. Now explain yourself."

She led me to the kitchen, and I gave Granny a hug. She tried to put on a good face, but I could tell she was worn out. Probably the midnight doctoring of Goose the night before had contributed to that.

"Get him some shine," Granny ordered. Mary grabbed a cup and poured me a few fingers. Whiskey with Rufus and moonshine at Granny's. No wonder I'd decided to stay.

"Well?" Mary said.

"I got something on McCauley."

"That's why you stayed?"

"I don't know why I stayed, okay? Maybe I got drunk and missed the flight. Or maybe I just like the weather. Either way, I'm here, and I found something on McCauley."

"Fair enough," Mary said. "I'd love to hear it. I've got nothing."

I told her about my fortuitous meeting with Rufus and our ensuing conversation that led us to the fishing shack. I described the place as well as I could and told her about the list with my name on it.

"Earl," she whispered softly, seemingly amazed by the revelation of my name being on the wall of the shack. It wasn't far from how I felt.

"So I asked Rufus if he'd ever heard about any map. He recalled a newspaper article from the early nineties."

"We'll go to the library tomorrow," Mary said.

"I've already been." I reached for my phone. "Got it right here." I unlocked the phone and pulled up the photograph. "Here," I said, handing it to Mary. "Read it out loud. I can't see this. You got young eyes."

She took the phone and frowned at it. She squinted and began to read:

Old-Time Religion Wins Against Mountain Drug Dealers

Robert Jackson Marcus, best known to his congregation as "RJ," still believes in the power of God. After being the head pastor at the Holy Flame in rural Coulee County in North Georgia for nearly twenty years, he's seen God work in ways that "will blow your mind." The latest—and, according to Marcus, greatest—example of God's power happened earlier this spring, deep in the mountains near the small town of Riley, when Marcus and some others, while on a spiritual search that led them to a spectacular waterfall Marcus calls "the tears of God," were accosted by some men brandishing weapons who told the minister the land was private and they'd need to move along.

"We are peaceful men," Marcus says. "We told them we'd be glad to move along, but that we'd be back after prayer and fasting if this was where God wanted us. See, I'd seen this place before in a vision.

Most people don't believe in visions or prophets anymore, but I'm not most people. Still, I gave them the benefit of the doubt."

Marcus is indeed "not most people." He's an imposing man with a deep, soaring voice and a faith that has stood the test of time.

"I've always been a believer, and I've always talked to God. Most people don't have the faith to listen, but I do."

After returning to his church, Marcus and his friends prayed about the land. According to members of the Holy Flame, they'd never seen their minister so dedicated to prayer and fasting. He holed himself up inside his church office for three weeks, only speaking to his closest friends and his wife. When he emerged, he said he'd heard the voice of God, who had instructed him to sketch a map. Marcus claimed if the men followed this map, God would keep them safe and lead them to a special place at the top of the mountain.

"I told the church that I was going back. God had showed me a well at the top of the mountain not made by the hands of man. He told me it was his well and I was to take it back for his people. I invited any of the elders to join me if they wanted to but made it clear I wasn't forcing them. Four of them came, including Daniel Edwards. He wasn't but twenty years old at the time."

Marcus and his men ventured into the mountains again with a renewed energy. Despite the implied threat of violence, none of them carried weapons. Instead, they were armed only with the map and what Marcus calls "the old faith." They moved into the region, more sure than ever they were approaching a holy place. As they neared the spot high in the mountains Marcus said God had showed him, they were fired upon. Young Edwards was hit and later died when he refused to seek medical help and instead insisted on continuing the pilgrimage.

Marcus's face grows dark when he speaks of that terrible time. "We begged him to let us take him back, but he was a true believer. Danny told me God's finger wasn't crooked." When asked to explain this, Marcus simply said it meant God didn't make mistakes. "What he touched was touched. There wasn't no accidents. That was what Danny believed. It's what I still believe."

Marcus and his men forged on ahead. Eventually, they stumbled upon the reason for so much resistance: a field of marijuana hidden in a secret meadow. Here, they encountered violence again, as several shots rang out, but none of Marcus's troop were injured, and they pushed on, using the illegal plants for cover as they continued deeper into the wilderness.

"Eventually, we reached the place I'd dreamed about, the well. It's hidden from all men lest they have the spirit of the Lord inside them, and even then it takes much prayer to see it. It's a place where the finger of God touches the earth, where God himself can touch a sinner and make them pure. We hunkered down there and prayed and prayed and prayed."

Despite the prayers, Marcus said the group hit a low point when Danny died. "It hurt, of course. Losing a man of God always hurts. We didn't lose faith, though. You never lose faith. You adjust. God is always asking us to adjust. Those with true faith can and will do that. He overcame the grave. The least we can do is overcome small adversities."

The drug dealers eventually found Marcus's encampment, a place he'll only describe as "fortified by God's righteousness," and during a great storm, Marcus commanded them to leave.

"The power of God surged in me, and it wasn't me speaking," he says. "It was God. They had guns. We had God. We won. There's a lesson there for all of us."

"It was the greatest display of God's power I've ever seen," says eyewitness and longtime friend of the pastor, Billy Thrash. "He called upon God for protection, and the Lord delivered fire from heaven. He saved us on that day, and I have no doubt in my mind it was because of the holiness of the man who led us and the sacred place he led us to."

After Marcus and his men returned from their sojourn, they reported the events to the authorities, who found the field of marijuana and seized more than five thousand individual plants. Four of the five suspects have been apprehended based on descriptions provided by Marcus and other individuals. The fifth suspect is still at large at the time of publication.

According to Coulee County Sheriff Hank Shaw, the operation Marcus uncovered was "significant."

"I'm not typically given to hyperbole," Shaw said, "but I've never met nobody like Brother RJ. The true power of the Lord is in him."

Marcus, who considers himself a "link" to the powerful religious past of North Georgia, is quick to point out his priorities.

"Every man, woman, and child must decide in this life. The decision is to leave sin behind and follow the Lord. It might be hard for some, but what those that continue on a road of sin will face in the next life is harder than anything they can imagine. I don't think there is anything more important than a man giving his life to God. Hell never ends. It never stops. It'll consume you and then consume you some more."

When asked what he'd say to the men who'd once used the mountainside for illegal drugs, Marcus demurred. "I would tell them the same thing I tell any man. Get it right. Get your life straight. Run from sin like it's on fire. Run to the Lord. Our doors are open every Sunday, and we believe in forgiveness."

The Holy Flame is located off Caldwell Mill Road (third gravel road on the right), and services are held every Sunday at 9:30.

When Mary finished reading, I was physically shaking. I took a moment to try to compose myself. There were so many conflicting emotions, so many things to unpack inside that article.

"Sounds like an advertisement for your father's church," Mary said.

I nodded. "Not surprising. It was probably written by a member."

"So much for objectivity in journalism." Mary handed the phone back to me.

But before I could say anything else, I heard Granny's voice. "The well," she said. "I heard of it before."

Mary and I both looked at her.

"When you're a midwife, you hear things nobody else does. A woman who never used a foul word in her life will go to cursing like she was getting paid by the four-letter word." She shrugged. "Some of them remember things they suppressed. Others just clench their teeth and fight an internal battle with nary a word. This girl—her name was Allison, if I recall—had come up hard; she was a fighter. I could just smell it on her. You know how I get those feelings about people."

Mary and I both nodded.

"Anyway, the baby was turned wrong, and she started panicking. I tried to calm her down, telling her I could do it, I'd done it before, and it would be fine, but she wouldn't listen.

"She started talking nonsense. Something about lightning at the top of a mountain. Saying something didn't work. Saying she was still angry at God, and it was her fault. It didn't work.

"I didn't shush her. I always just let them talk. Figure it's just nature's way of taking their mind off the pain. Sometimes, if it's really bad, I'll ask them questions. So that's what I did. 'Where was this?' I asked her. 'Where did you see the lightning?'

"She was hurting pretty bad at this time, but I'll never forget what she said: 'The well.' I remember because it didn't make no sense then or now. But I thought of it first off when your daddy said that about the well."

"Do you remember her last name, Granny?"

"I do. But you ain't gonna get to talk to her. She's dead. Long dead, actually. She died back in the late nineties."

"That would fit the timeline. The article came out in 1992."

Granny shrugged. "I reckon it does."

"What was her last name, Granny?"

"DeWalt. Allison DeWalt. Her people are from over on Small Mountain. I'll bet you there's still a few of them left."

"Want to ride out there tomorrow?" Mary asked.

"Is that aboveboard? I mean, I'm not really law enforcement."

"Look, if they're going to give me a case and then not help me at all, then I'll do what it takes. I'll plead ignorance if anything comes of it. I could say I thought your PI license gave you the right. You do have a PI license, right?"

"Not in Georgia."

"Like I said, I'm not worried about it."

"There's something else," Granny said, looking directly at me. I met her eyes and felt goose bumps crawling over my skin. "I think it might be important. She didn't just die."

"What do you mean?" I said, but I didn't really have to ask. I already knew before she said it.

"She hanged herself from a tree, not a mile from where she lived."

17

On the night Lester asked Maggie to marry him, I went down to Ghost Creek with a bottle of moonshine I'd been saving for a special occasion. I settled in on my usual rock and watched the moonlight streak the water as it slipped down the mountain. The evening felt charged with something supernatural and quick, something that touched my neck before sliding away like the nearly silent silver water, only to come back on the next breeze. I held off on the bottle, trying to be in the moment, sensing something big was about to happen. Daddy used to talk of his skin crawling, and I'd always wondered what that was like, but on that night, I felt it all over my body.

Soon, I found myself on my feet, bottle forgotten for the moment, following the creek up the mountain, trying to find its source—or maybe I was trying to avoid what was coming. It's easy to think back and say I knew, or if I didn't know, to believe I sensed what was about to happen. But the present always pulls the past into focus. Being in the moment offers little in the way of true clarity.

Whatever my motivation, I kept walking, and I resolutely tried not to think of Lester and Maggie. Since being effectively excommunicated by the church, I'd grown increasingly envious of Lester. Not only did he still have an opportunity to please our father, he also had Maggie, and I didn't even have to love her for this to drive me crazy.

Before long, I'd tired from my steep path up the mountain, but when I realized where I was, I decided to trudge on a little farther. I'd come to a forgotten place from my childhood, to the ruins of a little burial ground very few people knew about.

But I knew about it because my sister was buried there. Aida only lived for a few hours before succumbing to what we later learned was encephalitis. Just as he would do later with me and my mother, Daddy forbade even the suggestion of taking her to the doctor. Instead, he held her up to the sky in the middle of a powerful rainstorm, hours after her complicated delivery by the local midwife. He beseeched God to heal her of her "deficiencies" and make her whole again. The only answer was thunder and a crooked fork of lightning out over the valley.

"She'll die," the midwife I'd later come to know as Granny said. At the time, this woman had no name to me other than "the midwife." She'd delivered all of us, and Daddy told how she had once been a good Christian woman but had gone weak in the mind over the course of her long life and forgotten the fear of hell and the power of God to put you there.

"Leave me be, woman," he said. "I'll not have you corrupt my boys with that kind of talk."

"What talk?" the old woman said. "Just the truth. I've seen it before. She needs a doctor. She'll die before the night is out."

"Leave," Daddy said again, and his voice was deep and forceful, the way he spoke when he was calling out demons.

"I'll take that child with me," the old woman said.

Daddy slapped her, and she fell to the muddy ground. "You've done enough, woman."

Daddy held the naked child up again, and the rain beat against her tiny body as he asked for some mercy from the sky.

"Fetch an umbrella," Daddy said. "Get her out of here."

I didn't want to leave Aida, but I knew better than to argue with Daddy, so I went into the house and found the one and only umbrella we owned. When I came back out, the old woman nodded at me and took my arm. Together, we worked our way up across Houston's Pass and up the mountain to the little cabin where she lived, where I would live just a few short years later. She said nothing until we stood in front of her house.

Only then did she turn and face me. "When you go back, your sister will be dead. You should mourn her, but all isn't lost. It's the only chance your father may have."

I remember being utterly confused by her words. How could Aida's death be a chance for my father? I should have asked her, but instead I just helped her up the two steps to her darkened house and held the door as she disappeared inside and from my life for what I assumed would be forever. After all, if Daddy forbade her to come around, that was final. His word carried the weight of law in the mountains. How could I have known I would run to her years later because she was the only person I could think of who would not judge me?

She'd been right about Aida. When I came back, the house was completely dark. The rain had stopped, and there was only silence.

Inside, I found Lester sitting beside Mama on the couch, where she'd delivered just a few hours earlier.

"Where's Aida?" I asked.

A remnant of lighting flashed, and the windows filled with a brilliance that blinded me momentarily.

"Where's Aida and Daddy?" No one answered me.

Later, I would discover she'd died only a few minutes after I'd left. At first, Daddy wouldn't accept it. He screamed to the heavens, begging God to fix it, but when it became apparent he was wasting his breath, he took a shovel from the shed and started up the mountain with the dead child.

He didn't come back that night, nor the next day, until my mother sent me to find him. When I did locate him, he was in that graveyard.

Six years later, I'd recognized the little rock Daddy had laid atop of her grave. I wondered then if spirits could linger or if they just dissipated into nothingness upon death. Once, I'd believed in Daddy's versions of heaven and hell, but after the snakebite, I couldn't bring myself to believe in much of anything anymore.

A branch broke somewhere behind me. I spun around, nearly losing my balance and falling into the creek.

"Who's there?" I said. My voice sounded weak, scared. This was it. This was the thing I'd felt earlier. It was here.

I clenched my fists, ready to fight whatever creature might appear.

Then I heard a high, musical laugh, so light and silky smooth it might have just been the creek water against the grooved rocks.

It came again, followed by a voice that sent a shiver running from my scalp all the way to the tips of my toes. Maggie.

I saw her clearly as she stepped from the shadows and into a beam of moonlight. I swear the white dress she wore was so sheer, it might as well have been gossamer. Her whole body revealed itself to me in a glimpse of visual perfection I would never forget.

"Earl?" she said.

"Yeah. I'm here."

She stepped closer. I felt good. Dangerously good.

I had no idea why she was here with me, but I did have enough sense to know that Lester would have already made his proposal. "Congratulations," I told her, my voice stiff and harsh, betraying the jealousy I harbored.

Her face was difficult to read. She didn't look happy, but she didn't look particularly sad either. That would come later. Right then, she just looked like an alien to my seventeen-year-old eyes.

"You and Lester, right?" I said, beginning to worry I might have given his secret away. Maybe he'd taken ill or they'd gotten their signals crossed. It honestly hadn't occurred to me that she might have said no—until she actually told me she did.

"Lester and me are finished," she said. She stepped even closer.

"Finished? You've been dating for, what—a year?"

She shrugged, and one of the straps of her dress slipped down her shoulder. "I lost track."

"What are you doing here?" I said.

"I came to see you. I hope that's okay."

I felt the tingle again, and this time it was deeper, that same itch I'd tried and failed to scratch with the snake.

"Sure," I said. "It's fine. What's up?"

Except it wasn't fine. And I already knew exactly what was up. She moved closer to me still, and I did not back away.

To this very day, I wished so badly that I had.

18

Mary woke me up the next morning with a knock on the church door. Goose sat up and woofed loudly. Rufus cursed. I patted Goose's head and peeled his bandage back to get a look at the bite. Mary's friend had shaved the hair around it and told me to watch closely for signs of infection. It looked good.

The knocking came again, this time more insistent.

"You gonna get that?" Rufus said.

"Yep." I glanced over at Rufus. He was wearing nothing but an old pair of ragged tighty-whities. "You might want to put some clothes on."

He cursed again and stood. He stumbled over to a pile of clothes draped over Daddy's old lectern. He shrugged on a pair of overalls but didn't bother with a shirt.

I slipped down the aisle and out into the small gathering space. I slid the latch off the door and pulled it open.

"This is where you're staying?"

I smiled. "It's home."

"Invite her in," Rufus called.

"Is that your friend?"

I nodded and leaned in to whisper in her ear. "He's a little bit of a sight, but I promise he's harmless."

"Okay . . ."

"Come on in."

She stepped inside. "This was the old church?"

"Yep, it's where Brother RJ made his name by pretending to have that special pipeline to the Lord. Welcome to the Holy Flame. The only church where a man—and occasionally even a woman—can find salvation."

"Wait, the *only* church?"

"Daddy believed if you didn't go here, you were destined for hell. It didn't matter if you were Billy Graham or the Pope, you were lost."

"Jesus," she said.

"You can say that again."

She shot me a look that seemed to suggest she wasn't a fan of the way I was making light of it all. But I didn't care. It was one of the only ways I could deal with the past. The other options—withdrawal and bitterness—had not served me well.

Rufus stepped out into the gathering space. "I smell an angel," he said.

I sighed, sure Mary would be offended, but she smiled broadly. "Well, thank you, sir. It's just a little soap and some lavender-scented lotion."

"It's just about the best thing I've smelled all day," he said. He held out his hand. "I'm Rufus."

"Mary," she said. I was surprised to see she didn't seem put off by his appearance or his pervy old-man ways. "Earl says you've had some trouble out here?"

"I have, but I think he may have taken care of it for me."

She glanced my way, another nearly unreadable expression. It might have been irritation, or it might have been amusement. Either way, I liked it, which was beginning to be a trend.

"Well, I brought you something. It's what we call a burner phone. It's a cell phone with some minutes already programmed in. I've added my direct line to the contacts. If you have any more problems—that Earl can't handle—call me immediately. You shouldn't have to put up with those assholes."

Rufus smiled so big, it looked like his lips might split. "Oooh, I like you," he said. "I like you a lot."

"Thanks," Mary said brightly. "You mind looking after Goose today?"

"I don't mind at all. I'll be working in the cemetery most of the day. We can look out after each other. I've even got an old leash around here somewhere. He'll help me branch out. Maybe we'll take a walk."

We took Mary's Tahoe and drove over to Small Mountain. Following the GPS in the dash, we arrived at a cluster of mobile homes situated on the side of a hill. It looked like several of them were in danger of tumbling down the side of the mountain if not for some strategically placed rocks that had helped maintain a tenuous balance.

"According to the records I pulled, nearly all of these trailers are owned by a DeWalt. You got a preference?"

I took off my Braves cap and scratched my unkempt hair. I examined each of the trailers until I found one littered with empty beer cans. It was also missing a window, and the pickup sitting in front looked like it had been there since time out of mind. "There," I said.

"Interesting choice. I'd love to know why you picked the absolute roughest looking place."

"Yeah, I can tell you're not from around here. There's a lot that's changed in thirty years, but I can guarantee one thing hasn't."

"And that is?"

"Your church types are going to typically keep a neater house. Especially Holy Flame members. It was always one of Daddy's things: idle hands are the devil's playthings, a clean house helps keep a clean mind, all that bull crap."

"Gotcha. But why do we need to avoid church members? If you think there's some connection between what happened to your father and McCauley, the church folks might know best."

"They would know best. But the problem is those folks won't talk. Unless things have changed since Daddy's death, we won't get a damned thing out of them."

"So what you're saying is that your father's church—now your brother's church—is essentially a cult?"

I'd thought about that a lot over the years and once even went as far as signing up for a class at a community college about cults. I dropped out after the first one caused me to think of the old days pretty much constantly, and at that point in my life, it was just easier to let it go. So that was what I did. I let it go and stopped trying to decide.

"I'm no expert, but I think you're on the right track. Whatever you call it, the church I came up in was seriously messed up."

"I'm sorry."

I waved her off. "Let's go in."

"No, seriously, that sucks you had to grow up like that. Granny told me a little bit about what happened."

I clenched my jaw tightly. I did not want to do this.

"She doesn't really know much about it," I said. I tried to keep my voice even and low—I didn't want to be an asshole to Mary. I'd been an asshole to so many people over the years and ruined relationships because of how defensive the subject made me. I refused to let that happen with Mary.

"Well, she knows a little about it. I mean, she gave you a place to live after it happened."

"I think that came out wrong before," I said. "Can we just go inside now?"

She nodded. "Sure. No problem. Sorry if I overstepped—"

I didn't hear the rest. I climbed out and slammed the Tahoe door before she could finish.

Why couldn't I talk about it?

I sucked in a deep breath of mountain air and tried to clear my head. I heard Mary get out on the other side.

Change the subject, Earl.

"So," I said, trying to be casual, friendly, "who should lead this thing?"

Mary's face was noticeably neutral, and I feared she was trying to hide her true feelings of irritation at my prickliness. "It's your show," she said.

"Sure thing."

I knocked on the door.

It swung open an instant later, and we both stepped back. A man dressed in a tank top and a pair of tight pink briefs, carrying an oversized can of Colt 45, lurched from the trailer and knocked me aside. He stumbled down the hill, losing his balance twice before righting himself and leaning over, hands on knees, legs spread. He heaved once. Twice. Good Lord. He just kept vomiting.

I turned away and saw Mary was holding her nose and looking up at the clear sky.

A voice called from inside the trailer. "Shut the goddamn door! I ain't trying to cool the whole damned mountain!"

I looked over at the man—who I now noticed was at least my age if not older. He'd stopped vomiting, which was good, but then he did something even more nauseating: he lifted the can of Colt 45, took a big swig, and swished it around his mouth for a good fifteen seconds. For a moment, I thought he was going to redeem himself and spit it out, but the thought of wasting any must have been too much. With a shrug, he swallowed it all down.

"Ugh," Mary said. "Like I said, your show."

"Excuse me, sir?" I said.

He held up a finger while he swished some more around. He swallowed it again and turned to face us.

"Who are you?"

I looked at Mary. She just shook her head and looked right back.

"Sheriff's office," I said.

The man drained the rest of the can and tossed it against the trailer. "They got coloreds at the sheriff's office now?"

I glanced at Mary. She was surprisingly cool about the slur. I felt just the opposite.

"I'm going to ask you to rephrase that," I said.

He belched loudly. "There. Rephrased. Now get off my property unless you got some kind of warrant."

"We just have a few questions, sir." Mary's voice was pleasant and professional. I couldn't help but admire her grace. I decided to take a cue from her and attempt to keep my temper under control.

But I knew there wouldn't be much I could do if he insulted her again.

"What's this about?"

"We're trying to find out about a woman named Allison. Allison DeWalt."

Everything about the man changed in an instant. I'd heard of sobering news, but I'd always just figured it was an expression. In this case, it was the best way to describe his transformation. At the very mention of the name, he no longer seemed drunk.

"Sir?" Mary said. "Do you know that name?"

"This some kind of joke?"

"No, sir."

He shook his head and seemed to notice suddenly that he was standing in what passed for his front yard wearing nothing but a dirty wifebeater and a pair of pink briefs. "Goddamnit," he said. "Yeah, we're going to talk. We're going to talk for damned sure. Wait your asses right here. I'm going to put on some clothes."

He brushed passed me again, this time his gait steady, and when he bumped my shoulder, it was clearly done with purpose.

I let it go. Always easier to let slights go when they were directed at me. What did I care if he bumped my shoulder? But he was damn sure going to leave Mary alone.

When he went inside, he shut the door, and I looked over at Mary. Her eyes widened just a bit, and I had to chuckle a little. "Welcome to the Fingers."

When he came back, he was wearing a pair of jeans and some boots. A small woman stood behind him in the doorway, peering at us from the darkened trailer.

"I swear," he said. "If this is some kind of joke, I don't think I'll be able to control myself."

I glanced at Mary. She shrugged. "Man," I said, "we don't know what you're talking about."

"You said it was about Allison, right?"

"That's right. Did you know her?"

"Hell, yes, I knew her. She was my sister."

"Okay, that's a good start," I said. "Can we come in and talk?"

The woman had straight black hair that reached the rise of her hips. She scowled at us and jabbed a finger in my face. "You ain't stepping foot in my house until we get a goddamn apology."

"Ma'am," I said, "we haven't done anything that warrants an apology."

Her eyes nearly bugged out of her head. "You haven't done nothing? You haven't done nothing? Goddamn, that's the problem. It's been seventeen years, and *now* you want to talk?"

A quick glance at Mary made it clear she was just as confused as I was.

"Seventeen years," the woman said. "We couldn't get you out here then. We called and called. Went to the damned office. All those times, and it was always the same thing."

"Darlin'," the man said. He put a hand gently on her shoulder, but the woman shrugged it off.

"Don't even 'darlin'' me, Wyatt. You know as well as I do that it ain't right."

He nodded and put his hand down.

"Okay," Mary said, "I think I get it."

We all waited.

"You're disappointed in the way the sheriff's office handled your sister's suicide."

The small woman stepped forward and thrust her chest into Mary's. "Say suicide again. Say it one more time. I'll rip you apart!"

Mary stepped back as I reached forward to grab the woman. She screamed and flailed at me wildly. I pushed her away and into her husband. He nearly knocked her over in his zeal to hit me. Luckily his first swing missed.

And even more luck: the crack that nearly blew out my eardrum when Mary fired not one, but two shots into the sky was enough to throw my retaliation off. My punch landed harmlessly against the doorframe. Otherwise, I would have smashed his nose all to hell.

"Everybody just stop," Mary said, her voice still calm, but there was a clear *don't fuck with me* edge that you couldn't miss.

"We're all going to work this out. We're on your side," she said. The woman started to say something, but Mary shot her a stern look and she fell silent.

"Now," she said, "Earl, please explain to them why we are here."

Despite everything, I had to keep myself from smiling. It would have been wildly inappropriate considering the situation, but sometimes you meet a certain kind of woman who just hits all your buttons. For me, Mary was that woman.

"We're here because we wanted to find out a little bit more about the circumstances surrounding her . . . death. That's all. We weren't with the sheriff's office in the nineties. We don't know the details. It's why we're here."

The woman glared at me, but her husband nodded slightly.

"Maybe," I said, "if you'll just talk to us, we might be able to get to the bottom of things."

I probably shouldn't have said that. In my opinion, one of the worst things a detective—private or otherwise—could do was give false hope. It never paid off, but in this case, I decided it was a necessity if we were going to talk to these people at all.

"All right," the man said. "We'll talk to you."

His wife looked like she was ready to spit hot lava at him, or at least rip out his hairs one by one, but she kept her mouth shut. Her lips quivered with something like rage, but she managed to not say a word.

The man held out his hand. It was a begrudging, halfhearted kind of gesture, but it was something. "Wyatt DeWalt," he said. I looked at his hand, remembering the way, just moments earlier, he'd used it to wipe vomit off his chin.

Goddamn. I had to shake it. If I didn't, his wife might try to kill me again.

I grabbed his hand and pumped once, trying to hide my distaste.

When he turned to head back inside, I glanced at Mary. She was laughing at me.

19

"Just so we're clear," Mary said as we sat down at a flimsy card table inside the surprisingly immaculate trailer, "which one of you is actually Allison's sibling?"

Wyatt raised his hand and winced slightly. I was betting he had a headache from all that drinking. "That's me, but Patty and Allison was always close. I reckon Patty is the nearest thing Allison ever had to a mama."

Mary nodded, meeting Wyatt's eyes, and I could tell he was already getting comfortable with her, which was sort of amazing considering, just a few minutes earlier, he'd addressed her with a racial slur.

"Can you tell us what happened? Her story?"

Even Patty seemed to brighten a little at this. In my experience, almost everybody liked to tell their story, especially if it involved some injustice, either real or perceived. There were some exceptions. Me, for one. I'd just as soon bury my story and never think about it again, much less share it with someone else.

Patty was the one who told it, but every now and then, Wyatt would break in with a name or a date or would just grunt to let us know he was in agreement with what Patty was saying.

"Like we said, she didn't never really have no mother. A girl like that . . . well, she had some troubles. She went from this boy to the next one, but that ain't so bad. I had my own mistakes when I was a kid. I tried to warn her out of it, but kids—nearly all the ones I've ever known—have to make their own mistakes before they learn. Everything else is just a bunch of wasted breath."

"Noise," Wyatt said. "That's all it is."

Patty nodded at him. "Anyway, any fool could see she was going to get pregnant. And when it finally happened, she didn't know who the father was. She had some suspicions, but it didn't matter. Once she started showing, them boys that had been so eager to be with her, they disappeared like cockroaches when the lights come on. Scurried right on back to their holes. I told her me and Wyatt would take care of her. We'd help her out.

"That bucked her up some, but you could tell she was really sad. At the time, she was working part time over at the Magic Mart, out near 51. You know the little place at the foot of Pointer Mountain. Some fella came in there and invited her to church. She must have thought he was handsome or something because she ain't never been to church a day in her life, but she come home that afternoon just beaming because this man asked her, and she was going to go."

"I didn't see no harm in it," Wyatt said.

Patty shot him a look. "I told her not to go. There's some churches in these mountains that ain't about nothing good."

"Well, I didn't know this was going to be one of those," Wyatt said a little defensively.

"Which is why I told you—"

I cleared my throat and asked the question I already knew the answer to. "What was the name of the church?"

"The Holy Flame," Patty said, twisting the words in her mouth as if she couldn't stand to have them touch her tongue.

"I know the place," I said.

Mary glanced at me, then said, "Go on."

"So she went. And she changed fast. I mean, I thought that stuff took some time, but not with Allison. She became different, but she did seem happier, so I just told myself it would be a fad, and if it got her through the pregnancy and out the other side of them post–baby blues, I'd just shut my mouth."

Something strange happened then. Patty—previously so full of anger—began to cry. It wasn't an aggressive kind of crying like I would have expected from her, from a person who seemed to only have one speed, and that was full tilt. Instead, I might not have even noticed if one of the tears hadn't dropped onto the card table with a nearly silent smack.

She wiped her eyes, but the tears kept coming.

"She wouldn't talk about the man other than to say he was a 'good man.' Or sometimes she'd say he was a 'godly man.'"

"'He's looking out for me,'" Wyatt said. "That's what I'll always remember her saying. 'He cares about me.' Jesus Christ. I should have known."

"What was the man's name?" I held my breath, praying it wasn't my father.

"She wouldn't tell us. She could be so damned stubborn sometimes. She said if she told me, she knew I'd try to find him and meet him, and she didn't want that." Wyatt shrugged helplessly, and I saw him glance longingly at a half-empty bottle of whiskey sitting on the kitchen counter.

"Did she ever describe him, talk about what he was like? Anything?"

Wyatt deferred to his wife. "To hear her tell it, he was the nicest man around. Couldn't do no wrong. Said he hung the moon. Like I said, I was skeptical but just let it ride. Then she lost the baby. It was a terrible thing. Lost it a week before she was due. That did a number on her."

"Changed her," Wyatt said. "That's what it did. She weren't never the same after that."

"Did she continue to see the man from the Holy Flame?" I asked.

"Oh, yeah. She saw him more. She barely came around after that. Always gone. When we'd ask where she'd been, she just said, 'At the church.'"

Mary said, "I'm sorry for being unclear, but was Allison living with you?"

"Supposedly. She'd been with us for five, six years, but once she took to the church after the miscarriage, she was hardly ever here."

I swallowed, still feeling uncomfortable at the thought of this name-less man.

"Go on," Mary said.

"This is getting to the bad part. Eventually, she just kind of dis-appeared. We didn't see her. What was it, Wyatt, a month?"

He shrugged. "At least three weeks."

"I'd call it a month, but either way, she came back with these odd marks on her hands and up her arms too."

"Marks?" I said.

"They looked like tattoos," Wyatt said, "but they didn't stay. We tried to tell the sheriff's office about this before. But they wouldn't listen."

"Can you describe the marks in any more detail?" Mary asked.

"Hell, at one time, I drew pictures of them, but I threw all of 'em away when I finally realized the sheriff's office wasn't going to do anything." He shrugged. "I remember them being sort of red, and sometimes they could look like a rash, but they weren't like any rashes I'd ever seen."

"They was pretty," Patty said. "I'd of been proud to wear one as a tattoo, but they weren't that."

I glanced at Mary. From the look on her face, I could tell she was as perplexed as I was by these marks.

Exasperated, I said, "We can come back to those. Move us forward. What was next?"

"Well, next was her getting pregnant again."

"How long was this from the first?" Mary asked.

Patty pursed her lips and calculated. "From the miscarriage I'd say it was about a year."

"And the father?"

"That man," Patty said. "Had to be. 'Course she wouldn't ever say, but who else would it have been?"

"It was him," Wyatt said. "I know it was."

Mary and I both waited. The mood in the kitchen had grown heavy, and I could tell the worst was still to come.

"She had a little girl. Named her Jenny. She loved that little girl." Patty wiped at her eyes again. "I loved her too."

"What happened to Jenny after her mother died?" I said.

Patty glanced at her husband. "They really don't know."

Wyatt nodded. "You got your order wrong."

"How's that?"

"What happened to Jenny before Allison died? That should have been your question."

"Wait," Mary said, "is Jenny dead?"

Wyatt shrugged and looked at Patty again.

Patty's face was a mess. She looked stricken with grief. I suddenly felt really sorry for the both of them and was glad I hadn't retaliated earlier.

"It's possible. But the truth is, we don't know. One day, Allison just came home again. When she did, Jenny wasn't with her. We asked where she was right off, but it was like she couldn't hear us. Most I ever got out of her was when she said Jenny was okay."

"That's all," Wyatt said, nodding. "She wouldn't say no more. Just that she was okay, and we shouldn't worry."

"But we worried like crazy," Patty said. "I even went to the church to try to find her, but nobody there knew what I was talking about. Or if they did, they pretended not to."

"She raised hell," Wyatt said. "So much that the police came to us. Said there'd been complaints and we needed to stay away from that church."

"I told the police I had some complaints too," Patty said. "I told them we had a missing child. They wanted to talk to Allison. Wouldn't let us hear any of it, went in a back room and closed the door. When they came out, they said everything was fine. There wasn't no missing child."

"We felt helpless." Wyatt *looked* helpless right now. His eyes were downcast, his cheeks sallow and pale. He was sweating. Probably the drinking, though he sure did look like he could use another.

"I was the one that found her," Patty said. "She was up in the woods." She pointed to the window we were sitting near. "Out that way. No more than a half mile. Hanging from a tree."

It was too much for Wyatt. At that, he rose and walked over to the counter to retrieve the bottle. He unscrewed the cap and tossed it aside, as if he had no use for it anymore, and I fully expected that to be the case based on his hangdog expression and the way his eyes were locked on that amber-colored juice. I knew that look, had *felt* that look on my own face many times.

"We don't think it was suicide, though. We think it was that church. And I want to be clear, even if she hung herself, it wasn't suicide. It was murder. I'm convinced it wouldn't never have happened if not for that church. We tried and tried after she died to get somebody to investigate, but it wasn't happening."

Wyatt took a long pull from the bottle. "Once," he said, "Patty was sure she seen Jenny. Was about three years ago."

"Was only two years. Saw her walking on the side of the road over near Possible Mountain. I stopped. Told her who I was. Called her by name. I says, 'Hey, Jenny,' but she just looked at me like I was crazy. Told me her name was something else. Said she had a mama and a daddy, and she was happy. I had to let her go. But it was her." She gasped and covered her mouth to hold in a sob. "I swear it was."

Wyatt turned the bottle up again.

Mary looked at me. Her face was calm, but her eyes looked worried.

"I suspect," I said, "the lack of cooperation you felt might have been very real. I think it might have something to do with the sheriff being a long-standing member of the Holy Flame."

Patty nodded, her lip stuck in a painful-looking snarl. "That's what I said. But what do they care? Them deputies just do what he says."

"We'd love to help you figure out what really happened," I said, "but first we need some help from you."

Patty nodded. She seemed eager. Wyatt was deeply involved with the bottle now, his eyes nearly shut as he slumped in his chair.

"Either of you ever hear her say anything about a well in the mountains? Anything about lightning?"

Patty seemed to think. "I can't say that I do. I wish I could tell you something, but none of that rings a bell."

Wyatt opened his eyes. "When she came back after the miscarriage, she was afraid of storms. Didn't matter if there was lightning or not. Just rain made her afraid."

It wasn't very much, but I felt like it was a small strand I could tuck away for later.

"Anything else?" Mary asked.

They were both silent. After a few moments, Patty said, "What happened to Clint?"

"Excuse me?" Mary said.

"Clint. He was the only deputy that ever listened to us. He would check in now and again, but then he stopped."

"I don't know him," she said, glancing over at me. Her expression suggested she knew more than she was letting on.

"He was a good one," Wyatt said, slurring his words.

"I'm sure he was," Mary said. She smiled at Wyatt kindly.

"I just wished she'd never met that man at the Magic Mart," Patty said.

"Is there anyone else who might know about her situation?" I was thinking of one of the neighbors when I asked the question, but I should have seen the answer coming.

Patty met my eyes, and it almost looked like she'd divined my connection to the Holy Flame somehow, because she said, "You gonna have to go to that church and ask them. Somebody at the church knows. I guarantee that."

20

That afternoon, I sat in a folding chair under the high eaves of the burned-out church thinking about what Mary had told me as we drove away from the DeWalts' home.

"That's the deputy," she'd said.

I'd been lost in thought and didn't follow. "Say again."

"Clint Martin. That was the deputy I replaced."

"What did Shaw say had happened to him?"

"His exact phrasing was that 'he went AWOL.'"

"What's that mean?"

"I don't know, but it strikes me as a little ominous that the one deputy who tried to help the DeWalts is no longer around."

It struck me the same way. I wasn't ready to go so far as to believe Shaw was running a cover-up of some kind, but there was no denying the facts—at least the way the DeWalts relayed them—didn't look good.

I tried to clear my mind and concentrate on the storm moving in from the west. The view from my chair was the kind people would pay good money for, but it occurred to me I was enjoying it for free.

While in North Carolina, I hadn't believed home held anything for me except grief. But here I was, sitting outside the old church, and I felt something shift to the forefront, something I'd forgotten. I realized it was the hope of my childhood, the foolish kind of hope, uncorrupted by experience.

I watched as Rufus—led by Goose—crested the ridge just ahead of the storm. Rufus had tied a rope loosely around the puppy's neck, and the two of them had gone for a walk. Goose didn't seem to mind about the rope, and in fact, he appeared to have intuited Rufus's disability rather quickly. I laughed a little as Goose looked over his shoulder patiently as the old man picked his way around a large boulder.

As they approached, I closed my eyes and breathed in the scent of the oncoming storm. I needed to think. I needed to decide. I had cases waiting for me in North Carolina. Good, paying cases. Three times since Mary dropped me off at the church and made me promise not to leave without letting her and Granny know first, I had dialed the number to the airport to book a flight. And three times I had disconnected the call before anyone answered. The fourth time I tried—just fifteen minutes ago—I'd found my phone dead.

A sign?

That was laughable. This whole thing was laughable, really. Why should coming back home change my core beliefs? There were no signs in this world. The dead did not ascend. And whatever had happened to Allison DeWalt and Bryant McCauley was nothing to me.

But I knew that wasn't true. Allison especially. Her story reminded me too much of my past, and I had no doubt her fate was tied inextricably to my father's church. My *brother's* church now. Hard as that was to believe.

Sure, the world would continue to fall into the same holes, over and over again. It seemed the way of things, but invariably, it also seemed as if someone from my family was standing next to those holes, ready and willing to push the next fool in.

And I couldn't ignore that anymore.

I opened my eyes and saw that Rufus and Goose had switched directions and had wandered over past the graveyard and down to the edge of the creek. Goose was drinking from the water, and Rufus was standing straight as an arrow, oblivious to the rain that fell. He looked like a scarecrow weathering a storm, and I liked the analogy because Rufus was the same as me. He'd survived the Holy Flame. A little worse for the wear, but he'd broken free.

Others hadn't been so lucky. Daddy had always had a thing about letting go. Maybe it was why I still felt his hold on me even now. He must have never heard the song that said the best way to love was to let someone go. Daddy had always held on for all he was worth, and the worst part was how he'd done it with a clear conscience, because in the end, all he cared about was what happened in the next life. It was infuriating.

I stood to go back inside the church. Rufus and Goose could get soaked if they wanted, but I preferred to stay dry. I moved through the darkening gathering space and into the sanctuary, where I stumbled around until I found Rufus's sole gas lantern and struck a match.

Just before I lit the wick, I heard the movement on the other side of the sanctuary. It was coming from the front, near the place where Daddy had installed the snake pit.

When I was twelve, Daddy had made Lester and me help dig up the floorboards and put in a wire cage large enough to hold two or three rattlers or a half dozen cottonmouths. It was right by his lectern, where Daddy could pick one up at any time during the service. And even when he let them alone, you could always hear them moving—slithering over one another—in the quiet moments.

And that was what it sounded like now. The raspy slickness of cottonmouths twining together, rubbing the lengths of their strange bodies one against the other. I stayed very still, waiting, sure it was just my imagination. In the three years I'd lived with Granny, I often saw and heard things that weren't there. Granny called it the second sight and said it was both a blessing and a curse from the venom that had become lodged inside my veins. I didn't see any blessing in it and was more than pleased when the strange sights and sounds had seemed to dissipate and eventually stop completely when I moved to North Carolina.

Could this be another one? After all these years?

I lit the fuse, and the lantern brightened the sanctuary, casting its light toward the front. It fell on the lectern first, and it looked the same as it had earlier—still covered with blankets and quilts. I moved the lantern to the right slowly—toward the slithering sound—and saw the door to the snake pit was open, balanced upright. I felt my stomach fill with a heavy fear. I stumbled forward, afraid of what I'd find in the pit but unable to keep myself from looking anyway.

As I approached, I held the lantern at arm's length. I knelt, trying to catch a glimpse of what was inside.

Lightning flashed, and the stained glass window above me filled with light. The church blazed alive—on fire again. I dropped the lantern, and the light spilled over, finally illuminating the pit.

Inside, a mass of snakes tumbled over each other, writhing and hissing, their eyes set aglow in the lantern's light, and they were just as vacant as they had been thirty years earlier.

When I heard my name, it sounded like a whisper at first. Or maybe the storm was pushing wind through the savaged roof, making a desolate music that spoke to me. Either way, I turned around.

There was someone standing in the rear of the church.

"Hey, boy," the voice said.

I stepped back, edging into the front pew that Daddy had once kicked.

"Rufus?" I said, but it was just something to say, something to delay me facing the truth of who I knew it was. It was the only man I'd ever known who could defy death, who could haunt a man like an avenging angel and also dog his every step like a hound from the pit of hell.

"Daddy?"

"It ain't too late," he said.

"For what?"

"To find the Lord."

"You're dead," I said.

He shook his head and stepped closer. I could see him clearly now in a flash of lightning. He looked much as I remembered him from my childhood—stoic, handsome, unflappable.

"Ascended," he corrected.

"I don't believe that."

"That's always been your problem, boy. You don't believe nothing."

"What do you want?" A part of me understood that this could not be real, that it had to be another vision, a hallucination born of the snake's venom that had entered my flesh and was now pumped like blood through my veins. Another part of me understood that if he was really here, if he had ascended after his death, it meant everything he'd preached had been true, every proclamation, every backward prejudice, was not only true but sanctified.

I shook my head and stepped forward, determined to dispel the vision.

He laughed. "I want what I've always wanted, Earl. I want you to join the fold. It ain't too late," he said again. "Even the prodigal son returned eventually after seeing the world and learning there was nothing but emptiness."

I stepped forward again but staggered a little as the weight of his words sunk in. Nothing but emptiness. I thought of Maggie. I thought of Lester. Hadn't I screwed it all up? Maybe, just maybe, there was some comfort in the old ways?

That was when the lightning struck the church. I felt the air around me change, filling up with power and weight and a strange kind of heat the instant before the explosion.

When it came, I fell to the ground, heard Goose barking outside, Rufus's voice shouting my name. None of it mattered, though. I turned over to see if Daddy was still there. I half-expected him to be standing over me, ready to put another boot in my mouth, but he wasn't. He was nowhere.

That wasn't quite true. In fact, it was the opposite. I saw that now. Daddy was everywhere. It was almost as if, in death, he'd achieved the ultimate power; he'd become a god.

21

Rufus helped me to my feet.

"You okay?" he said. "Me and Goose heard it. Sounded like the roof came off this place. Anything on fire?"

I looked around. The snake pit was still open. Goose was heading that way, his body tense, his nose flexing as he inhaled some scent. Daddy was gone, but what about the snakes?

"Goose!" I said sharply. The dog stopped and fixed me with a look that seemed to suggest he knew his name. "Here," I said and patted the floor. He whined, looking back at the snake pit, and trotted on over.

"What the hell is happening?" Rufus said.

"I'm not sure." I pulled myself to my feet and picked up the lantern. The rain was pounding the roof now, and throughout the sanctuary, puddles were forming from all the leaks. I stepped over one and shone the light into the pit.

I recoiled at what I saw.

"What?" Rufus asked, somehow sensing the tension.

I looked again, this time holding my gaze on the pit long enough to really see. It was a toy. Not real.

Somehow I'd seen a mass of real snakes, writhing in the pit. In reality, there was only one, and it wasn't even alive.

Still, it proved something.

"Somebody's been in the church," I said.

"Who you reckon done it?" Rufus said.

My first thought was *Daddy*, but I left his name unspoken. Instead, I shrugged. Then, realizing Rufus couldn't hear a shrug, I added, "No idea."

"I wouldn't put it past them boys next door," Rufus said. "It wouldn't be the first time I caught them bastards in here."

I rubbed my beard, studying the toy snake in the open pit, thinking hard about why someone would want to sneak around this place.

"What's the story with that Thrash kid?" I said.

"Ronnie? He's just a little piece of shit that has found some smaller pieces of shit to follow him down the damned toilet. Trouble. Drugs. Booze. Guns. You know the type."

"Yeah," I said. What I didn't say was that the drugs, booze, and guns types scared me a hell of a lot less than the church types these days. "He mentioned that he was a big fan of mine. Not too much of a stretch to say he knows all about my history with the cottonmouth, right?"

"No doubt."

"I'm going to pay your neighbors a visit," I said. "See if I can't figure out who's responsible." I walked around the pit to the open door and dropped it shut. I bent over and clicked the latch in place.

"Want me to come along?" Rufus said.

"Nah. Stay with Goose. I think I managed to spook him."

"Either that or the storm," Rufus said.

I nodded. "Smart dog."

"Yes, sir," Rufus said, grinning. "I believe he is."

*   *   *

I took a slug of Rufus's whiskey before heading over and made sure my 9mm was loaded and stuck it in the back of my blue jeans for easy access. I pulled on one of Rufus's old jackets and set off into the early evening. My watch had 8:30, and in midsummer, Georgia was ordinarily still somewhat light out. But a heavy dusk had fallen because of the storm, and I pulled out the penlight I'd kept on my keychain for years.

Rufus followed me to the door and asked me if I was sure about this. I told him I was. I didn't tell him I had a plan that made me feel fairly confident about what would happen.

It would require some patience, but I'd sat for hours in my truck watching houses and bars and every other manner of building in North Carolina. I could do the same here.

I crossed the creek and edged around to the rear of the old shack. The two pickups were parked out front, and I could hear voices inside along with some slow country music.

I found a tree not too far from the creek that allowed me a good view of the outhouse and lay down on my stomach, trying to make myself invisible. I cut the penlight off and let my eyes adjust.

While I waited, my mind jumped all over the place—from Granny to Mary to Rufus—before settling, as it always did, on my father.

I tried to recall the news article Lester had sent me a few months back. It had come in an envelope without a return address, and the article—a poorly written one from the *Coulee County Reporter*—had detailed the circumstances surrounding the discovery of my father's body near the top of Pointer Mountain. What had he been doing back here? The church was gone now; he'd moved over to Ring like so many others. Why would he have come back? What had he been doing when he had the heart attack? The article claimed his body had lain in the sun—open to the elements, including the crows that destroyed his face—for nearly nine days.

I shook my head, remembering Lester's note, so formal, so distant.

Read article. Funeral Wednesday.

—Lester

That was it. Thirty years without speaking, and that was all my older brother could muster upon our father's death.

Not that I didn't understand. I thought of Maggie and remembered the way she'd looked that first night, wearing that see-through dress, when I saw her near Aida's grave . . .

It hit me then. Daddy had been visiting Aida's grave. That had to be it. There was a kind of poetic justice for him to die there, I thought. It was the only time he'd ever seemed mortal to me.

The back door to the shack swung open. Music drifted out into the night, followed by a loud belch. A big man stepped out and hurried across the yard, unbuckling his belt as he went. He disappeared inside the outhouse, and I let out my breath. It wasn't Ronnie.

More waiting. I shifted my position a little so I could keep an eye on both the outhouse and the sky, which was clearing. I saw starlight through the trees, smelled the wet soil clinging to my clothes, and I went back to that night again.

22

There was something in the back of my mind when I kissed Maggie. I felt like she was something I was owed. I felt like it was a moment that would make up for all the others.

And I felt like it was a middle finger to the church, to my father, to these mountains. So I ignored the part of me that said it was wrong, that I should resist. I did more than ignore it. I shut it off and threw myself into the moment the way an alcoholic gives himself to an evening of drunkenness after that first taste.

We were on the ground in seconds, and she was murmuring something in my ear about wanting me since she'd heard about the way I stood up to my father.

"My daddy thought he was warning me away from you," she said. "But he was really just warming me up."

I didn't say anything. I couldn't if I'd wanted to. Her mouth opened over mine again, and her tongue slipped between my lips, grazing my teeth, finding my tongue, and there was so much sweetness there, I felt dizzy with it.

She seemed to almost shimmy out of her dress in one smooth motion. I never did see another woman who could get out of her clothes like that.

Mine came off too. Soon, the soil of the mountain and our naked flesh became one. We built momentum, and I held on with everything I had, drawing the moment of escape out as long as possible.

And that was the only way to describe it. For a brief moment, we both escaped the soul-crushing, insular environment my father had worked so hard to instill in us.

But when it ended, I was still on the mountain, still my father's son, and my brother's girlfriend was on top of me. She stood up and slipped back into her dress. I couldn't meet her eyes, so I looked at the cemetery instead. *Aida. Poor, poor Aida.*

"What about Lester?" I said.

"What about him?" she said. "He doesn't own me. Besides, he never has to know. We can just meet here. Every night."

"I . . ." I wanted to tell her no. I wanted to tell her that this was a one-time mistake, but I couldn't. She was too beautiful. The first time had been too fast. *One more*, I told myself, because the damage was already done, right? What difference would it make to Lester if we did it once or twice? It was the same logic that would dog me with alcohol in the years to come. One drink, just a taste. Hell, I've already had the one, why not two, and having two, why not drink the house dry? I could always go buy more the next day.

"It's beautiful here, don't you think?"

I nodded.

"Then it's decided. I'll see you tomorrow night."

She started to leave but stopped before disappearing into the trees. "I ain't heartless," she said.

I nodded at her.

"I just need things. Lester didn't understand that."

Then she really did disappear into the trees. I was left alone, contemplating how I'd navigate the world without Daddy's strict rules to guide me. Had I already crashed and burned?

I didn't know. I just kept thinking about the moment before the release. I'd been somewhere else, somewhere far, far away from the Holy Flame.

I'd escaped, and maybe Maggie had too, if only for an instant.

*　　*　　*

We carried on long enough for my guilt to slide away. It was replaced by a warm pleasure as I got to know Maggie better and understand that, like me, she'd been scarred and damaged by her father too. Almost everything she did was in reaction to that.

"He tried to break me," she said once after we finished a frantic session. There was thunder in the air, and lightning blinked far away to the west, out over parts of the state where neither of us had ever been. "He couldn't do it," she said.

I kissed her, but she pushed me away. "I worry that Lester will find out," she said.

"Why?"

"He looks at me funny sometimes. It's like he knows something is going on."

"He couldn't know," I said. "We never even act like we know each other except when we're here."

"What about after we got off the bus the other day? You shouldn't have done that."

"What? You mean in the bushes? You liked that."

She smiled. "Of course I liked it, but it was too risky. I don't want him to be hurt."

It was what she always said, but I wasn't sure if I believed it. In reality, she often encouraged illicit behavior between the two of us when we were in public. Once, she'd sat next to me on the bus—something we'd said was off limits—and given me a hand job while Lester sat oblivious near the front.

When I'd groaned out loud at the end, she'd smiled and quickly slid across the aisle to the other seat, leaving me with the happy mess to clean up by myself.

But the most troubling aspect of our relationship came when I brought up the prospect of her getting pregnant. Like a lot of kids in the mountains—especially those raised in strict religious environments—I didn't really have what you'd call a good sex education. Hell, I didn't have any education at all, unless you counted the magazines Lester and I had found in the woods when we were kids. From those we figured out just enough to be dangerous. By the time I was with Maggie, I knew where babies came from, and I *thought* we were engaging in risky behavior, but I also deferred to Maggie on this topic. After all, she was the girl. She knew about those things.

Essentially, we were playing Russian roulette with a nearly loaded gun. It was only a matter of time.

When I looked back on it later, I realized it was what she wanted all along. Maybe there was a part of me that did too.

23

I lay near the base of the tree listening to the creek for nearly another hour before Ronnie came out. He lit a cigarette and looked at his watch.

He stood for a moment before unzipping his pants and pissing on the ground. That was no good. I'd hoped to catch him in the outhouse, where we'd be out of earshot from the other men inside the shack.

I was still deciding how to proceed when I saw the headlights coming through the trees. I stayed low and watched as Ronnie walked around the side of the house to meet the vehicle.

The headlights went dark, and the driver got out and walked over to greet Ronnie. I couldn't see the driver or hear what was being said, so I made a dash for the outhouse and knelt at the corner, trying not to breathe too hard.

I still couldn't hear, but I was close enough to see if I had some light. I thought about reaching for my penlight, but it would give me away. Instead, I waited, straining to hear the conversation, keeping my eyes on the man Ronnie was speaking with.

When I saw him, it was just the briefest of glimpses, his face illuminated in the orange flash as Ronnie sucked on his cigarette.

For a fraction of a second, I was sure it was my father. The nose and deep-set eyes were his, as were the slope of the shoulders, the thick neck, and his posture, but then I realized this man was mostly bald, wore glasses, and was too young. Much too young.

It was Lester.

He said something to Ronnie and put a hand on his shoulder. Ronnie nodded and pointed across the creek, back toward the old church. Lester nodded, said something else, and started back for his truck.

I watched as he got in and drove away. Ronnie stood there, smoking for a few more minutes, before heading back inside.

I felt as if all my energy had been sapped. I could hardly remember why I'd come at all. Finding out about a damned toy snake would have to wait. I needed to think, to figure out why my brother would have any need to come here to talk to a man like Ronnie Thrash.

*   *   *

The dream came that night. I'd been turning the crank and glimpsed the side of the bucket as it neared the top of the dark, womblike mouth of the well. On the side of the bucket was a dark smudge, some kind of slick fluid that I could not fathom.

Lightning blinked behind me, and I felt others there, easing closer to the well, hoping to see, but then my arms gave way and my hands slipped, and the bucket returned to the darkness.

24

The next morning, I drove out to Granny's before six, the dream lingering as I drifted carefully along the mountain roads. An early morning fog obscured the roads, and I had to drive at a snail's pace. Twice along the way, I thought I saw my father standing on the side of the road, only to realize as I drew closer that it was a mailbox, a tree, and once even a homemade cross commemorating a loved one.

When I pulled up to Granny's place, the fog was clearing, and I was surprised to see Mary sitting out front in one of the lawn chairs, sipping a cup of coffee.

She gave me what seemed like a particularly weak smile as I exited the truck. I hurried over, eager to join her and fill her in on the previous night's events.

But something about her body language—or lack of body language—stopped me short. "Coffee inside," she said. "Another chair too."

"Is Granny okay?" I said.

She shook her head and looked inside her coffee cup, as if the rough dregs at the bottom might hold some primitive answers. "She's in a bad way today. They said it would come. The pain. She's been dealing with it. You know Granny. Nothing can stop her."

Except that wasn't true. And I heard it in Mary's voice. The resignation stung me, and suddenly, I wanted to go back to North Carolina very badly. It had always been far enough away to make me forget—at least on a conscious level—the problems of home.

"Go in, give her a hug, grab your coffee, and then let's get after it. We've got a lot of ground to cover today." She smiled at me, and I decided there was a balance in staying a little longer. Love and death were always inextricably bound when a person went home. I felt the truth of it in my blood.

I headed up to the house and had the screen door halfway opened before pausing. "What exactly did you have in mind for today?"

"Well, I've got a list of people from the Holy Flame. I think we owe it to the DeWalts to get to the bottom of what happened to Allison. Not to mention trying to chase down the connection between Allison and Bryant McCauley."

"Connection?"

She gave me a sharp look. "Of course. The well? The newspaper article? The map has to lead to the well, right? The well that Allison mentioned to Granny, where she saw the lightning. Have you really not made these connections?"

Of course I had. But that was the problem. The connections were ripping me apart, in much the same way seeing Lester talking to Ronnie Thrash last night had. I saw all signs pointing toward my father's church. I saw them, and there was one side of me that couldn't wait to dive headfirst into the cesspool of memories and contradictions that made up my father's life's work, but then there was the other side of me that understood just how painful a journey like that might be.

"Earl?"

"Yeah?"

"Are you okay?"

I shook my head. "Just got a lot on my mind."

She nodded, and it was the best kind of nod, reassuring and empathetic. I felt a longing to be closer to her, for her to understand me, but understanding me meant understanding my past, and I believed no one—not even Mary Hawkins—could truly do that.

* * *

Granny put on a good face, but it was clear how bad she hurt. When I came in, she tried to sit up, gasped, and then settled back into the bed. She looked diminished and beaten lying there, and it was all I could do to keep myself from looking away.

Instead, I sat on the edge of the bed beside her.

"I don't reckon you hold much by prayer, do you?" she said, her voice a rasp that made me think of the snakes Daddy kept in the pit.

"No, ma'am."

She squeezed my hand. "You know what I think?"

"What?"

"We screwed it all up."

"Screwed up what?"

She gave me a weak and crooked smile. "Everything. Even prayer."

I was taken aback. Though Granny had always seemed a deeply spiritual woman, certainly a person open to the possibility of extraordinary events, I never knew her to pray or quote scripture or to even keep a Bible in her house, which definitely explained one of the reasons I felt so comfortable staying with her.

"I think of them like kisses," she said. "I prayed for you all the time you were here. Did you ever feel like you were being loved?" she asked.

I felt tears welling up. I set my mouth and looked away before nodding.

"Good," she said. "I just wanted you to know that I'm still kissing you, dear, every day."

I was flabbergasted. I'd just assumed she'd brought up prayer because she wanted me to pray for her. Instead, she had been praying for me. Something let go inside me, and I buried my face in her belly. She patted my head and let me weep.

After what seemed like a long time, her voice came back, pained, too long for this world, weary beyond any imagining: "I'm going to keep on," she said, "but you've got to promise me something."

"Okay."

"You won't quit."

"Quit?"

She ignored my question and bore her eyes straight into mine. "Promise."

I promised.

It was only later, much later, when I remembered the promise and truly understood what I'd agreed to.

25

Mary wanted to visit Lester first.

"Start at the top," she said as she turned into the Holy Flame parking lot. The new Holy Flame.

I barely heard her. I was in awe of how different a place it was than the old building where I'd been staying with Rufus, the old building where I'd spent every Sunday morning and Wednesday evening until I was seventeen.

The new Holy Flame was a massive, sprawling building that had more in common with a high school or conference center than it did the church many of its older members had attended.

Mary had to drive around the thing twice before she found the main entrance, a wide bank of six glass doors, flanked on either side by white brick, decorated with painted flames. It wasn't exactly subtle, but Daddy and the people who worshiped at his church had never been accused of being low-key.

Mary parked beside a couple of expensive SUVs. I noticed they sat in marked spots. One of them read, "Senior Pastor Lester Marcus." The other was reserved for "Associate Pastor Billy Thrash."

"You okay?" Mary asked. I must have looked pale because she put a hand to my forehead. "You're sweating."

I nodded. Took a deep breath. "I had a rough night."

She raised her eyebrows but didn't ask me to elaborate, which was good; I didn't want to tell her about Lester. I wanted to find out what he was doing over at Ronnie Thrash's myself. If it was as bad as it looked, I'd spill the beans then. Otherwise, there was no need.

"I need to talk to Lester alone," I said.

She nodded. "Okay. How about this: you go see your brother, and I'll go speak to"—she glanced at the sign in front of the big black SUV—"Mr. Thrash. Any relation to that asshole living by your friend?"

I nodded. "His grandfather."

She made a sound that might have been a laugh. "This just gets deeper and deeper."

"Tell me about it," I said. "I was supposed to be back in North Carolina two days ago."

We exited the Tahoe and headed toward the doors. It was a Wednesday but too early for services, and other than Lester's and Billy's SUVs, there were only a half dozen more cars in the whole lot. If there was going to be a scene like I feared, at least there wouldn't be too many people around to witness it.

Sensing my unease, Mary took my hand before we entered the building. She squeezed it gently. "You don't have to do this, you know."

"Actually, I do."

I was surprised to hear myself say it. Just a few short days ago, I wouldn't have even been able to think such a thing, but the confluence of events that had knocked me for such a loop over the last few days had made one thing clear: if I was going to work through any of this shit, if I had any hope of breaking the code my father had used to lock me down for years, I'd have to face Lester.

Sooner or later.

*   *   *

The church secretary—a woman who seemed to recognize me, though I couldn't say the same for her—buzzed Lester and then Thrash. She told them both they had visitors in the front.

Mary sat down in one of the chairs across from the secretary. I paced, circling the room, studying the framed photographs, all of which told the story of the old building, the original church my father had founded some sixty years earlier when he was barely twenty years old. The first photo showed him at close to that age, standing with a shovel, smiling. The placard underneath the photo read, *Brother RJ did much of the initial work on the first building by himself.*

The next photo showed the church taking shape and a half dozen smiling men posing for the picture. *Soon, he attracted followers who wearied of the world's sin and wanted to find a true path to God.*

It went like this for some time. There was a photo of him and Mama standing outside the finished church and another one of the two of them holding Lester when he was no more than a few months old. *Brother RJ was a wonderful father, who believed nothing was more important than making sure children were saved early in life, fortifying them against the sin of the world.*

I skipped ahead, looking for a similar photo with me in it. I wasn't sure why I bothered. There was nothing. It was as if I hadn't existed at all.

I moved past Mary, toward the end, where a photo showed a packed congregation and my father holding a large rattlesnake over his head. The caption read, *Brother RJ's last sermon, in which he reminded the body how far they'd come yet told them to never forget their roots because, like God, the church should be unchanging.*

The very last photo showed Daddy's grave beside Mama's and a headstone that read simply, *Who shall ascend into the hill of the LORD? or who shall stand in his holy place? —Psalm 24:3.*

"Well, as I live and breathe."

The voice—at once familiar and frightening because of the memories attached to it—nearly made me jump. I turned and saw Billy Thrash standing in the doorway. He was grinning—something I remembered him doing a lot. "Earl Marcus," he said. "Welcome home."

I nodded at him, afraid to even speak for fear of what I'd say.

He opened his arms wide and came across the office, wrapping me tight in a huge embrace. He patted my back, laughing.

"It is so good to see you, son. My deepest condolences on the passing of your father. You are no doubt aware he and I kept very close counsel, and he spoke of you often. He was in constant prayer for you in his last few years, and I want you to be assured that it was for your return to the faith, son. He truly worried about you, as all fathers do about the fate of their children."

"I'm not back for long, but I was hoping to speak with Lester."

Something changed in Thrash at the mention of my brother's name. It was nearly imperceptible, but I was attuned to Thrash's nuances and facial expressions despite the long absence. As a boy, I'd always found his unfailing good cheer a fascinating counterpoint to my father's dour and serious demeanor.

The change vanished nearly as soon as it had come, and Billy smiled even more broadly. "Your brother is doing a wonderful job. And of course you want to see him. This really warms my heart, Earl. It really does."

He turned for the first time and noticed Mary standing beside him.

"Can we go somewhere to talk, Pastor Thrash?"

"Please, call me Billy," he said. "And of course. Let's go to my office. Can I get you some coffee? How about a sweet roll?" He turned back to me. "I do hope we'll see you this Sunday, Earl."

I just looked at him. What kind of fool was this man? Did he really believe the past could just be erased like that? Did he really think I could step back into this faith without it crushing me alive?

I supposed he probably did. That was the difference between someone who still spent his days and nights under the heavy yoke of my father's religion and someone like me who had—

I cut that line of thought short. I realized there was actually very little difference between me and Billy Thrash. If there'd been so much, then why was I here? The answer was easy—because I'd experienced my father's heavy yoke too, and like him, I still labored under its burden.

It was just after this sad realization that I saw Lester through the office windows, walking through the lobby and heading this way. I hadn't seen him in nearly thirty-three years, but in some ways, he looked exactly the same. I think it was his expression. His mouth was closed tightly, his eyes were narrowed, and his body was tense as if trying to ward off some inevitability. He held my gaze for just a moment before looking away.

26

The rest of it felt anticlimactic. His reaction was not unlike his brief letter informing me of our father's death. He saw me, and his face went blank. He hesitated at the office door, waiting for Mary and Thrash to exit before poking his head in. "Can we make this quick?" he said, leaving all formalities by the wayside. "I'm on my way out the door."

He didn't wait for my reply. Instead, he let the door swing shut and walked outside. I followed him, not sure what I wanted to say or if I'd even be able to speak at all.

He leaned against the white brick. One of the pale-orange flames hovered above his head like a strange halo. He waited for me to speak.

I couldn't.

Finally he exhaled loudly. "What are you even doing here?"

A dozen replies ran through my head. *Why wouldn't I be? You're my brother. We need to talk. What were you doing at Ronnie Thrash's place? I came because something is going on with Daddy.* All of these and more.

But in the end, I only said, "I'm helping Deputy Hawkins on a case."

"Yeah, I heard from Burt you're some kind of detective. He kept up with you for a while but said you never return his calls anymore. Sounds about right."

I let that slide and tried to start over. "I also came back to apologize."

He shook his head, his lower lip stuck out in an expression that reminded me so much of our father, I wanted to close my eyes.

"Nope," he said.

"What do you mean, 'nope'?"

"I mean I'm not interested. What you did . . . it was absolutely the worst thing somebody could do. I don't want to be around you. You're just a walking, breathing vessel of betrayal, Earl. I can't be around that without getting angry. Go back to North Carolina. Find a church. I ain't like Daddy. I believe you can get saved in nearly any church. Get right with the Lord, because I don't think you'll ever be right with me."

It felt like a gut punch. I hadn't allowed myself to imagine what this moment would be like, but if I had, it would have never been like this. This was a door slammed right in my face. I felt an all too familiar resentment building inside me. How dare he call himself a preacher?

"You're more like Daddy than you know," I said. "You and him ain't preachers. You're power mongers, men who won't let go of even an ounce of their pride to forgive a member of the family."

That seemed to shake him a little. He pressed himself hard against the brick wall, his lip trembling.

"I've tried." He nearly spat the words at me. "I've tried so many times." He looked at his feet, deflated suddenly. "Please, just go back to North Carolina. There's things happening here . . ." He trailed off. "I've got to go."

"I saw you the other night," I said.

He raised his eyebrows.

"At Ronnie Thrash's. Why would a preacher associate with a thug like that?"

"I've got a question, Earl. What makes you think I owe you an explanation? About anything?"

"You don't. I'm sorry. I want to make this right."

"Then stay away from me. That won't make it right, but it'll be the best you can do."

I watched him as he headed toward the parking lot and his expensive SUV, resisting the urge to shout something else, something mean and insulting. In the end, I was glad I did. Lester—despite it all—still hadn't deserved what happened to him any more than I did.

*　　*　　*

129

I waited outside the church at a little picnic table nestled in a grove of trees for Mary to finish up with Thrash. It was a good piece of land, and I couldn't help but wonder how in the hell the church had paid for it. Daddy had always been big on tithing, often going so far as to shame certain members publicly if he didn't think they were contributing enough. Yet most of his congregation was poor. I can distinctively remember him complaining about money a lot when I was a kid. Sure, there had obviously been some growth, but it still seemed like a stretch. Hell, the land alone would have cost a million dollars or more, even in the late nineties.

I paced around a little, trying to make my mind work on the problems at hand. First and foremost, I needed to make up my mind about North Carolina. If I didn't go back soon, I'd definitely lose those clients. More than that, I badly wanted to go back. I'd long been programmed to escape when things got tough. I'd done it thirty years ago when I went to Granny's and then again three years later when I split for North Carolina. Both of those had worked out pretty well. Why shouldn't the same plan work now?

I kicked the picnic table, frustrated by my indecision. I'd always been a decision maker. Leap first, figure out where I was going to land on the way down. Now I felt paralyzed—impotent, really—to just pull the trigger and get the hell out of town.

I sat back down and held up a fist. One finger at a time went up until I'd ticked off five questions:

1. Where was Bryant McCauley?
2. What had happened to Allison DeWalt and, maybe even more important, Allison's little girl?
3. What was Lester doing at Ronnie Thrash's house?
4. Was my father alive or dead? I felt silly even posing the question, but there it was.
5. Depending on the answer to four, could I ever find a way to bury my father once and for all?

I looked at my open palm and realized there was no decision to make. As much as I wanted to go back to Charlotte—and at that particular moment, I wanted to go back very badly—I wouldn't find the answers to any of those questions there, and if I tried to continue living without those answers . . . well, I couldn't see much of a life for myself that way.

Before I had time to second-guess my decision, I called a PI buddy I knew only as Abernathy from Asheville and left a message asking him to call me back.

"I got some work I'm going to throw your way."

Abernathy, a large black man with no less than forty-four tattoos (one for each year of his life, he liked to explain) was the hardest-working PI I'd ever known. He'd take the cases, and he'd get them done. My clients wouldn't care as long as they got results. It was one of the advantages of working in this field—nobody gave a damn about technique, just the final score.

Next, I searched through my contacts until I found my cousin, Burt. He was a few years younger and had always sort of looked up to me. After I was kicked out of the Holy Flame, he was the only person who would speak to me when he saw me. Later, in North Carolina, he reached out and kept me updated on his family life, and I kept him updated on my lack of one. Compared to a lot of my family, Burt had been good to me, though I was also smart enough not to read too much into his apparent kindness. Daddy never let anyone go completely. I felt fairly confident Burt had been "encouraged" to reach out.

I found the number. I'd last dialed it in 2011. Had it really been that long? I tried to remember what we had talked about then. Probably his kids. He had two—Baylee would have been around twelve then, and her little sister, Amanda, maybe seven. He was proud of them, though I could have done without the reports of their successfully memorized Bible verses. That probably made me sound a little like a dick, but I had no illusions about my ability to see beyond my own hang-ups.

I pressed call and waited.

He answered on the third ring. "Earl?"

"That's right, Burt. How you doing?"

"I'm doing pretty good." Was there a pause? It sounded like there might have been. And if so, what did it signal? Probably nothing other than his surprise to hear from his self-absorbed, backsliding cousin.

"It's good to hear from you," he said.

"Yeah. You'll never guess where I am."

"In town."

There was an awkward silence. "Uh, yeah. How'd you know?"

"Word gets around."

"Was it Choirboy?" I said.

"No. I don't see him much these days. Did you run into him?"

"Yeah. Is this really a thing? Calling himself Choirboy?"

"It's just a nickname. You know how he is."

"How he was. People are supposed to change. You know, grow up."

"Not Choirboy."

I let that sit, still wondering how a fifty-something-year-old man could call himself such a ridiculous name.

Yet was it ridiculous? It certainly seemed to heighten his already ominous character.

"Earl?" Burt said. "You there?"

"Yeah. I was just . . . Look, I hate to invite myself, but I'd love to come by the house for dinner sometime. You know . . . I'm just trying to see some of the old guard." I hesitated, wishing I could just hang up. Why was it always so hard to confront my past?

"Sure thing," he said. "I was going to call you anyway. How about Friday night?"

"Okay."

"I'm by myself now."

"Excuse me?"

"Well, what I mean is . . . Jeannie left me."

"Oh, man. I'm sorry to hear that, Burt."

"Aw, it was a long time coming, but it's okay. The girls will cook us up a right nice meal."

"I don't want to impose. We could meet some—"

"No way. You're a Marcus. I'm a Marcus. We'll cook. Eat out? Come on, man."

"Okay. Fine." I laughed a little, and I hoped it didn't sound as forced as it felt.

"Six o'clock?" he said.

"I'll be there."

I ended the call and realized someone was in my peripheral vision.

I almost didn't want to turn around because I was sure it would be Daddy.

But when I did turn around, I saw Choirboy standing under the eaves of the church, staring out at me. He seemed to be lost in thought and didn't acknowledge me at first. Then he lifted one hand mechanically in what almost passed for a wave. When I didn't respond, he put his hand down and walked inside.

27

"Did you see that guy?" Mary said as we settled back into her Tahoe. "I saw him. His name is Chester Dunkling. We used to call him Choirboy."

"Choirboy?" Mary shivered. "It fits him, except in a creepy way."

"Tell me about it. We called him that as a joke. But get this . . . he's adopted the name now. And yet sees absolutely nothing ironic about it."

"Is he . . . I mean . . . I'm not trying to be rude, but is he . . . special?"

"Yeah, he's special, all right. But no. Not like that. He's plenty smart. And plenty mean."

"What was he doing?"

"Staring at me. We have a little history. He was sort of obsessed with my dad."

"And now he's obsessed with you."

"Apparently."

She shook her head and inserted the keys into the ignition. She didn't turn them though. Instead she said, "How was it?"

"What? Me and Lester?"

"Yeah."

"Bad. But nothing I can't handle."

"Did you learn anything?"

"Not really. Just stuff I already knew."

"Like?"

"Like he wishes I would just go back to North Carolina. He's not interested in salvaging our relationship."

"That's on him, then."

I shook my head. "No, it's on me." And then before she could follow up, I said, "What about Thrash?"

Instead of answering me, she cranked the Tahoe and started to back out before she stomped on the brake and brought the vehicle to a hard stop. "Want to go get a beer?"

"What?"

"A beer. I know it's not quite noon yet, but I could sure use one."

"Okay." I was more than a little taken aback by the sudden offer.

"We can get some lunch too," she said. "Then I'll tell you about my interview."

*   *   *

We went to Jessamine's, a square brick building on the side of Highway 57 that shared a parking lot with a shady video store called First Look Video. It had been there since the mideighties, and it had been a legitimate video store that did a pretty good business in soft-core porn in addition to the always popular new releases. Now it looked more like the kind of place you'd go to buy drugs or maybe to catch a sexually transmitted disease.

We parked in front of the video store and walked into the small tavern. Years ago, Jessamine had been a widow who took over her husband's bait and tackle shop—called Bait and Switch. She renamed it Jessamine's, cleared out all the old fishing stuff, and started serving po' boy sandwiches and soft drinks to the crowd of working men—loggers, power linemen, farmers, even the occasional sheriff's deputy—who frequently traveled the area's busiest road. When Coulee County finally went wet back in 1984, Jessamine quickly applied for a liquor license and saw her business more than double over night. It seemed nobody wanted to go to a piece-of-shit building by the side of the road for po' boys, but if you could also have a beer or even a shot of whiskey with that po' boy, well, that changed everything.

The place felt mostly the same as I remembered it, but the crowd was fairly light because it was midday. We sat in the back, and a pretty waitress with a single long braid of blonde hair came over to take our order.

We both ordered draft beers and hamburgers—no onions for me and extra pickles for Mary.

"So," I said, "what did Thrash have to say?"

"It was a very unenlightening conversation."

"I hate to hear that. Surely you learned something. What did he say about Allison? Did he remember her?"

"He said the name was vaguely familiar, but he couldn't place her. He said it was possible she'd gone to the church for a while. There were a lot of people that came and went."

"Yeah, that's pretty much the opposite of helpful."

She shrugged. "He told me a lot of stories. Little anecdotes about the people and the church. If I didn't know about your problems there, I'd almost be convinced it was a nice little place. Is there any way things might have changed?"

I thought it over. I might have allowed the possibility, but then I remembered Choirboy had been hanging around the church. He was enough proof for me to know there wasn't any significant change.

"What about McCauley?"

"He acted really surprised to hear McCauley was missing. He said he knew he'd been out of church the last few Sundays, but that wasn't too unusual for a man like McCauley."

"I asked him what he meant by that phrase, 'a man like McCauley.' He said it wasn't meant as an insult but that Bryant had problems."

"Problems?"

"Yeah, he said Bryant had been diagnosed with some psychological issues. He wasn't more specific than that."

"I don't really find that difficult to believe," I said.

"Yeah, I figured you wouldn't."

"Anything else? Anything at all?"

The waitress put our beers down, and Mary downed a third of hers before answering. "Damn, that is good. There was one thing. Nothing too concrete, but it definitely stood out. If Pastor Thrash told me once, he told me ten times how great a job your brother was doing."

"Well, that doesn't sound too crazy. That's just Billy. So positive it'll make you sick."

She was silent, studying her beer. "Maybe. But it seemed like something else."

"What did it seem like?"

"You a sports guy?"

I pointed to my Braves cap. "Baseball was my first love, but Carolina is basketball country, so I like that too."

She nodded. "Football for me. Both of my brothers played. The oldest, Jeff, got a scholarship at Auburn and went on to play two years for the Patriots before blowing out his knee. Anyway, that pretty much made me a football fan. College, NFL, hell, high school. I love it all. So here's something I've noticed over the years: when a general manager comes out and praises a head coach up one side and down the other, what do you usually think is about to happen?"

I laughed. She *was* a fan. "Easy. He's going to get canned. Probably sooner than later."

She snapped her fingers and said, "Bingo."

"But . . . that doesn't make sense. First of all, comparing Thrash to an owner simply doesn't work. He's only an associate pastor."

She shrugged. "I'm just telling you the way it seemed to me. It was weird. That's all."

It was a little strange to see Thrash so intent on that point. After all, what did Mary care about how Lester was doing?

My thoughts were interrupted by a sharp scream from the front of the restaurant. The place went quiet, and I followed everyone else's eyes to an old woman, steadying herself on the bar. She was pale and seemed out of breath.

Jessamine.

"I'll be right back," I said.

Jessamine tried to compose herself as I drew closer, but it was too late. Her eyes were still too wide and focused on me alone. Somehow, my presence had frightened her.

"Are you okay?" I said, taking her arm.

She nodded. "I'm fine. Just jumpy in my old age. Yours is a face I didn't expect to see. What's it been, twenty-five years?"

"Thirty."

"What would bring a man back after thirty years? I'd of thought you would have forgotten this place."

"It's not a place easily forgotten," I said.

"I reckon so."

"Why did I startle you?"

She patted my hand. "It was good to see you. I've got to get back to the kitchen."

"Why not have a seat and meet my friend Mary Hawkins?" I nodded at her.

"Another time." She pulled away.

"Okay. Sorry I startled you."

"Wasn't your fault. Don't give it another thought."

"Sure you won't come sit a bit?"

"No, I've got things to do."

I watched her walk back to the kitchen. She was lying, something that was hard for an honest person like her to get away with.

But why? What had frightened her?

I went back to the table with Mary and sat down. Our food had arrived, and Mary nodded at me over the hamburgers. "What in the hell?"

"Odd thing. That's Jessamine. Apparently seeing me gave her a start."

Mary grinned. "You are ugly, I guess, but not *that* ugly."

I ignored her joke and chewed my burger thoughtfully. My mind was churning so fast, I didn't even taste a damn bite of it.

*   *   *

138

When the waitress brought the check, I motioned for her to come closer.

"Any idea what that scream was about?" I said in a low voice.

She gave me a nervous smile. "Ms. Jessamine is getting old."

"Yeah, but something had to set her off."

"Well . . . between you and me . . . I heard her telling one of the cooks about it. Apparently there's somebody here whose father is supposed to be dead. But Ms. Jessamine's husband claims he saw the daddy out on a hike one day. Ms. Jessamine saw the son a few minutes ago—and apparently this fella looks like his daddy—and that was all it took. She was already wired up from her husband's story and then . . . bam. She got a scare."

"Okay," I said. "Thanks. I was just wondering. Glad to hear it was nothing."

"Yeah," the girl said. "Like I said, she's old."

I waited until she was out of earshot and leaned across the table. "I think we need to pay a visit to Jessamine's husband."

28

Jessamine's husband was an Atlanta transplant named Crawford Middleton, who'd come to Coulee County to die and ended up finding a new life after meeting his bride. At eighty years old, he'd arrived with stage three liver cancer and a pension the size of one of these mountains thanks to his years working in the Atlanta financial sector. His only plan was to buy some land and die while he watched the sun setting behind the mountains. Two months later, he met Jessamine, and a month later they were married. *Six* months after that, he was declared cancer-free, and these days, he spent all his time breeding golden retrievers, hiking, and leading excursions into the lesser known parts of the Fingers.

And apparently, he liked to hear himself talk. Or maybe he was just lonely. It was hard to tell. What was clear was his unrestrained joy at receiving visitors. He let us right in and didn't stop talking until Mary basically just bulled her way through the briefest of pauses.

"We're here about someone you claim to have seen on one of your hikes."

He sucked in a breath, ready to talk some more, but then stopped. "Which hike?"

Mary glanced at me.

I said, "Do you know who RJ Marcus is?"

He nodded vigorously. "Oh, I certainly do. I remember well when they found his body. Poor soul." He took a second look at me. "You're his boy. I see the resemblance."

"Yes, sir."

"You don't carry yourself like a preacher."

"Well, there's a good reason for that. I ain't one. You're thinking of my brother, Lester."

"Oh. I thought he only had the one son."

"It's okay. I've been gone for a while."

He nodded. "I see. Well, I don't mean to disturb you, but I saw your father. It was definitely him."

I felt something giving way inside me. How much longer was this nightmare going to last? Of all the things that haunted me about home, of all the things this trip could dredge up, finding out Daddy was somehow alive was by far the worst possible one.

No, I decided. There was one worse.

I steeled myself to ask the next question.

"What did he look like?"

"Good question," Crawford said with a wry smile. "I guess I'll say that he looked fair to middling—for a dead man."

I could sense Mary's confusion from where I sat. Or was it disappointment? I couldn't be sure, and I didn't really have the luxury of caring.

"When was this?" I said.

"Oh, let's see . . ." Crawford leaned back in his recliner. "I'm going to say it was April. I remember because I was leading a whole group of folks. It was one of my excursions."

Mary shifted in her seat. "Are you sure you saw RJ Marcus, Mr. Middleton? The Marcuses all favor. Earl and his brother look a lot like their father."

"No way. This was him. He was old. Looked sickly."

Mary—thank God because I was honestly too stunned to know how to proceed—took it upon herself to try to gather the relevant details.

"Did anyone else in the group see him?" she said.

"No. It was just me." He motioned toward his legs. "I keep in good shape. I crested the ridge first by a good bit. He was standing right there under this overhang. He saw me, nodded at me, and then ducked back into a crevice in the rocks. Hell, I didn't pinpoint him exactly, but I knew he looked familiar. I eventually put it together that it was your daddy. I mentioned it to Jessamine, and she told me they'd found his body a few months before. I didn't believe her. Figured she got her stories messed up, so I looked him up online, and damned if she wasn't right."

Mary scratched her head. I felt paralyzed. Except my knee. It was shaking so fast, it looked like I was having a seizure.

"Could you be mistaken?" Mary asked.

Crawford pinched his face up, offended. "No, ma'am. Now I'm old, but I ain't stupid. It was him."

"And you reported it to the sheriff's office?" Mary was all business, her voice quicker, her tone matter of fact.

"Well, no. I didn't."

"Why not?"

He rubbed his face with the side of his hand. "Jessamine talked me out of it."

"And how did she do that?"

He grinned. "That woman can do anything she puts her mind to."

"But how, specifically, did she convince you to not call?"

"Well, she just said she'd been in this area for a long, long time, and it was her opinion the best practice was always to stay out of . . ." He trailed off, looking at me apologetically.

"Out of what?" Mary pressed.

"No offense, okay?"

"I'm a big boy," I said.

He nodded. "Out of the Marcus clan's affairs. She said it just didn't pay."

Mary looked at me, as if to say it was my show now.

I got my knee under control and said the only thing I could think of.

"Can you take us there?"

29

After some negotiation, we decided on Saturday morning for the hike. I pushed for that afternoon, but Crawford quickly explained the hike would take us nearly four hours, and it would be best to start in the morning.

Mary said the next day was out because she had to meet with Sheriff Shaw for a performance review. That left Saturday. It seemed like a long time to go without investigating this place, but I had little choice but to accept it.

Mary drove me back to the old church that evening, but before I got out of the Tahoe, she stopped me with a question I had not been expecting.

"What happened back then?"

I didn't have to ask her what she was referring to. I knew without a doubt that she wanted to know about what happened when I was seventeen.

"I don't like to talk about that."

"Yeah, but I just thought . . . since we're sort of like partners . . ."

"Look, I appreciate you letting me tag along, okay? But it's a mistake to see me as a partner. I'm only here for Granny and to find out what happened to McCauley."

"Don't forget your father."

"My father's dead."

"I don't think you believe that. If you did, you'd already be back in Carolina."

She was right, and it angered me a little because it had been so easy for her to figure out.

"Look," I said. "It's not that simple. There's a lot of stuff you don't know about, so . . ."

"Which is why I asked."

I shook my head. There was just no way I could tell her. I'd never told anyone about those things.

Then she reached across to the passenger's seat and put a hand on my shoulder.

"I want to be there for you. I feel like . . ." She hesitated. Her voice had changed. It was softer. More intimate. I felt myself getting excited, but it was a lonely kind of excitement, because I knew I wouldn't pursue her. My relationships over the years had all been like Maggie—infatuation, followed by torrid lovemaking, ending all too quickly in irreconcilable difference or sometimes just plain old indifference. Mary was different. She was a woman I deeply respected, and what I felt for her might not be so easily dissolved in a few one-night stands.

Or maybe I was just too scared to try because of the possible part of me that would be vulnerable in a relationship. A real relationship.

"I feel like we need to be there for each other. But . . . you're keeping me in the dark."

She leaned closer, and before I realized it, her lips were inches from mine. I couldn't resist and closed the gap between our mouths, kissing her deeply. She moaned and relaxed, nearly wilting in my embrace.

She pulled away. "That was nice."

I nodded, trying to resist the urge to kiss her again.

"I don't think this is a good idea."

"You can trust me."

I took a deep breath. "I know. But like I said, this is short-lived. We shouldn't make too much of it. In a couple of days, I'll be back in North Carolina."

She looked genuinely sad. Sad enough that she attempted another kiss. But this time I dodged it and opened the door. I'd given in to Maggie so many years ago, and I turned that to utter disaster. I wouldn't make that mistake again.

"Earl . . ." she said, but I didn't hear the rest as I closed the door.

30

For about four months, Maggie and I were hot and heavy, whenever and however we could. Which was a lot. Teenagers are nothing if not resourceful about finding ways to have sex, especially when they live in an almost dystopian world of repression like the mountains we came up in.

Later, I wondered how long she knew before telling me. Probably a good bit. A month, maybe more. When she did get around to mentioning it, she seemed almost casual about it, resigned to her fate.

I was anything but.

We'd just finished a hot and sweaty session in the high grass beside Ghost Creek, and she was pulling her dress back on when I commented on her breasts.

"They're getting bigger," I said.

She nodded. "Other parts of me too."

"Yeah? What other parts?"

She rubbed her belly. I was too stupid to catch on.

"You look great."

"What are you going to do?" she said.

"Huh?"

"When you get out of high school? When you grow up?"

"Get out of here. That's for sure. What about you?"

"I'd like that."

"Well, let's do it together then."

She smiled. "What about tonight?"

"Tonight?"

"Yeah. We could leave right now."

It was actually an enticing suggestion. But even I realized how unrealistic it was.

"We don't have any money," I said.

"Yeah," she said and sighed. She looked grief stricken.

"Are you okay?"

"No."

"What's wrong?"

"I'm afraid things are going to change. With you and me. With us."

I shrugged. "I ain't planning on changing."

"But you will."

"Naw."

She was silent for a few moments. I watched as she pulled her dress up and examined her belly.

"You ain't fat," I said. "You look healthy. Hell, you ought to eat more."

She seemed to ignore my statement. Her thoughts seemed far away.

"You believe in any of the stuff your daddy preaches?"

"What? Hell no. You know that. Any man who hands his son a live cottonmouth is full of shit."

She nodded, but her face seemed uncertain. Usually, she loved to hear me curse my father. The rebellion turned her on.

"What if some of it's right though? What if what we're doing is wrong?"

"Don't feel wrong to me."

She said nothing, just continued to rub her belly.

That was when it finally hit me.

"Maggie?"

"Yeah, Earl?"

"Is something happening?"

She just looked at me, but the answer was in her eyes.

*   *   *

Our meetings became less frequent. Part of it was just being freaked out by the whole idea of being a father. Not to mention her moods.

Sometimes she was happy—nearly gleeful—but other times she was so morose, she'd talk about killing herself and the baby. There was no one for me to go to. There was no one to help.

As she started to show more, I knew it was only a matter of time before everyone in our tight-knit community knew. I spent sleepless nights trying to figure out how to handle it. I was scared and weak. I didn't want to be a man; I wanted to be a boy again and leave her to handle it alone.

But something inside me wouldn't let it go down that way. There was a burgeoning morality I felt inside me. Gone was the fire-insurance morality Daddy had tried so hard to instill in me. Now I simply wanted to do the right thing because I knew living with myself afterward would be too difficult if I didn't. Maybe there was still a kind of selfishness there, a self-centeredness that crippled me into only seeing things within the framework of my own life, but I was still convinced it was better than the empty promises Daddy preached.

I went to Maggie and told her I wanted to marry her.

But I was too late. When I arrived at her house, her father greeted me at the door. At the time, he'd only just been elected sheriff, but he was still an overwhelming and intimidating presence. Shaw punched me in the stomach and then stood me back up. He dragged me from his doorstep—physically dragged me—all the way to the church.

We went inside and found my father in prayer. When he looked up and saw me, he stiffened.

"I hope you brought him here because he's had a change of heart," Daddy said.

"No," Shaw said. "It's something else." And then, lowering his voice because even the sheriff was a little afraid of my father, added, "It ain't good."

"Well, go on," he said. "An unrepentant sinner always bears dark fruit. If we deceive ourselves and pretend to not sin, then there is nothing but darkness inside us."

"Amen," Shaw said. "His darkness has infected my daughter."

Daddy took this in, nodding his head very slowly. "He and your girl have had relations? How do you know?"

"She's come up pregnant, RJ. It took us half the day, but she finally told us he was one of them."

I think I gasped out loud. Daddy looked surprised too, and it took a lot for a person's sin to surprise him. He expected the worst in everyone.

"Did you say 'one of them'?"

"I did, RJ. I don't know where we went wrong with her."

Daddy nodded. He didn't look at me. I felt more like the physical embodiment of a sin than a son. I hated him more right then than I had ever hated him before.

"Who were the others?" I said.

"Doesn't matter," Daddy said. "You done your part. You lay with a slut. Pure and simple. You're just digging your path to hell piece by piece." It was the first thing he'd said to me since the day he kicked me in the face. It wasn't the last though.

He turned his attention back to Shaw. "Round up the other boys. I'll counsel them. Talk them through repentance. And then bring her to me on the morn. You know she'll have to do more than repent for this, don't you, Hank?"

Shaw looked at the floor.

"Hank?"

"Yeah, RJ. I trust your wisdom on it. I must have done something wrong."

My father shook his head. "Don't you worry, Hank. Most of the time, this kind of behavior can be traced to the mother. Besides, the one standing beside you is the one we need to focus on. An unrepentant sinner can infect an entire church. A community. Take him back to my house. Tell Josephine to put him in his room and not to let him out until I get home."

"Got it," Hank said.

He grabbed my arm and pulled me out of the sanctuary as roughly as he'd pulled me in. Daddy stayed at the church most of the night, and I was still sitting up in my bed, alone and seething, when I heard him come in quietly, lumber down the hallway, and pause ever so briefly at my door before moving on.

31

After a night of heavy drinking with Rufus, I woke up late.

I might have slept longer, but the sun came in hot through the stained glass, and I rose to find Rufus and Goose gone. I assumed they'd taken another walk and spent the next hour exploring what was left of the church, piecing together old memories.

I kept coming back to two places—both nearby: The small corner in the front where I'd lain for five days, oblivious to the pain waiting for me on the other side. The other place was not far away from there, just outside the church's double doors.

I'd stood there and addressed the entire church once.

I shuddered at the memory, the feelings of naked inadequacy as the congregation turned their eyes on me. The surge of adrenaline that I'd felt when I finally spoke the truth.

The painful realization that there were two things that often followed the truth: freedom and pain.

I'd had both, if only for a moment, and for that moment, I felt as if I'd been redeemed.

But not now. Now I felt as if I was covered in the blood of my family, that I bore not only my own sins—which were more than enough—but also the sins of my father and brother and, if possible, the sins of an entire church.

Realizing I had to leave the church or I would start drinking again, I pulled on my boots and walked outside. The day was already hot. Hot and dry. So dry it made my throat hurt. I glanced at the rental truck and figured I'd need to do something about that soon. It had already been five days.

I made a quick call to book it for another week, and when I hung up, I decided it was a good deadline. If I couldn't figure things out by then, I'd have to go back home.

At least that was what I told myself.

I drove down the mountain, thinking I'd head toward Jessamine's for breakfast, but I never made it to the bar.

At the bottom of Pointer, I noticed several sheriff deputy vehicles with their lights flashing. A group of deputies had gathered near the side of the road and were looking out over a jungle of kudzu and vines that crept from the road and over what appeared to be an old structure and the surrounding trees.

I spotted Mary standing next to Hank Shaw. She appeared upset, as if she'd just been reprimanded.

I watched as she raised a finger and pointed up past the kudzu to a little shack I'd passed dozens of times since coming home but had not really paid any attention to until now. It was in bad condition, and it appeared to have been years since anyone had occupied it.

Stopping my truck a little past the line of sheriff's vehicles, I got out and squinted into the morning sun for a better look. There appeared to be a trail in the kudzu—a sort of worn path—that led back up toward Pointer Mountain in one direction and past the shack toward Ring Mountain in the other. The path was barely discernible from the road. In fact, even standing where I was, looking down at the kudzu along the road, it was hardly noticeable. But it was there. Just the slightest depression in the vines.

Despite being overwhelmingly curious about what was happening, I decided it would be best to keep my distance and hope to get a better look later. I was heading back to my truck when I heard a siren chirp.

I ignored it the first time, but then a deputy shouted after me, "Get down on the ground!"

I dropped quickly and lay flat, cursing under my breath.

The deputy jogged over and put his boot on my back.

"Who are you?"

"Just driving by. Stopped to see what the commotion was about. You fellas find something?"

"I'm going to repeat my question. You've already ignored me once. Wouldn't do to ignore me again. Now who are you?"

"Marcus. My name's Earl Marcus. I'm from Carolina. Just visiting."

"Marcus, huh? Any relation to Lester or RJ?"

I thought about lying. Hell, I even opened my mouth, fully intending to say no, but then I heard Shaw's voice call out.

"What's happening over there, Roger?"

"Caught this one snooping around."

I waited, listening as several people approached. I was turned the wrong way. The only thing I had a good view of was the kudzu. I looked at the path again. It was barely noticeable. But it seemed important. Why would someone trek through there? It was a goddamn jungle, probably filled with all kinds of critters and bugs.

"Oh, Lord." It was Mary. I turned my head. She was standing beside Shaw, who was shaking his head.

"Get him up."

The deputy named Roger pulled me to my feet. He was a short, barrel-chested man with small eyes and heavy jowls and a thick neck. He glared at me, making it very clear he wasn't impressed.

Shaw looked at Mary. "Why is he here?"

She shrugged. "I don't know, Sheriff."

"Don't lie to me, girl."

"She ain't ly—"

Shaw turned on me viciously. "You close your mouth!"

"I'm not lying. We haven't talked yet. I was going to explain to him about our conversation earlier today, but I haven't had an opportunity yet."

I admired her ability to stay calm while not cowering in front of Shaw. As much as I admired it, I could tell it pissed him off.

"You got five minutes to explain it to him," he said. "But before you do, I got something I want to say to him."

For the first time, Shaw's eyes met mine. How old was he? In his early seventies, at least. His eyes were the same, and for an instant, I was eighteen again and powerless against Shaw, who, like my father, did not suffer doubts or constraint, much less temperance. His truth remained so unquestioned, it became a force unto itself; it was the kind of truth that could crush a man with more intelligence and therefore more doubt. It was evolution's cruel trick, but I refused to let it knock me for a loop again.

I returned his look.

"I don't have no idea why you're back here or why you're messing around with one of my deputies or interfering in the affairs of my county, but I'm going to give you the best advice I can. I think you'll remember me as a man who does not mince words."

"I remember you as a poor excuse of a man," I said.

He looked like he wanted to hit me. Instead, he just nodded, as if checking off some mental notification, some reminder for a later place and time that would alert him to what he owed me.

"You'd be wise just to leave town, but if you insist on staying, I'm going to insist you keep your distance from me and my deputies and any cases we are working on. Otherwise, I'll throw you in jail." He jabbed a finger into my chest. "And that's something I've been wanting to do for a good many years."

"Thanks for the heads-up," I said as nonchalantly as I could manage. "But I'm not going anywhere. Not until I get what I came for."

That was when Shaw began to laugh. At first, it just seemed like another intimidation tactic, but at some point, the laughter grew and became real, as if he genuinely found me nothing more than a foolish kid. "Okay," he said. "But you might not like what you find."

With that, he nodded at Mary and patted the other deputy on the back, guiding him away from the two of us so we could talk.

"What in the hell are you doing here?" Mary said.

"I was just driving by and saw the—"

"And you thought it would be a good idea to stop? Jesus, Earl. I told you Shaw wanted to meet with me. Well, we met, and he basically read me the riot act for messing with you. I tried to tell him you were a logical collaborator, but the more I tried to speak sense to him, the angrier he got. I'm only here because Shaw owed my old chief a favor, but I think Shaw's mad enough about this to fire me, or at least send me back. If that happens, I won't be able to be with Granny."

"I understand. We need to split up."

"You don't have to sound so happy about it."

"I just mean—"

She leaned a little closer. "Forget it. You're right. Splitting up is the best way to go. I can't risk this shit." She looked at the road. "Look, isn't this what you wanted anyway? I mean, last night you made it clear you worked alone. That you wanted to be alone." She said the last bit with enough feeling that I couldn't miss what she was getting at.

And maybe she was right. Besides, I couldn't allow myself to drag a good woman like Mary into the cesspool of my life. So we'd go it alone. That was okay. Right?

Sure it was. I *did* work alone. And besides, being alone would keep me safe—if not physically, at least emotionally.

It all sounded reasonable. It all sounded great. But why did I feel so miserable?

"I've got to go," Mary said. "I hope you get some closure on your father."

"Wait," I said. "At least tell me what's happening here."

She shook her head. "I'm not going to do it. It's not personal, but I need to keep this job. At least for a few more months."

"Okay," I said. "I understand."

I stood there for a moment more, taking in the scene. Several of the deputies had ventured into the kudzu now and appeared to be searching for something. Shaw was on his phone. He was holding something in a ziplock bag in his right hand. I couldn't tell what it was, but it seemed to be the color of flesh.

I started back to my truck, but just before getting in, I looked up at the shack again. One of the vines of kudzu moved, and I thought I saw a face in an open window. I stepped around my truck for a better look, but the vines fell back into place, covering the window and the face.

32

Rufus and I sat around and debated what it could mean the rest of the afternoon. His take—clearly more level-headed than mine—was it likely had nothing to do with McCauley or anything else I was trying to figure out. I appreciated him trying to calm me down, but it didn't work. I argued that the Fingers was a community too small to have disconnected crimes.

"Anything big enough to bring out the entire sheriff's department is something major. And anything major in this area is likely connected to McCauley."

"Lots of assumptions there," Rufus said. "Still, I reckon I've known you long enough to know you ain't going to change your mind."

I patted Goose's head, and he licked the bottom of my hand. "You've known me five days."

"Like I said, long enough to know." He spat out into the yard from his perch on the old steps. I was sitting on a log—one of several lying around the front of the church steps.

"What's up with all the logs?" I said.

"You probably wouldn't believe me if I told you."

"Of course I'd believe you. I've known you long enough to be sure you're only partially full of shit."

He nodded. "That's not too far from accurate. Okay. Here it is. In a couple of hours—right about sunset—there'll be about a half dozen to a dozen college kids pulling up. They'll gather around these steps to listen to my old ass hold court."

"Say that again?"

"I told you you wouldn't believe me."

"I believe you. I'm just trying to understand. Why do they come?"

"That, my friend, is a good question. I think they find me hip or cool or whatever the damned word is these days." He shook his head. "It started with some professor at Georgia who was doing a course on non-traditional living. Hell if I know how he heard about me, but he came up and asked permission to bring his class up on a field trip. I told him I didn't mind, as long as they didn't mind that I might be in the middle of something and that something could include getting drunk. I think that gave him a little pause, but he brought the class anyway. They asked me some questions about my life. They seemed to get a kick out of me. The way I gave up on religion yet I still live in a church and tend the dead. Next thing I knew, some of the kids from that class were knocking on the door the following weekend. I told them it wasn't safe up here because of them fellows across the creek, but finally I figured out if they'd just come on Friday nights, it would be all right. Ronnie Thrash and his buddies almost always go down to Riley and raise hell on Friday and Saturday nights. It's the weeknights when they like to stay home and raise hell." He reached out for Goose, and the dog scampered over to meet his hand. He grinned as he rubbed Goose behind his alert ears.

"Anyway," he continued, "they've started bringing me beer. They call it 'craft' beer, and it's really good. You should stick around if you ain't got plans. Should be a fun evening."

I told him I was going to be going to Burt's for dinner.

"Oh, I remember him. He was decent for a Holy Flamer. Was glad to hear about his daughter turning up."

"Wait, what did you say?"

"Oh, Holy Flamer. That's what I call them. It's just a—"

"No, what did you say about his daughter?"

"Oh, this was a month or two back. Spring, I think. She ran off for a few days. Made the news, but she came back. All's well that ends well."

"Did they say where she went?"

He shrugged. "Maybe. Sometimes I find it hard to keep up. No TV, no radio, no eyes." He grinned ghoulishly. "But people always talk to a blind man. I reckon they think I'm safer or something. Same thing with these college kids. They tell me anything and everything. Sex lives, drugs, you name it."

"You ever hear about anybody that lives in that shack up above the kudzu field out on 52?"

"It's been abandoned, grown over, since before I went blind. Why, you see somebody there?"

I told him about the face in the window.

"Sounds spooky. One of the advantages to being blind. Don't have to see that kind of shit."

I dug a boot heel into the dirt. "I probably imagined it."

"Like them snakes?"

"Yeah."

He nodded. "So you're working the McCauley and DeWalt cases now?"

I shrugged. "I'm working the whole Fingers. Working my past. Working it all. But not getting anywhere."

"Yeah, I can hear it in your voice, my friend. Let me see if I can offer you a little advice, considering how much you helped me all those years ago, even if you didn't know it."

"Sure."

"Focus on one thing at a time. It's always helped me. Too many things can be overwhelming. Follow one thread to the end."

"Sound advice," I said.

He grinned. "It's why the kids love me."

✴   ✴   ✴

Rufus's advice to focus on one thread and follow it to the end had been sound. But too often sound advice was the hardest to follow. As I changed clothes and headed over to Granny's to see how she was, I couldn't stop my mind from tangling itself in all the different threads I'd encountered since coming back to North Georgia.

The newest one perplexed me the most. What had been in the kudzu? And more to the point, what had been in the ziplock bag Shaw had been holding?

I knew I risked being late to Burt's, but when I reached the bottom of Pointer Mountain and saw there were no signs of any police vehicles, I decided to pull over to the side of the road for a closer look.

I didn't waste any time before sliding down the embankment into the kudzu. It was deeper than I anticipated, and soon I found myself falling through the vines and becoming completely submersed. Even though there was still plenty of daylight, it was nearly dark under the thick vines. With great effort, I managed to pull my way back to the surface and steady myself on a steep incline. From there, I saw the worn path I'd noticed earlier. It ran through the kudzu almost like a ditch. I moved toward it, half stumbling, half crawling. Once I reached the path, I was able to stand upright. I looked around. On both sides, the kudzu rolled away from me. Straight ahead, though, I had a clear view of the groove in the kudzu. It went on for a long time until it was too far for me to trace. But from the general direction, it appeared that it would eventually lead me to Ring Mountain, the same mountain Crawford and I were supposed to scale in the morning, looking for the place where he'd seen my father.

I studied the mountain closely, and I swore I could just make out a tiny crease—barely visible to the naked eye—running up the side. It was little more than a hairline, but I couldn't help but wonder if following this trail would take me there.

And if this was indeed a secret trail that led into the mountains, why had it suddenly attracted the attention of the Coulee County Sheriff's Office?

Was it possible the flesh-colored thing I'd seen in the ziplock bag had been a piece of Bryant McCauley's body? I thought back to all the esoteric bits of info I'd received from him over the last week.

The photo and the quickly scribbled note. What had it said?

Look at the time stamp. Compare with date of death. Proof he's alive. Need help finding him again. Please come.

So if my father had been at the top of Ring Mountain and this had been the path McCauley had been taking to get there, why did he need my help to find him?

The penciled notes on the wall of the fishing shack made things even more complicated. Like the note, I had committed the writing on the wall to memory.

—the girl
—find map (Miss Laney)
—Earl again

Again, if I was working under the assumption that someone had followed McCauley on his way to visit my father and decided to off him here in the kudzu—because why wouldn't you do it here where the body would be nearly impossible to find—then the idea of needing a map seemed sort of futile. Needing me was just as pointless.

Unless . . . unless McCauley only knew the general vicinity of where Daddy was located and needed me or the map or both to help him find the exact location.

Or Daddy had once been up on Ring Mountain, but then he'd moved somewhere else, somewhere McCauley didn't know about.

I shook my head, angry with myself. Of course, the most logical explanation of all was that McCauley was insane and I wasn't too far from it myself.

Daddy was dead.

Lester had seen his body.

I slapped a mosquito on my neck and then another on my forearm. It was time to get out. I looked up at the shack on the rise a couple of hundred feet away. It was abandoned. It had to be. The door was completely grown over with kudzu. I was a fool.

I climbed the rise, using the kudzu vines like ropes, before heading back to my truck, my eyes still locked on just the faintest hint of a trail on Ring Mountain.

33

Burt embraced me warmly and invited me in with a huge smile. I thanked him and stepped inside the old house, the same one he'd grown up in. The last time I'd been in this house was when I was sixteen, when we'd gathered to mourn the passing of his mother. Despite the reason for the gathering, I remembered the day fondly. Daddy had always thought a lot of his sister-in-law and spent the afternoon subdued, almost somber. When he was asked to talk, he didn't speak of hell or sin or any of his other tired themes. Instead, he remembered Aunt Julie with a stirring recollection of her many kindnesses. She'd been a special woman—not only because she'd had to endure all the bullshit that came with living in these male-dominated mountains, but also because she'd had to put up with my uncle Otis.

"It's a mess," Burt said and shrugged. "I'm still working on getting the girls to do the housework."

I looked around. Honestly, it looked anything but a mess. In fact, it looked meticulously cleaned. But that shouldn't have surprised me. Burt was like his father and mine, men who believed the state of a man's appearance or his house directly mirrored the state of his soul.

The house had been built in the 1940s by my grandfather, whom I knew very little about. Daddy would only say he was a carpenter, a good builder. If pressed further, Daddy would always get angry and tell me God didn't want us worrying about the past. When he'd died, neither my father nor Uncle Otis wanted the house, but Daddy, despite being younger, was the more powerful personality and tended to get his way.

The house was no exception. It is, perhaps, some indication of the level of pathos that existed between the two brothers that neither wanted the house, yet neither would sell it either. Because Otis was forced to leave the mountains and go to the valley, he'd always been seen as slightly less of a man than my father. Why he would not sell the place and just move back to the Ghost Creek Mountain, I'll never know.

Burt led me through the expansive foyer and into a dining room. There were four places set at the table.

"Let's sit in here," he said, pointing to a sitting room on the other side of the table.

I followed him in. There was a fireplace, a couch, and two recliners. No television. Everything was centered around the fireplace and the mantle lined with framed photographs.

"Make yourself at home. Can I get you a Coke or something?"

"Just some ice water."

"Coming up. I'll send the girls in to say hey."

"Sounds great. I can't wait to see them."

Burt stopped short of the kitchen. "Earl?"

"Yeah?"

"Just a heads-up. I told you about me and Jeannie."

"Yeah. I was sorry to—"

"It's been hard on the girls. Especially Baylee. She resents me. Blames me for her mother leaving."

"I'm sorry to hear that, Burt."

"I just wanted you to know because, lately, she's been sort of . . . distant." He smiled suddenly. "But we're going to get her through it. Prayer and staying in the word, you know?"

I just looked at him.

"That's right. I forgot. You still ain't come around."

I decided to change the subject. "How's Amy?"

He nodded. "Sis is doing fine. She got married a few weeks ago. Good man. Active in the church. Fellow named Brent Wallace."

I remembered the name, but I assumed he was much younger than me, as Amy was about fifteen years my junior.

"And how's the carpet mill?"

He shook his head. "Backbreaking. I'm on the late shift now. Includes Sunday through Thursday nights. You'd think they'd shut it down every once and a while, but people want their carpet. What can you do?"

The girls came in a few minutes later. I wasn't prepared for what I saw. Over the years, Burt had sent me photos, but apparently not recently. The older one, Baylee, had turned into an absolutely stunning creature. She was tall—a Marcus trait—but she had her mother's shapely figure and thick, almost oil-black hair that hung in long silken curls. Her skin was pale and clear, which seemed to come out of nowhere, as both her mother and father had dark complexions. She wore a simple pair of blue jeans, an oversized sweat shirt, and as far as I could tell, no makeup at all.

It didn't matter. Her beauty was completely natural and utterly disarming.

The other girl was still just a kid and looked like a Marcus. Dark skin, sandy hair, long and lanky. She definitely favored Burt.

"I'm Earl," I said and held out my hand.

"Uncle Earl, right?" the younger one said.

"Well, technically, I think we're cousins, but you can call me uncle."

"I'm Amanda," the younger one said and took my hand. "Daddy showed us your pictures. There's one of you holding a snake. I wish they let girls do that."

Burt came back in with my water. "Amanda, we've talked about that."

"Sorry, Daddy. It's just . . ." She screwed up her face. "I want to feel that too."

"Women serve in other ways," Burt said. His face was red, and I could tell he was uncomfortable with this topic.

I turned to Baylee. She tried to smile at me but faltered. Then she looked away and said, "I'm Baylee."

"It's good to meet you both," I said. There was an awkward silence while I tried to think of something else to say and failed.

"Here's your water," Burt said. "Why don't we sit?"

I settled into one of the recliners. Burt sat down in the other one and nodded at the girls. "Bye," Amanda said.

Baylee followed her out without saying anything.

"They're beautiful," I said.

Burt scratched his jaw. "Yeah, I'm real proud."

"Hey," I said, looking over my shoulder to make sure both girls were indeed gone, "did I hear something about Baylee being missing recently?"

Burt's mouth straightened out into a thin line. "What did you say?"

"Just something I heard. That she was gone for a while. Maybe it was just a rumor. Somebody said it was in the papers."

He seemed to relax a little. "It was a misunderstanding. That's all."

"Oh. Okay. Well, I'm glad she's safe. She's got to be getting close to graduating pretty soon. Does she have plans for college?"

He shook his head. "Baylee graduated in May. She's going to stay home for a little bit."

I nodded. Higher education had been viewed with suspicion among the Holy Flame community when I was a kid. And the idea of a girl going to college back then had practically been blasphemy. Based on Burt's reaction, I wondered if any of that had changed.

"Well," I said, "how is the church?"

"The church is fine," he said. "Never better, really. Your brother has done a fine job."

"It's hard to imagine Lester as a preacher. I mean, he just doesn't fit the type."

Burt nodded thoughtfully. "I hope you don't take this the wrong way, Earl, but do you really know Lester? How long has it been, after all?"

"Thirty years."

"That's a long time."

"Yeah, but I know him."

"If you say so. Either way, he's a good man. He's doing a good job."

I thought about what Amanda had said. "Does Lester handle snakes?"

"Sure. What would the Holy Flame be without snakes?"

"I guess that's a fair point."

"Earl?"

"Yeah?"

"What are you doing back?"

I hesitated, not knowing how much I wanted to reveal about my motivations. I decided to play it close to the vest. "I'm here because of Arnette Lacey. She's dying. Pancreatic cancer."

"The woman who took you in?"

"That's right."

"Look, I'm not trying to poke around in your business, but there's folks saying you're here for more than that."

"What folks?"

He shrugged. "Just folks. Some of them are saying you're here to tear down the church."

"Come on, Burt. Look, I wouldn't ever do anything like that."

"Why have you been hanging out with that deputy?"

"Mary? She's Arnette's granddaughter. We're just friends." I felt myself getting irritated. As much at myself as Burt. I was supposed to be asking the questions, finding out about the church, but instead, I felt like I was on the defensive.

"People are talking. That's all." He held up his hands, as if to distance himself from such rumors.

"What people?"

He waved it off. "I already told you, nobody special. You know how rumors go."

We were silent for a few minutes. I tried to think about the best way to bring up McCauley.

"You like chili?" he asked.

"Sounds great."

He made a face. "It's Baylee's first time cooking it."

"I'm sure it will be great."

"How's the PI business?" he asked.

I grimaced, remembering the cases I'd had to give to Abernathy. "On hold for the moment. I'm going to be here until Granny passes." It was the first time I'd acknowledged this, even to myself. But it sounded right. Somehow I felt like a weight had been lifted as soon as the words came out.

He nodded. "That's awful good of you." He shifted in his seat. "I've always wondered how that works for you atheists. I mean, why not just do your thing? Why come back here and sit by some old woman's bed while she wastes away? My faith tells me it's the right thing to do. But you . . . you got no faith."

"She took me in when nobody else would," I said. "How could I not come back? Are you crazy?"

He held his hands up again. "Hey, man, just asking."

"Daddy?" a voice called from the kitchen.

"I think supper is ready," he said. He stood up and extended a hand to help me to my feet. He patted me on the back. "It's good to see you again, cousin."

I just stared at him.

*   *   *

The chili wasn't very good. It wasn't offensive or anything, it just tasted bland, and I couldn't help but wonder if Baylee hadn't left out the chili powder.

Burt wondered the same thing aloud. "How much of the chili powder did you use?"

Baylee looked at her bowl. It was untouched. She hadn't even picked up her spoon yet. Meanwhile, Amanda was eating happily, having loaded her bowl down with sour cream, cheese, and crackers.

"Sweetie, I asked you a question," he said.

"I might have forgotten it."

Burt dropped his spoon. "Tastes like it."

"I'm sorry."

"Apologize to our guest."

"It's okay, Burt," I said. "I like it fine."

"I'm sorry," Baylee said, not meeting my eyes.

"Please, don't worry," I said. "With a little of this hot sauce on it, it'll be fine."

After dressing the chili out with hot sauce and cheese, it was better. We ate in silence.

I feared my time was running out to ask about Bryant McCauley and Allison DeWalt. I also wanted to get his take on the rumors about Daddy. None of these questions were really ideal to ask in front of the girls, but I felt like I didn't have any choice. I decided to go with the least innocuous one I could.

"Since I've been back," I said, "I've heard some crazy rumors."

"Yeah?" Burt said. "What kind of rumors?"

"Stuff about Daddy, mostly."

Baylee stiffened. I glanced over at her. She had her spoon almost to her mouth, but she stopped and looked directly at me.

"Your daddy?" Burt said.

"Yeah. People say they've seen him. You hear any of these rumors?"

He took a sip of his coke. "No, can't say that I have."

"I just don't know why anyone would say that kind of stuff," I said. I glanced at Baylee again. She was slowly chewing. Her body still looked rigid, as if she were undergoing some kind of deep internal turmoil and she could not let any of it out.

"Me neither," Burt said. "That's just the way people are."

I waited a moment. Baylee spooned up another bite, balancing it carefully on the way to her mouth.

"What about Bryant McCauley?" I said. "Word is, he's missing."

Baylee coughed. It was a half choke, half cough, and when he heard it, Burt rose from his chair.

"Baby," he said, "take it easy."

She coughed again, covering her mouth with her fist.

"Daddy?" Amanda said. "Is it happening?"

"It's fine, darling," Burt said. He walked around the table and put his hands on Baylee, helping her to her feet.

"We'll be back," he said. "She's had an upset stomach lately and—"

165

As if to punctuate his point, Baylee coughed again, except this time, she choked and gagged and spit up all the chili she'd managed to swallow earlier.

It went all over Burt's shirt. Amanda screamed. Burt shoved Baylee away in anger, and she collided against her chair. The collision seemed to set her off again. She gagged and leaned over her bowl, letting out a stream of yellow bile.

"Look what you did," Burt said. "Just look."

I decided I had to act. I went around the table and took Baylee by the shoulders and guided her toward the bathroom.

"It's okay," I said. "You're going to be fine."

I helped her kneel beside the toilet. She leaned over, readying herself for more. But it didn't come. My hand was still on her back, and I could feel her heart thrumming through her heavy sweat shirt. She felt like a panicked rabbit, shaking.

She wiped her mouth with the sleeve of her sweat shirt, and the sleeve rode up her arm, giving me a glimpse of her wrist.

I recoiled at what I saw. The flesh was torn and ragged from multiple cuts. I'd seen some botched suicide attempts in my day, but this was the worst-looking wrist I'd ever seen on a survivor. She'd clearly wanted to kill herself.

She saw me looking and quickly pulled her sleeve back down.

Burt was coming down the hallway. "Baylee?" he called. "Honey. I'm sorry I lost my temper."

She met my eyes. "Help me," she mouthed.

Then her father was standing there, and I moved out of his way while he got her to her feet and took her upstairs.

*   *   *

Back at the table, Amanda was crying. I put a hand on her shoulder.

"You okay?"

She nodded.

"Does she do this a lot?"

Amanda looked at me sternly. "Just when she's triggered."

"Triggered?"

"Yes. Why don't you just go back to North Carolina or wherever you're from?"

"Are you saying I triggered her?"

She just looked at me. I thought I saw hate in her eyes, which might have been the most perplexing thing that had happened all night.

I decided to try one more time with a slightly different line of attack. "Do you miss your mother?"

She seemed surprised by the question, and for a moment, her hard face softened a little. Then she seemed to remember herself and said, "No. Mama is a backslider."

I nodded. "Why did Baylee try to kill herself?"

That was when she started to scream. I tried to get her to stop, but she just screamed louder and louder. I decided it was time to make my exit.

Jesus, I still haven't lost my ability to totally disrupt a family, I thought as I slipped out into the warm evening. At least I had the consolation of knowing there was something already deeply wrong with this one before I ever arrived.

34

I decided to swing back by Granny's because I'd missed Mary when
I went by earlier. I also wanted to see how Granny was doing. Earlier, she'd seemed almost like her old self. She'd even tried to get me
to miss my dinner with Burt and just hang out and drink moonshine
with her.

It had been tempting to take her up on it, but I couldn't afford to
miss the time with Burt. Which had turned out to be quite a time, hadn't
it? I had no doubt something was deeply wrong with Baylee, and as I
pulled up to Granny's house, I was lost in thought, trying to make sense
of it all. Why had she tried to kill herself? Was it simply the separation of
her parents? And what exactly had prompted that separation? I realized
Burt had never exactly said.

There were several lights still on at Granny's, and I was pleased to see
Mary's Tahoe was parked out front.

I knocked lightly on the door. Mary appeared a moment later.

"Can I come in?" I asked.

"Granny just went to sleep."

"Oh."

She nodded. "Sorry about that. You can try again in the morning."

"Mary . . ."

"Please," she said, "don't make this difficult."

I pulled the door open. She didn't resist. I grabbed her wrist lightly yet
with some urgency. "It's already difficult. Everything is always difficult."

She waited. A breeze blew up from the valley and moved her hair back off her forehead. I could feel the heat from her eyes.

I took a deep breath and stepped away. "Something happened tonight at Burt's."

"Your cousin."

"Right. It's something I'm going to need your help with."

"Earl, I don't think that's going to happen."

"Just hear me out, okay? It's about one of Burt's girls."

She nodded. "Okay. Go on."

I told her about the throwing up, the trip I made with her to the bathroom, the fresh scars on her wrist, and finally her whispered plea for help.

"And," I said before she could react, "Rufus told me today that she'd been missing back in the spring. Do you remember that?"

"Baylee, right? Oh, my God, I do remember it. I'm so sorry for not putting it together before now that it was the same girl."

"What were the circumstances?"

"The circumstances were . . ." She hesitated, shaking her head. "They were just plain weird. The father never reported her missing. It was the school that notified us. She'd been absent for more than a week, and they'd not been able to round up a parent. I drove out to their house." She slapped her forehead. "Why didn't I think of it earlier?"

I put my hand on her arm lightly. "It's okay. No harm done. What happened at the house?"

"I met your cousin. He said his wife was at work. I asked for the girl, and he said she'd run away. Didn't seem very concerned about it. I asked him why, and he mentioned something about a boyfriend. He said she'd be back. She'd already called once."

"And apparently he was right," I said. "How long before she came back, and did you interview her?"

"Of course I interviewed her. It was maybe another day or two before we got word she was back in school. I felt like something suspicious was going on, so I caught her right after school that day. Interviewed her. She's a beautiful girl."

"Yeah," I said. "Which can make life pretty tough if you go to the Holy Flame. What did she say?"

"Not much. She checked out her father's story. Said she and the boyfriend broke up. She acknowledged the mistake."

"Did you see her wrist?"

"I can't remember. I definitely didn't notice any scars. I would remember that."

"Will you make a point to go by her place, just keep an eye out? She's in bad shape."

"Sure. Should I call protective services?"

I thought of Maggie then. The authorities hadn't helped very much with her, and Hank Shaw was still the man in charge.

"No. There's too many people in this area I don't trust."

"I'm beginning to think the same thing," she said.

"I need to know what was happening on the side of the road today," I said. "Can you at least tell me that?"

She looked around, as if there might be someone nearby listening.

"I'm going to tell you this, and that's the last of it," she said. "I'm off that case anyway. So this will likely be the last thing I know about it."

"You're off the case?"

She nodded. "I'm beginning to think they assigned it to me because they wanted me to fail."

"But you didn't fail, did you?"

She shrugged and walked across the gravel drive to lean against her Tahoe. "I wouldn't say I succeeded, but I think we found a piece today that might have been crucial for us."

"Us?"

"Yeah. That would have been nice."

I nodded. "It would have been."

"Change of heart?"

"Not really. I've always been a man in conflict with himself."

"I think I can see that."

"So what did they find?"

"A hand."

"Say again?"

"There was an anonymous call earlier this morning. Caller said he'd been walking in the kudzu with his dog early this morning. The dog ran off and came back with a hand. He sounded like a kid according to the deputy who took the call. Said he didn't want to leave his name. But he did give us detailed instructions on where to find the hand. We went right to it."

I settled in beside her, leaning against the Tahoe.

"It's pretty well mutilated, and the early evidence—at least as much as I was allowed access to—seems to suggest it was removed from the body after death, maybe by scavengers. Maybe even by the dog."

"And the body?"

Mary shook her head. "That's where things get weird. Shaw didn't seem particularly concerned about locating the body. We stood around for an hour while some deputies rummaged through the kudzu. He never brought in any dogs or search units or anything. When I asked him about it, he said for me not to worry. I suggested that the hand might very well belong to Bryant McCauley, and I was certainly going to worry about it. Then he tells me I'm not on that case anymore."

"He offer an explanation?"

"Nope. Just said I should go back through the files at the office, work on something else for the time being."

"Do you think the hand belongs to Bryant McCauley?"

"I honestly don't know, but there's definitely something that could tell us."

"What's that?"

"The hand had a tattoo on it, just below the knuckles."

"And?"

"I sneaked a look at it when Shaw wasn't paying attention. It looks like little lightning bolts with a date below it."

"A date?"

"That's what it seems to be. The numbers *one–twenty-eight–sixteen*. January twenty-eighth."

"Are you sure about the date?"

"Yeah. I memorized it."

"Thanks. I'm going to try to track down some of McCauley's family and see if anyone recognizes the tattoo."

"There's still something I need to tell you," she said. "But again, if Shaw finds out I've been helping you . . ."

"I get it. Don't worry. If I have it my way, I'll never speak to Shaw again, much less do anything that could hurt you with him."

She reached out and took my hand. "I know you wouldn't."

"So what is it?" I asked.

"You know how I said Shaw wanted me to work on old cases? Well, I spent the afternoon going through the files, and I found the perfect one. But when I took it to him, Shaw put the hammer down and quick."

"Which one was that?"

She gave me a wicked little smile. "Allison DeWalt's daughter, Jenny."

"Hot damn. What did you find?"

She shook her head. "Very little. Patty and Wyatt DeWalt filed a report, but Allison never did, which meant it was an easy one to over-look. In fact, there's no evidence in the file that anyone looked into it at all."

"Jesus. This whole county serves my father's goddamned church."

"I'm beginning to think you're right. When I took the file into Shaw's office and told him I wanted to work on it, he tossed it in the trash."

"Christ. Hank Shaw is in this mess shoulder deep."

"Yeah, and get this—after he threw the file away, I went back and found another case."

"And?"

"It was another missing girl. Her name was Millie Turner. All that was in the file was a report from the school about truancy and a report detailing an interview with her parents. I took that file into Shaw's office. He looked it over and then told me no."

"No? Why not?"

"Said that one had already been solved. She ran off with her boyfriend."

"Doesn't exactly sound solved."

"No. That's what I thought too. Something else, though. I didn't exactly follow Shaw's directions on that one. I dug a little deeper. Looked up info on her family. They've been going to the Holy Flame for years."

"You think she left because of the church? Because of some threat of . . . whatever Baylee and Allison experienced?"

"That's exactly what I think. And if it's true, if the church and the sheriff are in cahoots, what can we do?"

"What do you mean?"

"I mean, it's just you and me. Maybe we're in over our heads."

I squeezed her hand. "Not true. We've also got Rufus."

She laughed softly. "The blind guy. Okay. That's a comfort."

"Don't forget Granny."

That made her laugh even more.

"Hey, that woman would go to war for you."

"And you."

I nodded. "She's already done it once."

Mary put her head on my shoulder. "I can see why."

It felt nice to be out in the night air, to feel Mary's head on my shoulder, her hand wrapped tightly in mine. But it couldn't happen. I'd already decided that much.

"Mary . . ." I said.

"Shut up. Don't ruin the moment. We can talk about how you want to be alone another time. Right now, just close your damned mouth and enjoy this moment."

So I did.

35

The next morning, I met Crawford Middleton at his home in nearby Riley.

He was waiting for me in the driveway wearing short pants, hiking boots, and thick knee-high athletic socks. Over each shoulder he'd slung a canteen. He passed one to me.

"Jessamine thinks I'm meeting one of my hiking groups. She wouldn't be happy if she knew I was taking you, so you'll forgive me if I don't ask you in."

"I understand," I said. "Her policy is to stay out of Marcus affairs."

"That's right. Says she's lived here long enough to know better. I think she's just getting a little paranoid."

"You ever been to the Holy Flame, Mr. Middleton?"

"Nah. I don't buy all that religious stuff, myself. No offense."

"None taken, but if you had ever been inside the church and seen one of my daddy's services, you might appreciate your wife's wisdom in such matters."

We drove over to Long Finger Mountain and parked on the side of the road near an old portable toilet somebody had abandoned a long time ago.

"You up for this?" he said as I climbed out of his truck.

"Sure. Why not."

"It's a pretty stiff hike."

"I can handle it." Or at least I hoped I could. I worked out regularly in North Carolina, but most of my running was on level ground. It had been a long time since I'd really done any serious mountains. But I figured if an old guy like Crawford could handle it, I'd better be able to.

We'd only gone half a mile when I asked him to sit down for a rest.

We sat on a large, flat stone on the side of the trail, if you could even call it a trail. It seemed almost as if we'd been randomly trekking through the woods. If he was following a path, I hadn't yet seen it. Then I looked back down the mountain and saw the trail snaking through the trees and leveling off back down in the field of kudzu. It was definitely the same one that ran by the shack.

It was all I needed. The hand belonged to McCauley. It had to. And he'd been on his way to see my father—or at least where he thought my father was—when he'd been killed.

"Must be weird," Crawford said.

"What?"

"Me taking you up to the place where I saw him. I mean, you probably think I'm crazy."

"I think *I'm* crazy too. You're in good company."

He looked around, and if I didn't know better, I'd say he almost looked nervous, unsure of himself. "Maybe I didn't see him."

"What?"

"I don't know. I mean, maybe it was just somebody else."

I shrugged. "I'd say it probably was, but why the change of heart? You seemed so sure the other day."

"I don't know. I just don't want to see you upset for no reason."

"I'm a big boy. How much farther?"

He looked around at the dark trees, trying to judge. "Oh, we're close enough as the crow flies, but unfortunately we'll have to wind our way around hell and back to get there. Another two miles of walking, at least. I'll know more when we get out from these trees and I can see better."

I lay back and closed my eyes, remembering the previous night's gentle moment with Mary. A few short weeks ago, I wouldn't have believed a moment like that could have been in my future. Even now, I was more than trepidatious about the small portion of intimacy we were beginning to share.

"You ready?" Crawford said. "We don't get a move on, we'll risk losing the light on the way back."

"What? I thought you said it was only a couple more miles?"

"That's right, but the last mile is a doozy."

He helped me to my feet, and I was damned glad nobody else was around to see this old man absolutely wearing my ass out.

*   *   *

He hadn't been lying about the last mile. As we covered it, he must have asked me six or seven times if I wanted to turn back. I swear he either was trying to dig at how out of shape I was or had just decided we were wasting our time. All the enthusiasm seemed to have drained right out of him.

We emerged from the trees onto a steep rocky incline. It was grueling work, but despite his change in attitude, Crawford never faltered.

When we finally crested the rise, I thought I glimpsed something to my left. It looked like a person, but when I turned my head for a better look, there was no one there. I wrote it off as another random Daddy sighting. My imagination. Or the snake venom still playing havoc with my brain.

"All right," Crawford said after a little bit. "See that rock formation?"

How could I miss it? There were several gigantic shelves of granite laid on top of each other in cascading layers of varying shades of gray and tan. Most of the shelves were smooth and tan colored, but there was one jagged rock at the very top, giving the entire formation the vague semblance of a head wearing a rusted crown. There was a dark crevice between the two largest rocks, like the entrance to a cave.

I recognized it from the photo McCauley had sent me. Daddy had been standing right in front of the crevice.

"He was standing right there. Right in front of that little hole. See it there? Follow the brown rock at the top all the way down."

I nodded, too stunned to speak.

"He was just standing there, looking sick as a dog, but he was alive."

"Right," I said, finding my voice. "And what happened? Tell me again."

"He stepped back inside that hole when I saw him. Nobody else in my group saw it, so I couldn't convince anyone to investigate. But I saw him, by God."

"Okay," I said. "Let's go in."

"I don't know about that," he said. "Those kinds of crevices ain't always safe. Maybe we should turn back."

I ignored him and trudged on up. I hadn't come this far to just take a look and go back. I wanted to investigate.

When I looked back, he was following me, albeit reluctantly.

We covered the last twenty yards to the opening of the crevice. As I neared, I saw the opening was deeper than it first appeared and was more of a tunnel leading off for some unknown distance.

I pulled out the penlight I kept on my key chain and turned it on.

"You coming?"

"No, sir," Crawford said. "I think I'll wait out here. Like I said, it ain't safe. I'd advise against you going in yourself." His face looked strained, and for a second, I believed he was suffering a stroke, but then it cleared and he looked away.

I shrugged. "Okay. I'll be out in a minute or two."

"Be careful."

I nodded and walked inside, holding the penlight out in front of me.

These were the moments that frightened me. Ronnie Thrash and his buddies were little more than chaff blown in the wind. This dark corridor, though, was something else.

Upon entering, I immediately detected a smell. It was pine and clove and something more elusive, something like oil. It smelled like the old church. Like Daddy. I was no more than a few steps inside before I stopped to take a deep breath. To consider.

I had to go on. There was no other option. I moved slowly, cautiously, one hand on the cool wall, the other hand holding the penlight. I followed its illumination deeper into the mountain, all the while aware the distance back to the entrance increased with each tentative step I took.

The corridor was very narrow for a while, but eventually it seemed to widen out. I couldn't see much with the penlight, just plain rock all around me. I half-expected to see some ominous graffiti etched in blood against the white stone. But there was nothing. Except the smell of Daddy.

Eventually I became aware of two things: there was light somewhere far ahead of me, and somewhere behind me was the sound of what I believed to be footsteps.

"Glad you decided to join me," I called. "Keep on coming." I held the penlight up. "Follow the light. And speaking of light, I see some more up ahead." I tried to sound confident, but in truth I was frightened by the sound of the steps.

The footsteps stopped at the sound of my voice. Maybe I'd just imagined them?

Then I heard them a second time. Except now they were quicker, louder. And there was no doubt they were footsteps. Heavy. Close.

"Crawford?"

The steps continued. I heard breathing too and then tight-lipped laughter.

I reached for my 9mm with my free hand. I shone the penlight into the darkness with my other hand.

"I've got a gun," I said.

The laughter came again. I waved the light around, trying to see who it was, but all I saw were stone walls in every direction.

The footsteps stopped.

I decided I'd move toward the light that I'd seen in the distance. At least there, I could see who I was up against.

I walked backward, not easy when you know your surroundings, damned hard in a dark, curvy tunnel, but I didn't dare turn my back on the footsteps behind me.

They came closer. More breathing. An actual grunt. I resisted the urge to just turn tail and run toward the light. But it would be unavoidable soon. Moving backward was slowing me down. My pursuer was gaining by leaps and bounds.

I stopped again.

"I'm going to shoot," I said, trying to sound like I meant business even if I had my doubts about the futility of trying to fire inside a winding passage like this one.

The footsteps fell silent.

Someone exhaled softly. Whoever was following me was very close now, maybe just a few yards away.

I raised the 9mm. "I'm warning you. Identify yourself or I'll shoot."

The only sound was the low, pinched laugh.

My finger twitched on the trigger. I knew a shot in this narrow tunnel would likely kill or maim whoever was following me or hit solid rock and ricochet back toward me. Not to mention what it might do to my ears. I decided to keep moving. If my pursuer came much closer, I'd be able to see his face. And the light had to be coming soon.

I inched backward again.

It felt like he was within a few yards. I began to move faster, trying to reach the light, which I could now feel on my neck and shoulders.

In my haste, I stumbled. I landed hard on my back and dropped the 9mm. It slid across the rocks and out of the tunnel. I tried to turn over and scramble after it, but that was when someone jumped on me and shoved my face into the ground.

I felt the barrel of a gun pointed at my head.

A voice whispered in my ear, "I got a gun too, Earl. Now we're going to do what I should have done a long time ago."

I turned to see my attacker and wasn't at all surprised to see Choirboy on top of me, grinning. I was amazed to discover I felt relieved. Relieved it wasn't Daddy or Lester.

"Get up, Earl. Let me show you the legacy you missed out on."

He pulled me up and led me out into the blinding sun. I tried to locate my gun, but I couldn't do anything but squint my eyes against the bright light.

"Look around you," he said.

I blinked again and tried to open my eyes. What I saw made me do a double take. We seemed to be inside some kind of walled temple. All around us was smooth rock that rose anywhere from ten to twenty feet in the air. We stood in the middle of a circle, facing a crude stone altar consisting of a flat slab of rock laid across two large boulders. On the rock wall behind it, someone had hung a cross made out of deadwood. No fewer than three cottonmouths moved listlessly about in the sun.

"I know he was here because I love him more than anyone else. I followed him to this spot so many times. I knew about the prayers he gave the snakes he kept up here. Ain't that something? I knew about this, and his own boy didn't." He smiled at me and cocked his head to one side. "Now I get to do what your daddy never could do because he was so purehearted."

"And what's that, Chester?"

"I get to send you to hell."

I nodded.

"You followed us? How did you know?"

"God has been speaking to me, Earl. He's told me you are a virus come home to infect us all. Now walk over there with that snake. That one there, the one near the altar." He leveled the gun at me.

I eased over to the snake, trying to locate my own gun. I saw it as I neared the suspiciously languorous creature. It was at least fifteen yards away. He'd put three bullets in me before I reached it. I turned my attention to the snake. I'd have to survive it.

Somehow.

An idea came to me, but it had very little chance of working. Still, I knew I had to try.

"Closer," he said. "I'm going to want you to pick it up."

I had a feeling that was coming, and as badly as I didn't want to do that, I also believed it was my best chance for survival. After all, if Daddy had spent time with these snakes, they would be inured to humans. At least that was what I hoped.

"You're not even going to give me a chance to repent?" I said.

"Your daddy said it was too late for you."

"My daddy, huh?"

"That's right. He speaks to God."

"What, God opened up the sky? Showed him a picture? What?"

"He speaks. Your daddy listens. I done told you that."

"I don't believe you."

"You wouldn't."

"I think somebody is using you, Chester."

He jabbed the gun in my direction. "You're a fool. Ain't nobody using me but God above. Now pick it up, Earl. We're going to put your life in the hands of God now. He spared you once, and all you did was spit in his face. You got hell coming now. Go on."

I turned and regarded the cottonmouth. It barely acknowledged my presence. I bent down, reaching both hands out. It turned an eye on me, an uncurious, nonchalant eye.

I knew when it struck there would be no warning.

I thought of Daddy, up in front of the church. I saw him sweating from his hairline all the way down to his round chin. I saw him holding the cottonmouth, the same one that had bitten me. As a kid, that had been the snake I feared the most because Daddy had picked it out for me, promised me to it, the way some fathers promise their daughters to future spouses. Daddy always grabbed it up without a care or thought, no single instant when you could see any sign of hesitation or doubt. Took it and caressed it, which always gave me a chill. He loved that snake because it was an evil so tangible, you could feel it. He loved that snake because it made his God, so frequently hidden from the senses of man, a real thing. A powerful thing. And the more powerful his God was, the more powerful my father was, the less he cared about consequences. And therein lay my father's strength, his ability to do so well what so many other men would not even attempt.

I closed my eyes, breaking the languid gaze of the snake. I breathed slowly, easy, tasting the dust in the air, the scent of faraway rain on the wind.

When I opened my eyes, the snake had inched forward. I shifted my weight and leaned past his head to grab his tail. He struck at nothingness as I swung him out away from my body.

Choirboy barely had time to laugh before I spun and tossed the snake at his chest.

He put up the hand not holding the gun to ward off the flying creature, but it wasn't enough. The snake wrapped itself around his arm and bit him in the face. He fired off three shots before he fell. All of them went over my head.

I sprinted toward the tunnel and my own gun, but there was another cottonmouth lying near it. I slid along the smooth rock, keeping my distance from both the gun and the snake, deciding I'd rather leave a thousand guns than ever touch a snake again.

I watched as Chester struggled with the snake. His body was shaking, but he still held the pistol, and it seemed like he was trying to hold the muzzle against the cottonmouth's head.

Because I was watching his struggles, I almost missed it when the snake nearest me charged. I kicked out at it, missing, but warding it off momentarily. I didn't wait to see what else it would do. I sprinted back into the tunnel and didn't stop running until I'd come out on the other side.

36

Crawford was gone when I emerged again, but that didn't surprise me. It actually made sense now why he didn't want to go in. He knew what was happening. Hell, there was a good chance he'd helped set it up.

What I couldn't figure out was how or why.

Crawford wouldn't have connections with Choirboy. He didn't even go to church. And Jessamine had made it clear she didn't want any dealings with the Holy Flame.

And why would Crawford *want* to help Choirboy snuff me out? As I picked my way back down the rocky face, I came up with what seemed like the most plausible theory.

Crawford had been forced to help. That was the only explanation. Someone found out about our trip and saw it as a great opportunity to get rid of me. Hell, Crawford might have only been told to not go inside and to leave as soon as we parted. It was entirely possible he hadn't even seen Choirboy going in after me.

But the first question still remained: How? If Crawford hadn't told anyone, how did Choirboy find out? Crawford must have mentioned it to someone. Maybe one of his hiking buddies.

There was a lot to figure out, perhaps nothing more pressing than how I was going to handle the situation I'd just barely escaped. I knew the right thing to do was to go to the sheriff's department and tell them I'd been attacked. Then I could take them to the place where I suspected they'd find Choirboy's dead body. But there were two flaws in this approach: first, I wasn't completely convinced Hank Shaw wouldn't have been perfectly happy to see Choirboy succeed, and second, I couldn't be sure they wouldn't try to implicate me in his death, if for no other reason than to get me out of the state. Or lock me up. Either way, the backslider was gone, and the church was free to do whatever the hell it was doing.

Because it *was* doing something, right? If I truly believed Choirboy wasn't acting on his own, then that meant me poking around about McCauley was really pissing off somebody at the church.

Lester?

It didn't fit, but I certainly couldn't rule him out. He *was* the preacher, the de facto head of the church. And he hated my guts.

And if not him, who? Billy Thrash seemed far too easygoing to engage in such drastic measures.

Hank Shaw? Like Lester, he hated me, but he'd never seemed like a true believer, just one more person hoping to catch a little bit of the wave my father created in this area with his prodigious gifts for initiating and mobilizing unquestioning hordes of followers.

Still, involved or not, I couldn't trust Shaw to handle this situation fairly. I'd have to go another route.

When I made it back to the side of the road and the portable toilet, I tried my phone to see if I had any service yet. A bar showed up, and I immediately called Mary.

I didn't know anyone else. Rufus, but Rufus didn't have a phone other than the burner Mary gave him. Or a car. Not to mention vision.

Mary picked up on the third ring.

"Could you give me a ride?" I asked.

It was only when she'd agreed and I stood leaning against the old portable toilet that I remembered there was another possibility I hadn't considered about who might have put Choirboy up to snuffing me out.

Maybe it really was my father.

*   *   *

Thirty minutes later, night had fallen, and I was sitting inside Mary's Tahoe, trying to convince her the best plan of attack was for me to make an anonymous phone call.

It didn't take long before she relented. As much as she wanted to trust the organization she worked for, it was becoming increasingly harder to do.

She made me repeat the tale three times before she finally seemed to accept it.

"So this Choirboy," she said, "he's like . . . what? A fundamentalist hit man?"

"I hadn't thought of it like that," I said. "But yeah. Good way to put it."

"Do you think he might have killed McCauley?"

"I don't know. It's possible. I'd definitely put him at the top of the suspect list."

"I hope he's dead," she said quietly. "There's something deeply off about that man."

A few minutes later, Jessamine's came into view. The lot was filled, but I scanned every spot until I saw Crawford's truck. He was inside the bar. I reminded myself that I'd decided on the anonymous call. That was the safest bet. I pointed to the payphone at the far end of the lot, and Mary let me off there.

I called the sheriff's office and reported what had happened without leaving my name.

"Well?" Mary said when I came back to the Tahoe.

"I reported it. We'll see if they do anything. My guess is that Choirboy is already dead."

She followed my eyes to Crawford's truck. "What are you staring at?"

"He's inside Jessamine's."

"Are you thinking about confronting him?"

"I am."

"Maybe you should slow down a little, Earl. If you're right about Shaw and the department, it really is you and me out on an island."

I heard what she was saying, and what's more, it even made sense to me, yet I couldn't seem to stop myself from doing what I wanted to do.

"Maybe you should just stay here," I said.

"Nope. If you go in, I go in. From here on out, we don't split up."

"Wrong. After this, we totally split up. You can't afford to be seen with me."

She pursed her lips. Her nostrils flared, and her eyes narrowed to two dark beads. She looked fierce, and I realized she was exactly the kind of person I needed in my corner. "Somebody tried to kill you today, Earl. I'm not leaving your side. Especially not to let you walk in there on a Saturday night."

She had a point. The lot was filled with pickup trucks. It would probably be a rough crowd in there, but at least I could take comfort in the knowledge that my father's followers would never let themselves be caught dead in a bar.

"Stay," I said again, but mostly just to make myself feel like I'd tried. She was coming, and I could see there wasn't any way to stop her.

37

Country music and the chatter of forty or fifty buzzed or drunk folks rang in my ears as I pulled open the front door. I wasn't two steps inside before sweat broke out on my back and under my arms. Dozens of pairs of eyes looked me over and then darted quickly to Mary, and I realized it was one thing to come in here at lunch with a black woman, but it was altogether different at night, with the crowd like this.

And it really was a rough-looking crowd. There's not very many ordinary folks in these mountains. People tend to go one of two ways: there's the fundamentalists, with all their psychological problems and misogynistic culture, and there's the heathens, who tend to wash away their guilt for not being in church with gallons of whiskey and beer. Drugs too. Both populations are dangerous and thrive off violence and intimidation. Both groups are angry. Both groups have a history of racial prejudice and are more than willing to engage in violence.

The good thing about a bar is you knew which group you are dealing with.

Mary and I found the last two open barstools and slid onto them. The bartender threw a glance our way, and I held up two fingers and said, "Beers."

The beers came, and I sucked mine down, not realizing how thirsty I'd been from the hike, not to mention the near-death experience.

I turned around on the stool to look the place over. It didn't take me long to find Crawford. He was sitting at a table over in the corner with Jessamine and a couple of other folks.

I elbowed Mary and nodded in Crawford's direction.

"What are you planning?" she whispered.

"Just a chat. Nothing more."

"Good, because there are two deputies at the other end of the bar who would like nothing better than to bust your ass, not to mention show me up."

"Come again?"

She pointed to her left, and I made the deputies immediately. They both had short dark hair and five-o'clock shadows. They were both big dudes. One of them big with muscles and the other just big. They were tossing back boilermakers and laughing.

"Now why would two fine gentlemen like that have it in for me?"

"Are you kidding? Shaw has told everyone at the station about you. He's got them convinced you're the Antichrist or something. And they hate me just as bad or worse. See, I'm your friend. And I'm a black woman. Right now, those are just about the two worst things a person can be in this county."

I stroked my beard and tried to put myself in Mary's shoes. I couldn't. Basically, I would have turned tail and run a long time ago. She was damned tough.

"I appreciate it," I said.

"What's that?"

"You sticking with me."

"Yeah. It hasn't been easy. Especially because you won't even tell me why everybody hates you so much."

"I'm sorry," I said. And I really was. For the first time, I realized what a prick I'd been for not telling her. Yet even as I understood that, I found myself resistant to the idea.

I scanned the bar one more time, my eyes roaming to the farthest reaches of the big room. That was when I spotted Ronnie Thrash sitting at the table where Mary and I had eaten lunch a few days back. He was surrounded by his boys, and he was looking directly at me.

I nodded at him.

He looked away.

"Wish me luck," I said. I pushed off the barstool and made my way slowly over to Crawford and Jessamine's table.

As I got closer, I grabbed an empty chair from a nearby table and set it down across from Crawford.

"Howdy," I said and sat down.

The two people on either side of me slid apart to make room. They were both women somewhere north of seventy, and one of them tutted at my rudeness.

Crawford's eyes were wide. He didn't speak.

"We don't want no trouble, Earl." It was Jessamine.

"Neither do I."

I kept my eyes on Crawford.

"Baby," he said, "why don't you and your friends go back to the kitchen and let me and Earl talk about our hike?"

Jessamine bristled at this. "I told you it was trouble to get involved with them."

"No trouble," Crawford said. "Just a misunderstanding."

Jessamine stood, and her friends followed suit. Just before leaving, she leaned over and whispered in my ear. "I got a shotgun in back. I ain't afraid to use it."

I nodded, still keeping my eyes on Crawford.

Once they were out of earshot, I said, "I expect you're a little surprised to see me."

He shrugged. "Don't know why I should be."

"I'm like the second dead man you've seen this year, huh?"

"I don't even understand why you'd say that."

"Sure you do. What I want to know is two things: Who came to you? And how did they know?"

He took a swallow of beer. "I don't know what you're talking about, Earl. I waited for you outside the tunnel, but you never showed."

"Cut the horseshit, Crawford." I leaned across the table. "There's a sheriff's deputy ready to arrest your ass if I just say her the word. But if you'll tell me what I need to know, then I'll call her off. Easy as that."

He grimaced. "Listen, I'm in a bad place here, okay? I don't know how they knew—because I didn't tell a damned soul about the plans for our little hike—but these two guys paid me and Jessamine a visit. One of them . . . Shit. One of them wasn't right. He had these eyes, big and bugged out of his head. He never blinked. Kept quoting scripture at us and actually went through our bookshelves and pulled out some of my books. He threw them on the back patio and set them on fire. Said they weren't 'holy books' and he couldn't in good conscience be around them."

"Was he tall? Wears his pants hiked high? His shirt tucked in? A bad dye job and a comb-over?"

Crawford nodded.

"I know the guy. What about the other man? Who was he?"

"That's what I meant by being in a bad place. The other guy . . ." He leaned forward and pushed some empty glasses to the side. He motioned for me to meet him halfway.

"The other guy's sitting right up there at the bar."

He nodded to the two deputies. Both were turned, facing us.

"Which one?"

"The stocky one."

I recognized him now. Shaw had called him Roger. He was the one who had caught me snooping around the kudzu. My back was still sore from where he'd ground the heel of his boot into my spine.

"He's a cop. What can I say to a cop?"

"So, what, they threatened you?"

"I'm really afraid right now," he said. "They're looking over here."

I nodded. "Okay. I understand. We may talk more later."

"Where are you going?"

"To talk to these assholes."

"Please don't. They'll know I told you," he said, nearly whining the words.

"They already know," I said as I slid the chair away from the table.

*　　*　　*

When they saw me coming, both deputies turned around and focused on their boilermakers. There were no seats available, so I actually had to tap Roger on the back to get his attention.

"I'm drinking," he said. "Come back later."

"I need a word with you," I said.

"Here's two: fuck off."

I grabbed the back of his shirt and dragged him off the barstool. He was damned heavy, like trying to tug a couch across the den with one hand, but once I got his weight shifted, gravity did the rest.

He landed hard on the floor and tried immediately to get up, but I stuck my boot over his throat and pressed it down. He gagged on his words.

The other deputy seemed too surprised to react, which was what I hoped would happen. He was going for his piece when I put an elbow into his chin. He fell back against the bar.

I let off Roger and bent down to get his gun. He was still trying to find his wind when I got his piece out and pointed it at his head. "You and me, Roger. Outside. Right now."

He said nothing as he clambered to his feet. I pointed to a side door, and he nodded. He was coughing, still trying to clear his airway.

I checked the other deputy. He had his hand near his jacket. "Don't," I said. "Unless you're stupid enough to think I won't shoot him. Then go ahead and take a chance."

He held up, watching as I pushed Roger toward the door. I scanned the bar as we headed out. Every eye in the place was fixed on me. I tried to find Mary. She was sitting on the stool, a look of resignation across her face. I shook my head sharply when she started to rise. She sat back down. Good move. She couldn't afford the trouble she'd get in if she actually helped me do what I was about to do. I pushed the side door open and motioned for Roger to step outside.

*   *   *

"You know this ain't going to end well for you, right, asshole? You have assaulted a sheriff's deputy and taken his firearm, and now you're pointing it at him. You are a stupid, stupid prick."

"You left out the part about you helping to organize a fucking hit on me. I think that might be a factor if this shit ever goes to court," I said.

191

"Maybe. But this is Coulee County, Mr. Marcus. We do things the way we do things. Sheriff Shaw said you did his daughter wrong a long time ago. He said you were a fucking bacteria that Coulee County couldn't afford to host."

"So Shaw put you up to this?"

"Man, I don't know what you're talking about."

I punched him right in the mouth. I'm not going to lie—it felt really, really good.

"It ain't Shaw," he said after he'd spit out a tooth.

"Then who?"

"It's the same man it's always been in this county. Don't matter who you are, where you go, what you believe, this man calls the shots."

"Who, goddamnit?"

He spat a glob of blood onto my boots. "Seems like you of all people would know, Earl. It's your daddy."

I hit him again.

38

I left Roger on the ground, bleeding and mumbling to himself. It was too much to process. My father was dead.

He was, goddamnit.

I kicked a trash can into the alley between First Look Video and Jessamine's. It clattered across the pavement and rolled off into the grass behind the parking lot.

Heat lightning flashed over the mountains, and my world flickered as if I'd become little more than an actor in an old film. I had to make some kind of progress. As much as I didn't want him to be alive, there was too much that suggested otherwise to ignore the possibility. If my father was alive, if he was indeed "calling the shots," I had to find him. I had to look him in the eye. And if he wasn't, then I had to know that too.

I went back over to Roger and knelt beside him.

"Where is he?" I said.

"Hell," he said, "if I knew, do you really think I'd tell you?"

"If you know, you damned well better tell me."

"Only thing I know is when word comes down, you got to do it. There's problems for those that don't."

"Problems?"

He rolled over. "Yeah, problems." He grinned. "I reckon you'll find out soon enough."

I broke down his pistol, leaving the gun with him. I put the magazine in my pocket and walked around to the front of the bar.

I figured the place would be swarming with deputies soon, so I wanted to get Mary and get the hell out. I had my hand on the front door when I heard the sirens.

I stopped. I was a marked man. If she came with me, she'd lose her job, her income, her ability to stay with Granny, and possibly her life.

Letting go of the door handle, I jogged away from Jessamine's and cut across a meadow, heading for the cover of trees.

*   *   *

I walked for most of the night, originally setting a course for the old church and Rufus, but eventually I changed my mind and stayed near the highway until I came to the kudzu field and the old shack that loomed above it.

It had been raining for the last couple of hours, and the idea of getting out of it sounded good. I made my way through the kudzu and up to the shack.

I had my hand on the door before I noticed the light flickering within.

Shit. I guess now was as good a time as any to figure out who I'd seen inside the shack the other day.

I knocked on the door.

A dog barked and voices began to whisper.

"I just need to get in out of the rain," I said.

A moment later the door swung open, creaking loudly. A kid—no more than nineteen or twenty—stood there on one foot, leaning his weight against the doorframe of the tiny shack. His other foot—or maybe it was his leg—must have been injured from the way he held it just off the floor. Behind him, a mangy golden retriever poked his head out and wagged his tail amicably.

"We don't want no trouble," he said. He had curly blond hair that he wore long. He was wearing a pair of sweat pants and a tank top. He was scrawny enough to make me wonder when his last meal had been.

"Neither do I. I'd just like to get out of the rain."

"Who is it?" a female voice said from inside.

The kid grimaced and hopped back a little, rebalancing his weight.

"I don't know. Might be one of them you saw earlier."

"Your leg okay?" I said. I saw now his knee was swollen something awful.

"I'll live."

"Let him in," the girl said. "But tell him to put his hands up."

The kid started to repeat what she said, but I waved him off. "I heard."

He hopped out of the way, and I stepped inside, out of the rain. The dog licked my hand and shook his tail wildly.

"Much obliged," I said.

"Hold on," the kid said. "You got to get your hands up."

Not sure what was happening, I put both hands in the air and turned the corner.

The girl was braced back in the far corner of the room, her legs shoulder width apart, her eyes hard marbles of determination, her hands gripping a shotgun that looked nearly as heavy as she was. She aimed it right at my forehead, and I knew from the way her body shook she was just frightened enough to pull the trigger.

The boy shrugged. "Sorry."

"Look," I said, "why don't you put that down? You don't look like the kind of folks that want to hurt nobody."

"No, but I will," the girl said. She was just a tiny little thing, no more than seventeen or eighteen by the look of it. Her hair was short, lopped off in a messy cut that almost looked like it had been done as a purposeful stylistic choice, but not quite.

The boy hopped past me and settled down on the floor next to where she stood. He patted one of the girl's painfully thin thighs. "He don't look too bad," he said.

"Looks don't mean nothing. And besides, if you'd have listened to me, he wouldn't be here."

The kid shrugged. "You can't know that."

"I can too. Sometimes the right thing is the wrong thing."

"I don't believe that and neither do you," he said.

The girl just shook her head, as if she'd seen way more of the world and it's evil ways than he had. She looked at me again, tightening her grip on the shotgun. "What's your name?"

"Earl," I said.

"You look like somebody I knew once, Earl. You from around here?"

"A long time ago."

"Why are you walking around in a damned rainstorm? Answer quick," the girl said. "Don't you dare think about lying."

"I knocked out a cop," I said. "I'm in trouble."

"So now we're in trouble," the girl said. "They'll follow you here. Shit, Todd. What are we going to do?"

"They ain't following me. I mean, they're looking, but they won't come here." I hoped it was true.

"See? He ain't one of them, right?"

"He might be. Look at him. Who does he look like to you?"

Todd looked at me and shook his head. "So what. He's dead anyway."

"Excuse me," I said. "Are you talking about Brother RJ?"

"Shit," the girl said. "Shit. Shit. Shit. He's one of them." She spread out her already impossibly wide stance, as if bracing herself to fire off a shot.

"Easy," I said. "I'm not one of them. RJ is my father. I quit the church a long time ago."

The girl just stared at me.

Todd said, "Why don't you tell us about it?"

"Sure. Okay. Could you just lower the shotgun first? Then I'll be happy to."

"No," the girl said. "Talk or get the hell out."

I nodded and told them as briefly as I could about being bitten by the snake and later leaving the church. I left out everything with Maggie. Because what was the point?

When I finished, the girl had lowered the shotgun, though she still gripped it with both hands.

Todd shook his head. "I'm sorry, mister. This ain't what we're usually like."

"I understand. I'm a stranger. You've obviously been through something."

And then it hit me—Mary had said the hand had been found by a kid and his dog.

"You found the hand," I said.

"We don't know nothing about no hand," the girl said.

"It's okay," I said. "Really, I'm not with the police. Like I said earlier, I kicked a cop's ass. They hate me."

"I'd like to believe you," the girl said, "but I can't let myself."

I nodded. "Okay. I understand that. What if I just rest a minute or two?" I started to put my hands down, but the girl grunted.

"Up."

"Okay. Maybe I should just go then."

"I think that's the best thing. But before you go, do you have anything to eat?"

I looked at the girl. Her eyes told the story: they were hungry.

"I know you understand what it means to need help," I said. "I need some. Badly."

Both looked away, and I knew they felt my misery. From the looks of it, they felt it ten times over.

I nodded at Todd's knee. "When did it happen?"

"This morning. I was on the way back from the payphone where I called the police about the—"

"Shut up," the girl said between clenched teeth.

"Why? He knows, okay? He already knows."

The girl said nothing but kept her eyes—and the shotgun—trained on me.

"Anyway, we was all set to get the hell out of this place. People around here ain't right. This place wasn't safe anymore after that business with the hand. Was running back from the gas station about two miles down the road, trying to hurry so we could get Millie and leave, but then I tripped not ten yards from the shack. Tore it up pretty good." He grimaced, then smiled. "I'll be good to go in the morning though."

It was clear he wouldn't be, but I decided to let it ride. "How long have you been hiding out here?"

Todd looked at the girl. "I think we should tell him, Millie."

Where had I heard that name?

"No," she said. "You already said too much, and if you'd listened to me about just staying out of it, we could already be gone."

"It was the right thing to do. You of all people should want to help."

She took one hand off the shotgun and rubbed her face. She looked like she was about to break down.

"Don't worry, Todd," I said. "I think I already know."

"You do?"

I nodded. "Millie. That's the name of the girl who disappeared with her boyfriend a while back. You went to the Holy Flame."

Millie finally lowered the gun.

"Yeah," she said. "Your daddy died, and that place went to shit."

"You mean . . . my brother . . . ?" I wasn't even sure what I wanted to say.

She shrugged. "The whole place. People say your father is still alive. Said he was displeased with the youth and wanted to straighten them out. I saw what they did to one of them. I told Todd, and he said we'd get out."

Todd grimaced. "Just ain't made it very far. Yet. We was going to stay here until we could get some food for the road, but . . . that didn't never seem to happen. We just kept eating whatever we could get our hands on."

"You said you saw what they did to another girl. Can you explain?"

Millie sat down and put the shotgun across her lap. The dog wagged his tail as if relieved some of the tension had dissipated.

"Her name was Hannah. She was so pretty, and it was almost as if that was a strike against her. After your daddy died, people said he was still alive in the mountains, and he was going to clean up the young people, get them right with God. But seemed like the only ones needed cleaning were the pretty girls. Anyway, Hannah fit that mold. One day, she just disappeared. Stopped coming to school. I asked about her, but nobody was saying nothing. I'd say she was gone a week, maybe more. When she came back, she was changed. It was awful. She'd been happy before they took her. But then she came back, and she started talking like she was one of them big believers, but it wasn't real. She was sad." Millie dropped her head. "I didn't want that to happen to me."

"Did she say what they'd done to her or where they'd taken her?"

Millie shook her head. "No. She wouldn't give any details. She just said she was 'fixed,' but she wasn't nowhere near fixed. She was off. Scared of her own shadow."

I thought of Baylee and remembered the desperation on her face when she'd asked me to help her. And so far, I'd failed her. I resolved right then to help Baylee as soon as I could.

"I understand." Unfortunately, I understood all too well.

"How many years did you say you been gone?" Todd asked.

"Thirty."

"And you come back because you're trying to find this fella, and you think it might be his hand Cloverfield found?"

"Cloverfield?"

The boy nodded at the golden, who seemed to sense we were talking about him because he beat his tail against the dirt floor twice.

"It's a movie," Millie said.

"Oh."

"So why did you beat up the cop?"

"He and another fella tried to kill me."

"What did the other fella look like?" Millie asked.

"We call him Choirboy. He looks like one too, but taller than a tree and his eyes look like glass. Ain't nothing in them but hate."

Millie let go of the shotgun and set it on the dirt floor.

"I saw you the other day," she said. "Out on the road. That cop made you lie down. Stuck his boot on your back. Was that the one you beat up?"

I nodded. "His name is Roger. He's one of the men that tried to kill me."

"You should tell him everything," Todd said.

"Let me think."

"I trust him, Millie. Besides, you got a better idea? He said he'd help us out. If we stay here for my knee to heal, it could be another couple of weeks. Somebody's going to find out we're here, and if it's one of them men you saw . . ."

"Shut up, Todd."

"He's got a point," I said. "I'm not one of them. I'm on your side."

Millie studied me carefully in the flickering light.

"Okay," she said. "But you got to promise."

"I promise," I said. What I didn't say was I planned on helping them regardless. This wasn't any place for a couple of kids, especially two who'd run away from the Holy Flame. It was a hard place to escape.

I knew that all too well.

"Okay," she said. "After they done that silly little search—which anybody could tell wasn't no real search—I figured they'd be back. Me and Todd would have split if not for his knee, but since we had to stay, I figured I'd sit up with the gun. Just to make sure. I'm sort of protective."

"I noticed."

"Don't be cute," she said.

I started to say something cute back but thought better of it. The shotgun was still within easy reach.

"So what did you see?"

She smiled, pleased with my compliance. "I saw them down in the kudzu, arguing. This was late, real late. There was a full moon, and I've got night eyes because in another life, I used to be a cat. Unfortunately, I didn't get the ears because I couldn't make out everything they were saying, but it sounded like one of them—the older one—was giving the younger man a really hard time about something. Then—and I couldn't believe my eyes—I saw that they were digging. And pretty soon, they had a body, and they carried it back to their truck and drove off."

I needed a drink. Hell, I needed five or six.

"Did you recognize either man?" I said.

"Nope. I didn't really get a good look at them. It was dark. One of the men was tall and sort of stood weird."

"Weird how?"

She scratched her head. "I don't really know. Not like a person. Too straight. Too stiff. It seemed off in a really big way."

"Okay." I had to assume this was Choirboy, who seemed to be involved in doing everybody's dirty work.

Nope, just one man's dirty work.

I tried to banish the voice as quickly as it had come. But it was no use. The seed had been planted. It would be foolish to ignore it. Daddy was alive or he wasn't. That almost seemed inconsequential in the grand scheme of things at this point. Either way, his influence was far reaching.

Of course, there was nothing inconsequential about that question for me. For me, that question seemed to matter more than anything else in the world.

"What about the other man, the older man?" I held my breath, waiting for her answer.

She shrugged. "I couldn't tell. He seemed older. That's all."

I let out the breath. It could be Daddy. Or it could be anyone.

"Anything else?" I asked her.

"Are you some kind of detective?" Todd said. "I mean, it's cool if you are. It's just I've never met a detective."

"Yeah," I said. "I'm a detective. Private. Thank you for trusting me."

Millie nodded at the shotgun. "I'm still gonna keep it by my side."

Todd grinned. "She ain't half as mean as she seems."

I had to admire them. They seemed happy. And that was something that was extremely elusive. They'd also managed to do what I had not. They'd escaped the Holy Flame unscathed.

I thought that was the end of it. They both seemed sleepy and lay back down on the blankets after peeling one off for me. Cloverfield lay down beside them and began to lick Todd's knee.

I sat up, looking out the window, still wishing for a drink. I might have asked if they had anything, but they looked so content lying there, I let it ride.

And then when the rain had fallen away to a mist and the shack was quiet and the flares of lightning seemed to be moving farther and farther away from the little shack perched adopt the field of kudzu, Todd sat up.

"Oh, man. The map. You didn't tell him about the map."

39

"What did you say?"

"Show him," Todd said.

"I was planning on keeping that for later," Millie said, shaking her head in disgust. "Ain't you never heard of keeping something up your sleeve? If I didn't love you so much, Todd Bell, I'd slap you silly."

She sighed and reached for one of their bags. She dug inside for a moment before pulling out a piece of yellow folded paper. "I saw it fall off the body when they lifted it," she explained.

I moved over to the gas lamp and held the paper close as I unfolded it with shaking hands.

It was a map, though it was a very crude one. At the top of the page, it read, *The Well: best guesses. Note: not original.* Below that, someone had sketched out all five of the Fingers. Three of them had stars beside them—Pointer, Ring, and Longfinger. An arrow pointed to Longfinger. Beside the arrow, someone had scribbled, *Highest point.* And below that was a single sentence: *Lightning always strikes the highest point.*

I studied the map some more, looking for any telltale detail, no matter how small.

I didn't see anything. The three mountains that were starred and the notation beside Longfinger. That was all.

I turned the paper over. On the back were some notes. It appeared to be the draft of a letter:

Your daddy predicted they'd do this. He told me weeks ago to get in touch with you. I tried and tried, and then one day, I went back to his hiding place, and he was gone. Left me a note said he'd be at the well. He'd told me how to get there, but I can't remember. Never been good at memorizing. I'm in a bad place. The other side has got some guesses. I'm trying to work it out, but I hear you're a detective now. Maybe you can help. There's Old Woman Laney, but she ain't never liked me too much. I've done everything I can do. I need you here to help. I know there ain't

It stopped right there, as if something had distracted him from his writing.

I shook my head, trying to process it all.

"So this fell out of his pocket?"

Millie nodded. "I guess so. Is it a treasure map?"

"No," I said. "I think it's a map to a torture chamber."

*   *   *

One of the reasons I drank like I did was to keep the dreams away. There was nothing like a fifth of Wild Turkey to put a man into a deep, dreamless sleep. Sometimes the dreams still came through, but they were fragmented enough to dismiss.

That evening, lying on the floor of the little shack without a drop of alcohol in my system other than the beer I'd had hours earlier, my dreams played catch-up with my subconscious and wreaked havoc on my nerves.

First, I dreamed of Granny's funeral. Mary and I stood over a large hole in the ground waiting for her coffin to be lowered inside.

A machine roared nearby, cutting through the silent morning like a guttural scream. I watched as the machine deposited her coffin right before us. Mary held me tight and put her face in my side as she cried.

But there was something wrong with the coffin. The lid was missing, and there was a blanket pulled over Granny's body. Mary reached for it and pulled it back for one last look.

We both gasped—the body inside the casket was not Granny's. Instead, it was my father's faceless body. I saw where the scavengers had eaten his eyes out and torn up his cheeks and pecked at his lips until what remained was little more than an eyeless mask. I forced my eyes away from his face and scanned the rest of his body. He was dressed in a brown suit, a color I never remembered him wearing in life. His shoes were black and polished so well, I could see my reflection in them. But when I looked closer, it wasn't me I saw in the mirrored black—it was Lester.

I stepped away, looking at my hands, my clothes, my suit. Somehow, I'd become my brother in my dream, and the feeling was so cloying, I had to scream out loud.

I kept screaming until Mary squeezed me and told me it was okay. "We found him. Finally."

"Found who?" I asked. She pointed back to the open coffin. It was McCauley now, his face frozen how I remembered him best: wild eyed and far too desperate for someone to take him seriously. I reached out to pull up the blanket, to see if his hand was missing, but Mary stopped me.

"It's in your pocket," she whispered.

Repulsed, I tossed it into the coffin with him as faceless men picked up shovels and scooped dirt into his open grave.

When it was finished, everyone sang a song. It was an old gospel song that went on forever. At the end of it, I realized I was alone in the field of kudzu. No, not quite alone. Goose was there with Cloverfield, and they were playing among the twisting vines. I watched a thunder-cloud building in the sky over Ring Mountain. Lightning flashed out of it like electric pitchforks, impaling Ring Mountain and sparking a blaze that circled the peak and rose into the sky, an inferno that could touch heaven.

A hand fell on my back.

"Them dogs have found something."

I started to turn to see who the voice belonged to, but before I could, I heard the dogs barking and dancing around a well that had emerged from the kudzu.

I walked over, as if compelled. I began to turn the crank, as I always did in the dream. Behind me, the voice—a voice I recognized but could not name—offered encouragement.

"It's almost there, boy. Come on, put your back into it."

The rope creaked. The bucket came into view, but it was tipped away from me, and I couldn't see what was there.

"Crank it again. One more, boy."

I bent my back into it and turned the crank another full revolution.

What I saw woke me up and sent me back to a time I'd nearly forgotten.

40

There were some things I didn't think about anymore. My sister, Aida, was one of them. When I dreamed of her small, dead body inside the bucket, I woke up with a memory I had chosen to repress—or maybe I was just too afraid of what I'd discover if I thought on it too much.

But what *did* it mean? Seeing her in the bucket had to be important, but for the life of me, I couldn't say how. I lay on the floor of the little cabin, listening to the rain falling outside, trying to make a connection between her short life and my present-day predicament.

It had happened after I'd returned from escorting Granny back to her house in the rain. I was soaking wet and angry when I came into the darkened house and saw Mama and Lester sitting expressionless on the couch. A few days later, Mama sent me up the mountain to look for Daddy.

I followed Ghost Creek until I found him at an old children's cemetery, way up near the peak of Pointer Mountain. He was sitting on a big rock, looking at the little markers in the cemetery. His back was to me, and he seemed startled when I called his name.

A boy always remembers seeing his father cry. I suppose it's a result of the deeply ingrained patriarchy I grew up in, but men—especially men like my father—did not cry. They prayed. They stood tall, Bible in hand, facing down the devil. There was no physical or spiritual damage that this world could send their way at which they couldn't shout, "Get behind me, devil," and then move forward, untouched, as if all trials in this life were made up of only weak-willed, obedient demons flung by a spiteful wind, incapable of touching the human spirit.

Even though the snakebite was responsible for galvanizing my rejection of my father's faith, the doubts go back much further than that. The doubts began when he turned around and I saw his face streaked with tears.

"Daddy?"

He was clutching a wooden box to his chest. It was the size of a shoebox, something I'd seen him keep baby cottonmouths in before. I understood without having to ask that Aida was inside it now.

He laid the box on the ground and stood up, his legs trembling, his body wavering. For a moment, he didn't seem real. He seemed like an electric ghost, a hologram of a father, and then he steadied, and I saw his eyes and understood that if there was a way to put a demon behind you, if there was a way to "pray" something away, he'd have already done it. But the pain there, the real hurt in his downcast, bleary gaze, told me there wasn't. Not this time.

He didn't say a word to me. Instead, he reached behind him for a shovel I'd not seen earlier.

He stuck it in the dirt and began to dig. He didn't have to dig too far because the box was small. He was crying again—sobbing, really—as he laid it carefully inside. He scooped the dirt back over top and smoothed it out carefully.

When he was finished, he sat back down on the rock heavily and closed his eyes.

"Mama . . ." I started, but my voice caught, and I realized I was crying too. I'd seen something on that day that had taught me more about life than any sermon Daddy could ever dream up, more than any stomping on any stage or any snake held above any head. I'd seen a man weep.

"Mama said to find you."

"Well, you did."

"Daddy?"

He said nothing.

"I'm sorry."

"Ain't we all."

I almost couldn't process it. His daughter, my sister, was dead. He'd just laid her in the ground, yet he'd said not one word to or about God.

I waited for more, for some admonition for my own life, for something I could do to avoid such future grief, for something about Aida being in a better place, for something about how we should all wish to be so lucky, but he didn't say anything else.

And I left him like that, my real father—stripped of the religion he wielded like a shield and a sword, but mostly, I realized for the first time, like a mask.

*   *   *

But what did it mean? Why was Aida in the bucket? Why would I suddenly remember that from so long ago? Was it my subconscious, still trying to look for a way to connect to my dead father, or was it something more, some kind of intricate code I could not decipher?

Throughout the years of my life, I'd come to believe in something at work in the world. It was as subtle as faraway music on the breeze, but it was there. All of my experiences made it impossible to deny. I knew Daddy would say it was God calling me back home. And I wasn't ready to say it might not be. But if he was calling me anywhere, it was back to myself, back to the memories and the experiences that made me who I was. Maybe even back to the single spark of divinity that had lit me up so many years ago. I'd felt it each and every time I'd defied my father, and I felt something like it now, remembering Daddy and Aida in that broken state.

I let my mind drift through the dreams again, the memories, looking for something my subconscious already knew but that had been locked down by my conscious mind.

I saw Daddy holding the snakes. I saw him lifting them high and shouting down demons within the congregation. I saw him weeping beside the little box.

I saw Aida in the bucket.

Then my mind drifted to the coffin. Granny's coffin, except the players were interchangeable, weren't they? Granny became Daddy and Daddy became McCauley. It was like Maggie becoming Allison and Allison becoming Millie and . . .

Baylee.

I remembered my resolution from the night before and felt a new urgency. Maggie and Allison were dead. Millie had run away.

There wasn't any time to waste. I had to help Baylee.

I sat up quickly. The room was still. Millie and Todd breathed in a heavy rhythm. Only Cloverfield paid me any mind as I pulled on my boots, scribbled a note for them explaining my abrupt departure, and left it on the floor next to them with my credit card on top of it before slipping out into the overcast morning.

41

Hungry and sore, I didn't have much choice but to hike up to Rufus's place. He'd have something I could eat. Besides, I wanted to touch base with him so he could let Mary know I was okay and get her over to pick up those kids. I'd left them a note, suggesting Millie hike up to the gas station and use my credit card to buy something to eat, but I hated to think of someone from the Holy Flame spotting her.

My own plan was simple: get something to eat, rest during the daylight hours, and head over to Burt's house that night, when he'd be working the night shift at the carpet mill.

After several stops to catch my breath, I eventually made it up the mountain and to Ghost Creek. I followed the creek for a half mile or so until I came to the church.

Right away, I knew something was wrong. My rental was gone. The place looked too quiet. I expected to hear Goose barking as I walked up, but there was only silence. Even the birds in the trees seemed asleep, or maybe just waiting for something.

The creek slipped by behind me, grooving the mountain with its deceptive force.

I walked forward, sure that when I stepped inside that church, I'd see something that would haunt me forever.

A voice came from behind me.

"He's gone."

I nearly jumped out of my skin. I spun around, consumed by an irrational onset of fight-or-flight adrenaline, fists clenched, jaw set.

"Easy there, tiger."

I relaxed a little. It was Ronnie Thrash. He was shirtless with a pair of old sweat pants and flip-flops. He was holding a can of Bud Ice. He tipped it back, drained it, and tossed the can in the creek.

"What do you mean gone?" I said.

"Sheriff's deputies got him. They come up and towed that rental car of yours. Then they arrested the blind motherfucker. Him cursing them out all along the way." He slipped his foot out of its flip-flop and touched his toe to the running water. "I figure you're really the one they want, but I reckon he'll do for the time being."

"What about Goose?"

"He's inside with Walt and Beard."

"Thanks," I said.

He shrugged. "Don't mention it. He's a good dog. You're in deep shit, you know. I saw you drag Roger Peterson out of the bar last night. They say you fucked him up pretty good. That true?"

"What if it is?"

"Then I'd say congratu-fucking-lations. The sheriff's office in this town is as corrupt as that church your daddy started."

I nodded. "I think you're right about that."

"I'm right about a lot of stuff."

"That so?"

"Yep. Don't you remember, the first night we met?"

"I remember you showing up trying to act tough."

He scratched under his arm and leaned into a loud fart. "I did send them boys home, but I wasn't really talking about that. I was talking about what I told you."

I didn't have time for this. Then again, I didn't really have any place to go. Not without some more sleep and something to eat. Maybe he could provide some if I played my cards right.

"And what was that?"

"I said me and you are a lot more alike than we are different. Remember?"

"You said something like that, but it ain't no more true today than it was then."

He grinned. "We'll see."

"I guess it always comes out one way or the other."

"That it does." He nodded slowly.

"I need to know something," I said.

"All right."

"Did you put a toy snake inside the church to try to scare me away?"

He laughed, rubbing his belly. "You got me confused with somebody from the Holy Flame. I won't even touch a fake one after they made me hold the real one when my daddy died. Soon as I found me a place to stay, I ran away. Lived with Beard. He and his daddy ain't never been nothing but heathens." He grinned. "Like you and me. See, another little piece of common ground."

"You're full of shit."

He shrugged. "Maybe. That don't change the fact that me and you are a lot alike."

"Okay, fine. We're a lot alike. Now answer me another question."

"I'll try."

"What the hell was my brother doing at your place the other night?"

This seemed to catch him off guard.

"What?"

"I saw Lester and you talking the other night. Why?"

"Maybe you better come inside," he said.

I shook my head.

"Suit yourself. But I reckon the last place they'll look for you is with me." He pointed at the church. "And don't think they won't come back for you there. They will."

I stared at him.

He smiled. "We got the same enemies, Earl. Hank Fucking Shaw and that damned church that tried to fuck us over. How's that saying go? The enemy of my enemy is my best friend . . . or something like that."

He was right. I decided to go inside. At least I might get some insight into Lester. Besides, I wanted to see Goose.

42

Goose was fine. In fact, I was surprised to see Beard and Walt playing keep-away with him using a tennis ball. Goose trotted over to me and actually jumped into my arms. I hugged him and let him lick my face before setting him back down.

"That's Beard and Walt," Ronnie said.

Both men nodded in my direction, raising their eyebrows just enough for me to see they disapproved but wouldn't say so in front of Ronnie.

"Want some bacon or eggs or something? We just had breakfast, but there's a shitload left over in the cooler."

I nodded. He sat down at a card table and nodded toward the cooler. I rummaged through and pulled out a plate of eggs and a plate of bacon, both covered in plastic wrap.

I put them on the card table, and Ronnie handed me a fork.

I ate the eggs first and chased them with the bacon. Ronnie tossed me a beer. I was damned glad I'd come in. It was the best I'd felt in a couple of days.

"Lester contacted me a few months ago. Asked me if I was willing to be his eyes and ears."

"Eyes and ears? What were you looking and listening for?"

"Rumors, plots, all that shit."

"I don't understand."

He cracked another beer open for himself. "Well, you wouldn't. Truth is, I didn't understand either. Not until he filled me in. See, after your daddy 'died,' there was some turmoil about—"

214

"Why'd you do that?"

"Why'd I do what?"

"Make those air quotes when you said *died*?"

He flashed me a big grin. "You ain't heard? Your daddy done rose from the grave, Earl. You can't tell me you didn't know the rumors."

"I heard some stuff. I guess the problem is I don't really know if they're true or not."

"Let me ask you something, Earl. Do you think a man can rise from the dead and ascend into the fucking mountains?"

I hesitated. Of course I didn't think that was possible.

Did I?

"Are you seriously having to think about it?" he said.

"No." I brought my fist down on the table for emphasis. "Of course not."

"Well, there's your answer then. He's deader than a doornail. Lester saw the body. Lots of people saw the body."

"But the face—"

"Was missing. I know. But it was your daddy. Ain't nobody with a lick of sense disputes that."

"But there's a lot of folks out there without sense." *You're one of them, Earl.*

"Bingo. And Lester—he's worried because he says there's a faction in the church that claims your daddy's displeased with the job Lester's doing. They keep spreading these things around the church about how Brother RJ said this or Brother RJ said that. And they don't mean before he died. These people are saying he talks all the time. Of course, if people say it, people will believe it. So long story short, your brother don't know if your daddy is alive or if these people are just using his death as a way of fucking with him. You know?" He shook his head and blew out a laugh. "Fuck, I hate fucking religion. Don't you?"

I shrugged. Hate wasn't exactly the right word to describe my feelings about it.

More like *feared*.

"Lester says people come to him all the time and wanna know why he ain't being more respectful of his daddy's wishes. Sad thing is, your brother can't let him go. He's got this . . . I don't know, guilt, I guess. Wants to talk to your daddy one more time, all that shit."

"Who's behind it?" I said.

"What's that?"

"Who's telling him Daddy's saying all these things?"

"That's the thing. He can't really pinpoint who's behind it. That's where I come in."

"What's your granddaddy say?"

"My granddaddy don't speak to me anymore. Besides, he's a fool. All he does is smile and say everything is okay. Smiling and pretending everything is right ain't never helped nobody. But Lester ain't too worried about him. Says he's in full support."

"So who then?"

"Well, from what I can tell, Hank Shaw's about as corrupt as they come."

"Tell me something I don't know," I said.

"I'll bet you didn't know your brother was having a hard time with it all. He's trying to do right, but I think it might kill him first."

I looked up at him.

He nodded. "I don't buy the religious fuckery, but I know he's trying to change the church. He's trying to move it into the twenty-first century. Stop all the crazy shit that's going on. But he can't 'cause some folks just refuse to let your daddy die."

I gave him a skeptical look. "You expect me to believe you really care about my brother and his struggles?"

He shrugged. "Believe what you want. But I hated your daddy for what he did to mine. I hate him for what he did to you and your brother too."

"My brother? What did my father ever do to Lester?"

Ronnie seemed like he didn't hear me. Or maybe he was just pretending not to.

216

"He's got a good heart, you know?" He studied me closely, smiling just a little. "He's a lot like you. Just can't get out from under Daddy's shadow."

"You don't know me."

"Maybe. Maybe not. But Lester does. And he's mad, Earl. Damned mad. My daddy told me about that girl. Maggie Shaw. Jesus, he said every boy wanted her, but it was you that got her."

I was ready to change the subject but couldn't think of anything else to say.

"'Course when two brothers want the same gal . . ." Ronnie shrugged. "I never did have a brother. Just a little sister. Granddaddy and me don't talk. I'd try just about anything I could to keep a brother. Even if he was a fucked-in-the-head preacher."

"I'll keep that in mind. Look, I hate to impose, but would you mind if I used your phone?"

He pulled out a cell and held it out to me. I reached for it, but he pulled it back. "Who you going to call, anyway?"

"A friend."

"That black woman?"

"Her name is Mary."

"Fine. Mary. You tapping that?"

I tried not to let myself get angry. As bad as it was to say, at that very moment, Ronnie Thrash was the closest thing to a friend I had in the whole world.

"Can I use your phone or not?"

"I'm going to say not on that one."

I felt my face flush. It would feel so damned good to punch him.

"Why?"

"Like I said, I don't trust Hank Shaw."

"She ain't nothing like Shaw."

"And I ain't nothing like my granddaddy or these nut jobs I hang out with, but that didn't stop you from judging me."

I decided to let it drop. I had a plan, if a person could rightly call the impulse to do something based on a weird dream a plan, but it was all I had.

"Is there a place I could rest for a little, Ronnie?"

He shrugged. "Rest wherever you want. I don't give a good damn. Like I said, Earl, you and me . . ." He held out his hand with two fingers crossed.

I nodded and went to look for a place to sleep the day away. I had a feeling I'd be needing all my energy soon.

43

When I woke, it was already dark, and I heard voices outside. I looked at my phone for the time, but it was dead.

I got up and dug through the cooler for something else to eat. I found some ham and wolfed it down hungrily. I knew I might have a long night ahead of me, so I scooped out some of the ice with a cup and took it with me. I'd need to stay hydrated.

Ronnie, Walt, and Beard were sitting in a semicircle around a cooler in lawn chairs. A couple of their friends had joined them.

Everyone fell silent as I stepped into the ring of chairs.

"I need a favor," I said.

*　　*　　*

Despite his claims that we were a lot alike, Ronnie didn't hesitate to seize the opportunity created by my neediness to see what he could get in return.

"I'll help you out if you'll help me out." We stood over to the side of the group, not too far from where he'd met Lester a few nights earlier. He shook out a can of Skoal and loaded a huge plug between his lower lip and gum.

"Well?" he said. He spat and grinned at me, his teeth nearly blacked out by the strands of dip clinging from them like charred vines.

"You need to be more specific."

"It's simple. You need a ride. I need some information."

"You might be asking the wrong man. I'm wandering in the dark these days."

He spat again, this time precariously close to my boots.

"I hear you and that colored gal been poking your nose in all kinds of business."

"We're trying to find someone."

"Huh. I figured you was doing some detecting. Who you looking for?"

"If I tell you, will you give me a ride?"

He laughed. "Shoot, that sounds fair."

"Bryant McCauley."

"That's what I figured. Any leads?"

I shook my head. "I already answered your question. Now let's go."

"Well, shit, I ain't taking you unless you got something else. I mean, it ain't like I haven't already let you stay at my place, eat my food, drink my fucking beer. You are one bold motherfucker, Earl Marcus."

"I get it from my daddy," I said.

That made Ronnie laugh, and he patted my back hard enough to make me cough.

"I'll tell you what—I'll take you to your cousin's house, but you got to answer one more question before we get there. If you answer it, I'll even come back and pick you up."

I thought about it and didn't see that I had much choice. When you beat a sheriff's deputy's ass outside of a crowded bar, you don't really have the luxury of being choosy about who helps you out. Between Rufus's arrest and my desire to keep Mary clear of this shit, Ronnie was all I had.

"It's a deal," I said.

*　　*　　*

Ronnie didn't say much as he drove, at least not at first. As we drew closer to Burt's place, he cleared his throat.

"What are you planning, exactly?"

I shook my head. "That your other question?"

"Aw, shit, Earl, I'm just making small talk. You don't trust me?"

"I don't know who to trust."

He sighed and kept driving.

"Burt and Shaw seem to be pretty close," he said.

"Yeah?"

"That's right." He tapped his head with his index finger. "People think I'm stupid, and maybe all the damned beer and pot has killed some cells, but I ain't no dummy. You going to visit Burt has got me intrigued. And now I can't decide what question I want to ask."

I nodded. I couldn't figure what to make of Ronnie. He was crazy, but crazy was still a long way from evil. His association with Lester still troubled me, and I even believed his story about Lester's need to have somebody on the ground, listening.

What I wasn't sure about was Lester's motivation. Seemed like that was the real question.

"You never told me what my father did to Lester."

"You mean besides fucking up his entire childhood?"

"Yeah. Besides that."

Ronnie grinned. "You'll have to ask your brother about that. Not my place to get in the middle of family squabbles."

"You're an asshole," I said.

"Kindred spirits," he shot back.

We turned onto the road where Burt lived, and I motioned to some trees on the side of the road. "You can let me out here."

I opened the door and started to get out.

"Hold it," he said.

I stopped. "Your other question?"

He nodded, a small grin playing on his lips. "My other question."

I waited, irritated because sometimes I almost found myself liking Ronnie, even if the rest of the time, I found his presence detestable.

"What was it like?"

"What was what like?"

"Standing up to him?"

"My father?"

He nodded.

"It's hard to remember."

"That's hard to believe."

He had me there. I remembered it vividly.

"Okay. It felt good. Like there was finally something right in the world after all those years of wrong."

He nodded slowly, taking it in. He looked satisfied, like a man who'd just taken a big hit off a joint. "I can dig that. Thanks." He seemed sincere, and for the first time, I found myself wondering if maybe he wasn't at least partially right.

Maybe we did have something in common.

I shut the door and leaned into the open window.

"I think McCauley's dead. And I think the Holy Flame is behind it. You can tell that to Lester."

Ronnie stared at me. "I'll do it. But I think you don't know your brother anymore. He's got nothing to do with all that."

"Maybe. But I know his church."

I patted the door and walked into the trees.

44

I confirmed Burt's car wasn't there before knocking on the front door. When no one answered, I knocked louder and rang the bell.

Still nothing. Glancing around to make sure there were no witnesses, I decided to see if the door was locked.

Surprisingly, the door handle turned, and I was able to push it open with little resistance.

The house was silent. Almost. As I stepped in and pulled the door shut behind me, I heard soft music coming from nearby. I stepped through the dining room where I'd talked to Burt a few days ago and into the kitchen. A small radio was tuned to a soft rock station.

I slipped past it and through the den toward the steps leading upstairs.

Pausing, I tried to listen for voices. I heard none. Could the girls be asleep? Or were they even home?

I started up the stairs, and as soon as my weight shifted to the first step, it groaned loudly.

"Daddy?" a voice from upstairs called.

I nearly pissed my pants. Twenty-plus years as a private investigator in North Carolina, dealing with real baddies without ever losing my cool, and now the voice of a teenage girl was about to cause me to piss my pants?

I steeled myself and started on up.

"Daddy?" the voice said again, this time with a hint of fear creeping into it.

I thought it belonged to Baylee's sister, Amanda. I was pretty sure it did. I remembered Baylee's voice as deeper and somehow less sure than her younger sister's.

I winced and stayed very still, not sure how to proceed.

When I heard the footsteps, I knew I needed to think quick to avoid scaring the poor girl to death.

"Hello?" I said. "Amanda?"

The footsteps stopped. "Daddy?"

I sighed, waiting for the inevitable.

She stepped into view. I waved at her, and she started to scream and point at me.

"Easy," I said. "Take it easy."

She backed away, holding her hands out, as if to ward me off.

My decision to advance up the steps to calm her down probably wasn't one of my better ideas—she screamed even louder and threw the book she was holding at me. I tried to tell her it was okay, that I wasn't there to hurt her, but she was screaming so goddamn loud, I knew she couldn't understand a word I was saying. I sprinted up the steps and caught up with her right before she reached her bedroom. I grabbed her as gently as I was able—which wasn't very gently given the circumstances—and put a hand over her mouth. She bit it.

Now it was my turn to scream, which I did without letting go. I spun her around so she could see my face, and she lunged, trying to bite my nose.

"Stop it! Just listen!"

She screamed again, and I shook her. Hard. Her eyes grew large, and she tried to pull away, but at least she stopped screaming.

"I don't want to hurt you. I'm here to help."

"Please let go of me," she said.

I complied, and she backed away again.

"That's fine," I said. "You can go in your room. You can shut the door. I just need to talk to Baylee."

"Leave my sister alone," she said. "Leave us all alone."

I turned around and saw what had to be Baylee's door on the other end of the hallway. I did a double take when I saw there was a padlock on the door. "What's happening? Why is she locked in her room?"

"It's for her own good."

"What are you talking about?"

"Daddy said I wasn't supposed to talk to you."

"I need to use your phone."

"No."

I saw a cell phone on the desk in her room. When she saw me heading for it, she grabbed my arm.

"Who are you going to call?"

"A friend."

"No, please no. Daddy says if anybody finds out about Baylee, there'll be trouble."

"Trouble?"

"I don't know what kind. I promise, I don't, but I know it's bad. It's scary. Everything has been scary lately."

"You're going to need to get more specific." I shrugged her off but stopped short of picking up the phone. True, a girl was being held in her room, but I'd also broken in. I had to make a sound decision here. Not a rash one.

"Please just leave us alone," Amanda said, but I ignored her and grabbed the phone off her desk.

She screamed again.

"I'm not going to call anyone," I said. "This is just to make sure you don't either." I walked down the hall and stood outside the padlocked door to Baylee's room.

"It's Earl Marcus, Baylee. What's going on? Why are you locked in your room?"

"Don't call anyone," Baylee said. Her voice was loud, and I knew she was pressed against the other side of the door.

"We're going to help you."

"I want to live."

"I want you to live too."

"Then leave. Leave right now. Leave and pretend that you never knew me. They know about you. He knows about you. He mentioned you by name the other night. If he thinks I told you anything, I'll die. He told me that."

"No, not if you let me help you. Baylee, I—"

She screamed. I felt the door vibrate with the power of the wail. It was one word, and it resounded inside me emphatically: *No.*

"Okay," I said, willing myself to stay calm, "the other night, you asked me to help. I'm sorry it took so long, but I'm here to do that now. You need to tell me who's behind all this. I know it's somebody in the church."

She was quiet for a moment.

"Baylee," I said, "I'm going to break the door down. I don't want you to be afraid."

"Please don't." She was sobbing now, deep, guttural bellows. The sound of them gave me pause. But the padlock was too much. I'd seen this sort of thing before, and I wasn't going to let what happened so many years ago happen again.

I stepped back and then charged hard, leading with my right boot. I heard the door crack, but the padlock held.

I'd need something to bust it open.

Amanda was standing behind me, weeping.

"Listen to me," I said. "I'm going to get you and your sister out of here. I'll take you someplace safe, and then I'll come back and deal with the mess in this county. But I need your help. Where does your daddy keep his tools."

"The basement," she said, her lips trembling.

"Let's go," I said.

"What?"

"You're going to take me down there."

She started to cry again.

"Stop it. Please. I'm not going to hurt either one of you. I'm here to help."

She shook her head but started down the steps.

I followed her into the kitchen, where she opened another door and led me to the basement. She turned on the light, and I found a huge red toolbox sitting on a bench. There was an oversized hammer on the top shelf. I picked it up, weighing it, and decided it would probably do the job.

"Back upstairs," I said.

"You're making a mistake," Amanda said. Her tears had stopped now.

"I'm doing what I have to do."

"You'll see how bad a mistake it is."

"Upstairs," I said firmly.

We went back up to the second floor and Baylee's door.

"Okay," I said. "I'm coming in."

She didn't answer, but I heard her breath still hitching from the sobs.

"Step back."

It took me a couple of dozen swings to break the padlock. I pushed the door open.

The lights in the room were out, but the blinds were drawn and light from the full moon shone in, illuminating everything in a pale light.

The room was bare, just four walls and the carpet. Baylee sat in the corner, naked, her knees pulled up to her breasts, her head down, her hair flung forward like a tattered gown.

I gasped and stepped back, stunned by what I saw.

"Where are your clothes?"

Her voice came, and it almost sounded disembodied. "Daddy says I'll hang myself with them." She looked up, nodding toward the window. "It's why they put the bars up too."

"Jesus. Are you planning on hurting yourself again?"

That was when she rose and stepped into the patch of moonlight.

I turned away, shielding my eyes from her nakedness.

"You don't understand anything, do you? I don't want to hurt myself. I want to stop the hurting. I want the pain to end. I want the world to go away."

"I'm going to get you some of your sister's clothes, and then we're going to get you out of here. Okay?"

"No. I need you to see me."

"What?"

"I heard you say you were going to stop them. I heard you tell Amanda that. You have to see what they can do first."

"What are you talking about?"

"Look at me."

"What? I'm not going to do that, Baylee. It's not right."

"Look at me. They marked me. *He* marked me. You *have* to look."

Despite myself, I looked. She was right—I had to. I'd come all this way, taken all these chances. If she meant to show me something, I meant to see it.

She'd turned her body sideways to show me her profile. Moonlight filtered around her, sharpening the lines of her silhouette. She pointed to her left hip, but it was too dark for me to see from where I stood, and I didn't dare get any closer. I pulled out the penlight I kept on my keychain and flicked it on. I shone it on her side, careful to keep it away from her breasts.

I found what she wanted me to see and dropped the penlight. It hit the floor, but somehow the light remained on her side—or maybe I didn't need the light anymore, maybe the image was burned into my brain, maybe she turned just enough for the moonlight to catch it.

A dark tattoo-like pattern had been grafted against her skin. It ran from the bottom of her left breast all the way down her leg. It shimmered an electric red, like the inside of the skin turned out, slick and soft and gleaming, an intricately crafted welt, a scrape beneath the flesh, branching and flowing toward her hips in fernlike striations.

I thought of Allison DeWalt, the mark that her brother said he'd seen on her.

"What is it?"

"It's the mark of God," she said. "Where he touched me with his finger."

I picked up the penlight and stepped closer, determined to get a better look, but just before I could, I saw her eyes go wide with fear. Someone spoke from behind me.

"I told you to leave our family alone."

I turned, but not fast enough to dodge the hammer as the small girl brought it crashing down into my forehead.

45

I woke to the smell of death—deep and overwhelming. It was well past my nostrils and had seeped into my lungs. There was no escaping it. That was my first realization.

My second was the darkness. Darkness so deep, there was a moment in which I couldn't determine if my eyes were opened or closed. I lay on my stomach, my right cheek pressed against the ground.

I blinked a dozen or more times, trying to orient myself, trying to make something out, but if there was anything else near me, it was hidden from my sight so thoroughly, it might as well have not been there at all. No shape or form came clear in the viscous blackness.

I remembered my penlight. I slid my hand down to my pocket, lifting one hip slightly so I could dig out my keys. I was surprised to find they were still there.

Just before flicking the light on, I felt something soft brush past my right pants leg. I reached for it with my free hand and touched the skin of something alive. Repelled, I rolled away only to land on what felt like knotted rope or maybe thick roots.

Then I felt that move too.

I screamed and scrambled to my feet, flicking the penlight on. My hand was wild—it shook with fear and exhilaration—and I couldn't see anything but quick flashes at first, the staccato lightning of my deepest fears.

The tiny light reflected off their shiny backs as they heaved in a unified mass. I glimpsed an open mouth—needle fangs framing an endless corridor of clean white throat. The light touched a living wall of the creatures, so entwined they pulsed as one great heart, an organ whose arteries had wrapped it in a blood-black knot. There were eyes too—the tiny soulless couplets that knew me, that recognized me as a fellow traveler through the underworld, knew we were just pawns, really, held before a God who'd long stopped paying attention to the evil that men do in his name.

I steadied my hand and held it close as I cut a wide swath with the penlight.

There must have been twenty or more cottonmouths. On one side of me, the majority of them were engaged in a mating orgy so intense that even in my fear, I was stunned into wonder.

And that was the moment everything came back to me—the ride with Ronnie out to my cousin's; the encounter with Amanda; the lock on Baylee's door; my forced entry; the deep, resinous abrasions that flowed beneath her skin and fanned out across her hips like the wet tendrils of a creeping vine.

The tiny girl lifting the hammer.

And now I was here. With the cottonmouths. Waiting to die.

I shone the light up. There was a trapdoor at least ten feet over my head.

I was fucked.

I stumbled away from them and into the side of the pit—because that was exactly where I was, a snake pit. I pressed my body against it and shone the light out like a torch.

*   *   *

My dreams—or rather, my nightmares—over the years had been largely devoid of snakes. There was always the seed of one in every fear, every quivering moment of unexplained anxiety. I tried to pluck them free like splinters, but—also like splinters—they were nearly impossible to grasp and extract. Snakes didn't so much make an appearance in the films of my subconscious but rather *slithered* among the shadows, always just out of sight, ghosts sure enough of their power, their hold over the haunted, they need not do any more than move languorously across the scaffolded fabric of my stupor.

And even in this way, they were able to grip me with panic, to control me with hidden strings. My encounter with them in Daddy's sanctuary on Long Finger had been bad but bearable enough because there was space to separate myself from the vile things. Even picking up the cottonmouth and swinging it toward Choirboy was less an act of confrontation with my inner fears than simply an act of pragmatic survival.

Now—seeing the ground not only move but squirm beneath me—I realized I'd become immersed in my deepest fear. Worse, I realized this was how I would die.

I tried not to breathe. I tried to consider my options, but I didn't have any.

One of the snakes not engaged in the orgy was making its way over to me. I shone the penlight at its eyes, and it stopped, transfixed.

I could buy some time. Maybe. But that was all.

I tried to make my mind work. I worked my way back to Burt's house. The hammer. How long had I been out before Amanda got in touch with her father? And who did he get in touch with to bring me here?

And where was here?

The snake retreated, and I took the opportunity to move the light around the pit again, this time not so much looking for snakes but checking its dimension, hoping to see something I'd missed before, something that would help me escape.

The walls were poorly delineated in the dark, but eventually I gained a sense of my surroundings. The pit was big, as snake pits go, probably about fifteen feet by fifteen feet. The snakes covered nearly half of the pit. I kept to the other half, pressed against the earthen wall.

I swung the light back to my right. Something gleamed white in the beam. I leaned in—too afraid to risk movement—hoping for a better view.

Something caught the light and threw it back into my eyes. A metallic object lay several feet away.

I did another sweep with the penlight. The orgy had grown, and I realized when that ended, my chances of survival would go way down.

I decided to risk the move and slipped quickly to my right, the penlight tracing my path.

I knelt, shining the penlight on the reflective object. I did a double take when I realized what I was looking at.

A badge.

I picked the star up and read the inscription.

Deputy Sheriff Coulee County

The light caught something else. The gleaming I'd seen earlier. I pocketed the badge and moved the penlight slowly across what appeared to be a skeleton covered loosely in tattered clothes.

And that was when I understood why the snakes weren't particularly interested in me. They'd been fed well. Most of the flesh had been picked clean, but a little still remained on one leg.

I didn't need anything else to understand who this was. Mary had told me on the very first day I met her that she'd taken over for a missing deputy. Well, at least I'd managed to find him. I wondered what he'd done to end up here and remembered how the DeWalts had said there was one deputy who'd actually tried to help them, and it all made sense.

What didn't make sense was who exactly was pulling the strings. If it wasn't Shaw—and according to Roger the night I'd dragged him out behind Jessamine's, it wasn't—then that left my father. But . . . shit. Always back to the same problem. He was dead. He had to be.

Or maybe I was just fooling myself. Maybe it was time to face the truth. He lived. Somehow, he had survived. The body had been identified wrong, or it was an elaborate ruse.

I swallowed hard. Maybe it was all true. Maybe he *had* ascended and now his spirit resided at this mythical well, and it was from here that he had been manipulating everything, including my own return to the mountains.

It was a scary thought. It was a thought that made me question everything.

It was a thought I could not—*would* not—allow myself to entertain.

So were there any other possibilities?

Only one. What if he'd faked everything? He certainly had the resources at his disposal. Hank Shaw would help. Billy Thrash and Lester would help. But how? How would something like that even be possible? And just assuming it *was* possible, there was still another pressing question that needed to be answered:

Why? Why would he do such a thing?

I was extrapolating quite a bit now, but it seemed to me that if I were my father, if I had his unique mind-set, there could be a couple of reasons I might do something like that.

One, he'd do it because it would prove God's power. I once saw my father try to pick a lame child up and force her to walk after he laid hands on her. When she fell over, he picked her up again and this time held her by the belt loop of her blue jeans and tried to make it appear as if she were walking on her own. The message was unmistakable: when my father believed God was going to do something, he truly expected it to happen, and if it didn't, he wasn't going to hesitate about making it happen himself. No, he had no compunction whatsoever about fooling the church if he believed it would make their faith stronger.

Two—and I wasn't completely sure this wasn't just an extension of the first reason—he'd do it as some twisted way to gain more control over the congregation. The folks in these mountains craved religion and God, but even more than that, they craved the inexplicable, the articulation of power through supernatural means. Look at the way they ate up the whole snake-handling shtick.

And maybe there was a third option too. Maybe Daddy had always wanted to be more than a man. I saw that in him as far back as I could remember. The way he soaked up the adulation, the way he welcomed the praise and the hyperbole about his legacy. He wanted to become a legend, to linger in these mountains in a way that gave him the ultimate power. The power of an unseen, all-knowing God.

And if it was true, if he really was alive, he'd succeeded.

Something moved nearby. I jerked the light and saw a cottonmouth exiting the hollow of the deputy's skeletal eye socket. It launched itself at me, and I flailed wildly to meet its attack. I got my keys and penlight up in time to knock it down before it struck, but unfortunately, I dropped the keys and penlight in the process.

Scrambling back, I was forced to leave the light where I'd dropped it.

I pressed myself to the wall again, creeping backward to the far left side of the pit. That was when I stepped on something that cracked beneath my boot.

I turned around, no penlight now to show me what I'd stepped on. There was something large below me. I knelt, feeling with both hands. I touched fabric and then cold skin. I moved up to a face and then to thinning hair.

Something made me find the right arm and trace my way down past the crook of the elbow to the wrist and to . . .

Nothing. The hand was missing.

I backed away, returning to the one spot I'd found that seemed safe. A cruel song lyric drifted across the dark of my consciousness—*Clowns to the left of me, jokers to the right.* Except now it was a dead deputy to my right, Bryant McCauley's corpse to my left. And everywhere else? Snakes.

Fucking cottonmouths.

At least I'd found McCauley. Finally.

So whoever had brought me here had also moved his body here. More food for the snakes? Probably. Not to mention a safer place to hide his corpse.

I thought of the deputy again, and suddenly I realized Mary might endure the same fate if I didn't manage to get out and warn her.

But how?

I didn't even have a light anymore. If the snakes came for me now, there was truly nothing I could do but die.

46

"When you die," Daddy said, "there's an immediate rush of light. For some it's a brief, fleeting glimpse of what they might have had if they'd just listened to the Gospel. After the fleeting glimpse of all the wonder they'll be missing, the universe goes dark."

"There ain't no fire?" I asked. I was six or seven, and we were alone out in the woods, looking for a pig that had escaped from the pen.

"Oh, there's fire aplenty," he said. "If that's what you fear. If it's drowning you fear, there's water. Satan is downright mean. He'll hit you where it hurts."

I nodded in serious contemplation of Daddy's words.

"But the Lord has told me he has a special plan for me."

"Special?" I asked.

"Special. Upon my death, I'll ascend to these mountains and lead the church from a special place. It'll be a holy place, and I'll speak with God daily."

At that age, I listened to Daddy with awe, unsuspicious of any hidden agenda in his words. It was in this spirit I asked my next question: "How can you know that will happen?"

He grabbed me by the shirt collar and twisted me around.

"How can I know? Hell, boy, I know because God told me."

I remembered being afraid of him then. Not just because he'd grabbed me so roughly. At that age, I'd already become so accustomed to such behavior as to barely notice. No, it was his eyes. They were so demented, so otherworldly. I didn't have the words to express what I saw in them then, but they came to me later.

He believed what he said. Not just in the religious sense too, which I'd learn so many times meant people *wanted* to believe something so badly, they fooled themselves into it. This was different. He believed he talked to God the same way an ordinary person believed in the permeable world that existed before our very eyes. He believed when he died, he'd ascend.

But what if he got impatient? What if he decided to speed things up?

It sounded like a stretch. How *did* one go about faking one's own death?

"He talks to you?" my seven-year-old self persisted, trying to wrap my head around the possibility.

He put me down. "He does. It started when I was a boy not much older than you. He told me it'll happen with you or Lester too."

I swallowed hard. I did not want God to talk to me. As bad as I feared hell, I'd come to fear God and heaven more.

The moment ended with him asking me to kneel and pray with him. When we rose, he was smiling again.

"What?" I asked.

"God told me where that pig was."

And he was right too. We found the pig a few minutes later, and I watched—memorizing the look of smug accomplishment on his face— as he picked it up by its legs, ignoring its pitiful squeals for mercy, as only a true man of God could do.

*   *   *

Everyone in the Holy Flame believed my father was special. It was undisputed. If someone expressed doubt in his ability to discern God's word or to even hear it, Daddy had been known to excoriate them in front of the entire congregation. Most left and never came back. A few were changed by the experience and, more often than you'd expect, went on to become some of Daddy's most ardent supporters.

Around the time he called for Hank Shaw to bring his daughter before him, Daddy was at the height of both his powers and his popularity. His word was iron, and it didn't matter how crazy the things he said were, people treated them as law.

I heard about it secondhand, piecing it together from rumors and innuendo to draw a picture of what went on that night.

I knew the meeting was brief. I knew Maggie was forced to stand in front of the church the next Sunday and apologize. Afterward, she was made to stand in the churchyard while elders from the church walked past her offering blessings. I watched this from the top of a large maple tree a couple hundred yards away. Based on the expression on her face, I wondered if the men weren't really offering curses.

She kept her mouth shut tight, her lips trembling while tears streamed down the sides of her face. At one point, she said something back to one of the elders, and Daddy—standing off to the side and observing the proceedings—stepped in and slapped her face. She fell to the ground crying. He stood over her, shouting words down with such anger, I could almost see them striking her. I cringed as I watched it all take place, and as bad as I'd feel later when everyone turned on me, it never got worse than what I felt at that very moment.

I was a true coward. I knew it in my bones. I could not look away, but neither could I muster the fortitude to do what I should have done, and that was to climb out of the tree and go help her.

*   *   *

A few days after that, Lester came by my room. He sat down on my bed. I'd taken to spending most of my time when I was home in my room, the covers pulled up tight, in a futile attempt to keep the deranged world of my family away.

I expected him to slap me, to scream at me, maybe even to try to kill me. But he did none of that. Instead, he just asked me how I was.

I nodded, still wary.

"I think me and Maggie might make it after all," he said.

I wished I could have seen my own face then. I was sure I must have looked shocked. It was the very last thing I expected him to say.

"She's got a demon in her, Daddy says."

"A demon?"

He nodded. "Daddy said God told him about it. She needs something to get it out."

I shook my head, nearly speechless. Was he talking about the baby? Our baby?

"He said she's going away for a little bit."

"Where?"

"Daddy said he'll tell me when the time is right." He slapped my knee. "You got to get out of bed, Earl. Can I pray with you?"

I was too stunned to tell him no, so I closed my eyes as he said his prayer. I'll never forget one part of it.

"And, Lord, please show Maggie the error of her ways, as you've showed so many of the women in our community. Help her to come back whole and repurified."

I didn't ask him what he meant by that, but I wished I had.

*   *   *

The problem was she never came back. Not really. Her body came back, but her spirit—her soul—never truly did.

I followed her home from the bus stop one day just to speak to her. She saw me coming after her and started to run. I sped up, sprinting hard until I was able to grab her arm and slow her down.

"Please," she said. "I don't want to talk to you, Earl."

"What did they do to you, Maggie?"

"They fixed me, Earl. I see that now." She spoke in a different voice—lighter, more airy, with none of the sexual gravitas she'd exuded before.

I grabbed her arm again. She didn't resist. Instead, she was simply limp.

"You didn't need fixing."

"Oh, but I did. I'd shut out the Lord's light."

"Let's leave," I said.

"Leave?" Was there a glimmer of something in her eye, just the barest hint of possibility?

"Tonight. You and me."

She opened her mouth to speak but then closed it.

I touched her face gently. "Maggie, we can get out of here. Tonight. This life . . . it's not worth living. Not like this."

Before she could respond, a voice called my name sharply.

"Earl?"

I turned. Lester was standing in the clearing, looking at me strangely.

"I gotta go," I said. "Ten o'clock. Meet me in the cedar grove west of Ghost Creek."

She didn't respond, but her eyes grew wide. I wanted to believe it was an expression of hope, but the years have showed me it was probably something else.

I trotted off into the trees. I turned around once when I thought I was in the cover of darkness and saw Lester talking to Maggie. He seemed to be upset.

I disappeared into the woods and didn't go back home again.

I spent the rest of the afternoon and evening walking the length of Ghost Creek, thinking about where we'd go. I just knew she'd show up. There had been something in her eyes. It had been hope. I convinced myself that was exactly what it was.

When my watch showed 9:50 by the glow of the half-moon, I followed the creek back toward the church. About a half a mile before the church, I crossed over and walked along a ridgeline until I could see the cedar grove up ahead.

Under the moon, the cedar trees looked like wrist bones, their roots knuckling into long, slim fingers. The moon's glow seemed unnatural for a moment, but then the clouds shifted, and the night went nearly dark.

Something moved. Maybe just the breeze, but it sounded like a person creeping through the grove.

"Maggie?"

There was no answer. I braced myself for disappointment as I slipped past the first couple of trees into the lush canopy of leaves and early dew.

The breeze filtered through the trees, rustling leaves and agitating a branch here and there. Something creaked as the wind picked up.

I wished the moon would come out again. Without it, I was flying blind, moving on feeling and scraping against the rough bark of the cedars, grasping for something solid.

"Maggie?" I said again, this time more desperate. I didn't believe I could go on watching her act like she'd been the last few days. It had been like watching a once free wild animal become confined to a dirty cage.

The wind picked up again, and the creaking grew louder, followed by a muffled thump. I waited.

Creak.

Thump.

Creak—the sound of a rope stretched to the breaking point, weighed down by something heavy—

Thump.

Something brushed my waist. I flailed out with both hands and felt naked skin, human flesh. It was wet and cold and slick.

I fell backward, gasping, wiping my hands against my blue jeans.

I peered up through the impossible dark. There was someone looming above me.

I didn't have to wait for the clouds to clear to know it was Maggie.

*   *   *

The clouds did eventually break, and I saw her in the moonlight—naked, hanging from the double-braided rope, her eyes stuck in an upward glance, perhaps to find the moon, to find something in the moment of her last breath.

It was another moment before I came to my senses enough to see what she'd carved on her belly.

When I did see the incomplete message, I threw up right where I sat. I rubbed my eyes, praying it would go away when I looked again, but it was still there.

Earl, it read. There was something else underneath, but there was too much smeared blood across her abdomen to make it out.

Later, I'd see it clearly by the light of day, the blood all wiped away. It was simple and damning, and it was the worst sentence I'd ever heard in my life.

Earl, you were right.

Perhaps I would have joined her in death then. It did cross my mind. I was so beside myself, so absolutely disgusted with everything I'd come to know as my life that I considered taking her down, removing the rope, and wrapping it around my own neck.

But I never got the chance.

"Earl?"

I turned around and saw Lester. The moonlight lit him up like pale fire. He moved slowly past me and touched the blood on Maggie's bare stomach.

I had no idea what to say, so I stood quietly while he began to cry. He wrapped his arms around her legs and tried to lift her, but it was far too late for that.

When he finally let go, he turned around and faced me with the heat of hate written across his face.

"It was you," he said.

"I wasn't the only one."

"It doesn't matter. You're the only one that's my brother. You're the only one whose name is . . . is . . ." He broke down again. Without thinking, I reached for him, hoping to embrace him and apologize.

He flailed out at me, connecting a solid blow to my mouth and splitting my lip.

I wiped away the blood, spat on the ground, and looked at him. He was half sick with grief, half mad with fury.

I made a decision—I would not fight back.

He screamed something as he lunged into me, driving us both into one of the cedar trees.

I didn't try to get up. I didn't try to talk. I lay there—for the first time in my life—and did not fight back as he pummeled me over and over again. He beat me senseless. I woke sometime later, and her body was gone. I was alone. In many ways—both significant and otherwise—I've remained that way ever since.

*   *   *

Several men came for me at dawn the next morning. I had not moved from the spot where Maggie had hung herself. They lifted me to my feet and pushed me along Ghost Creek back to the church.

I saw the throng of people before we were even across the creek. They stood on either side of the path leading to the church, leaving me a single lane to walk through on my way to the doors.

Daddy stood near the front of the church, flanked by Hank Shaw and Billy Thrash.

"No," I said and tried to turn around. I wanted to bolt. I did not want to do this. But they carried me toward the church.

When they held me before Daddy, he nodded for them to put me down. Then he looked at Shaw, who reached for the handcuffs he kept on his belt loop. He latched one over my right wrist and the other one to the church door.

"Brothers and sisters," Daddy began, "I present to you my son."

Not a soul said a word. The only sound was the wind coming through the trees near Ghost Creek.

"You're probably wondering why I called you all here to see him. Why I've had Hank here secure him to the church door. He's not under arrest. He has committed no crime, at least not in the eyes of man."

Daddy clasped his hands together under his chin, a prayerful gesture. I wanted to spit at him, and I might have if he'd been a little closer. It was as if instinctively he knew to keep his distance from me.

"But as you all know, we don't serve a man. And we don't serve man's law. It's one of the reasons Hank and I get along so well. He does his job, sure, but he never forgets the supreme law, and that's the Lord's."

Daddy cleared his throat, shuffled his feet, and looked up at the sky and the newly risen sun. He nodded to himself, completing the practiced dramatic pause.

"My son has broken the laws of God. He's not only broken them repeatedly, he's flaunted them; he's reveled in his lawlessness, his sin. Fornication is one thing." He smiled slightly. "The Lord is not pleased by sexual promiscuity, but at least he can understand how a boy might fall into that hole. After all, God designed us. He made the male full of desire for the female, and even though the righteousness of that desire can only be found in the fulfillment of marriage, there are young boys who are tempted by harlots."

"Amen," Billy Thrash said.

Daddy nodded.

"And while the dead girl was certainly a harlot, a slut, a bag of flesh set upon this earth seemingly by Satan himself as a temptation to the Godly man . . . while all of this cannot be denied, a miracle had taken place. God had touched her with his own finger. He'd touched her and said she was good again. She was pure."

"She was always good," I said.

All eyes turned to me. Except Daddy's. His stayed focused on the creek, where several more men were coming across. They carried a makeshift stretcher with Maggie's naked body on it.

One by one, the crowd turned and saw the men coming. As the group walked between the two masses of people, I heard gasping and muttering. They'd cleaned the blood off her stomach and were carrying the stretcher low enough to read what was written there.

Earl, you were right.

Jesus, it sounded like I'd encouraged her to kill herself.

"I didn't want her to do it," I said. "I just wanted her to leave with me." Eyes swung back to me. They were full of the most contemptuous judgment I'd ever seen.

"She hanged herself," Daddy said. "At the request of my son."

"No," I said. "That's a lie."

Daddy stepped swiftly across to where I stood and slapped me hard enough to knock my head back into the church door.

"Silence your lying tongue."

I used my free hand to wipe away the blood from my cheek. Daddy turned around to address the crowd again, but I was done. Done with his pious attitude. Done with his church. Done with his God. Done listening to his shit. Done with every part of my father. I spat at his face. The glob of saliva landed on his cheek.

He paused, not moving for a moment as it dripped down to his neck and fell off onto his shirt collar.

Then he grinned. "See, this is what life looks like when God has turned his back on a man." He nodded, still smiling, as if he were discussing something pleasant instead of the subjugation and ultimate rejection of his own son. "This is what a man controlled by Satan looks like."

"You are Satan!" I shouted.

He still did not look at me.

"I believe in a God more powerful than the devil. I speak to him daily, and he tells me of his plans. I saw Earl's unwinding coming from when he was a young boy. I saw the demons take up residence inside him, one after another, until dozens fought within his soul for dominion, until one defeated the rest. The Lord hath told me the name of the demon that resides in him now, and it is Andromalius; he entered a few months ago when my son held the serpent and God turned his protection away. Legions followed, but it is Andromalius, the demon thief, that controls him now. He has stolen my son's soul, and now he has stolen Maggie Shaw's life."

Everyone was silent. I closed my eyes, unable to bear the gazes any longer.

"Yet," my father said, his frown loosening, his eyes filling up with tears as he actually smiled at the congregation, "God's mercy and love know no limits. He has spoken to me and said that even the demons of hell are under his control. Lo, even Satan himself will bow down to the Lord God Almighty one day. 'For it is written, As I live,' saith the Lord, 'every knee shall bow to me, and every tongue shall confess to God.' Amen?"

The people said amen. I just glared at my father, trying to understand what was happening.

"And if God can make the devil himself bow down before him, why not this boy, this poor, poor boy, led astray by the sin of this world, the rebellion inside him, the heart of sin that we are all born with."

He turned to me.

"God said he won't turn his back on you, Earl. All you need do is kneel before him and accept this gift and all will be forgiven."

Daddy nodded at me. The congregation was so silent I could hear the creek moving over the rocks. I realized they were waiting on my response.

To this day, I believe my father was sure I'd kneel, that I'd give in, come back into the fold, and there was certainly a strong urge to do just that. And I might have if not for remembering Maggie. I turned and looked at her dead body again, slung carelessly onto the ground.

"That's great," I said, "but what about Maggie?"

"What about her?" Daddy said. "She had her choice, and she chose hell."

There was something in the way he said those words, something so nonchalant, so full of arrogance. I couldn't take it.

I turned back around. "I'll never kneel to your God."

Daddy's smile disappeared. He had not intended for it to go like this. No one ever got away from him. He controlled everything, every person, every decision, even the ones made in the dark hollows of these mountains. And now, he couldn't even control his own son in front of his own congregation.

His face turned red, and he began to shake with anger.

"You need to reconsider," he said.

"Never."

"You'll burn in hell. The demon will eat you alive."

"Probably not as quick as you will."

There was a murmuring in the crowd. They were unsettled, not sure how to take my blatant rebellion in the face of redemption. Daddy must have sensed it too because his face shifted smoothly from troubled to relaxed. The congregation quieted. He held up his hands.

"God can do everything but make the decision for us. We have free will, and my son has exercised his. It is a sad, sad occasion."

"Heathen!" someone shouted.

"Backslider!"

"Possessed!"

Daddy quieted the crowd again. I could see the smug expression was back. Things had not gone as he'd planned, but he'd managed to avert disaster. He was still in control.

"What I need from you," Daddy said to the congregation, "is simple. I need you to respect his decision the way God will respect it. If you turn your back on God and live a life of sin, you suffer the consequences. Therefore, I admonish you to shun Earl. Do not speak to him, do not acknowledge him, do not offer him food if he is starving to death. In this way, and in this way only, the demon will die as it will be unable to feed on your kindness, your mercy. Shun him completely as you would shun any evil thing. Only then will the demon weaken enough for Earl to defeat it. It remains to be seen, of course, if Earl will let go of his own pride enough to ask for the Lord's help in defeating the demon, but that is something I cannot help him with. But let it not be said I am giving up on my son. I will never give up on him, but neither will I tolerate his rebellious spirit in this community. The decision is his."

All heads nodded in agreement.

"Now unlock him, Hank."

Hank Shaw walked over to me, and without meeting my eyes, he removed the handcuffs from my wrist.

"Now look to what is good, to the sky, to your savior," Daddy said. "Do not grieve for Earl Marcus. He may one day be my son again, but until that day comes, he is truly lost."

Everyone turned around to look at the rising sun, leaving me unwatched. I stood there for a moment, wondering where Mama was.

Surely she wouldn't abandon me. Surely, she'd say something. I searched the crowd of people for her but didn't recognize her among all the turned heads. Later, I'd learn Daddy had made her stay home because he didn't want to risk undermining his little ceremony with her support for me. Just one more small manipulation.

I stood there for a while, just watching everyone's backs. They were so stupid, so easily led, like dogs following a person with a treat. But there was no treat at the end. I saw it clearly now. There was only a master who wanted to control each and every one of them completely.

He couldn't control me, so I had to leave. It was that simple.

So I did.

But not before I had my say.

When a man like Ronnie Thrash says we have a lot in common, it's most likely because of what I said to my father on that day.

It came from somewhere deep inside me, from a deep well I didn't even know I had. None of it was planned. It was completely spontaneous. If I'd tried to plan it, I wouldn't have said it. The things I said to my father were unthinkable, unforgivable. Yet I said them.

"Turn around," I said.

He didn't move, probably thinking he was still in control of the situation. A man can spend his whole life in control of every situation and fool himself into thinking that's just the natural order of things, but sometimes the order gets upset. Sometimes a man has to learn the world is not what he thinks it is.

"I saw you," I said. "Crying for Aida. Turn around."

He stiffened at this but did not turn around.

"Why didn't God heal her? Why didn't he save her?"

"It's time for you to go." A few of the congregation turned back to look at me. Daddy pointed at them, and they looked away. "Go now. The demon in you is worse than I thought."

"There's no demon inside me," I said. "It's just me. It's Earl. I'm a person. I screw up, but so does everybody else. Why did God let that happen to Aida?"

More people turned around. Daddy didn't stop them, but he continued to face the creek as he spoke to me. "God willed it. It was for the best. There's a lesson there for those who will see it."

"You're lying. You didn't believe that. Not then. Not when I saw you burying her. You were broken. God didn't speak to you."

Daddy swung around, and I saw his face was twisted with a cold wrath. "You lie."

"No," I said, pleased I'd won my first battle with Daddy—he'd turned around. "You lie to all these people."

Everyone was looking at me now. I had their attention. Whatever I said now mattered. "My father is a con man," I said. "His religion is a sham. He loved his daughter more than anything else in the world. God didn't take her from him. She just died. And he was just a man, unprepared to deal with the grief. He doesn't talk to God. If there's a God at all, he wouldn't waste his words on a man like my father."

There was a cold silence. It seemed to echo across the mountainside. No one spoke. Daddy's face was turned down. I walked past him and through the line of congregants, who all stepped away from me as I approached, as if they might risk their own damnation by getting too close to mine.

*   *   *

That was how I came to spend the next three years with Granny. She accepted me without any questions. She fed me, she clothed me, she loved me.

And it was the memory of Granny that comforted me as I lay in the snake pit. The thought of her gave me the strength to know I was ready to die.

Why shouldn't I be? I'd seen what this world had to offer—its cruelty, its twisted power plays, its brutal dismissal of human life. But I'd also seen the way a person can touch another person, can reach past the baser instincts of our kind and, through selfless acts of love, show another a small, refracted glimpse of the divine.

47

I must have died a thousand deaths inside that pit. The first one happened when the penlight went out. Dozens more occurred as I lay on the cold ground, my head and arms pulled tight under my shirt. I lay very still as first one snake and later two more slinked into my personal space. One of them brushed past my pants and curled itself over my boot. Even when the next two moved across my hips and traced a path up my back, I didn't move.

And soon, without light, without movement, with only the subtle creeping sensation of serpents roaming over me, I felt as if I had died.

I felt as if the demon had won.

That was when I did something I hadn't done in more than thirty years. I prayed.

It wasn't a prayer to my father's God. It was a prayer to Granny's. To the God of goodness, the God of second chances, and the God who might not care. I understood that even as I prayed. But it still felt good. Somehow, it still gave me a little moment of peace.

I lost track of how many snakes moved over me. The only thing worth keeping track of was how many had bitten me. The answer was still one. Thirty-three years before. Nothing since.

My mind turned to the mysteries at hand, reeling through the myriad of clues and layers of deceit I'd uncovered so far.

McCauley was dead. Could there be any doubt after what I had seen in this pit? But what about the map he had made? What had it said?

Something about the well and Daddy trying to reach me. He mentioned Old Woman Laney too.

What could she possibly have to do with all this?

I thought hard, trying to connect her with all of this. Rufus said she'd started coming after I left. He also said she'd been the first person to start taping the sermons.

That was when I remembered something else, another clue McCauley had left, maybe without even meaning to: Mary had said there was a tattoo on his hand. A date. January 28. I felt sure if I opened up a calendar, I'd see that it was a Sunday.

Miss Laney had all the sermons. There must have been something in the one from January 28 my father wanted me to hear. But why hadn't McCauley just told me that in the letter then?

I might never know, but I believed I had a good guess. McCauley was in over his head. It was clear from both of his letters and the scribbling at the fishing shack that he was confused by the whole thing. Hell, why shouldn't he be? I felt the same way.

If it wasn't so sad, it would have been funny. I'd finally realized he wanted me to hear that sermon, and there was nothing I could do about it now. I'd never get out of this hole.

Yet my mind continued to work, even while the rest of me shut down. I was hungry and thirsty, but I hardly noticed anymore. Instead, I moved inside my own mind, leaving everything else behind.

I thought of Maggie again. Where had they taken her? Some place that made her suicidal, that changed her irrevocably. Just like Allison. And now Baylee. Granny had said Allison spoke of the well and the lightning on top of the mountain. Something else hit me then: the marks on Baylee and Allison. I remembered reading an online article once about something commonly called "lightning treeing." These were symmetrical marks left on the skin after a lightning strike. I'd long since forgotten the science of it, but I felt sure it was what I'd seen on Baylee now. I'd be willing to bet Allison had had the same marks.

So someone was taking them up to the top of a mountain, the mountain with the well, and . . . what? Shocking them? Calling lighting out of the sky to strike them? It sounded insane.

But it also sounded familiar. Where had I heard such a thing before? It wasn't lightning exactly . . . no . . . it was fire.

The newspaper article written by one of the members of the Holy Flame. Thrash was quoted in it saying something about "fire from heaven."

Lightning. According to the article, my father had called upon God to save him from the drug dealers at the well, and God had sent lightning.

It was too much to believe. My father was a fraud, so complete he'd even swindled himself. I would not allow myself to believe anything else.

But that wasn't really consistent, was it? After all, I'd seen firsthand how my own dreams had come true, how a "new" side of me had been *unleashed* after the snakebite.

What if it were all true? What if my father could call the lightning, and what if he could defeat the grave?

Before I could give that chilling thought any more consideration, I heard what sounded like a dog barking far away.

I let out a breath I hadn't even realized I was holding. A snake slithered over my neck and back onto the ground. I waited for the sound to come again.

When I heard the next bark, it was closer than before. I let myself hope. Just a little. Could it be . . . ?

The next bark answered the question. It was Goose. Goddamnit, it was Goose.

A few minutes later, I heard a voice. "I can't see, dog. Just hold your horses, okay?"

"Rufus?" I said, but it was barely a whisper. I'd have to do a lot better than that.

I rolled over, still keeping as much of me as I could covered in the fabric of my shirt. Another snake dropped away from my legs. A third disentangled itself from my boot.

I stood up and cupped both hands over my mouth.

I shouted Rufus's name as loud as I could.

Goose barked a reply, and Rufus said, "Well, I'll be goddamned."

48

It wasn't easy, but eventually Rufus helped me get out of the pit. After he got the door open and my eyes adjusted to the harsh morning light, I was able to see the snakes. They seemed to be blinded by the sudden light, and I encouraged Rufus to move quickly.

"I need something to stand on," I said. "Or a rope."

"Got an idea," he said.

He stepped away from the square opening above me. Goose leaned over and barked at me. I laughed. "I knew I saved you for a reason."

He barked again, as if to say we were even.

A few seconds later, I saw something drop through the opening. It was a piecemeal rope consisting of Rufus's shirt, blue jeans, socks, and his belt.

I had no idea if it would hold me or if Rufus would even be strong enough to haul me up, but I grabbed the end of it anyway, determined not to let go.

"Give me a sec," Rufus said. "Let me get a good grip."

I waited until he called out that it was time.

Fist over fist, I strained to pull myself up. I'd gone no farther than a foot or two off the ground when I began to hear the fabric ripping.

"Come on," Rufus said. "You better hurry."

I reached out as far as I could with my right hand, grabbing the blue jeans. The T-shirt ripped away, but I held onto the jeans with one hand, and somehow Rufus held on too.

Goose barked at us both, and with his encouragement, I worked my way back up to the surface.

Alive.

Demons and all.

*   *   *

I lay there for a long time, trying to breathe, trying to answer Rufus's questions. When I finally caught both my breath and Rufus up on what had happened to me, he patted around for me on the ground.

"Here," I said and reached for his hand. He helped me to my feet.

"How'd you find me?"

He laughed. "That damned dog found you. Soon as they let me go from the jail—you can thank your girl Mary for that one—he found me and wouldn't let me rest until I took him on a walk. He kept sniffing the whole way. I had to stop and rest six times before he got to you."

I looked around. "Where are we, exactly?"

"About a half mile from home, but to get here, you got to traipse through all kinds of weeds and rocky terrain. It's pretty well hidden."

"Can you get us back?" I said.

"You're kidding, right?"

"No, I don't have any idea where we are."

He shrugged and picked up Goose's leash. He held his other finger up to the wind and then pointed to his right. "That way."

I followed him.

*   *   *

"What're you going to do?" he said when we reached Ghost Creek. "I ain't sure coming back to the church is the wisest plan."

"Right." I looked around, trying to think now that I had my bearings. I remembered the connections I'd made while in the pit. "I need to pay a visit to Miss Laney. Remember her?"

"Lady that tapes the sermons? Of course I do."

"Think she'll see me?"

He thought it over. "Not sure, but it's worth a shot. You're going to need some food and water."

"Yeah."

"And you ain't got no truck anymore. They confiscated it."

I sighed, trying to think.

"You could call that deputy gal."

"No. I want to keep her out of this. It's not safe for her."

"You mean because of the fellow you found in the pit?"

"Yeah. He must have crossed the line. These people don't play."

"They never have," Rufus said. "So you got any bright ideas?"

I thought about Ronnie. He might be willing to give us a ride again, but there would be a price to pay if he did. He wasn't the kind of person to do things out of kindness.

"I guess we'll have to walk," I said.

"Naw, I know somebody. Let's just see if that phone still works."

*   *   *

I found the burner phone Mary had given Rufus sitting on Daddy's old lectern. I turned it on and saw it only had 5 percent left. I handed it to Rufus. "Do your thing."

He made a call to a girl he said he knew. When he finished, he handed the phone back. "She'll be here in a half hour."

I looked at the phone and saw there was now just 1 percent left.

"Didn't she give you a charger?"

He shrugged. "No. She told me she'd bring it next time."

I dialed Mary's number quickly. It went to voice mail. I waited for the beep and said, "I'm okay. Getting closer to the end of this maze. Don't try to help. Save yourself. Don't make waves. There's one thing I need you to do though." I told her about the two kids in the shack out by the kudzu field. "Get them out of the county," I said. I took a deep breath. I wasn't sure how far to go, what to tell her exactly. I decided against mentioning the deputy or McCauley. If I knew Mary, she'd take it straight to the top. And if I knew Shaw, she'd be the next one in the snake pit.

"And just don't try to find me, okay? I'll find you when it's all over. I promise."

I tried to disconnect the call, only to see that the screen was already black. I wasn't sure how much of my message recorded before it died. Hopefully enough.

49

The girl drove a vintage red Pontiac convertible. She was probably in her midtwenties and wore her hair in a throwback bob. Her sleeveless shirt revealed dozens of intermingling tattoos on each arm. Her skin was pale and clear, and she was just about the prettiest thing—short of Mary Hawkins—I'd laid eyes on in a good while.

"What the hell," I muttered when she stopped the car and hopped out, revealing form-fitting pink yoga pants and a navel ring peeking out from just beneath her knotted shirt.

"She look as good as she smells and sounds?" Rufus asked.

"Better," I said.

Rufus grinned. I wanted to ask him how in the hell an old blind man pulled something like this off, but she was right there, and it might have been rude. Besides, I thought I already knew—Rufus was the walking embodiment of the North Georgia gothic. He was a mystery, an enigma, and just a tad bit dangerous without being mean about it.

As if to prove my point, the girl ran up and gave him a huge hug. She kissed his lips and then his neck while he just grinned at her ministrations.

"This is my friend, Earl," he said. "Earl, this is Marsha. She's a grad assistant down at UGA. She's been coming up on Friday nights to hear me bullshit for the last few months."

"Pleased to meet you," she said. Her voice was deeper, more mature than I expected based on her youthful, almost bubblegum appearance. "Rufus said y'all needed a ride?"

"Yeah. If you don't mind."

"I don't mind. I'm off today. Plus, anything to get me to the mountains. I love this place. Did you grow up here?"

I nodded, trying to keep my face neutral.

"We better go," Rufus said. "We ain't got time to waste."

I whistled for Goose, and he came running out of the trees, wagging his tail. Marsha knelt to pet him, and he licked her lips and face, her grinning through it all.

Rufus and Goose sat up front, and I lay down in the back seat.

*   *   *

She stopped at a McDonald's by the highway and went in while Rufus and I waited in the car. She came back with two hamburgers for each of us and one for Goose. I ate greedily as she drove us to Miss Laney's place over on Ring Mountain.

The sky was growing dark. I hadn't seen a weather report in days, but it was clear a big storm was coming.

I wondered if we'd see lightning.

*   *   *

When we arrived at Miss Laney's house, Rufus told Marsha to wait outside with Goose.

"You see any cops, just go ahead and go, okay? There ain't nothing you can do by staying."

She gave him a worried look and then glanced at me. "What are you two caught up in?"

"The past," I said.

She looked at me blankly as I climbed out of the car and started toward the house to knock on Miss Laney's door.

50

Miss Laney did not speak when she saw me. She just stood there, glaring at me.

"You probably don't know who I am," I said.

"I know exactly who you are. I've been expecting you for some time."

"You have?"

"You're here for the sermon, right? Your father said to only give it to you."

She seemed in poor health, her face pockmarked with age spots and scarring. Her hair was a brittle shade of gray.

"He said that?"

"He never did give up on you. Those of us closest to him always knew that." She looked at Rufus. "Why is he here?"

"He's helping me figure all this out."

"He's a bad influence."

"Well, I reckon I can take that as a compliment, Miss Laney," Rufus said.

She craned her neck to see past him. Marsha smiled and waved at her from the front seat of the Pontiac.

"They need to leave," she said. "I won't let you hear it until they're gone."

"They're my ride, Miss Laney. Can they just wait outside?"

"No. You aren't ready until you put away these worldly friends. Don't forget, I wasn't there the day you rejected God and your father, but I know the story. He's a more forgiving soul than me, I know that. If you had been my child, I'd never want to see you again."

I felt like getting angry, but I'd been through too much to let this foolish woman stop me.

"Okay," I said. "I understand."

Rufus laughed. "This must be some kind of joke."

"You and Marsha can go," I said. "Take care of Goose for me."

"You sure about this, Earl?"

"Yeah, I'm sure. I think things will make a lot more sense soon."

He put a hand on my shoulder. "I'll be back to check on you."

"No," I said. "Don't." I tried to sound angry, dismissive.

I sensed Miss Laney's approval and added, "Stay away, Rufus. Far away from me. I'm trying to get things right."

I wished he could have seen me. I believed he would have seen the pain in my face as I pretended to reject him. It was my only chance. I hoped he understood.

*　　*　　*

She led me to a room whose walls were lined with bookshelves holding hundreds of cassette tapes. Each was labeled on the case with a date.

"I started taping in 1984. These represent every sermon your daddy gave since that time up until February of this year. Thirty-one years, nearly two thousand tapes." She bowed her head. "I only wish I had access to his sermons now."

"That's impossible," I said without thinking. "He's dead."

"*Was* dead," she said. "He lives again. He's in the mountains, hidden away, waiting for you. Your father was the only man I ever knew who could discern God's most intimate plans. Even on that day you rejected him, he saw the greater plan, how God would bring you back."

I had to resist arguing with her. I wanted to tell her if this was God's plan, God wasn't nearly as brilliant as advertised. Or as loving, when you considered all the collateral damage done just to get me to come back home again.

"Do the people at the church—at the Holy Flame—believe this, that he's risen again?"

She shrugged. "I left the Holy Flame. Your brother is not your father. His failings are beyond comprehension. He is as possessed by Satan as you ever were."

"Andromalius," I said.

She nodded. "Satan has many names."

"You think Lester is possessed?"

She narrowed her eyes. "I do. He is attempting to tear your father's church apart piece by piece. It's only the presence of good men like Billy Thrash and Hank Shaw that give the church any hope." She smiled. "And you. I think you have come back to save the Holy Flame."

I almost laughed. Nothing could have been further from the truth. Still, as amusing as I found her words, the suggestion was deeply troubling. There was a sense that even in death, my father had orchestrated a plan so intricate, so manipulative, I was now walking headlong, eyes wide open, right where he wanted me to go.

"The tape?" I said.

"Of course. You just need to tell me which one. He said you'd know."

I told her the date that had been tattooed on McCauley's wrist. She nodded, pleased with my answer, and walked over to one of the shelves. She plucked one of the last tapes free and placed it into an old tape recorder.

"It was one of his last, right after your uncle died."

She pressed play.

"I'll leave you now. Your father has requested that no one else hear it."

She closed the door, and I listened to the hiss of static and then the strains of Aunt Mary Lee's piano fading into the background. Heavy steps trod across a stage, and then that voice—that awesome, soulful voice that had ruined so many lives—began to speak.

51

The sermon was short and relatively simple. It was—dare I say it—tame, at least in comparison with the ones I remember as a kid.

He spent most of it speaking of family, of the importance of looking out for one another. He worked his way around to a story about him and his brother, Otis, when they were boys.

"Otis died last week when his heart gave out. I spoke at his funeral two days ago, and I'll repeat now what I said then. He was a good man, a godly man. In the end, nothing else matters."

He paused for what seemed like a long time. Someone from the congregation shouted, "Amen," but Daddy still didn't say anything.

The quiet continued for an abnormally long time.

When Daddy spoke again, his voice was low. "I miss my brother. But God has a plan. It's hard to believe sometimes, but God will use his death for his glory."

"Amen!" It sounded like Billy Thrash, forever Daddy's right-hand man, forever giving him backup when he needed it most.

"There's another death I don't talk about much. Some of you remember when my little girl, Aida, died."

I sat up as a chill snaked down my spine. I'd never heard him speak Aida's name since the day I found him crying over her grave.

"I loved that little girl, and when she died . . ." His voice broke a little. "When she died, I questioned God. I did, brothers and sisters. I questioned how God could do that. How it could possibly further his kingdom. But I just had to trust that it did. Well, recently, brothers and sisters, recently I've been in prayer. And God has showed me the future."

The crowd began to murmur excitedly. I remembered, as a kid, they'd do the same thing before he inflicted another bullshit prophecy on them.

"He showed me how a bad thing can lead to something good. It may take years and years and years. But eventually it will happen." He fell silent. I imagined he was pacing now, his hands clasped together in front of him, a prayerful gesture. "I still think of my son, Earl. Many of you were here years ago when I sent him away. I haven't given up on him, and neither has God. Mark these words, brothers and sisters: what God destroys and man buries, God can use again if we are willing to keep his grounds."

That last bit was such an odd line, so unlike something Daddy would normally say, I rewound the tape and listened again.

What God destroys and man buries, God can use again if we are willing to keep his grounds.

What did it mean? Was it a clue?

I didn't know. The tape played on, and Daddy moved on to sin and immoral behavior—two of his favorite topics—and it dawned on me how far I'd come in a few short weeks. I was sitting inside a little old lady's home listening to a tape of one of my dead father's sermons in hopes of . . . what exactly? What was I hoping to hear?

He was winding down the sermon when he said something else that struck me as odd.

"Long-standing members of this congregation know I'm not a man who quotes other sources besides scripture, and if I do, there's a reason for it. Well, I'm going to quote one now. There's an old saying. Maybe you've heard it. 'Familiarity breeds contempt.' This may not be directly stated in the word, but I think the truth of it is in there. Consider Jesus's own life. At first everyone was amazed by the miracles he performed, the wisdom he displayed. But soon enough—when he turned that wisdom and that unerring moral compass on them—they began to grumble and question his authority. Eventually, they went so far as to crucify him."

He paused to chuckle playfully. "Well, that didn't work out so well for them, did it?"

The congregation laughed. Somebody whooped an amen, but I didn't think it was Billy Thrash this time.

"The thing to remember is that God and his son, Jesus, and any man who has their spirit cannot fall victim to petty jealousies and small minds. It just won't happen. Can't happen. Not in this life or the next.

"I can hear you now . . . 'Preacher,' you're thinking, 'it sounds like you might be calling somebody out.'"

There was a long pause. I could picture my father nodding solemnly.

"If that's what you're thinking, then yes, you're right. In a way. I'm not calling them out. I'm reminding them. Reminding them what, you ask? Simple. God wins in the end. And all that is holy will overcome the grave, and all that has been set asunder will be set to rights again."

The tape ended, and I sat quietly, trying to clear my mind, trying to think.

Otis had died the week before. He talked about him briefly before moving on to Aida and the mention of me. Then the line about keeping the grounds . . .

It hit me. If there was a message here for me, it had to be there. I thought of my dream, of the crank finally reaching the top, of Aida's tiny body filling the bucket. She'd only lived a few hours, but she still haunted me nearly thirty-three years later.

And she haunted Daddy too.

It was what we shared.

And suddenly, I knew I had to dig up her grave, because that was what the line meant. That was what he wanted me to do.

I should have felt good about finally making some sense out of it all, but I didn't. Instead, I felt like I was playing directly into my father's hands. And I felt like there was more. All the stuff about "familiarity breeds contempt" at the end. Who had that been meant for? My first thought was Lester. Hadn't Ronnie said my brother had reason to be angry with Daddy? Had the two had a falling out? There was so much to think about, but I just didn't have the luxury of sitting still.

I ejected the tape and put it inside its case and back on the shelf.

I went over to the single window in the room and opened it up. I kicked out the screen and climbed through.

At the road, I looked both ways for cars—especially police vehicles—before crossing and starting the long trek to my sister's grave.

52

It was raining when I arrived, and not having a shovel, I was a muddy wreck by the time I found the tiny little box where Daddy had put her body. I hesitated before opening it. I wasn't sure I was ready for what I'd see.

And smell.

But before I could pry the lid off the box, I noticed something on the other side. I turned the box upside down and saw a plastic bag attached to the bottom with some kind of adhesive. Inside the bag was a piece of notebook paper.

I tore open the bag and unfolded the paper.

It was a map. *The* map.

Finding cover from the rain under some of the shadier trees, I studied the map in my mud-covered hands.

An *X* marked the spot near the top of Long Finger Mountain. Written by the *X* were two words in my father's tortured script:

The Well.

I flipped the paper over. On the back were some scribbled instructions on what to do when I got closer. Below that was a list of names that didn't make a lot of sense.

Lester
Earl
Earl

266

Lester

Lester

Earl

And then a short sentence that seemed to be mostly nonsense:

After Earl, follow the light.

If this was supposed to mean something, it was lost on me.

I read it again and again until lightning flashed in the distance and I looked up to see that the sun had disappeared. It was time to get moving. I knew where I was going now, and I was pretty sure I wasn't going to find anything good.

*   *   *

I made it back to the highway before the rain and lightning forced my hand. I had to take cover. I ended up crouching under a bridge while the storm continued with all the force of a heavy metal band.

I waited for a half hour or more until there was a lull, and as I was about to step away from the bridge and continue on my path to Long Finger, I noticed a car coming down the road. I hit the ground and rolled down the embankment into a nearly washed-out plain, hoping the driver either hadn't seen me or didn't care to.

No such luck. The car slowed and a door swung open. I felt panic jolt my body, and I struggled to my feet to make a break for it. I hadn't gone far when I heard the chirp of a siren. Ignoring it, I plowed across the muddy field, my eyes fixed on a line of dense trees a couple of hundred yards away. I might have made it if I hadn't slipped.

I sprawled into a pool of floodwater and decided to just stay there, keeping my head under.

I made it for nearly two minutes before I had to come up for air. When I did, I heard Hank Shaw's voice.

"Earl Marcus," he said. "You should have listened to me when I told you to leave town."

He stood a few dozen yards away, flanked by two deputies. One of them was Roger Peterson. He held a rifle aimed at my face.

"You're under arrest for the rape of Baylee Marcus," Shaw said.

53

They sat me at a table, facing a one-way mirror. I wondered who was looking at me from the other side. Hank Shaw? Almost certainly. Daddy?

I shuddered at the thought.

Some time later, Roger Peterson came in and sat down across from me. I could see the bruises on his face from where I'd kicked him. He put a laptop down on the bare table and looked at me directly.

"When we found the note, I figured that alone would be enough to convict your sorry, sorry ass, but then your cousin told us about the security camera he installed. I watched the video of you coming in the house, Earl." He smiled. "You do know what happens to pedophiles in prison, right?"

I said nothing. The truth was, I was unable to completely follow what he was saying. I got stuck on his first line—when we found the note.

What did it mean? Who had written the note? Baylee?

He pointed at my head. "That where she hit you with the hammer?"

I nodded.

"Jesus, are you even going to deny it?"

"Deny what?"

"Fucks sake. Are you going to make me show you the video?"

"Video? Video of what?"

"Of you entering the house and going upstairs?"

I shook my head, still trying to understand. "What was the note? Is Baylee dead?"

"Maybe you should tell me. Nobody's seen her since she was with you. But we got all the details from the little sister. She told how you promised her she'd be next. And how you laughed and laughed while you were doing it." He leaned in. "What kind of man does that?"

"I didn't do any of that. You may not know it, but Shaw does. They've cooked all of it up. I want to know where she is."

Before he could answer, the door opened, and Shaw said, "I want to be alone with him."

"Sure, boss." Roger stood up and nodded at me. "I'll get you back for the other night. Just you wait and see, old man."

Shaw pointed toward the mirror. "I want everyone out of that room. Everyone. You understand?"

"Yes, sir."

"And turn the cameras off."

Roger smiled. "Yes, sir."

"And before you go . . . cuff him to the table."

Roger came over and slammed the handcuff on my wrist far too tight. He hooked the other one to a little ring drilled into the heavy table.

Shaw waited until he was gone before coming over and taking the seat across from me.

"Feel familiar?"

"I don't know what you're talking about."

He unwrapped a stick of chewing gum and folded it before putting it in his mouth. "Sure you do. The day your daddy called you out for what you were. A sick individual. He had me cuff you then too." He nodded at my wrist and shrugged. "Sorry, I thought it would be best if you weren't able to fight back." He chuckled, and then, as if remembering something—maybe Maggie, maybe just the simple fact that he hated me—he darkened considerably.

"I think that was the first time me and your daddy didn't see eye to eye on something. I thought you deserved what Maggie had. Hell, worse. But no, your daddy always had a plan. He called it God's plan, but I've come a long way on that kind of thinking. Now I think the only thing God is good for is controlling folks. Come to think of it, that's about all your daddy's ever been good for, keeping the population in line. He did it better with religion than I ever could. All except you." Shaw shook his head. "See, there's always somebody who won't fall in line, somebody that can't operate under the constraints of society. Being a lawman all these years taught me what I wished your daddy had known."

"And what's that?" I said.

"Some folks only respond to a good old-fashioned beatdown."

With that, he rose from his chair and stepped over to me.

Desperately, I tried to think of something to delay him, as much because I wanted to hear more about his problems with Daddy as to avoid the inevitable pain.

"I didn't rape her," I said. It was all I could think of, and it sounded weak. He already knew I didn't rape her. None of what was about to happen had anything to do with Baylee. It had everything to do with Maggie.

He rolled up his sleeves and removed his tie. I needed a different tact.

"You know he's still alive."

He glanced at me. "What?"

"My father. He's still alive, and he'll make you pay for this."

"Earl, your daddy's the one who told me to do this."

I opened my mouth, maybe in surprise—it had been the last thing I'd expected him to say. I never got a chance to respond.

His knuckles caught my top teeth, and I felt one of them ping off the back of my throat. I leaned over, trying to cough it out, but his second and third blows landed near the same place his first had, and I swallowed it.

"What did you tell her? What did you say that made her do"—he hit me again, this time in the gut—"what she did?"

I gasped and tried to speak. The words came out like wheezes. "I told. Her. We needed to get out. Of that community. We needed to leave because we didn't have a future there. I was. Right."

"You were wrong." He kicked my legs out from under me. I fell, at least until the handcuff caught me, digging into my wrist. "Stand up, you piece of shit."

I tried to stand up, but I was turned around wrong, and the handcuff was making it difficult to move. I tried to stall again.

"So why torture the girls, Hank? You of all people should know the consequences of that."

He kicked me in the face.

"Maggie killed herself because of you. So shut"—he kicked me again—"up!" The next kick made me almost lose consciousness.

He paused to catch his breath.

I tried to reposition myself and brace for the next onslaught.

But the next onslaught never came. He had just caught his breath and straightened up when the door swung open.

A deputy I didn't recognize stood in the doorway, his mouth open in shocked awe.

"Sheriff?" he said.

"I had to," he said. "He's a rapist. And he killed my little girl."

The deputy shuffled his feet and looked at the floor. "Want me to take him to a cell?"

"Yeah. I want him to live at least long enough for him to get what's coming to him in prison."

The deputy came over, obviously nervous, and unlocked the handcuffs. He guided me out of the room and down the hall into a cell.

I collapsed on the hard bed, moaning in pain. But it was more than just physical pain. It was the knowledge of time wasting.

As if to remind me of the storm's increasing fury, there was an explosive crack of thunder that shook the cell and caused the single bulb hanging above my bed to flicker and go out.

The darkness lasted just long enough for me to see my father standing in the corner of the cell. His body glowed with something like radiance, and his eyes glared at me, unblinking. Just as the lights returned, I realized he was a demon too.

It was quite possible we all were.

54

I was asleep when I heard Mary's voice.

At first I thought it was part of my dream, especially when the cell door swung open and she kissed my cheek.

I blinked my eyes and sat up, taking the smell of her in, feeling an untimely sense of arousal at her presence.

"I came as soon as I heard."

"It's not true," I said. She hugged me tightly, pressing her body into mine.

"I know. I don't believe any of it."

"Thanks."

"But I need you to fill me in."

"Okay."

"On everything."

"Sure."

"No. I don't think you understand. I need to know what happened in the past. It's like I'm playing cards without a full deck here. It makes getting to the bottom of this thing nearly impossible."

"I thought you were off the case?"

"I am." She stood up and took off her badge and tossed it on the floor. "I'm completely off all cases. I'm only here for you now, and for the victims of these mountains."

I shook my head, wincing. "Are you sure about this? What about Granny?"

"I've got enough money saved to stay with Granny. And I refuse to work for a corrupt sheriff. Now talk. Tell me everything."

I had to admit, even when I made up my mind to tell her, it was hard, especially when I came to the stuff about Maggie. She listened attentively, putting her hand over mine when I got to the part about meeting Maggie in the cedar grove. When I faltered, telling her about the sound of the breeze moving the rope, she put a finger to my lips.

"I understand. You don't have to talk about it."

But it was too late. I *did* have to talk about it. In voicing my past, something unexpected was happening: I didn't feel so powerless in the face of my regret.

I pushed on, telling her everything, only stopping after I'd made it to the part about staying with Granny.

When I finished, she didn't say anything. The rain was coming down harder now. The thunder and lightning had ceased for the time being. There was only the sound of the constant downpour on the roof of the jail. We were alone. There were no other prisoners in the other cells. The nearest person was the desk sergeant, and he was several solid walls away. I felt myself unwinding. Everything that had been inside me, curled up tight like a swollen fist, opened up and was set loose, as if a dam had been breached and the pressure alleviated.

Still not speaking, Mary leaned in and kissed me lightly on the lips. It hurt a little from where Shaw had punched me in the mouth, but it didn't matter. It felt so good, the pain was far away.

She locked her eyes on mine.

"I'm not sure if this is . . ."

She kissed me again. I worried about the impropriety of me being fifty and her being nearly fifteen years younger. I worried about my busted lip—was it still bleeding? Would she care? I worried about hurting her. Most of all I worried about my own inability to let somebody in.

Except I'd already done that, hadn't I? I'd just told her everything. There was nothing I'd held back, and this, along with the sensory overload of her lips and tongue and her body pressing itself so urgently against mine, was enough to make me give in.

I slid my hand across her flat belly, and she murmured encouragement. I pushed under her shirt and cupped a breast beneath her bra. My other hand moved down to her thigh, and the friction my palm made against the denim of her jeans burned.

The rest of it happened fast despite the lingering pain from Shaw's beating. Somehow the pain hurt a little less as we locked our bodies together and found a pace I could only describe as frantic. And perfect. Most of my encounters over the years had been fast like this one. One-night stands, acted out without real passion, only lust. Sometimes the one-night stand turned into a month or two, but the passion, the true feelings, had been absent. Not so now. I wanted her body, sure, but I also wanted her, some nearly unattainable essence of her that I longed to release and absorb.

As I began to climax, she squeezed both of my hands and moaned loudly. I kissed her, silencing the moan, but I still felt her vocalizations reverberating inside my mouth.

When it ended, I tried to move off her, but she pulled me back. "Stay. Just a few more minutes."

I understood. It felt safe here, our bodies intermingled. When it ended, when I had to pull myself away, there would be a hard and bitter world waiting.

As if to remind us just how hard and bitter and full of danger, a low rumble of thunder shook the jail cell.

"We better get moving," she said, standing and pulling her jeans back up.

"Moving?"

"Yeah, we're leaving."

"We can't just walk out the front door." I looked at her. She was already by the cell door. "Can we?"

"When I came in, Shaw had just left. That means there's only Crowe at the desk and Winston around back. I'll distract Winston and meet you out back."

"That easy?"

"They don't even know I'm here. Why would they think you'd be able to walk out on your own? Give me ten minutes and then head for the back door."

She started to leave but stopped.

"I'm sorry you had to go through all that, Earl."

"Don't be. I have to take responsibility. If I hadn't ever slept with—"

"You were seventeen. No seventeen-year-old should be held accountable for an act like that. Especially one who'd suffered through what you did."

I wanted to believe her. I really did. But then I thought about my encounter with Lester a few days back. His dismissiveness, his complete unwillingness to even talk things through.

She came back over to the cot where I was laying. She leaned over, breathing on me.

"Kiss me," she said, her lips already grazing against mine. I reached for her hand and held it and the kiss for a long time.

She pulled away. "Ten minutes. Wait for me out back."

"And then what?"

"Then we go to that well on your map."

"Not yet," I said, realizing there was something else that couldn't wait.

"What do you mean not yet? Baylee could be there right now."

I nodded. "I know. Which is why I plan to make this quick."

"Plan to make what quick?"

"The visit to Lester."

"Are you sure that's a good idea?"

"No, but I have to." I looked at my watch. It was a little after midnight. "If he's not home, I think it will tell us a lot."

"I don't understand."

"I think it could be happening tonight. The lightning. The storm. If he's involved, he'll be at the well."

"Okay, what if he is home?"

"Then I want to ask him where he stands. I want to ask him for his forgiveness, and I want to ask him for his help."

55

Lester's home was in the city limits of Riley, nestled in a patchwork subdivision of trailers and regular houses. He had one of the houses, and one of the nicer ones, at that.

Mary pulled into his driveway behind a pickup truck. A single light was on inside.

"Should I wait?" Mary asked.

"Yeah. I'll try to keep it short."

I gave her a quick kiss before jumping out of the car and sprinting through the rain to his front door. I had no intention of coming back. If Lester wasn't home, I'd slip away into the trees behind his house. Go do what had to be done on my own. If he was home . . .

I decided not to get carried away. One thing at a time.

I rang the doorbell.

After a few moments, I rang it again and knocked on the door with my fist.

A light came on in the back of the house. I breathed a sigh of relief. He was home. Which meant he wasn't somewhere in the mountains torturing Baylee. There was no guarantee he hadn't done it before, but at least, at this moment, his presence made clear one of two things—he wasn't involved or Baylee wasn't presently being tortured.

Another light, this time in the foyer, came on, and I saw him walking toward the door. He looked old, far older than he should have. He would be fifty-two now, but he looked ten years older. He pressed his face to the glass on the side of the door and shook his head when he saw me.

"Can we talk?" I said.

His expression was unreadable through the glass, and for a second, I feared he was simply going to turn away, leave me on my own to deal with whatever it was I was about to experience, but then he reached for the door and he let me inside.

*   *   *

I sat on the couch in his den. He fixed us both coffee and then sat in a recliner opposite me.

"I'm here to apologize again," I said.

He stared at me. "What happened to your face? Looks like you took a beating."

"Never mind that. I want to tell you how wrong it was of me to do what I did with Maggie. I was a stupid kid."

"Stupid kids don't convince girls to kill themselves."

"I didn't do that, Lester."

"I saw you talking to her the day of the suicide. She carved your name on her body, Earl. Do you really expect me to believe you had nothing to do with it?"

"No. That would be foolish. But I also want you to see that we all had something to do with it. Every person in that community. But nobody more than our father."

He swallowed some more coffee and looked at the rain-streaked windows behind me.

"She'd still be here today if you hadn't gotten her pregnant," he said. "That's on you."

"Would she? Do you really believe a girl like Maggie would have made it much longer in that environment?"

He rolled his tongue over his front teeth. He was uncomfortable, which meant he was considering that I might be right.

"Why are you here?" he said.

"Because I need your help."

"I mean why are you in Georgia? Why even come back?"

"I came back for Granny."

"The woman who took you in?"

"That's right."

He looked like he wanted to say something hurtful, something mean, but there was nothing to say.

"But you stayed," he said.

"I did."

"Why?"

"I also came to find Bryant McCauley. He contacted me in North Carolina. I simply wanted to tell him to leave me alone."

"Bryant McCauley." He said the name with disdain. "He's the fool that started all of this. I don't reckon you found him?"

"Oh, I found him. He's dead. Killed by Chester. Remember Choirboy? 'Course you do. He was hanging around the church the day I came to visit you. What do you mean when you say McCauley's the fool who started all of this? All of what?"

He ignored the last question and instead answered the first one. "Chester still goes to the Holy Flame, but I'll be honest with you, Earl. I wish he didn't. I'm trying to change the church's image. I want to put a positive spin on things. Stop living in the past and making everything about hell."

"What's stopping you?"

He stood up and walked over to the window before pacing back to his chair. He didn't sit though. Instead he continued to move around as he spoke.

"There's resistance to it. Some people—especially the older folks—say I'm a false prophet. There's also some . . ."

"Go on."

"Some who say Daddy is still alive. Bryant McCauley was one of them. But there's others. I hear most of it secondhand, you know, but that doesn't mean it's not true. I know Choirboy is involved, and I'm pretty sure Hank is too, but that's all I can figure."

"Where's Thrash stand on the issue?" I asked.

279

He shrugged. "I don't really know. The truth is we haven't had a real conversation in months. He just glad-hands folks on Sundays and sings my praises as far as I can tell, but he doesn't have much to say to me."

I thought about it. "Seems like the same ones who you suspect are in the 'Daddy is alive faction' are the same ones who are out to get me."

"How so?"

"Choirboy tried to kill me recently. Wanted to leave me for dead with some cottonmouths."

"But you escaped?"

"Yeah, it went the other way. He was the one that got bitten."

"Explains why I haven't seen him lately."

"Shaw is out to get me too. He's saying—" I stopped, unsure I wanted to mention the accusations to Lester. Our peace—if you could even call it that—felt extremely tenuous.

"Saying what?"

"That he wants me out of town." I gestured to my swollen face. "He made sure I got the point."

"Well, that shouldn't surprise you."

"No, I guess it shouldn't." I took a deep breath. We seemed to have reached a stalemate. "Well," I said, "I wanted to apologize again. I never intended to hurt you."

He sat there.

"I also wanted to asked for your help."

"My help?"

"Yeah. I think they're doing it again."

"Who's doing what again?"

"Torturing the young girls. Like they did Maggie. And I've found out about more too."

"And what, you're going to stop this torture?"

"I'm going to try."

"You're a fool, Earl. Always have been."

"Okay," I said. "I've said my peace. I apologized." I stood up and looked at the back door.

"One more thing," I said.

280

He just looked at me.

"Go on."

"Do you think he's alive?"

Lester looked away. A single tear dropped down his cheek. He seemed to be fighting hard not to break down.

"Well?"

"I need to tell you something," he said, wiping his face with both palms.

"Okay."

"I think it's important."

"I'm listening."

"They're blackmailing me."

"What? Who is blackmailing you?"

"I'm not sure. I think it might be Shaw. Sometimes I think Thrash is involved." He shook his head and kicked the couch. "Maybe even Daddy."

"I don't understand."

"Sit back down. Don't leave. You're the only person I can tell."

56

"I saw his body with my own eyes," Lester said. "His face had been pecked apart, but it was him. Everything about the body screamed 'Marcus.'" He gestured to me. "You and me aren't exceptions. The thick neck, the hairy arms, all of it. He had on his wedding ring, Earl. It was him."

"Okay. I believe that."

"And he was dead. No two ways about it. Not a breath left in his body. Then we had the funeral, and he hadn't been in the grave more than three days before Bryant McCauley—stupid fool that he was—started telling the whole world that RJ Marcus was alive, that he'd 'ascended.'"

"Did people believe him?"

"At first I think most of them didn't. But that changed when he came to church that day talking about the well."

"What about the well?"

"He said Daddy had told him about it to prove that he was still alive. It worked. Suddenly everybody thought he was alive." He looked at me closely. "Do you know something about the well?"

I took a chance. "I think it's where they took Maggie. And maybe the others, maybe Baylee."

"What did you say?"

"I think the well is the place where they punish the girls."

"No, not that. Did you say Baylee?"

"Yeah, our cousin's girl."

"Baylee?" He seemed very agitated now, and I felt the air shifting in the room. The temporary peace might have been over before it had really begun.

"What about her?" he said through pinched lips.

"She's missing. I think she may be at the well. Again."

"Again?"

"I saw marks on her. They were consistent with the marks that were seen on a woman named Allison DeWalt, who we also believe went to the well."

At the mention of Allison's name, he went rigid.

"Are you okay, Lester?"

"I'm fine. I just need a minute to process . . ." He stood up and walked into the kitchen. I waited for what seemed like a long time for him to come back. I was about to go look for him when he rounded the corner holding a bottle of Wild Turkey. He unscrewed the cap and took a long pull. He held it out to me, and I took one as well.

"I didn't know you drank."

"There's a lot you don't know about me, Earl."

"Like what?"

"I'm a father."

"Excuse me?"

He nodded. "Got a daughter, but I don't even know her. Have barely even seen her."

"Who's the—" I was about to say *mother*, but then the answer dawned on me.

"It was you. You're the man Allison was dating from the Holy Flame."

He nodded.

"What happened to the little girl?"

"Daddy sent her away. After Allison killed herself . . ." He let that hang there long enough for me to truly understand the horror he'd been through. Not one, but two women he'd loved had killed themselves.

"After that, Daddy wouldn't hear of me raising the girl. He promised me he'd place her with a family in the church and we could stay in touch."

"Why did you let him do that? He had no right."

Lester looked at me like I'd lost my mind. "You're the only person I've ever known who stood up to Daddy. Mama couldn't do it. Hank Shaw—the meanest S-O-B I've ever known—couldn't do it. Choirboy? Putty in Daddy's fingers. And me? Oh, God, Earl, I was the worst. I wanted to please him so much. And even when that urge finally stopped, when I couldn't do anything but loathe him, I still couldn't stand up to him. I was still afraid."

He began to sob, and my first instinct was to look away. It was simply the way I remembered our relationship working as young boys. We respected each other enough to pretend that our emotions, our fears, our paranoia that Daddy had instilled in each of us so deeply, none of it really existed. But we weren't boys anymore. We were old men. Old and deeply broken. Both of us.

I went to him, and though he pushed me away at first, I persisted. Eventually he relented and let me embrace him.

The moment was brief, but when I straightened back up and released him, I was slammed with the certainty that it was one of the best, most right moments of my life.

He wiped his eyes clean and looked at me directly.

"Earl, the little girl . . . my little girl . . . it's Baylee."

57

"**B**urt wouldn't let me see her," he said after I got over my shock. "He said I was a two-time loser. That something about me caused females to commit suicide. I wondered if he wasn't somehow right, and I didn't fight it. Maybe, I reasoned, it was better for her not to know me."

"No," I said. "The common denominator with all three of those women isn't you, Lester. It's the church."

He nodded. "I suspect you are right. Which brings me to the black-mail situation."

I'd almost forgotten the blackmail he'd mentioned earlier.

"It started around the same time when people began to talk about Daddy being alive. I received letters with no return addresses. Inside were details about my relationship with Allison. And several other women I had . . ." He sucked in a breath again, and for a second, I thought the sobbing was going to come back, but he managed to stifle it and continue. "I had a problem. There were a lot of women. I didn't think Daddy knew. But he did. He knew everything. He knew about the prostitutes, the one-night stands. He knew it all. That was what the letters said, that Brother RJ had told them of my dalliances."

"Jesus," I said. "What did they want?"

"That's the thing," he said. "It didn't make sense. All they asked was that I keep doing my job. Don't leave. Don't rock the boat. I think one letter specifically requested I 'keep my ears shut' and not stick my 'nose where it isn't wanted.' I was relieved. At first. I could do those things.

But then the rumors started about the well. And then Bryant McCauley disappeared. Now I'm not sure what's going on."

Neither was I. But what seemed clear was that we had at least one of the same goals.

"I'm going to find Baylee tonight."

"How?"

I pulled the map out of my blue jeans and handed it to him.

He shook it out and looked it over. "Let me get my gun," he said.

When he came back a few minutes later, he was dressed in dark jeans and a lightweight raincoat. He scratched his head, hesitating.

"I want you to know," he said, "that I forgive you."

"You don't have to say anything else," I said.

He held up both hands. "Wait. Let me speak. I forgive you, and I hope you'll do the same to me."

"For what?"

"For this," he said and lifted the back of his raincoat and took out his handgun.

"What are you doing, Lester?"

"I'm sorry. But they called just before you showed up. Said you'd escaped from jail. They said if you came by to hold you until they came back. I don't believe you hurt Baylee, though."

"Then why in God's name are you doing this?"

"For the same reasons I've done everything in my life, Earl. I'm afraid. More afraid than ever because Daddy's alive."

"I don't believe you," I said.

"It's true. I have proof. They told me where he was. Said they had pictures I could see."

"You can't see that they're lying, Lester?"

"Maybe they are, but McCauley told me the same thing. And I sense it too. I've got to find out. They promised if I helped them, they'd let me see him."

"You hate Daddy, Lester. You just told me that."

He began to cry again. "I do hate him. But I also love him. In the end, aren't they the very same thing? Don't they both take a back seat to what you fear? That's who I am," he said. "I'm a man afraid."

"So are you going to shoot me? I wouldn't advise that. There's a sheriff's deputy sitting in the driveway."

He shook his head. "I don't think she's going to be a problem, brother. I really don't." He was crying harder now, and I didn't think I'd ever seen a soul more tormented. Not even Maggie.

"Daddy promised me if I did this, I could also talk to Jenny."

"Jenny?"

"Baylee!" he said, swinging the gun wildly. "My daughter. Her real name is Jenny."

"Okay," I said. "Just calm down. I don't know why you think Mary isn't out there anymore."

"I never said that. Look out the window."

I walked over to the window and peered out.

Mary's Tahoe was still parked in the driveway, but there was another car behind it. There was something on the ground in the front yard. I leaned in squinting and understood it was Mary. Someone else walked up and kicked her hard.

The doorbell rang.

"I'm so sorry, Earl. I really am." He walked over to the door and swung it open.

58

After the shock wore off of seeing Choirboy alive again, I couldn't stop looking at his face. I saw now I'd been lucky when the cottonmouth had bitten me. I still had scarring, but most of it was hidden beneath the scraggly gray of my beard. Choirboy's face was rotting away before my very eyes. While the left side seemed normal, the right side appeared to be in the midst of a metamorphosis. The white of his cheekbone was exposed, and much of his flesh had turned black and scabrous like charred meat. Except for one area, just to the right of his lips that had turned white and was riddled with tiny pustules, mushrooms blooming in the scorched field of his face.

Despite it all, he smiled, causing the right side of his face to crack and ooze white puss down his chin. He wiped it away like it was an afterthought, and with his other hand motioned at me with my 9mm. The same gun I'd left with him in my father's sanctuary, truly expecting not to ever see it or him ever again.

"Hey, Earl," he said. "It's time to meet your maker."

"You already tried that twice," I said. "Seems like you would just give it up."

"Third time's a charm," he said. "Snakes . . ." He shook his head, and for a horrifying instant, I thought a charred piece of his cheek was going to slip free, but it only shifted and stayed attached to the rest of the necrotic tissue. "Snakes ain't always the most efficient way of getting a man to see the error of his ways. But lightning . . . it's the very crooked finger of God. It'll make you fear the Lord." His wound split open as he smiled, and more pus oozed out over his lips and teeth. "Or it'll kill you." He leaned around me and saw Lester standing in the den. "Hello, Lester. I thank God you came around. I know it's tough to turn on your kin, but the Lord said, 'Fear not them which kill the body but are not able to kill the soul: but rather fear him who is able to destroy both soul and body in hell.' That's from the gospel of Matthew."

A voice called out behind him. "We ready?"

"Ready," he answered.

Choirboy led me outside to where Hank Shaw and Roger Peterson stood over Mary. Her eyes were open, and she seemed calm. I saw no marks or bruises. But I'd seen one of them kicking her. A rage was kindled inside me. At that moment, I would have killed both of them if given the chance.

Mary must have seen the look in my eyes because she said, "I'm fine, Earl. Don't do something you'll regret."

Hank Shaw laughed. "His whole life has been nothing but one regret after another. Stubborn little bastard. You should have just stayed in jail. When I heard they were trying to kill you, I thought it would be a better solution, less mess for me to clean up, but then the word came down."

"From who?" I asked.

He glanced at Lester and grinned. "Your daddy, of course. God's right-hand man."

That was when I understood. Daddy wasn't alive, but it helped Shaw and Choirboy if everybody believed he was. Who could question the authority of an ascended RJ Marcus?

"You're full of shit." I turned to Lester. "They're playing us both."

"Oh, come on now, boys," Shaw said. "Don't be doubters. You know your father never could tolerate a doubter."

"My father is dead," I said.

"Correction—he *was* dead. But now he lives atop Long Finger Mountain. He's ascended and become God's true voice in the wilderness." I let it go, mostly because when I looked at Lester, I could see he was on the verge of falling apart. If it helped him to think Daddy was alive, let him think it. There was something else too. Something that nagged at me. Something that didn't quite fit the narrative, the one that suggested it was all just a hoax perpetrated by Hank Shaw. Why have McCauley contact me? Unless he went rogue and did it on his own. But that didn't fly either. McCauley was a follower. He never did anything on his own. Which brought me back to the possibility that Daddy was still alive.

Could it be possible Shaw didn't know?

59

We followed a road so narrow, Shaw was forced to keep his speed under five miles an hour to avoid sliding off the side of the mountain. The road was muddy, and the rain continued to fall, making each moment more hazardous than the last.

Mary and I sat on either side of Lester in the back of the Tahoe. Roger and Shaw were in front, while Choirboy rode in the very back, his presence hard to forget not only because of the fetid smell of his rotting face but also because of his breathing, which I noticed had become more and more labored. I wondered how long he had left and made a mental note to attack him first when the time came.

I didn't know exactly what they had planned for us, but I knew two things: it would almost certainly involve lightning, and it wouldn't end well.

Lester was quiet as we drove. He seemed severely agitated and continued to slap at his neck and give me sidelong glances.

I put a hand on his knee and squeezed. I wasn't angry at him. He'd done what he had to do. If anyone could understand Daddy's power, it was me. To be angry at him would feel like the ultimate betrayal of the only person in the entire world who could ever really understand me. We'd been born into this shit together, just a year and a half apart, and I knew exactly why he had done what he did. He did it for the same reason I'd done so many things in my life—because I was still desperate for my father's love and approval. More than that even, I wanted to understand the man, to affix some causality to his nature. Maybe that was the faith I

291

needed to find. Maybe it was simply an assurance that there was a reason my father had burned my world down and had taken without hesitation everything he could from every person he'd ever met and been able to manipulate.

Maybe we were both afraid he might have been right all along. After all, as enlightened as I liked to think I was, I'd allowed a "dead" man to lead me along by the goddamn nose. How had that happened unless there wasn't a part of me that believed he had overcome death, that he'd fulfilled his own prophecy and grown omnipotent in his second life?

But if he was still alive, how did that jive with Shaw's cavalier and insulting attitude toward my father? Hadn't Shaw alluded to a falling out over my punishment? Was it possible he'd been waiting all these years to capitalize on my father's prophecy of ascension?

It made sense on so many levels. Choirboy would be easy enough to manipulate. Lester was a bit of a problem, but the blackmail had done the trick. And the torture? What better way to make it seem like Daddy was pulling the strings than to do what Daddy did best: torture young girls.

But there was still a piece that didn't fit. More than a few, actually. Why the map? Why the clue about the sermon I'd listened to?

The sermon. I remembered suddenly the part of the sermon where Daddy spoke of familiarity breeding contempt. He'd seen their rebellion coming. I felt like I was close to getting my head around it when the Tahoe slowed to a stop.

"Go on," Shaw said.

I peered through the rain and tried to see why we'd stopped. Roger climbed out, and I watched him walking out in front of the headlights to swing open a wooden gate festooned with barbed wire. Lightning broke the darkness suddenly, revealing the mouth of a cave behind the gate.

Shaw pulled the Tahoe through the gate and stopped the vehicle.

"Get them out," he said to Choirboy, who dutifully jumped out of the back of the vehicle and came around to open my door.

I had a mind to punch him as soon as the door opened but decided not to at the last minute. Roger and Hank both had weapons. It would be too easy for one of them to shoot me and Mary before I was able to retrieve his gun. No, there would have to be a better moment. I'd be patient, wait it out.

Choirboy pushed me around to Mary's side of the truck. He got her out, and Roger came back holding his own weapon. Together they escorted us toward the mouth of the cave.

I thought of the map in my back pocket, thankful none of them had tried to search me yet. All that pain and suffering to find it, and in the end, I didn't need it at all.

Except . . .

I thought of the strange list of names on the back. What could it mean? It was yet another code I hadn't been able to crack.

Inside the cave, Shaw lit a lantern and hung it on a sharp outcrop of rock. The space was smaller than I'd expected, just a tiny gathering area with three openings—corridors, which I suspected led farther into the mountain. There was also a wooden crate near the far left corridor. Roger walked over to it and took the lid off. He rummaged around for a moment before coming back with two long strands of thin wire.

He held one of them out to Hank, who turned to Mary with it. "Put your hands out," he said.

She did as requested, and he looped the thin wire around her wrists and tied a knot. Then he tightened it so hard, she gasped. Blood crept around the edges of her wrist and onto her palms.

"You're going to kill her like that," I said.

"Shut up," Shaw said as he took the other piece of wire from Roger. "Out," he said.

I refused to put my hands out. He nodded at Choirboy, who grinned and knocked me on the forehead with a balled fist. Not expecting the blow, I lost my balance and fell to the cave floor. Shaw leaned over me and wrapped the wire around one fist and then the other before pulling it tight and drawing my wrists together. He didn't stop pulling when I screamed; in fact, it seemed to encourage him to pull it tighter. I felt the wire dig through my flesh and made myself be quiet. Finally, the tightening stopped. My hands went numb. I watched as both Roger and Choirboy pulled on thick, insulated gloves. Then they each took one of the wires like a lead—Choirboy grabbing mine and Roger grabbing Mary's—and pulled us toward the far left corridor.

Shaw carried the lantern, casting the light out in front of us as we were pulled into the darkness. Somewhere overhead, I could hear rainwater rushing down the side of the mountain and thunder rolling out like a rapid beating of a large drum.

We turned to the left again, and the new passage was more narrow than the first. I felt the slick walls on each of my arms as we squeezed through.

We took two more turns before they pulled Mary and me to the left. This corridor was wider, and light flickered all around us. We were close. The thunder grew louder. I suspected we were near the end of the tunnel and I'd see the well of my dreams soon.

It didn't take me long to find out. The corridor opened up into the sky, and we were pulled out into the rain, onto a narrow ridge where the air itself felt alive with a charge of power that prickled my skin and made my hair stand on end.

There was so much to see, it took me a moment to process it all. The first thing was the lightning. I couldn't take my eyes off it. It struck over and over again in the same spot, once every couple of seconds, each time blinding me anew, making me shield my eyes, disturbing my equilibrium.

When the barrage of lightning finally lapsed, I was able to take in the rest of the ridge. The well. It was much like the dream, except the roof of the well and the hand crank for drawing up the bucket were missing. Instead, someone had inserted a long metal pole into its mouth. It rose some forty or fifty feet into the sky, and it was at the top of this where the lightning struck.

Behind the well, I saw three girls all wearing sheer white dresses. They were on their knees, facedown as if in prayer or mourning. One of them was Baylee. I recognized her deep-black hair, even as soaked and wild as it was now.

Finally, there was a single figure standing to my right. He was tall and faceless because of a hood he wore pulled tight to hide his features.

I felt a chill thrum through my body. If it was Daddy . . .

The figure spoke, his voice piercing the rain and thunder. It was a wild, nearly inhuman keening that felt as if it had been elevated somehow to a place of supreme and unquestioned authority.

But the voice didn't belong to my father. That should have given me some relief.

It didn't. There was too much evidence staring me in the face that he lived.

I made myself focus on the words of the hooded man. He turned to me, revealing his face. I gasped when I saw it was Daddy's closest advisor and Lester's biggest supporter, Billy Thrash.

"I've spoken to your father," Thrash said. His usually jovial tone had vanished. His voice sounded solemn, as if he were imparting news of a great tragedy. I supposed in a way he was. "As always, his faith demands we not give into our irrational hatreds and instead let God above be the judge of these sinners."

"Amen," Choirboy shouted. "He is good! He is just!" I wasn't sure if he was talking about God or my father, but I decided, in the end, it didn't matter much.

"Hook them up," Thrash shouted.

Before I could argue, Choirboy lashed the end of my wire over a little spike in the pole protruding from the well. Then he reached for Mary's to do the same.

"Leave her out of it," I said. "She's innocent. Just me."

There was a pause where no one spoke. Then Thrash said, "No. He has ordered them all to be judged."

Choirboy hooked Mary up. Shaw had moved to the other side of the well and was working on doing the same for the three girls.

He latched Baylee's wire to the pole last, and her face was pitiful to behold: resigned and defeated. I understood in a sudden flash of insight exactly why Allison and Maggie had killed themselves. This was the kind of trauma you didn't run away from. Not that it had ever been easy to run away from the Holy Flame, especially if you were female.

"Now!" Thrash shouted. "Let there be lightning!"

Shaw and Choirboy shuffled away, moving to the far side of the ridge, putting as much distance as possible between them and the well. Thrash did the same, though he took his time, moving with a deliberate pace as if unconcerned about the possibility of lightning striking before he wanted it to.

For a moment, nothing happened. The worst of the storm appeared to be over. I scanned the other faces—the hopeless misery in the three girls who had been here before, who obviously knew the pain that was coming; Lester's confused countenance, no less miserable than the girls; and finally Mary's. She was looking at the sky.

Waiting on the lightning? Or was she looking for something else?

I followed her lead and looked up. An awesome thundercloud churned above us, and it was easy to imagine it as the anger of an indignant God. But what or who was his anger directed toward? The answer to that question seemed to be the key to everything, the difference between hope and despair, life and death.

I felt it before I saw it. A charge in the air, a prickling of every inch of my skin, and then the sky was alive, alight, scored with the greatest power I'd ever seen.

The ground jumped up and smacked me in the face. My body felt like it was on fire, and my hands flew apart, the wire on my wrists disintegrated. I was too dazed to move. The lightning coursed through my body in spasms of heat, or maybe it was just my muscles continuing to contract because of the electric shock. Either way, I'd never felt like this before. Every piece of me was charged and buzzing, and inside my skull, I felt a thousand ants crawling.

Time slipped away from me, and my senses registered only light and staccato bursts of sound and waves of deep, bone-rattling vibrations.

Some interminable time later, Choirboy leaned over me, leering, the white pus from his cheek threatening to drip onto my skin. "Alive," he said. "He's even awake."

"Lash him back up," Thrash said.

Choirboy produced a new wire and reached for my hands. As he did this, I heard Roger, or maybe it was Shaw, say, "Dead."

I struggled to rise in order to see who he was talking about. I prayed it wasn't Mary or Baylee. When I sat up, I saw him dragging one of the other girls out of the way. Mary was sitting up nearby, as were Baylee and the third girl.

As they prepared us for another blast, Lester complained loudly, "I want to see him. You promised me I'd get to see him."

"He doesn't want to see you anymore," Thrash said. "He said to tell you that you need to ask for forgiveness for your sins again."

"I've done that," Lester said, and his voice was surprisingly strong. "Either God forgives or he doesn't. I want to see my father."

Thrash laughed. "You want the truth? He told me today he was disappointed in you both. He said he was at the point where he couldn't understand why God had inflicted such boys on him, and then the Lord spoke. He said the two of you were trials for him, nothing more."

"That's not true," Lester said. He charged at Thrash, and Choirboy had to let go of me before he got the wire tied properly. I struggled to my feet, and the wire fell away. Roger shouted when he saw me going after Choirboy, but he'd laid his gun down too in order to lash Baylee back up. Choirboy turned to ward off my charge, but it was too late.

I was already swinging. My fist landed in the waste of his wound, and I felt the splintering of bone beneath my knuckles. He dropped into the mud, not making a sound. I believed I might have killed him.

Something too sharp to be thunder sounded nearby. Roger grabbed his gun and shot at me. I dropped into the mud beside Choirboy and found my 9mm tucked into his waistband.

I sat up firing, my first shot hitting the well, beveled stone exploding in all directions like shrapnel. My second shot hit Roger in the leg and spun him around. I was about to finish him with the third when I felt my

297

skin prickling again. I looked up in time to see it, another God-almighty blast from heaven. The entire sky seemed to turn to lightning, and it was daytime for an instant. In the daylight, we all looked so absurd—Thrash wearing his hood while Lester punched him in the face, Mary's face aghast as she looked at the wire on her wrist, Baylee and the other girl waiting patiently like handmaidens on the king.

And the king, I realized, was in the sky.

It hit, and the world went sideways. I saw fire, angels and demons, a great bird careening among the stars above, shaking left and right, dipping its sharp wings dangerously close to us all. I felt the blast in the top of my head, my hair standing on end, and I heard Lester still pounding flesh with his fists.

The rain slowed, and the fire rose. I focused my eyes in the near dark and saw that one of the girls—not Baylee—had slipped out of her dress, which now rose in the wind. I watched it float away like a ghost into the rainy sky.

I spotted Baylee. She was free from her constraints and standing near the side of the ridge, precariously close to stepping off into nothing. I shouted at her, but she ignored my call.

Someone grabbed my shoulder.

I turned, ready to fight, but it was Mary. She flashed me a worried smile. "He never got the other end hooked up," she said, holding out her wrists. They were still tied together with a thin wire.

I started to help her get them off, but she stopped me. "Forget it. Go after him."

"Who?"

She was about to answer when a sound I'd been hearing but not really recognizing grew louder. We both looked up.

A helicopter was trying to land.

"I'll get these girls clear," Mary said.

I nodded and looked around. Choirboy was still down. So was Roger. But where were Lester and Thrash?

And Shaw?

I glanced back at the chopper. "Georgia State Patrol" was printed on the side. I didn't have any idea how Mary had contacted them, but it was a damned miracle.

"Make sure these girls are okay," I shouted to her before trotting back inside the mountain to find my brother and Billy Thrash.

And maybe even my father.

60

I didn't have a light, but it didn't take me long to find them. There was the blood for one thing. I felt it streaked against the cavern walls, traced it with my fingers as I moved in the blackness. Then I heard their ragged breathing, the grunts and moans as the two men fought.

Occasionally, Lester would beg to see Daddy, and Thrash would try to say something, but then he'd never get the words out. I assumed because Lester had punched him again.

I was still shaken by the two blasts. The first had gotten under my skin, made me tingle and ache. The second had thrown me to the ground with a concussive blast strong enough that my ears were still ringing. But I was alive. Mary was alive. Baylee too, at least for the moment, was alive.

Only time would tell if she would remain so.

I rounded a corner, and there they were, blocking the passage, trading blows, staggering like heavy shadows in the deep dusk of the cavern.

"Lester," I said, "it's Earl. I've got a gun, but I need to get a clear shot."

A body flew against mine, knocking me back. I recovered and aimed the gun down at Thrash.

"Shoot him," Lester said.

"I plan to."

Thrash laughed. "You boys came all this way, but I have to tell you something . . ."

"Go on," Lester said. "Say it."

"Ain't nobody seen your father. Bryant McCauley was just a fool. I thought maybe he was right for a little bit, but then I realized he was full of it, and I decided I could play that game better than him. He didn't even know where the well was. He'd been going to your daddy's old sanctuary on Ring Mountain. It was easy to convince Choirboy that McCauley was just crazy, that I was the one who really had your daddy's ear. God, it was so easy. And you know what? It was right too. I served your daddy for so long while he had all the power. While he made all the decisions. Was only fair for me to get a chance."

I almost pulled the trigger, but I had one more question to ask.

"But why do what you're doing to these girls? What's the point?"

He laughed. "You've always been so stupid, Earl. I'll bet your brother knows. Tell him, Lester."

Lester was silent for a moment. Then he said, "Because it was what Daddy would have done. It made everyone believe."

That cut me to my core, and suddenly I didn't want to shoot Thrash anymore. I wanted to shoot myself. I'd come from that man, and even though he was a fool, there was no questioning his capacity to do evil in this world. I'd fallen victim to it myself. All my rebellion, all my anger, and all my guilt was because of him.

"Get up," I said.

"What?"

"You heard me."

He struggled to his feet.

"Where are we going?" Lester said.

I took a deep breath. "Back out to the well. It's time to put an end to this."

61

They found Shaw's broken body a few days later on a rocky ledge some fifty feet below the well. It wasn't clear if he jumped or simply fell. I like to imagine Baylee pushed him. She had been standing near the ledge where he fell.

If she did push him, she wasn't talking about it. In fact, the last I'd heard, she wasn't talking at all. She and her sister had been moved to a foster home in Riley. I'd tried to visit them the other day, but when I showed up and the mother—a nice-looking woman who seemed well-intentioned enough—saw my bruised face, she shook her head and refused to let me see either girl. I took this as a good sign. At least she was being cautious.

Lester, Thrash, and Roger were all taken into custody, and the Georgia Bureau of Investigations moved into the sheriff's office and provided a police presence in the tumultuous days that followed.

My own first couple of days after that night were tumultuous too, so much so, they later became a blur to me. I did remember being in a hospital bed and looking at my arm and seeing the same marks I'd seen on Baylee, except mine were deeper, more like my blood vessels had snapped and all the blood had risen to the surface of the skin in some preordained pattern. I remembered Mary coming to see me once or twice and then a stream of investigators taking statements, making notes, and asking follow-up questions.

I explained it all the best that I could, including what I'd been doing at Burt's place. Eventually, all the charges against me were dropped, and the investigators, mostly state police, even stopped treating me like I was some kind of pervert.

As I explained my story to the investigators, all of it seemed to make sense.

Almost.

McCauley was a madman, an extremist who couldn't take my father's death, so he kept him alive, deluding himself and—to some extent—Lester and me, not to mention many others in the church who so badly wanted to believe in my father's immortality. It was funny because all I ever wanted was to see my father as a man.

Billy Thrash believed it too but decided to verify it, and when he realized McCauley was simply pretending, he stole the idea and ran with it, using his connection to Daddy to exert power over the church and to become the true authority in all matters, even while Lester was still the figurehead. Like Hank Shaw, he had long resented my father but had lacked the courage to confront him in life. My father had that effect on people. But once he'd died, Thrash didn't hesitate to capitalize, gaining all that power and more because, as I'd suspected, the congregation responded to an "ascended" preacher even better than they did a living one. Of course, he had to get Hank Shaw on board, but that was an easy thing, considering the sheriff's own resentment against my father. What the two men ultimately wanted to accomplish with this power was beyond me. Like my father, Hank Shaw and Billy Thrash were men driven by forces I didn't believe even they understood.

I believed Thrash's mistake was when he started going after the young girls again. It wasn't the kind of thing that could happen in today's world. Maybe for a while if you had the sheriff on your side, but not long term. Still, without some good luck and foresight from Mary, he might have continued the torture, and with the threat of torture came an absolute kind of power that must have been too much for Billy Thrash to resist.

Mary's foresight was one of the things I thought about the most in the days I lay in the hospital bed. Even when they released me and Mary showed up to take me back to Granny's, it was the first thing I asked her about.

"I went with my gut. When you went inside your brother's house, I had some time to think. I figured we were going to be heading into the mountains. I also figured we might not be coming back. So I called a friend at the GBI. Told him if he didn't hear from me within the next two hours, to send out a chopper."

"And he didn't question you? I mean, that's some trust," I said.

She smiled and turned onto Granny's gravel drive. "We have history," she said. "He knows me."

I nodded, willing myself not to feel jealous. I wasn't sure where I stood with Mary exactly. We'd had the one night in the jail cell, but there was still the age gap, and the last thing an older man should do if he wanted to be with a younger woman is get jealous. So I let it go. At least I tried to let it go.

Hell, I tried to let a great number of things go, but I couldn't quite do it.

One thing still bothered more than the rest.

But before I could say anything to Mary about it, Granny's place came into view. The day was mild for late June, and Granny was sitting in the cast-iron rocker in the front yard. Beside her were two kids I recognized. Maybe I should have been surprised to see them there with Granny, but I wasn't. This was who she was. Who she would always be until she was no more. A helper, a guide. A friend when everyone else had abandoned you.

Millie noticed me first, and I cut down the window and waved. Todd got up from his seat and limped over to the Tahoe, grinning proudly at how well he was moving.

I got out of the car and reached to take his hand, but he bypassed my hand and went for the big embrace. When I let go, Millie was standing there waiting for the same thing.

She kissed my cheek and whispered, "Thanks." Then she held out my credit card. "We only charged a few things on it. It comes to seventy dollars. I'm going to mail the money back when we get it."

I shook my head. "No, you're not. Don't even think about it."

She blushed and pulled her hair back. It was hard to see her as the same girl who'd held the shotgun on me in the shack just a few nights before. She seemed revitalized, and she glowed with an interior light that made me feel good inside.

My mind turned involuntarily to Baylee. The good feeling went away when I realized Millie had just barely escaped. So many—Maggie, Allison, and now Baylee—had not been so lucky.

I walked over to see Granny next. She had struggled to her feet to greet me, and I embraced her, nearly lifting her wasted body off the ground as she clung to me with all her might.

"Thank you," she said. "Thank you." I was pretty sure she wasn't talking to me.

*   *   *

I visited Lester in his cell a few days later. He was in bad shape, and I could see why Mary said they had him on suicide watch. He was a man possessed—not by a demon, but instead by a dead man. He'd never get his chance to see Daddy again, to please Daddy again. Most folks wouldn't understand why this was so important, but I did. For the first sixteen or seventeen years, Daddy was how I measured myself as a man. He was my role model, everything I aspired to be. For Lester, this feeling had lasted a lifetime, boring itself into his very identity. He'd become a shell without Daddy's approval.

Worst of all, he was still convinced Daddy was ascended somewhere in the mountains.

Which was why I didn't stay long. Just a few minutes, enough time to tell him I didn't hold any grudges. Enough time to tell him I was sorry again for what had happened with Maggie. And Allison. And to update him on Baylee. It was only when I mentioned Baylee that he seemed—if only briefly—to be his old self again.

It was a moment I'd come to treasure.

"They shouldn't be holding you," I said. "You weren't involved. I've told them over and over again."

To this, he just shook his head, his eyes wild with his pain. It hardly mattered to him, I realized, where he was miserable. I understood. Every woman he'd loved had been taken from him. Even his daughter had not really been his.

Just before leaving, I gave him a hug. I think he might have hugged me back. It was hard to tell.

62

What followed was a tenuous peace. Everything should have been right in my world. I spent my days out at Rufus's place, trading stories, talking philosophy, drinking. My nights were spent at Granny's, spending time with a woman I loved and another I believed I might love soon.

When Todd's knee healed up enough, I gave them five hundred dollars and bus tickets to Florida, the place Millie dreamed of going. Nobody tried to stop them. I would have been the most likely to urge them to stay, but I had memories of a girl who'd stayed too long. If only Maggie and I had left before it all went bad. My life would have been so different. She'd still be alive.

A few more days passed. Mary and I fell into a rhythm. We made love at night and then sat outside and looked at the stars, Goose napping nearly silent at our feet. We talked about everything and nothing at all. There seemed to be no future or past. There were only these moments. And I wanted them to last forever.

I almost let the thing go that had been gnawing at me.

It took Granny's death to shake me free from the dreamlike state. It was only then that I made myself reconsider the puzzle of my father's life and death, but it wasn't until her funeral when the last piece fell into place.

*   *   *

In the backdrop of those days, mostly hidden beneath the layers of goodwill and intimacy Mary and I shared, were the inconsistencies of the whole ordeal. Nothing really made sense. Why had the map been inside Aida's grave? Why had the sermon—the same one McCauley had tattooed on his hand—been so clear if I wasn't supposed to hear it? What did the names mean on the back of the map? And most troubling of all—if my father hadn't instructed McCauley to contact me, who had?

All these questions seemed to come raining back down on me full force when I went by after a Thursday afternoon of drinking with Rufus and found Granny dead.

Seeing her stiff, frail body did something to me. Something inside me got wrenched around, and I realized life was too short to pretend, even if pretending took the all too pleasurable form of lazing around with Mary Hawkins. I needed answers. Even if I didn't like where they might take me.

In the days leading up to her funeral, I flailed around, not getting much accomplished. I pulled out the map I'd found in Aida's grave, reading the back so many times, I had memorized it:

Lester
Earl
Earl
Lester
Lester
Earl
After Earl, follow the light.

I tried all kinds of theories—he was leaving me some mathematical equation based on the differences in our ages, he was trying to tell me I had to get Lester's help to find him, and on and on—but each one fell flat under scrutiny.

Eventually, I let it go long enough to attend Granny's funeral.

The day was sticky with humidity, and everyone in attendance was sweating through their formal clothes. Mary had arranged for Granny to be buried down in Riley, and a dozen or so people stood around her open casket, paying final respects before they lowered her into the ground.

When it was my turn to stand over her, I was surprised to feel a sense of déjà vu overtake me. Had I done this already? It wasn't possible. A person could only die once. Yet the feeling was strong enough to make me step back and try the approach again. No change. I was sure I'd seen her lying in this coffin before.

That was when it hit me. The dream I'd had that night in the shack with Todd and Millie. I'd seen her in the coffin, but only briefly, right? Because then she'd changed. Then it was my father in the coffin, and then Lester, and then finally McCauley. I remembered the polished shoes and seeing Lester's reflection in them but not even realizing it wasn't my own at first because . . .

All the Marcuses favor.

Mary had said that once, and it was true. We all favored. That was when I remembered something else. The sermon, one of Daddy's last, had been right after his brother's death. If he were ever going to fake his own death . . .

I felt lightheaded with sudden understanding. I stepped away from the casket and sat down hard in a folding chair.

Mary came over and draped an arm over my shoulder. "Are you all right?" she whispered.

"No," I said, "but I think I will be soon."

*   *   *

Rufus and I walked out to the graveyard beside the old Holy Flame with two shovels.

I stood over Uncle Otis's grave and stabbed the still soft ground with the shovel. It had been a wet summer, and the digging was easy enough.

With both of us working, we hit the coffin within an hour.

"They already put a new guy in as sheriff," Rufus said.

"How do you know all the news in these mountains before I do?" I asked.

"Blind men have to pay close attention. We ain't spoiled like the rest of the world."

"Having eyes means you're spoiled?"

"Among other things."

I nodded and tapped the wood with my shovel. "You know this new sheriff?"

"Nope. But I do know one thing about him."

"What's that?"

"He never went to the Holy Flame."

"Well," I said, bending to open the casket, "that's a point in his favor."

"Ain't that the damned truth."

The casket was empty, which was exactly what I'd suspected. Daddy had left Otis's body in the mountains and carefully removed the face. He knew Hank Shaw wouldn't really investigate, especially if Otis was wearing Daddy's clothes, which he had been.

"Well?" Rufus said.

"It's empty. Which means they never found my daddy's body. They found Otis's."

"You mean . . . ?"

I nodded. "My daddy dug up his own brother to fake his death."

"Why would a man do such a thing?"

I thought about it for a moment. "I think he believed it would give him more power. Around here, there's no power like the afterlife."

Rufus nodded. "I believe you have broken the code, my friend."

63

The next morning, after a sleepless night, I rose silently and left Granny's house before dawn. I took the map and my 9mm and drove Mary's Tahoe back up to the gate where Shaw had taken us a couple of weeks earlier. The gate was locked and covered in police tape, but I didn't see any officers around. I jumped over the gate without much effort and headed for the cavern where Shaw had instructed Roger and Choirboy to put the wires around our wrists.

Here I encountered more police tape blocking the way. Beyond the tape were two corridors. The one we'd taken to get to the well was on the right. More police tape covered this entrance. The one on the left was open.

I pulled out my penlight and the map. I turned it over and read what I'd already memorized.

Lester
Earl
Earl
Lester
Lester
Earl
After Earl, follow the light.

I looked at the two corridors again.
Lester.

Left.

It almost made sense. But what about my name? Did it mean *right*? It had to. An idea hit me, and I stepped back out into the sunlight. It was still morning, so the sun was low in the east. I faced the cavern, the same direction I'd be facing if I was still inside looking at the two corridors.

The sun was on my right. My right was the east. *East* for *Earl.*

I went back inside and took the left corridor. Even with the penlight, it was slow going. The corridor seemed to go on and on, winding mindlessly into the mountain. Because of the limited range of my light, I moved at a snail's pace, not wanting to miss anything.

A few moments later, the corridor widened, and I was presented with another choice. I didn't need to look at the map to know it was time to go *Earl,* east, to the right.

I followed the instructions, moving slowly through the caverns for at least half an hour until I came to the last *Earl.* Here there were three corridors, but only one could be considered on the eastern side, so I took it.

When I saw light ahead and smelled smoke, I knew I was close.

Inching forward, I came to a large cavern illuminated with a flickering light. On the far side, there was a massive hole in the mountain the size of small church, and a great expanse of stars shone in the predawn. A snarl of smoke drifted among them, and I followed it back to its source, a campfire, built out on the ledge. There was an animal roasting on a spit.

My father sat with his back against a rock, taking in the stars, and it was the most beautiful vista I'd even seen. I stood frozen by the view, by the knowledge that my father was indeed alive.

"Daddy?" I said.

He turned to me slowly and nodded.

"I prayed that you'd come," he said.

I didn't know what to say, how to proceed. Everything that had happened over the last few weeks seemed a blur, unimportant. My father was alive. My father was sitting here, roasting some wild animal in the early morning dark.

"Come on out. Let's talk."

He waited as I made my way out on the ridge. From here, the view was even more spectacular. The stars seemed to go on and on forever, an ocean in the sky. Over past a few more mountains, there was the first light of the sun, straining to bleed over everything, to light a new day. But the night held on. A kind of peaceful stasis manifested itself. I sat down and watched.

"I never miss a sunrise," he said.

I nodded.

"You look like you've had a go of it." His voice was the same sonorous timber, the same captivating sound of the divine it had always been. His physical presence had diminished. His body had wasted away, and his hair had fallen out. He seemed to be some ghost version of himself, and in my awe, I wondered if he'd really ascended. There was so much I didn't understand.

"So," he said, "I saw the police tape. Must mean they got Hank and Billy. Probably that choirboy too. What about your brother?"

"What about him? He never did nothing but try to please you."

He smiled. "True enough. But the spirit wasn't on him. You know God works in mysterious ways. The proof is your very presence. I told Bryant to contact both of you. My hope was that you'd both come, but he didn't make it, did he? Just you. All the way from North Carolina. You came when I called. Ain't that something?"

It was *something*, but I didn't know what exactly. The truth was, I hated him for having this power over me, for manipulating me from inside this mountain.

He shrugged. "It had to be done. Once upon a time, I believed he was special. God teaches you, though. He taught me that no matter how much I wanted something, I couldn't make it be. That's why I decided to reach out to you both. Let God decide who was worthy. And look what he decided. That's twice by my count the Good Lord has saved you, brought you back 'round for a shot at redemption."

"Redemption?"

"Of course. You didn't think God had given up on you, did you? He don't never give up."

"So you brought me here?"

He smiled. "I follow the Good Lord's example. Like him, I don't never give up on a sinner. Especially not my own flesh and blood."

"You had McCauley contact me?" I said, still trying to get my head around it.

"You think that fool ever came up with an idea of his own?"

"Why be so vague? Why not just tell me where you were? Why hide at all?"

Daddy grinned. "Why indeed? Lots of reasons, but let's just say I wanted to remain hidden until Billy and Hank were out of the picture. I've known for some time now that they would betray me. Just like I knew you'd come back to me if I did it just so. God showed me. He sure did, Earl. He showed me I'd get my son back. He showed me you'd come back to the fold. All I had to do was leave some clues, and here you are."

There was silence. I was aware of the 9mm pressing against my calf. It felt cold and persistent. I wanted to kill him before he said more, before he convinced me my life—at least the last thirty years of it—had been a sham.

"It's time to step up to the plate, Earl. Decide who you are, what you're going to be."

And that was really the question, wasn't it? Who was I?

The son of a North Georgia preacher. The boy of a legend who called the lightning, and looked upon God's face, and lifted serpents into the air like they were harmless. A man who couldn't betray his past, his father. A man who had been manipulated by the master, by the one man nobody could stand up to.

Except that wasn't quite right, was it? I heard Lester's voice inside my head. *You're the only person I've ever known who stood up to Daddy.*

Yet I still felt caught under the shadow of his towering existence. I feared that version of me was gone. I feared all the heartache I'd endured had killed the little bit of life I'd once had.

After all, didn't I need to be redeemed? Hadn't I sinned early and often and even seen the long-term effects of those sins on my life?

I felt like a man being split apart by the lightning. One side of me knew it was all bullshit, it had to be, while the other side of me was sure it was the truth and that most of my life had been a lie.

It wasn't until Daddy said the next part that I came to my senses.

"It's always the females," he said. "They ruin everything. They make a godly man live in sin, a good son turn on his father. But in the end, it all works out to good. I've said it so many times, but it's true: God does work in mysterious ways." He smiled at me then as if the matter was settled, as if that was all it would take for me to forgive him for a lifetime of fear and subjugation, as if his simple yet deeply flawed logic would be irrefutable.

The sad thing was I almost wanted to just let it ride. It would have been easier to do just that.

Instead, I reached for the 9mm.

"What's this?" he said.

"A gun," I said.

He smiled at me as if I were offering him more bread at the dinner table.

"You ruined lives," I said. "Mine, Lester's, Maggie's, Allison DeWalt's, Baylee's. Many more."

"You would give me so much power? I say again, the Lord makes all things come out to good."

"What about Aida?" I said. "Nothing good came out of that."

He sighed. "You never learn, do you, Earl? You never let go. I admire that. Well, *would* admire that if you applied it to faith. Instead, it's just one more aspect of your personality I don't understand. God has offered you everything, yet you continue to reject him."

"You don't know God," I said. "I've seen God."

"Have you now?"

"Yes, sir. I saw him in Arnette Lacey when she took me in after you deserted your own son."

"That nigger midwife? You are a corrupted soul, Earl." I saw the first glimmer of irritation in his face. He'd been so sure that if he could get me here, the rest would be easy. I'd accept his faith, turn to his religion.

He'd win in the end by controlling me. Because that was what Daddy's love had always been about: control.

He stood up then, and for the first time, I saw what had been lying on the other side of him. It was a sawed-off shotgun. He picked it up with one hand but kept the twin barrels pointed toward the ledge.

"You'd shoot your father, Earl? After all I've done for you? No, I don't think so. Put down the gun. Let's pray. I love you."

"You're a liar. What kind of love is it that makes a father hand his son a snake? What kind of love does . . . all of this? I mean, think of the wasted lives just to get me right here. Just so you can have the satisfaction of knowing I never got away?"

"If you don't put that gun down, son, I'll be forced to defend myself. In a firefight, I'm going to win. Even if I die. I go to heaven. If you die, though . . . well, that's the rub, ain't it? I want you to think about that. Think about it hard."

"I should have killed you a long time ago," I said. "I should have done it while you were sleeping. Think of all the misery I could have saved."

"You don't know misery, boy. Not the kind that hell will bring." He lifted the shotgun. "I'm afraid one of us is fixing to get shot."

I aimed the 9mm at his head. "It might be you."

"So be it. I'm prepared. It's you who will have to answer for your sins. Just remember, God's judgment is harsher than any lightning. I see the marks on you now, but God will leave a mark on your soul. He'll blister it and—"

He fired. The shotgun pellets ate up the entire left side of the cavern, narrowly missing me. I felt the heat of them on my arm and neck, and when I twisted away from the blast, I lost my balance and fell onto the hard ground. I hadn't been expecting that. Daddy always said his peace, was never one to cut his own speech short. But not this time.

Still, I managed to hold on to the gun. I aimed it up at him. My first two shots went wide, out through the side of the mountain.

He kicked the gun out of my hand.

"It's a good thing I love you," he said. "Otherwise, you'd already be in hell. But no, your father just keeps on trying and trying and trying to make you see." Something in him had snapped. He began to kick me repeatedly. My side hurt so badly, I could hardly process the kicks.

I was seventeen again, lying in the floor of the Holy Flame sanctuary. I was a kid, being forced to pray for my mother's forgiveness. I was a man standing outside of the church, commanding him to turn around.

I'd stood up to him then.

Somehow, I had to find the strength to do it again. I rolled over and reached for his legs. His next kick caught me near the sternum and knocked the breath out through my throat in a great whoof. But I held on.

I continued to roll, knocking him off balance and into the fire. The animal on the spit tumbled over the ledge, leaving streaks of flame in the air.

Daddy stood up, even as the flames rose up around him like wings, and he was finally the physical manifestation of the demon he'd been all along.

The fire seemed to come from within him and all around him at once. His entire body was consumed until the top of his head became a torch. I swear as his skin burned, he grinned at me, and I realized he was already in hell, and somehow he liked it.

I staggered to my feet and ran at him with every ounce of strength I had left in me.

My shoulder caught fire on contact, and he tried to hold on to me, to take me over the side with him, but his hands—more fire than flesh now—couldn't hold on. I fell onto my belly beside the fire, my chin hanging over the ledge, my face in the open air of morning, and watched him fall and burn until he hit a creek below and disappeared.

He was gone. At last.

*   *   *

No, not quite *gone*. But he was *faded*. Sometimes—in the months and days that followed—he came back. I saw him in the shadows at dusk, heard his voice whispering on a breeze, felt his judgment when I did something I knew he wouldn't approve of. But these were just agitations, visits from ghosts. The man was dead.

And when the ghosts did bother me, when I found myself filled with doubt, I reminded myself to have a ghost, one must be dead, and this is where I found my comfort.

64

On the day Rufus and I had found the empty grave, he'd told me I'd broken the code. But that wasn't true at all. Maybe I'd messed with it some, maybe I'd even gotten some of the numbers right, but the truth was the code was still largely unknown to me. I still didn't understand my father or my brother. I barely understood myself.

I only told one person. It wasn't Lester or Mary or even Rufus. I figured one day I might tell Lester, but at the moment, he didn't need any more mention of Daddy in his life. His trial date was a few months away, and his lawyers were optimistic he might get off. I wanted him to go back to a normal life. The shit that had happened inside the mountain between me and Daddy was anything but normal.

As for Mary, I wanted to tell her, but the time never seemed right. It wasn't hard to hide the burns I'd suffered when I knocked him off the mountain, but the bruises on my ribs from his kicks were more difficult. I had to lie to cover those. It was just for a little while, I told myself. Things were good between us, and each time I thought about telling her the truth, I decided to wait. There's a certain point you reach with a thing like this where it becomes too late, where a deceit creates its own momentum, and the consequences of that momentum grow with each passing day. Bringing it up would just make her wonder why I waited so long. In the end, once I'd more or less healed, I decided there really wasn't any worthwhile reason to tell her anymore. It was just something that had happened to me once. I'd deal with it alone and save her the pain. My father was a part of my past I was leaving behind. Mary was my future. What good could dredging all that back up possibly do?

The person I did tell surprised even me.

He came by the house a day or two after I watched Daddy fall to his death. Mary and I were cleaning out Granny's room when she nodded toward the window. "Looks like trouble."

I crossed the room and peered through the window. A silver pickup was sitting near the old rocker. Ronnie Thrash got out and started toward the front door. He'd cut his hair and grown a beard, but it was definitely him. I would have recognized that cocky strut anywhere.

"Wait here."

I met him at the door and led him back out to his pickup. "What do you want?"

"Well, it's good to see you too," he said.

"Cut that. I don't want you coming around here."

"Well, that's not very neighborly of you, Earl."

I glared at him.

He grinned. "Fine. I'll get to the point. I just come by because I wanted to tell you . . . good job. I'm glad to see my grandfather is going to get what's coming to him."

Suddenly, I remembered the other side of Ronnie Thrash. The side that actually did have a good bit in common with me.

"I just hate your own daddy wasn't alive to get his comeuppance." He shrugged. "Anyways, I just wanted to thank you. I feel like I got a new lease on life without my granddad and Shaw around. I was so obliged, I even forbade Beard and the boys from messing with that old, blind fool. Much as it pains me to do so." He patted my shoulder. "Much respect, Earl."

I rolled my tongue over my teeth and nodded at him.

"What's the plan? Gonna stay and make an honest woman of that cute little deputy or head on back to Carolina?"

"You want to go for a ride?" I said.

He nodding, thinking it over. "I'm always up for a ride with the great Earl Marcus."

*   *   *

We stopped by Rufus's and got a couple of shovels, the same ones we'd used to dig up Otis's empty grave. Rufus didn't ask me why I needed them, and I didn't volunteer the information. I couldn't say for sure why I'd decided on Ronnie's help and not Rufus's. Maybe because this was the kind of secret I didn't want to put on a good man like Rufus. Maybe because Ronnie would appreciate what we were about to do more than anyone else I knew.

I had him park on the side of the road nearest the creek where I believed we'd find Daddy's body. We hiked around for half the afternoon looking. While we looked, I told him about what had happened. He didn't seem to believe me until I spotted the body hung up on some rocks in the nearly dry creek bed.

"Well, if that don't beat all," he said. "You killed Brother RJ. And it looks like he even burned in hell."

I had to smile at that one.

*   *   *

We buried what was left of the body not far from the place it had landed in the creek. The dirt was moist and easy to dig. When we finished, Ronnie leaned on his shovel and looked me over with admiration.

"I envy you," he said.

"Don't do that."

"No, seriously, I wish I could have done it."

"I didn't want to. He didn't leave me any choice."

Ronnie screwed up his face, as if he were thinking it over. "Maybe, but if you really hadn't meant to do it, I don't think you'd look so proud right now."

I hated him for saying that. The last thing I needed in my life was more regret. But like it or not, I'd found some.

65

The next afternoon, while continuing to clean out Granny's room, Mary asked me two questions, both of which completely caught me off guard.

"What are you going to do?" That was the first one.

"I thought I'd finish Granny's room and maybe take a nap on the couch. Then fix some dinner. What about you?"

She smiled at me. I wanted to kiss her. She was so damned smart. I didn't deserve her. She'd saved both of our necks with the call to the GBI.

"That's not what I mean. I want to know what you're going to do next. I mean, you still have a business in North Carolina."

I put down the box of clothes I was carrying and sat on the couch. "I was thinking of moving the business," I said.

She nodded. "That's surprising."

I shrugged. "Is it?" It felt anything but surprising to me. It felt right. "I think it's time to come back." I reached for her hand. "You're here. I got Rufus." I smiled at his name, and she did too. "Not to mention, Goose said he loves these mountains." Hearing his name, Goose perked up. He'd grown a lot since I'd found him nearly six weeks ago. He was going to grow some more, and I knew Charlotte wouldn't be any place he'd be happy.

And I wouldn't either. These mountains were home. And now that I was sure Daddy was gone and I'd confronted my past, not only could I come home again, but I could stay here.

"About that," she said. "I need to up front with you."

"About what?"

"I'm moving back to Atlanta."

I just looked at her. Was she breaking up with me already?

"I'm sorry, Earl. I've been meaning to tell you for a while now, but every time I start to tell you, I just can't. You've been through so much. Granny and everything with your father's church. Lester. I just didn't want to hurt you anymore."

"Well then be quiet," I said. "Don't say another word."

She smiled at me sadly.

"I came for Granny. You know that. She's gone now. It was a wonderful surprise . . . and quite the adventure meeting you, but I promised my chief in Atlanta I'd be back." She looked like she was close to tears. "I've got to honor that promise."

She straddled me then, wrapping her legs around me and leaning in to kiss me on the mouth.

"I want to try to make this work," she said. "Just because I'm going to be in Atlanta doesn't mean it can't still work."

I nodded. That was better. Still not great, but I understood. And I was overjoyed she wasn't dumping me.

"And," she said, "I want you to stay here."

"Here?"

"Sure. It's perfect. It's paid for. You won't have to pay me rent, so that will allow you to get on your feet. Plus, I love making love to you on this couch." She smiled, and I reached for her again as she moved her hips on my lap seductively.

It was a slow, sweet session. Afterward, we lay there and laughed when we realized Goose had been watching the entire time.

I was just about to drift off to sleep when she asked me the second question. It was one I didn't have a good answer for, one I still consider nearly every day.

"After all of it," she said, "what do you believe?"

I might have told her that somehow, despite it all, I still believed in God. Not my father's god, nor the god most people thought of when they heard the word. But instead, I believed in Granny's God. The God of hospitality and acceptance. The God who saved a little kid from his father's hateful and vengeful religion and put him right here on this couch, with something resembling a future, even if he was fifty years old and still not completely over his daddy issues.

I might have told her all that, but if I had, I still would have had to explain what Granny taught me about prayers that day in her room, how they were kisses, but I just didn't have the energy right at the moment.

But it was something to think about. If there were kisses, there might be prayers, and if there were prayers, there had to be a God.

But I would never claim to know for sure.

Acknowledgments

Writing a novel is a lot like being stranded in an ocean of ever-intensifying waves. You can try to make it to land all by yourself, or you can send out an SOS and hope someone else might be willing to lend a hand. During the writing of *Heaven's Crooked Finger*, I would have certainly drowned miles from the shore if not for a few kind souls who gave willingly of their time to keep me afloat.

I owe a huge debt of gratitude to friend and writer Kurt Dinan, who has been a first reader for me for more than ten years now and knows better than anyone else when I'm doing it right and when I'm just mailing it in. Thanks for your friendship and the way you continue to bring out the best in me.

Another early reader who deserves special mention is Jamie Nelson. Jamie read a couple of early drafts and asked me the question that led to my most important narrative breakthrough. Thanks, Jamie, for your sharp eye and willingness to help.

There were so many others who read drafts or offered advice during the process, but I'll try to limit myself to the most noteworthy. These include Barry Dejasu (always willing to read or just chat); Sam W. Anderson (an old friend and probably the most loyal individual I know); the Boston brothers (who may or may not live in Boston anymore, but that's how I'll always think of them)—Bracken MacLeod, Chris Irvin, and Errick "Danger" Nunnelly—and Paul Tremblay (who has always been far too kind to me and, come to think of it, may actually live in Boston but definitely hates pickles).

On the business side of things, I'm extraordinarily lucky to have Alec Shane as an agent. Each time I sent him a draft, he pushed me to take it to the next level. When the manuscript was (finally) finished, he sold it *and* book two, which I hadn't even properly started yet. I don't think a writer can ask for much more from an agent.

Two ladies have been instrumental in helping me establish an online and promotional presence. Thank you, Jana White and Julie Trelstad. You are both saints for putting up with my ineptness and (at times) reluctance to embrace promotion, digital and otherwise.

Finally, I want to thank the fine folks at Crooked Lane Books. Faith Ross Black is an ideal editor—easy to get along with, efficient, and deeply respectful of the process as well as the product. Thanks to her and all the others at Crooked Lane who helped make this book a reality. A special shout-out to Jenny Chen and Danny Constantino, whose precision copyedits made a world of difference in the final product.

And, of course, none of this would be possible without my wife, Becky. She's my best reader, critic, emergency responder, cheerleader, and friend.